The Coronation of Prince Malock

Book Four in the Prince Malock World

by Timothy L. Cerepaka

An Annulus Publishing Book

Annulus Publishing, Cherokee, Texas, 2014

Published by Annulus Publishing

ISBN-13: 978-0692335338

ISBN-10: 0692335331

Contact: timothy@timothylcerepaka.com

Cover by Elaina Lee of For the Muse Design
(http://www.forthemusdesign.com)

Acknowledgments

I would like to thank my uncle, James Wilhite, once again for helping me get this novel into publishable shape. I would also like to thank my family for supporting me while I wrote this novel.

Chapter One

CROUCHING LOW IN THE snow, ignoring the wetness clinging to the soles of her boots, Jenur Takren, former member of the Dark Tigers' Guild of Ruwa, drew her white coat more tightly around her body as a freezing cold wind blew through the valley. Her stomach growled, but she ignored it as she peered out from the boulder which she hid behind. Her prey was not yet here, but she had studied the habits of this particular pale deer for days and had only set up the perfect trap to capture it when she was confident that she memorized its habits.

Of course, if this fails, Dad and I will go hungry again, Jenur thought. *For the third time this week.*

Jenur tried not to think too much about that. Ever since she and her adoptive father, Quro, who was also a former member of the Dark Tigers' Guild, had come to the Great Berg—a massive cold land located far to the north of the much more temperate Northern Isles—they had struggled to meet their basic daily needs. There was only one town here on Urma, one of the very few islands in the Great Berg that was capable of supporting human life, and the town—known as

TIMOTHY L. CEREPAKA

Yurima—was miles away from where Jenur and Quro had set up their home, which was why they had to rely on hunting and fishing to feed themselves.

Maybe we should have rethought asking Skimif to send us to the Great Berg, Jenur thought, rubbing her gloved hands together to generate warmth. *About the only good thing about this place is that the Dark Tigers don't ever come here. Still, would it really be so hard for Skimif to give us a warm summer every now and then?*

Of course, Jenur knew that Skimif was too busy in his new role as the God of Martir to cater to her and her father's every need, no matter how pressing it may have been. Jenur had long ago learned that you couldn't rely on the gods for everything, that if you wanted anything in this life, then you had to get it yourself.

Which was why Jenur was out here, in the middle of a steep valley known for its avalanches, keeping as quiet as possible, waiting for the pale deer she had been stalking for the past few days to show itself. Any minute now, she knew, the pale deer would appear at the west end of the valley and walk down to the valley floor, where it would attempt to get a drink of water from a small stream that flowed through the place. Once it stopped by the stream—and always in the same spot, as pale deer were creatures of habit and predictability, rarely ever straying from routine except in dire circumstances—it would step on the wooden trap that Jenur had devised.

Though the device was currently covered under a thick layer of snow—which Jenur had done herself, to prevent the pale deer from seeing it—she had no trouble remembering what it looked like. She had modeled it after the jaw of a baba raga, wide and strong, though

2

she had to make the two sharp, wooden stakes that would cut straight through the pale deer's neck short in order to hide them under the snow. Assuming it all worked out correctly, the pale deer would die in an instant, Jenur could clean its body, and she and Dad would be eating well that night. As this particular deer was rather fat in comparison to its fellow deer, it might even give them enough meat to last two days.

At that moment, the pale deer—her prey and future dinner—appeared on the ridge to the west. Trying to keep her mouth from watering, Jenur remained as still as she could, watching the pale deer walk down the valley. To her knowledge, this pale deer was a loner, which was unusual as most pale deer tended to travel in packs. She suspected it may have been the lone survivor of a pack of pale deer that had been slaughtered by a group of baba raga a while ago, as the first time Jenur had seen this deer, it had been sleeping among the corpses of several other deer. This deer may have been traumatized by the attack and so had never tried to join up with any other deer pack, even though there were plenty around and most were generally willing to accept new deer into the fold.

Why am I analyzing a pale deer's psychology? Jenur thought. *None of this will matter when he steps into my trap and, later, into my stomach.*

The pale deer made its way down the slope easily enough and walked directly to the stream of water, which shone in the sunlight. The pale deer didn't even look around at its surroundings, which meant it must have been very thirsty. It licked its lips, its eyes focused solely on the stream flowing before it.

Jenur rested her hand on her knife. The pale deer was only feet away from the trap now. Once it unknowingly rested its two front hooves on the pressure-sensitive trap, the trap would shut around its neck and kill it. The crunching of the snow under its hooves as it walked just made Jenur all the more impatient to eat.

Then a smell like fried fish entered her nostrils. It was a familiar scent, one that stirred Jenur's memories. The smell reminded her of Ruwa, her home island and the headquarters of the Dark Tigers. The Dark Tigers had almost always had fried fish for breakfast, lunch, and dinner, but that didn't explain why she suddenly smelled it now. Was she so hungry that she was beginning to imagine the scent of fried fish?

Then the sound of a knife being drawn—its blade cutting slightly against its leather sheath—made Jenur whirl around just in time to see a long, silver blade come at her face. Jenur ducked her head to avoid getting stabbed in the face, but then another knife came at her, forcing her to jump back—awkwardly, due to the fact that she was still crouching—and roll backwards to avoid the second one.

Jenur shook her head and dusted the snow off her shoulders as she looked at her attacker, saying as she did so, "What the—"

Standing before her was a tall, bulky aquarian wearing the black robes and tiger mask that all Dark Tigers wore. The assassin carried two long, silver blades in her fishy hands, her yellow eyes glaring out from the eye holes in the mask. Jenur at first thought it might have been her father, Quro, playing a practical joke on her, but one glance at the assassin's prominent breasts told her that her attacker was indeed another Dark Tiger, which made no sense at all.

"How did you—" Jenur stopped mid-sentence when she heard the sound of hooves beating against the snow. A glance to the right told her that the pale deer had either seen or heard their fight because it was now sprinting back up the slope in an effort to escape the valley.

"Oops," said the Dark Tiger, her gurgle-y aquarian accent making it difficult to understand her at first. "Did I scare off your dinner? Sorry. I didn't mean to."

The Dark Tiger's voice was eerily familiar to Jenur, prompting Jenur to say, "Wait a minute ... Kura? Is that you?"

"So the child finally recognizes me," said the Dark Tiger, immediately confirming her own identity. "I was wondering when you would show the intelligence of your father. Guess all those years of raising you finally paid off."

"How did you even find us?" Jenur said, drawing her own knife out of its sheath at her side as she spoke. "No one knows we're out here."

"A client hired me to kill you two," said Kura. She raised her blades. "Of course, I would have done it for free, seeing as you and Quro broke the Rules, but getting paid to do something you want to do is just as good as doing it for free."

Jenur's stomach growled, but again she ignored it. She knew just how vicious Kura could be. Back when Jenur had been a member of the Dark Tigers, Kura had gained a reputation among the others for the absolute cruelty she showed towards her assigned targets. Once Jenur had heard that Kura had drowned the baby of one of her targets simply for the fun of it, although she had never been able to confirm that rumor herself and really didn't want to.

Despite that, Jenur didn't feel frightened of Kura. Over the past six months, Jenur had faced beings far more powerful and vicious than Kura could ever hope to be. As long as Jenur was smart and didn't give Kura any openings, she figured she'd survive this.

So Jenur raised her serrated knife and said, "Wirm must be getting sloppy if he only sent you to kill us. As good as you are, Kura, you do realize you can't beat me and Dad, right?"

"Idiot," said Kura. "Of course I know that. Why else do you think I attacked you here, in the middle of nowhere, well away from that pitiful shack you and Quro call a house? Besides, I could never harm Quro. He's too handsome for that."

Jenur scowled. Now she remembered the real reason she had always disliked Kura. For whatever unholy reason known only to the Powers, Kura had taken a liking to Quro. As far as Jenur knew, Kura had always had a thing for her adoptive father, but the assassin had refused to show any of that same affection toward Jenur. Not that Jenur particularly wanted it, but it had sometimes felt like Kura considered Jenur competition, which was as ridiculous a thought as any.

Then again, who said Kura was rational? Jenur thought.

"Well, if you can't harm Dad, then I guess Wirm must have been an idiot for sending you after us," said Jenur. "Is that coot getting senile in his old age or is he a lot more incompetent than I remember?"

Kura shook her head. "Oh, I didn't come alone. Wirm himself came with me. He wanted to make absolutely sure that Quro and you were dead. Right now, he should be driving a knife into Quro's throat; regrettable, but as much as I love Quro, I know better than to cross the Grand Tiger's path."

Jenur's eyes widened. Though Nijok Wirm, the Grand Tiger of the Dark Tigers, the organization's founder and leader, was an older man and rarely took on any assignments himself, Jenur had grown up hearing all kinds of legends about Wirm's legendary assassination skills. Supposedly, Wirm had slain over 100 major political figures from various human and aquarian nations in the Northern Isles over his lifetime, and the bounty on his head was said to be so high that it exceeded the combined wealth of the entire Northern Isles twice over. Not to mention that Jenur herself had once run afoul of his temper, earning a beating she still tried to block out from her memory to this day.

Thus, real fear entered Jenur's soul as the thought of Wirm himself killing Dad dominated her mind. She had to get back home fast, but then she remembered that Kura was in her way and that the only way she could have any hope of rescuing Dad was if she killed or defeated Kura.

"Wirm can't be here," said Jenur. "You're just saying that to scare me."

"No, it's true," said Kura. "The Grand Tiger himself is on the hunt. We even used his personal boat to get here. He is quite serious about making sure you and Quro sleep on the ocean floor tonight."

The hunger pains in Jenur's stomach were too distracting, but Jenur once again ignored them. "Wirm never leaves Ruwa, not even to take on paid jobs. You're lying."

"You broke the Rules," said Kura. "I know you have a hard time wrapping your mind around that simple concept, but breaking the Rules has consequences. Didn't you learn that when Wirm beat you senseless for being a lazy slob?"

For a moment, Jenur only saw Nijok Wirm—a large, muscular human man, with long, thin white hair, his brass knuckles shining in the candlelight—before her, beating her face in with his fists. She could feel his brass knuckles shattering her nose, bruising her cheeks, and smashing her forehead and making it bleed, as though it was happening right now.

It had been a long time since she last thought about the beating. The thought itself was enough to send fear pumping through her veins, fear unlike any she had felt before. All she wanted to do now was run from Urma and get away from Wirm before he found her again.

Then Jenur shook her head and beat down her fear. Running would not help. She needed to stand her ground. Dad needed her and she couldn't just abandon him, even if she did fear Wirm more than all of the southern gods combined.

So Jenur said, "If what you say is true, then all I need to do is kick your ass and go after Wirm myself."

"You're a lot braver now," Kura said. She crossed her arms, the blades of her knives facing toward Jenur. "I thought you were going to run away when I mentioned that Wirm was here."

"I'm not going to abandon Dad," said Jenur. "Especially not to someone like you."

"I'm hurt," said Kura with the most sarcastic voice possible. "Not.

But I'm genuinely glad you're not running this time, you little witch. I've wanted to teach you a lesson for a long time now about respect."

"This isn't school," said Jenur. "So you can forget teaching me anything."

"Idiot," said Kura. Then she shook her head. "It doesn't matter. You'll be dead soon anyway, which is what you always should have been."

With her blades flashing, Kura charged at Jenur. As Kura ran at Jenur, she kicked up the snow in front of her, sending it flying toward Jenur. Ducking to avoid the snow, Jenur ran at Kura and slashed at her with her own knife.

Jenur's blade met Kura's twin blades in midair and for a moment the two women struggled against each other. Though Jenur was in good shape, Kura was stronger due to her aquarian body and she was succeeding in pushing Jenur down, despite Jenur's best efforts to hold her back.

Biting her lower lip, Jenur lashed out with her right foot, striking Kura's legs and knocking the Dark Tiger's feet out from under her. Kura fell to the snow flat on her back, giving Jenur time to bring down her knife directly on Kura's chest.

But Kura rolled out of the way just in time, causing Jenur's knife to impale the snowy ground underneath. Jenur had no time to pulled it back out, however, because Kura had rolled to her feet and lashed out with both of her knives. Jenur was forced to leave her knife in the snow as she jumped back to avoid getting her hand cut off, causing her to skitter backwards in the snow as she did so.

"Dropped your weapon?" said Kura as she stood up, her chest

heaving up and down. "That's not good. I guess I'll just have to add it to my own collection when I'm done with you here."

Jenur scowled but didn't say anything. Her knife was her best weapon, but it wasn't like she was totally unarmed. Dad had once given Jenur a bag of pepper powder pellets, pellets that exploded into a red powder when thrown into the target's eyes. Kura probably didn't know about it, which was why Jenur said nothing about it.

Kura dashed at Jenur, her blades once again flashing through the air like lightning bolts. Jenur stood her ground, however, remaining perfectly still, calculating the ever-closing distance between her and Kura as fast as she could. She had to make sure not to throw the pepper powder pellets too early or Kura would have time to dodge, but too late and Jenur would be dead.

Just as Kura got within five feet of her, Jenur stuffed her hand into her coat's left pocket, grabbed a handful of pellets, and hurled them directly at Kura's eyes. The pellets flew through the eye holes of Kura's mask, causing Kura to screech to a halt, kicking up snow everywhere as red powder exploded from within the eye holes of her mask.

"My eyes!" Kura screamed, dropping her knives as her hands flew up to the mask. "Good gods! My eyes!"

Kura ripped her mask off her head and threw it into the snow, revealing her eel-like face as she rubbed her eyes. Jenur, seeing an opening, ran at Kura and slammed into her midsection with her shoulder, sending the assassin falling backwards onto the ground.

Kura crashed onto the ground with a shout, but Jenur didn't give her time to react. She scooped up Kura's knives and pinned the Dark

Tiger to the ground, straddling her enemy's body with both legs. Jenur then stabbed both knives directly into Kura's hands, causing Kura to scream once more before Jenur slapped her in the face.

"Shut up," Jenur said, her voice as low and threatening as she could make it. "Or I'll jam those knives into your throat, you old witch."

Kura had enough sense in her to listen to Jenur's command, because she stopped struggling underneath her and went quiet. Kura now looked like a mess, with her hands bleeding and her eyes bloodshot from the powder. Jenur doubted she would live much longer.

"You ... evil ... whore," Kura said, saying each word slowly and carefully. "Are you gonna kill me now? Finish me off? I know you want to. I can see it in your eyes."

Jenur, deciding that Kura was not going anywhere, stood up and walked around the assassin to get her knife. It was still stuck in the ground; in fact, it must have been embedded in the earth quite deeply because it took a few seconds of tugging before Jenur succeeded in removing it.

After checking that the blade was still intact, Jenur turned and walked back over to Kura, who had not moved from her position. Not that she could, considering her condition, but Jenur knew that deception was one of the best weapons in any Dark Tiger's arsenal. Combine that with sheer determination to see an assignment to the bitter end and Jenur was surprised that Kura had not already freed herself.

Kura's bloodshot eyes, the powder covering them like badly-applied makeup, looked up at Jenur as she walked back into her view.

"You didn't answer my question," said Kura. She winced and groaned, probably at the pain in her hands. "Kill me or not?"

"I'm not really into the whole 'killing my enemies' thing anymore," Jenur admitted as she flipped her knife in her hand. "But at the same time, if I let you live, you'll probably just come after me later. Unless Wirm gets me, but I doubt he will."

"Wirm will get you, even if I don't," said Kura. "Wirm always gets what he wants, no matter what it is."

Kura's words made Jenur realize that every minute she spent here, deciding whether or not to kill Kura, was another minute that she was not heading back home to save Dad. Killing Kura would probably take time, even if she did kill her instantly by slitting her throat in just the right spot. Jenur couldn't waste any time making sure Kura was dead, especially when Kura was in such a pathetic state as she was.

So Jenur sheathed her knife and said, "You know what? I'm just going to leave you here. I don't have time to waste killing you when I could be using that very same time saving my Dad."

"Coward," Kura hissed. "I swear by the gods that you will live long enough to regret this decision."

That seemed like a strange thing for someone in Kura's position to say, but Jenur knew that Kura was not a normal person. With gray, rumbling storm clouds rolling in overhead and a strong breeze picking up, Jenur didn't have time to question Kura's response. She did, however, kick Kura in the side once for good measure.

So Jenur turned and ran toward the eastern end of the valley, the part of the valley closest to her home. She would have to run with all of her might to even hope of getting there in time to stop Wirm.

And even if she did get there in time, a part of her feared that she wouldn't be able to stop Wirm at all, making her wonder if taking out Kura hadn't guaranteed her survival, but had instead only delayed the inevitable. Those thoughts didn't make her slow down, but they hardly helped her feel better about coming face to face with Wirm, either.

Chapter Two

PRINCE TOJAS MALOCK, SON of King Halock and Queen Markinia of Carnag, Crown Prince of the House of Carnag, and former captain of the *Iron Wind*, took his seat in the Carnag Box besides his father as the rest of the delegates from other islands entered the Meeting Hall. The Hall was noisy, but not crowded, as it had been designed to hold all of the hundred or so delegates who came to the Northern Summit, held on the island of Rane, once every five years. Malock was not a quiet person himself, but he usually enjoyed the noisiness of parties, not the noisiness of various politicians and delegates speaking in different languages, sometimes rather loudly, in a chamber that, while not small, had no real openings for the noise to escape to. It would all go down in time, he knew, once the actual discussions between the various delegates started going, but he still found it annoying.

The chair he sat in was soft and comfortable, with just the right back support. It was a chair he had sat in many times since he had first started coming to Northern Summit meetings with his father, King Halock, fifteen years ago, and the chair always felt exactly the same as it did now. He sunk into it as the First Queen of Nikos briefly stopped by their box to talk to King Halock, taking advantage of this time to think back on all that had happened over the last few months.

After Skimif's ascension to godhood, Malock had returned to Carnag. There he had seen exactly how much damage had resulted from Skimif's fight with Grinf, the God of Justice, Metal, and Fire, which had been far more than Skimif had told him. Malock remembered well how terrible the Stadium, where part of the battle had taken place, had looked, with its ceiling caved in and its field blackened by flames, as well as the various other buildings that had been damaged during the battle.

Thankfully, only a small portion of Port Blasan had been damaged. Still, it had only been just recently that the city's resident etimancers and the construction workers who worked under them had finished repairing the streets and buildings, and it would be at least another couple of weeks before the evacuated citizens would be allowed to return to their homes. Malock had supervised the entire rebuilding effort, partly because as Prince of Carnag he felt it was his responsibility to make sure Port Blasan was rebuilt, partly because he had told his parents about his association with the Brotherhood of Heathens—an organization dedicated to ending worship of the northern gods in the Northern Isles—and they had forced him to supervise the rebuilding of Port Blasan as a kind of punishment.

Granted, that's better than being disowned or tossed into prison for my beliefs, Malock thought, glancing at his father, who was now chatting with the Head Councilman of Kikasa. *It still wasn't that fun, though.*

Ever since Malock had returned from World's End, his relationship with his parents hadn't exactly been as stable or good as it had originally been. Both his mother and father had been worried sick since his disappearance, despite having left them a note explaining where he had gone and what he was going to do, and when he had returned, they had been very angry. They became even angrier when he revealed his new Heathen beliefs to them, as both of his parents were devout worshipers of Grinf. They simply could not understand why Malock no longer respected the gods, which Malock had tried to explain to them but which they had both failed to listen to.

Thankfully, as Malock had just thought about, they had still accepted him back. The only difference now was that Malock had been asked to keep his Heathen beliefs to himself, at least for now, because Carnag was still recovering from Skimif and Grinf's battle and they felt that the majority of Carnagians would not take kindly to the news that their Prince no longer worshiped the gods. Additionally, many of the other Northern Isles were also dealing with sudden changes in the way of the world; in particular, Skimif's ascension to godhood.

As a matter of fact, that was why Malock and his father were on the island of Rane today, attending an emergency Northern Summit. The last Northern Summit had been held only two years ago, and it was tradition to hold a new one every five years, but with Skimif's ascension to godhood—among other notable, major changes to Martir that would affect nearly every nation in the Northern Isles—it was only logical to begin another Northern Summit right away.

Of course, this Northern Summit hadn't actually happened 'right away.' The Carnagian Royal Family had received a letter of invitation from the Northern Summit Committee—the group of individuals, one provided from each Northern nation, that organized the Norther Summit and kept the island of Rane from falling into disrepair during the non-Summit years—two months ago, asking them to attend the next Summit. The letter had to be sent out at least two months beforehand in order to give the various delegates time to prepare for the journey to Rane, because, while the island may have been in the geographical center of the Northern Isles, it was still quite a long ways from most other islands.

In fact, Malock and his father were among the last two delegates to arrive on Rane, having only arrived on the island about a day ago. They had intended to come much sooner, but due to the rebuilding efforts in Port Blasan, they had had to delay their arrival by a week. They had almost missed it when their ship had been caught in a sudden, unexpected storm when halfway between Carnag and Rane, but thankfully they had weathered the storm and arrived before the Summit officially began.

As Malock looked around the Meeting Hall, he was reminded of the Throne Room of the Gods, back on World's End. He was actually surprised—a little disturbed, even—at how closely the Meeting Hall resembled the Throne Room. The Meeting Hall, while much smaller and not nearly as grand as the Throne Room, had a similar construction to the Throne Room. Around one hundred boxes stood around the edges of the room, similar to the hundreds of thrones in the Throne Room of the Gods. While each throne on World's End had been crafted to fit with whichever god happened to sit there, these boxes all looked more or less the same, except for the symbols of each nation attached to them to signify which nation the box belonged to and the amount of seats per box, as some nations sent more delegates than others. In some ways, the Meeting Hall looked more like a pitiful mortal copy of the Throne Room, although to Malock's knowledge, the original architect of the Meeting Hall had never been to World's End and therefore couldn't have known what the Throne Room of the Gods looked like.

A strange coincidence, if ever there was one, Malock thought. *Or maybe it's just my imagination at work, making me notice more similarities than there really are.*

"Tojas?" said Father, breaking Malock out of his concentration.

Malock looked over at Father. Father was looking at him with tired, old eyes that reflected his age. He even looked a little sickly, though Malock dismissed that as old age simply creeping up on Father. He had been looking this way ever since Malock had returned from World's End, but as Father had not complained much about it (aside from his usual complaints about his aching back), Malock never saw any reason to bring it up. He had asked Friyu, the Carnagian Royal Family's resident panamancer, to keep an eye on Father, though, just in case.

"Yes, Father?" said Malock. "What is it?"

"Councilman Nikar told me that King Fabadi is not here yet," said Father. "He said that it's unlikely Fabadi is going to come because Fabadi is still angry about Raya's assassination happening on Carnagian soil and that he's angry we still haven't executed the assassin."

Malock groaned as the delegates began taking their seats in their boxes all around. "That's right. I almost forgot that he wasn't here. Doesn't he know that Jenur didn't kill Raya, that it was Hollech's servant?"

Father looked skeptical. Not surprising; after all, it had been Jenur Takren, one of Malock's friends, who had been found with the knife that had been used to murder Raya. Indeed, the only reason Jenur was still alive today was because Malock had managed to convince his parents and King Fabadi that Jenur had been framed for the assassination of Raya. Though when Malock thought about it, he realized he had little proof of that claim except for the knowledge that Jenur had no reason for killing Raya whatsoever.

That was the explanation he had given Father, Mother, and King Fabadi at the time, but he had always been aware that his parents only half-believed him and Fabadi didn't believe him at all. Maybe if Fabadi had known Jenur as well as he did, Fabadi would have, but Fabadi didn't, which made Malock glad that Jenur and Quro had vanished from the public eye. Otherwise, he was sure that Fabadi would have sent the entire Shikan Army to kill them or at least kill Jenur.

"It's not my fault that Fabadi can be an irrational old fool," said Father. "He's always been that way, even before you were born, Tojas. When Fabadi gets an idea in his mind, he rarely lets go of it, even if you offer him proof that it is a bad idea."

"Then again, I guess it's not that surprising," said Malock. "The Shikans have been acting increasingly unfriendly towards us ever since Raya's death. I have even heard rumors that Shikan pirates have been targeting Carnagian vessels to the exclusion of the ships from other nations."

Father shuddered. "Let us pray to Grinf that Fabadi doesn't decide to go to war with us. He's so angry that I doubt it would take much to convince him to declare war on Carnag."

Then Father looked at the surrounding boxes and their delegates, a frown on his face. "That was why I was hoping Fabadi would be here. I hoped we could calmly and rationally discuss Shika and Carnag's relations, but if he refuses to come, then that complicates things quite a bit."

Malock nodded. "It certainly does. After this Summit, we should send an envoy to ask Fabadi for a meeting."

"I tried that while you were away," said Father. "But he didn't even let the envoy enter Castle Shika. This behavior on his part does not point to a bright future for the relations between Carnag and Shika, that's for certain."

"We just need to be smart," said Malock. "After all, Father, you were the one who taught me that you shouldn't give your opponent any ammunition to use against you in negotiations, right? As long we don't do anything to provoke Fabadi intentionally, then I think we can avoid a full-fledged war with Shika."

Father sat back in his chair, but he did not slump, as to do so in the presence of so many other delegates and royalty would be to invite ridicule and mockery. "Sometimes, Tojas, even if you do the right thing, everything can still go wrong. The world doesn't always reward the diligent and careful. Sometimes, it does the exact opposite."

"Maybe that will change," Malock said, "now that Skimif is in charge."

The mere mention of Skimif's name caused Father's eyes to flash with absolute loathing. His old fingers gripped the arms of his chair tightly and his face twisted into a scowl so foul that it made Malock lean back slightly.

But then Father took a deep breath and said, in a restrained voice, "Yes. Perhaps."

Malock had no trouble discerning Father's true feelings about Skimif. Back when Skimif had been a mortal, he had been the leader of the Brotherhood of Heathens and as a result had come into conflict with the Justice Enforcers, the primary law enforcers on Carnag who happened to be followers of Grinf. Malock knew that Father and Mother had always disproved of the Brotherhood, especially Skimif, which was why neither of them had been happy to learn that Skimif was now the God of Martir. Not that there was anything that either of them could do about it; even so, Malock could just imagine the hatred and rage Father felt toward Skimif for being given the highest title in all of Martir. It must have seemed like a slap in the face to him, making Malock feel a bit sorry for Father, even though he didn't feel quite the same about Skimif's ascension as Father did.

Of course, it wasn't like Malock was totally happy for Skimif. Sure, he was glad that his friend had been granted such an honor and he knew that Skimif would be a good god, but at times, he felt a little jealous. It was irrational jealousy, he knew, but sometimes, he wondered why it seemed like everyone around him was given certain honors that he wasn't.

First, the gods choose Kinker to become one of them, Malock thought, *Kinker Dolan, a simple fisherman from an obscure island on the edge of the Northern Isles. And then the Powers choose Skimif, a farmer from an obscure aquarian town, the name of which I cannot recall because it's so obscure, to become the most powerful god of all. What makes them so much more special than me?*

Granted, Malock didn't like dwelling on these thoughts. All they did was make him bitter and resentful towards people he liked and respected. Still, at times, when Malock lay in bed alone at night, trying to fall asleep but failing due to the Burn of Grinf on his face keeping him awake, he would wonder just why he was never chosen or destined for that kind of greatness.

I guess, if I understood that, then I would also understand the gods and the Powers, Malock thought. *And few mortals can honestly claim that, even I, someone who has had extensive experience with both.*

Just then, Father tapped Malock's shoulder and whispered, "Tojas, the Summit is about to begin. Pay attention, now."

Snapping out of his thoughts, Malock looked toward the center of the Meeting Hall. A bald, middle-aged man with a large mustache stood in the platform in the center of the room. He wore the long, flowing white robes of a member of the Northern Summit Committee; in fact, the man was Foram Yudra, the current chairman of the Northern Summit Committee. His face was small and almost child-like, but despite that, Malock knew from experience that Yudra was not a man to mess with, as he also happened to be an audimancer and was not above using his magic to make a point.

By now, all of the delegates and royalty in the Meeting Hall had gone quiet. Their eyes were on Foram, who was standing at the marble podium which went up to his waist. He was shuffling through some papers, perhaps his notes, with a frown on his face. Sweat dripped from his forehead, even though it was not very hot inside the Meeting Hall.

Then Foram looked up. Wiping the sweat off his brow, Foram said, "Welcome, delegates from the various human nations of the Northern Isles, to the twenty-fifth annual Northern Summit. For the new delegates who may not know, I am Foram Yudra, Chairman of the Northern Summit Committee. I am a loyal follower of Amare, Goddess of Sound, having served her for well over two decades now. I also hail from the island of Itrija, which is located on the northern tip of the Friana Archipelago; nonetheless, I strive to treat all delegates equally, regardless of their homelands, and always do my best to follow the rules of the Northern Summit Committee."

No one challenged Foram's claims, although Malock knew that not everyone believed that. Other delegates had claimed that the Itrijan dwellings on Rane were better kept than the dwellings of the other nations' delegates, but as far as Malock knew, such accusations were false. Chairmen of the Northern Summit Committee were usually picked by a vote from the various Northern delegates, to ensure that no one nation had more power over any of the others. Malock had not been here when Foram had been elected—which had been twenty years ago—but he knew that Father had cast one of the deciding votes in Foram's favor, which was why Malock respected the Chairman and didn't believe the rumors of partiality that circulated around him.

"With the introductions out of the way, allow me to read from the minutes of the last Northern Summit," said Foram. He held up a stack of paper and began reading from the top of it. "In the last Northern Summit, King Fabadi of Shika and King Halock of Carnag had agreed to sign a ten-year-long peace treaty between their nations that would officially end all the hostilities that have existed between the two nations for years."

Doesn't look like it's going to last even five, Malock thought, *if Fabadi remains angry with us.*

He glanced at Father, who seemed to be having the same thought as him. Unless Malock's eyes were deceiving him, Father's dark complexion was becoming progressively paler, prompting Malock to whisper, "Father? Are you all right?"

Father didn't look at him, but he nodded and whispered back, in a harsher voice, "Yes, Tojas, I am fine. Now shut up and listen to Foram. We can discuss this later."

Malock leaned back in his chair as Foram continued. "Then Councilman Aruga, Head Councilman of the Free Council of the Republic of Kikasa, agreed to extend Kikasa's trade agreement with five other Northern Isles nations, including—"

"Enough!" said a loud voice, causing almost all of the delegates to jump in their seats. "Are we honestly going to waste time recapping information everyone already knows, when there is much more important news to be discussed?"

Malock looked around and spotted King Fabadi standing at the exit. His silver-blonde hair poked out from under his white crown, while his equally white royal robes hung from his elderly body like a second skin. He looked absolutely enraged, as if someone had just insulted his family.

"King Fabadi," said Foram, forcing a smile. "We didn't think you were going to come."

"I wasn't," said Fabadi, gripping his silver scepter as he looked around the Hall. "But then I decided that this Summit was too important for me to miss; at least, I originally thought that, but if all we're going to do is sit around and talk about what we did—or didn't do, as is often the case—last time, then perhaps I wasted my time coming here all the way from Shika."

Many of the other delegates were sighing, some even shaking their heads. Most just looked surprised, as no one had ever interrupted a Summit like this, especially not a king like Fabadi. The King of Shika did not seem to care, however, because he didn't look at all intimidated or afraid of the delegates' obvious disapproval.

Next to Malock, Father sat upright, his eyes focusing on Fabadi. There was no telling what Father might have been thinking, but based on Father's expression, he had to be at least as surprised as everyone else.

"King Fabadi, with all due respect, this is how Northern Summits have always begun," said Foram, his tone level. "By discussing what we did last time, it gives us a context into which to place our current plans."

"Last time, Martir was not ruled by an aquarian and there was only one pantheon of gods," Fabadi said shortly. "I cannot be the only one who has had to rethink all of his future plans in light of this development. What we did or didn't do in the last Summit is irrelevant. What we need to do now, is."

Malock could not recall ever seeing Fabadi quite this way before. The King of Shika had always struck him as a subtler man, less prone to dramatics and theatrics, unlike some royals. Perhaps Fabadi was acting this way because he honestly believed his words or maybe it was because he was still grieving Raya's death or maybe both.

Either way, by now many of the delegates were muttering in unkind tones. They were too quiet for Malock to make out what they were muttering about, but it was quite clear just who was the subject of their conversations.

Foram, in an obvious attempt to get things back on schedule, said, "Yes, King Fabadi, I absolutely agree that we need to discuss these two very important changes to Martir that have happened since the last meeting, but rules are rules and—"

Fabadi actually laughed at that. "Rules are rules? What rules? The rules don't matter anymore, not when our entire world has been turned upside down. I say we skip the minutes—which I think we can all agree are utterly irrelevant to our current situation, whatever we may have discussed at the last Summit—and move on to the topic of discussion that all of us really want to discuss: Skimif and the southern gods."

Although there was still quite a bit of discontent among the delegates, quite a few were now nodding in agreement with Fabadi. Even Father was nodding, though whether it was because he agreed with Fabadi or because he was doing it to earn Fabadi's trust, Malock wasn't quite sure.

Foram looked a lot less confident than he had a few minutes before. He opened his mouth, closed it, then shuffled through the papers again, before finally saying, "All right. We can move on to Skimif and the southern gods, then. I'll just have my scribes make sure to hand out copies of the minutes from the last Summit to the delegates when you all return home. That way, you may all read the minutes even if we never get to discuss them."

With that, Foram flipped his papers face down and said to Fabadi, "King Fabadi, would you please take your place in the Shika box?"

Fabadi shook his head. "No. I wish to stand and speak to the rest of the delegates. Allow me to take your place. Now."

Foram looked annoyed at the request, but he nonetheless bowed and stepped away. Fabadi walked across the Hall, ignoring the many looks and murmurs from the other delegates. Fabadi strode forward with his back straight and his head held high, like a much younger ruler.

When he climbed onto the podium, he didn't even look at Foram or thank the Chairman for giving him a platform from which to speak. He just placed his scepter in his belt, put his hands on the podium, and looked around at all of the delegates, his eyes sweeping across them all like the judging eyes of Grinf.

Drumming his fingers against the marble podium's surface, his silver nails clicking and clacking against the marble, Fabadi said, "My fellow delegates. Some of you I have known for years, some as friends or allies, others as enemies. I see some new faces here, new delegates or young royalty sent to represent their kingdoms and peoples. No matter. In the end, what matters most is that we are all here, together, and that we live on this world, this world that is no longer the same."

Something about Fabadi's demeanor made Malock uneasy. It was

27

like a force had come over Fabadi, as though the King of Shika was being controlled by someone or something. More likely, Malock was just not used to seeing Fabadi act so passionate, as his past encounters with the King had made him think that the Shikans were generally reserved.

Even more amazing was the complete and utter silence that reigned over the Meeting Hall. At this point, there was usually lots of shouting and name-calling as random delegates brought up the grievances that their nations had against the nations of other delegates. Once, Father had gotten into a heated argument with the Natachan delegate about the quality of Carnagian boots that were delivered to Natachan (the delegate seemed to believe that the Carnagians had been intentionally designing the boots they sold to the Natachans badly, though to Malock's knowledge, the Carnagians never knowingly designed bad boots).

Fabadi gestured at the ceiling. Painted upon the ceiling was a map of every island in the Northern Isles, not counting the aquarian cities beneath the Crystal Sea. It was highly detailed, with each island appropriately labeled in Divina. It even had trade routes drawn on it to symbolize the primary chain that connected all of the islands together.

"We are all connected," said Fabadi. "By trade, by political alliances that have lasted, in some cases, for centuries, and by blood. And despite all of our differences, we all strive to serve the gods as best as we can, despite the difficulties that we as humans have faced from those who would rather we not."

Malock felt Father glance at him, but Malock didn't return the glance. Fabadi was clearly referring to the Brotherhood. Malock had forgotten that the Brotherhood had members on every island in the Northern Isles, not just Carnag, making him wonder just how the Heathens on Shika were doing in comparison to the Heathens on Carnag. He supposed he would have to ask Aqur, the current leader of the Brotherhood of Heathens, when he returned to Carnag, assuming he could get in contact with her, as she had not been very communicative with him since Skimif's ascension. That problem made him scowl.

"But now, everything has changed," said Fabadi. "The gods are no longer the highest powers in this world. They now must answer to Skimif, the God of Martir itself. This is completely unprecedented in the entire history of Martir. Not only that, but Skimif revealed to all mortals in the Northern Isles that there exist many more gods outside of the Northern Pantheon, gods who live in the southern seas, who are kept from killing us because of some 'Treaty' that appears to dictate the relations between the gods. All of this appears to be true, which is yet another massive revelation on top of Skimif's ascension. No doubt everyone here—or the leaders who sent the delegates here—have been trying to learn how these two major changes will affect us and our people and what we should do in response to them."

Almost every head in the Meeting Hall was nodding now, again including Father's. Malock nodded along as well, as he, too, had been wondering just how different things were going to be from now on, even after hearing Skimif's plans for the gods personally only a couple of months ago. He had not spoken to Skimif since World's End, so he didn't know for sure how well Skimif's plans were going along. He had not seen any disturbances in the world, nor heard of the gods causing any trouble, so he had always assumed that things were going fine.

"I have spent much time thinking on this matter and praying to Nimiko, the God of Light and the patron god of Shika," said Fabadi. "Yet the gods seem to be silent. Nimiko has not spoken to me. Nor has he spoken to any of our priests, many of whom have spent countless hours trying to contact him. Are we Shikans alone in this or have other nations also heard this deafening silence from the gods?"

"It is the same with us," said the Head Councilman of Kikasa, his voice deep. "The Council has sought guidance from the three gods whom we worship, but so far, there has been no response from any of them. It is worrisome."

The other delegates said nothing, but based on their expressions, it was clear that they, too, had heard nothing from their own gods.

Fabadi looked around at them all. "Is not that quite strange? As soon as Skimif takes over, the gods cease speaking to us mortals. It is almost as though Skimif is trying to separate the gods from the mortals. This should worry us all deeply, no matter what island we represent or rule."

Malock knew that there was some truth to what Fabadi said. Back on World's End, Skimif had said that he was going to make sure that the northern gods did not interact with mortals as much. It was to ensure that the northern gods would focus more on their actual purpose—maintaining the various domains and elements of Martir— instead of constantly fighting or bickering over minor issues. Malock wondered why Fabadi was treating this like a big revelation, however, when Malock was pretty certain that Skimif had made sure everyone on Martir knew of his plans.

"But this isn't an entirely terrible thing, is it?" said the Natachan delegate whose name Malock had forgotten. She was an older woman, with short gray hair, and beside her the other two Natachan delegates were nodding. "Doesn't anyone here remember the message? Skimif said he wanted to make sure the northern gods worked more diligently at their jobs, rather than interact with us mortals."

Exactly, Malock thought, but he kept the thought to himself, seeing as he had nothing more to add than what she had said.

"So he said," said Fabadi. "So he said. But can we believe him? Skimif was the leader of the Brotherhood of Heathens. He was known for his utter disrespect and hatred of the gods. What if Skimif is instead abusing his new power to weaken the gods so that he can conquer us all?"

Anger coursed through Malock, causing him to stand up and say, "That's a lie. I know Skimif. He is not a power-hungry tyrant like you make him out to be."

Fabadi's eyes shifted to Malock, as did the eyes of the other delegates. This was the first time Malock had ever spoken out in a meeting like this, as he had only ever come to past Northern Summits to prepare him for the day that he would become king. Having all of those eyes on him—some hostile, most curious—was a lot more nerve-wracking than he thought it would be, but Malock kept up a confident demeanor, not backing down in the slightest.

"Knew him?" said Fabadi. "How did you come to know the leader of a dangerous social movement, Prince Malock? Did you invite him up to Carnag Hall for brunch once?"

Not certain it would be wise to reveal his affiliation with the Brotherhood of Heathens to so many people at once, Malock said, "Because I was there when he was ascended. The Powers chose him to become the God of Martir because of his honest nature. Skimif only has our best interests at heart."

The delegates began muttering among themselves, mostly about Malock's revealing that he had been there when Skimif had ascended. Malock couldn't hear exactly what they were saying, however, because he felt someone tugging on the sleeve of his robes and, looking down, saw Father looking up at him. Father's face was paler than ever and sweat glistened on his forehead.

"Tojas, please," said Father. His voice was alarmingly weak. "There's no need for you to get involved in this."

"Actually, Halock, there is," said Fabadi, his own voice much stronger than Father's. "Your son is grown. He can stand for himself. No need to defend him, not when he obviously has much to say."

"I said my part," said Malock, looking back up at Fabadi. "Skimif has only our best interests at heart. He is a truly compassionate aquarian who cares about all mortals, whether they care about him or not. I agree we should discuss what changes his rule will bring, but I can confidently say that they will not be negative changes."

Fabadi snorted. "Are you a Tinkarian prophet, like Hanyu? Can you see the future? Of course not. Only Tinkar knows what our ultimate fates will be. I do not see how you can confidently say that the changes Skimif brings will be positive; in fact, I would argue just the opposite, that rather than help us, Skimif is working to harm us."

"What do you mean?" said Malock. "How will he harm us? What has he done so far to cause any of us harm?"

"The southern gods," said Fabadi. "You know, the gods who want to eat mortals? I sincerely wish that they were a myth, but they are very much real. Skimif has allowed them to cross into the Northern Isles much more often than they have done in the past, according to him. Yet why would he do that if he only had our best interests at heart?"

Malock's face began burning, causing him to involuntarily rub his face as he said, "Skimif made it clear that he intends to unify the gods. To do this, he is encouraging the gods to cross over into each other's territory more often than they have in the past and learn to work together more effectively."

"So he claims," said Fabadi. "But what if Skimif is instead using the southern gods to cow us into submission? Tell me, how much trade has been lost in recent months since the southern gods have been allowed to travel this far north?" He looked around at the rest of the delegates, all of whom wore expressions that told it all. "Shika cannot be the only island to have seen its trade drop to nearly half of what it was when the southern gods never crossed the Dividing Line. And I imagine it will only get worse as time goes on, making us weaker and weaker, unable to stand against Skimif and his southern gods."

Malock could not believe what he was hearing. "This is insane. The southern gods are forbidden by the Treaty from eating or attacking mortals who live beyond the northern half of the Dividing Line. Have you heard any news of southern gods attacking or harming any mortals in the Northern Isles?"

"Yes, I have," said Fabadi. "One week ago, a Shikan trading vessel was attacked and sunk by a massive kraken just off Shika's north shore. The Kraken Goddess—a southern goddess—was seen in the area around the same time, having allegedly come to rein in that beast. It was obvious, however, that the Kraken Goddess was behind it, because krakens do not live off the shores of Shika due to the water's temperature."

"And two weeks ago," the Natachan delegate spoke up suddenly, like she had just remembered something, "a serial killer calling herself the Southern Worshiper appeared on Natachan and killed a dozen men and women. When we apprehended her, she said she was working for the southern gods, who were planning to abuse their new freedom by causing chaos in the Northern Isles."

"See?" said Fabadi, gesturing at the Natachan delegate. "It is not Shika only that is under threat from the southern gods, Prince Malock. No doubt many of the other delegates here also have stories to tell about the southern gods and how they have harmed or threatened their people within the last two months."

Malock looked around at all of the delegates. Most were nodding in agreement, as they had been for most of the discussion. Others looked disquieted, perhaps worried that their people, too, might soon run into similar problems from the southern gods. The Frianan delegate, in particular, was glancing at the clock on the wall, as if he was frightened that every moment he spent here was another moment not spent back home on Friana, helping to make sure his island was safe.

"How do we know that the southern gods are actually behind any of these events?" said Malock. "I hate the southern gods as much as anyone else, but maybe the Southern Worshiper was just a crazy woman who thought the southern gods were telling her what to do. And maybe that kraken was just a kraken that somehow got lost and attacked that Shikan trading vessel because it was frightened or hungry. None of this implicates either Skimif or the southern gods."

Fabadi placed his scepter on the podium length ways and said, "But there is one story that implicates Skimif. Months ago, as everyone here—including you, Prince Malock—is aware, my daughter, Raya Kabadi, was killed by an assassin, at the time believed to be a servant of the god Hollech. A young woman named Gaharna Vicin was caught with the murder weapon in hand, but she was not punished because she claimed that it had actually been a servant of Hollech who had murdered Raya and that she had been framed for the assassination. Although I was skeptical of that claim, it was Prince Malock who defended her, saying that she was innocent and that he believed her story, despite the almost complete lack of proof of the existence of this Hollechian servant that Vicin claimed had framed her for a crime she didn't commit."

Fabadi's story was accurate, despite the obvious insinuation that Malock had unknowingly defended a murderer. Malock had indeed defended 'Gaharna Vicin'—really Jenur Takren, using a false name to protect her identity—despite Fabadi and everyone else believing that she was behind the assassination. Granted, Malock had not seen the Hollechian servant himself, but he knew Jenur well enough to know that she would never kill someone who, like Raya, had not been a threat to anyone.

But Fabadi didn't quite seem to believe that. His voice shook with emotion and his hands gripped the podium as he spoke of his daughter's death; nonetheless, he still managed to retain a leader-like appearance and confidence in the faces of so many delegates, despite the obvious grief he was experiencing as he relived the night on which his daughter had died.

"But recently, I have learned the truth about this Gaharna Vicin woman," said Fabadi. "A trustworthy informant—who has requested to remain anonymous for his own safety—has given me new information about her. I was told that Vicin was in fact a Dark Tiger hired by Skimif to kill Raya for no reason other than to strike fear into the hearts of us Shikans. My informant told me that Skimif had been planning to extend the Brotherhood's presence into Shika, but did not think he could succeed unless I was grieving too much to stop him and his petty band of fools that he calls a movement."

Gasps erupted all around the room, but Malock held up his hands and said, "Hold on. Who is this informant? What proof did he offer of this claim? This is the first time I've heard of this."

"The proof, Prince Malock?" said Fabadi. His tone had become sharper than a steel blade now. He reached into the folds of his robes. "The proof is this document, written and signed by Skimif of Tunya, detailing the exact amount of money he was to pay the Dark Tiger Gaharna Vicin for killing my daughter."

With a flourish, Fabadi pulled out a folded piece of brown paper, which he unfolded and held up for everyone to see. Fabadi was too far away for Malock to read the note, but its blue ink shone in the light of the chandelier above his head, blue ink which reminded Malock of Skimif's room back in the former headquarters of the Brotherhood of Heathens on Carnag. Fabadi turned in a circle, making sure that all of the delegates could see the paper, holding it high above his head with shaking hands.

"This was the proof that the informant gave me," said Fabadi. He then lowered it and flipped it around so that the text was facing his face. "For the skeptics among us, shall I read it aloud, so that everyone may know exactly what Skimif has written?"

Before anyone could object, Fabadi began reading the paper aloud: "*To: Gaharna Vicin. Upon completion of the assassination of Princess Raya Kabadi, the Princess of Shika, on the day of her wedding to Prince Tojas Malock, Prince of Carnag, I will pay you the second half of the five hundred coins I promised to pay you for the work. Signed, Skimif of Tunya, leader of the Brotherhood of Heathens.*"

Fabadi's fingers shook as he read that. Nonetheless, his voice was steady and clear, and when he finished, the angry tears in his eyes were so thick that Malock was surprised Fabadi could see at all.

Looking up from the note, Fabadi said, "Is this the man we wish to rule over not only us, but our whole world? This conniving, coldhearted revolutionary who could care less about the lives of others if they get in the way of his ideology?"

Malock could hardly believe his ears. "King Fabadi, are you certain that the letter was written by Skimif? What if it was forged?"

"Forged?" said Fabadi. "This is no forgery, I can assure you. I had some of my mages look it over and they all agree that it was written sometime before Raya's death. This is one hundred percent genuine, and is clear proof of Skimif's treachery."

Malock shook his head even as the rest of the Meeting Hall erupted into mutters and whispers. "May I read the note? I would like to see its contents myself."

"Not right now," said Fabadi, clutching the letter close to his heart. "What matters now is that we must act against Skimif if we are to have any chance of freedom or survival. He is a dangerous person, whether as a mortal or as a god, and I doubt that his ascension to godhood has made him a better person."

"But what do we do about him?" said the Frianan delegate who Malock had noticed earlier. "And the southern gods? How do we mortals fight gods? Furthermore, how do we fight the God of Martir himself?"

"Who says we need to fight them?"

The voice that asked that question made everyone look in its direction. The owner of the voice sat in the box next to Malock and Father's box, in the Kikasa box. It was a middle-aged man with a short, brown beard, with tiny silver hairs starting to show, and wearing large, crimson pants who had spoken. He looked cross, with a frown on his lips, and it took Malock a moment to recognize him as Nikar Aruga, the Head Councilman of Kikasa and the Kikasan delegate.

"What was that, Nikar?" said Fabadi, a hint of annoyance in his voice.

"You heard me," said Nikar. His voice was tinged with that strange accent all Kikasans had, which sounded like he had gravel stuck between his teeth. "I admit that I don't like the sound of things and I certainly don't want Heathens like Skimif running the world, but I think it might just be best for us to accept it. If we fight, who knows what kind of damage Skimif and the southern gods could inflict on our people?"

"If we don't fight, who knows what kind of damage they *will* inflict on our people?" said Fabadi. "Make no mistake, Nikar—or any of the other delegates who may harbor doubts, for that matter. Skimif and the southern gods do not come in peace. They seek to enslave, conquer, and perhaps even destroy us."

"Now that is jumping to conclusions," said Malock. "We have no idea if that letter was forged or not. You have no proof that Skimif is planning anything. You're just—"

Malock felt Father tugging at his robe sleeve again, causing him to look down at Father once more, annoyed at being interrupted. His annoyance quickly turned to concern, however, when he saw just how pale and sweaty Father's face and hands were.

"Tojas," said Father. His voice was so weak that, although he obviously wasn't whispering, he might as well have been. "My health ... it's ..."

Without warning, Father slumped forward in his chair, his forehead hitting the rim of the box in front of him.

Malock dropped down to his seat as the rest of the Meeting Hall erupted into shocked shouts and gasps. Fabadi actually abandoned his position behind the podium and walked over to the Carnag box, while Foram stuck his head out the door and yelled for Rane's panamancers to come and check out Father right away.

Father's eyes were closed and his heart was barely beating. His skin was so sweaty and pale that he looked more like a Shikan than a Carnagian now.

"Father?" said Malock, shoving Father's shoulder to see if he could wake him.

Father didn't move.

"Father!" said Malock. "Wake up. What's wrong?"

Again, Father didn't move at all.

By now, Fabadi had reached their box, a look of concern on his face as he reached for Father's arm. He felt Father's pulse, which Malock didn't object to him doing, and his concerned face became even grimmer.

"Your father is sick, Malock," said Fabadi, looking up at him suddenly. "He is terribly ill, but not being a doctor or a panamancer, I can't tell what illness he may have come down with."

At that moment, a couple of panamancers entered the Meeting Hall, their cloaks embedded with the symbol of the Northern Summit. They dashed across the Meeting Hall to the Carnag box, where Father's unconscious body still slumped forward like a paper doll. The panamancers immediately began waving their wands over Father's body and muttering chants under their breaths, but despite that Father didn't seem to be getting better at all.

"We'll have to move him out of the Meeting Hall and to the atikan," said one of the panamancers to Malock. "This is no place to heal him. If you can come with us and tell us what symptoms King Halock was showing before he collapsed, that would be great."

Malock nodded and climbed out of the box as the panamancers

used their magic to float Father out of his seat. Even as he did so, however, Malock did not have a good feeling about this, which was why he made sure to follow right behind the panamancers floating Father out of the Meeting Hall, ignoring all of the mutterings and whispers from the other delegates as he passed them.

Chapter Three

J ENUR CUT THROUGH THE snow like a knife on her way to rescue her Dad. Her legs burned and her boots felt heavy on her feet, but she didn't allow any of that to slow her down. Huffing and puffing, ignoring the frightened snow rabbits that she sent scurrying when she zoomed by, Jenur at last reached the final hill between her and her and Dad's home. It was not a terribly tall hill—indeed, it was closer to a mound than a hill—but it had snowed recently and her clothes and boots were so heavy that it was harder for her to climb over than it should have been. Not to mention she was still tired from her fight with Kura, which added to the difficulty of climbing the hill.

When Jenur reached the top of the hill, she put her hands on her knees and panted as she looked down at the beach below. For one frantic moment, she couldn't see the house, but then she spotted their tiny hut—short and stout, the wooden roof peaking out from under the thin layer of snow covering it—and also saw smoke rising from the front window. Someone had left the door open, but there were no footprints in the snow before it, nor was there any sign of anyone else having been there, either. The smoke alone almost drained Jenur of all hope, but she didn't turn and run away.

Instead, Jenur ran down the hill to the beach, where their house was located. The ocean waves crashed against the rocky beach, which she hoped would be loud enough to hide the sounds of her boots against the snow. She didn't know if Wirm was still there or if he might have left after finishing off ... she didn't even want to think about it.

Until I see Dad's corpse for myself, I can't let myself think that, Jenur thought as she drew closer and closer to the hut. *And Wirm very well might not be there at all. I mean, he sent Kura after me. Maybe he thinks Kura killed me and so he went to go find her or something.*

Jenur walked doubled over to the hut, hoping that her coat would help her blend in with the snow. She could now see through the open door, which swayed slightly in the wind, but there were no lights on in the hut and she couldn't hear any noises from within.

In a few seconds, Jenur finally reached the hut, but she didn't enter immediately. She sidled up against the outside wall, holding her breath, feeling the heat radiating off the exterior, trying to be as silent as possible. She inclined her head toward the open doorway, trying to hear the slightest noise, but to her disappointment, all she heard was the sound of the wind blowing through.

But the stench of smoke burned her nose. It had been months since Jenur had last smelled that smoke. Wirm had been a capnomancer; in fact, Dad had once told her that one of Wirm's favorite killing methods was using smoke to choke his targets. She had never actually seen Wirm do it, but knowing his brutal nature, she had no reason to doubt it.

Just go inside now, Jen, Jenur thought, her fingers rubbing against the cold stone walls. *You can take Wirm. You've faced actual gods before and survived. He's just a mortal; a mortal who can turn into smoke, maybe, but still a mortal. What's the worst that he could do?*

She shouldn't have thought that. Once again, her mind briefly returned to the day Wirm had beaten her for her laziness. He had mercilessly broken her face. He had ultimately spared her life, that was true, but Jenur froze just thinking about him. What if he beat her again? He was a legendary assassin, better and more experienced than the rest of the Dark Tigers' Guild put together. Jenur was good, but even she knew that she was no match for the Grand Tiger himself.

Then Jenur shook her head. *The longer I stand here, worrying and letting my old fears and memories constrain me, the more likely it is that Wirm is killing Dad. It doesn't matter how I feel. I'm the only person who can save Dad from Wirm and I have to do it now.*

Drawing her knife out of its sheath, her hand heating the handle from her gripping it so tightly, Jenur took a deep breath and stood in the doorway.

"Wirm," Jenur said, her voice as firm as she could make it, although it trembled slightly despite herself. "It's me, Jenur. Jenur Takren. You know, the girl you beat up a while ago? Quro's adopted daughter?"

No response. The hut was completely dark and incredibly smoky. The smoke must have been thick because she had to step back to avoid inhaling too much of it. Not to mention that the smoke burned her eyes, making them water, forcing her to wipe the tears away.

"Wirm?" said Jenur again. "I'm here. Where are you? Are you just going to sit there in the smoke and choke to death? Because that would be really convenient for me and considerate of you, you know, since you're a worthless scumbag who isn't worthy of even half the respect that the other Tigers always gave you."

"And you, girl, are not worth even half of the life that your father gave you," said a low, yet cunning, voice behind her. "Allow me to take it."

Two large hands gripped Jenur's arms and lifted her off her feet before she could do anything. The hands were trying to move her towards the open door, but Jenur lashed out backwards with her feet and felt her boots strike a soft, pudgy face, causing Wirm to cry out in pain and drop her.

Falling to her feet, Jenur rolled to the side, avoiding both of his massive fists as they smashed into the ground where she had stood previously. Getting to her feet, Jenur held her knife before her defensively as Wirm lifted his hands off the ground and turned to face her.

Wirm had not changed a bit since Jenur had last seen him. He was still unnaturally huge, almost as big as the late Bifor Kamon, a mage who had tried to kill her a while ago, which didn't endear her to him very much. His massive fists were thicker than rocks, the bronze knuckles on them gleaming in the faint sunlight above. The knuckles themselves had the words 'DARK TIGERS' carved into their surface. Those were the same knuckles Wirm had worn when he had beaten Jenur and just seeing them made her want to turn and run, but she held her ground just the same.

His hair was short and trim, like a tiger's coat. A thick, heavy winter coat hung off his body, its surface dotted with dozens of pockets that no doubt carried a variety of assassination tools for whatever situation Wirm found himself in. His left eye was red and swelling shut, probably from Jenur's boot earlier, but despite that, he looked at her with an amused smile on his face, the same smile he had worn when he had first beaten her not long ago.

"Jenur Takren," said Wirm, wiping away a line of blood dripping from the corner of his mouth. "As prone to playing dirty as ever, I see. Your boot did not taste very good."

Smoke came from the corners of Wirm's lips as he spoke, which didn't help Jenur's nerves at all.

"Where's Dad?" said Jenur.

Wirm's smile continued, almost as if Jenur had asked him how he had slept last night. "Quro is dead. I came upon the traitor as he was fishing for dinner for the two of you. He put up a good fight, but he was easy to subdue and even easier to kill."

Wirm ran a thick finger along his neck as he said that.

"You should have seen the blood," said Wirm. "It was ugly and messy, as blood always is, but I never get tired of seeing aquarian blood. You never know what color it will be. His was black, you know."

"Where's Dad's body?" said Jenur. Her voice shuddered as she said that and her heart felt empty, her motivation draining like the heat from her body.

"In the hut," said Wirm, gesturing at the smoking hut. "I put it in there and started a fire in your pitiful little stove. I was worried it might burn to the ground before you got here, but I see that I was wrong."

"How did you know I would even be here?" said Jenur. "What if Kura had killed me?"

Wirm's smile never left his lips as he said, "Kura is a jealous fool, silly and shortsighted. Though she is older than you, I did not think for even one moment that she would be able to defeat you, no matter what advantages she may have had. Tell me, what sounds did she make when she died?"

"I didn't kill her," said Jenur. "I just left her to die back in the valley."

Wirm tilted his head to the side. "That is a very merciful thing of you, girl. If I recall correctly, your favorite method of disposing of your targets was to slit their throat in just the right spot, thus killing them instantly. But of course, you are too weak to stomach the sight of death anymore, aren't you?"

"I'm not weak," said Jenur. "I just had enough sense in me to see how wrong the Dark Tigers are. I knew I didn't want to be part of that life anymore, no matter how much I may have been used to it."

"Youth always believe they know better than their elders," said Wirm, shaking his head. "Youth never appreciate the things they are given until they are taken away from them. That is why you betrayed us, you spoiled child, after the many years we allowed Quro to raise you, despite the Rules explicitly stating that no children are allowed in the Den."

"After you beat me, did you really think I wasn't going to run for it and never look back?" said Jenur.

47

"I was disciplining you," said Wirm, holding up his bronze knuckles. "I discipline all lazy, traitorous Tigers. This is yet another thing youth dislike. Youth find discipline disagreeable, but never realize or understand that it will help them in the long run."

"That wasn't discipline," said Jenur. "That was abuse and you know it, you psycho."

Wirm laughed; actually laughed, smoke streaming from his mouth like a chimney. He slapped his belly, laughing so hard that it seemed he had let his guard down completely. Not that Jenur bothered to take advantage of his seeming defenselessness. She knew him well enough to know that Wirm never left his guard down even when he was laughing uncontrollably.

"Oh, my young, pathetic little girl," said Wirm in between chuckles. "I have been called many things in my life. Murderer. Opportunist. Killer. Hater of the gods. Greed's consort. Lover of gold. Obese baba raga. Blood farmer. Woman beater. And many, many others that would make your skin crawl. But psycho? My, that is the tamest insult anyone has ever called me. I suppose Quro didn't teach you very many good insults, now did he?"

Jenur gritted her teeth. Her eyes darted to the hut, which was still smoking. If Wirm was telling the truth, then Dad was already dead and there was nothing she could do for him. Jenur would just have to defeat Wirm, somehow.

But what if Wirm lied? Jenur thought. *What if he only thought he killed Dad? Maybe Dad is still alive in there, but only barely.*

Of course, the idea was dead to her before she even finished thinking it. There were a lot of things you could say about Wirm—

most of which Wirm had already said himself—but he was not one to leave any of his victims unless he was absolutely certain, beyond a shadow of a doubt, that they were dead. Jenur remembered hearing rumors from the other Tigers that Wirm had once been a doctor prior to founding the Dark Tigers' Guild, which would explain how he knew so much about killing, but whether he had or hadn't been one, he was by no means lazy or hasty.

"No comebacks?" said Wirm. "You surprise me, girl. I remember you always having a snappy retort for any occasion. I imagine it must have died when you learned that Quro was dead."

"I was thinking," Jenur said, "about how your corpse is going to make an excellent meal for the local baba raga when I'm done with it. Though it might not be entirely healthy, seeing as you're what, eighty or ninety percent fat? I'm surprised you even came out this far. It must have taken you hours to recover."

Wirm's smile never faded. "Insulting my weight is a little better than insulting my sanity, but not by much."

Then Wirm spread his legs and slammed his fists together. The bronze knuckles echoed loudly through the quiet winter air, their clanging sound reminding Jenur of how Wirm had prepared to beat her the first time. That sent her heart rate soaring and her face sweating.

"Enough banter," said Wirm. He pointed at Jenur and said, "I have a lot of business awaiting me back on Ruwa and I left Corze in charge. I accepted this mission only because you are the only Tiger to last longer than a day when you decided to quit. Well, you and Quro, of course, but you have lasted longer than him."

"Who hired you?" said Jenur. "How did you find this place? How did you find us?"

Wirm's smile widened. "Your questions just gave me a brilliant idea, girl. Why don't we make a deal?"

"Great idea," said Jenur. "How's about this: You leave, right now, and never, ever come back or send anyone else after me or tell anyone else where I am. This way, you can get back to your business on Ruwa and I can live. It's a win-win situation."

"No, that would be silly," said Wirm. "My offer is simple. If you defeat me, I will tell you who my client is and how I found you two. If I defeat you, however ... then you die."

Jenur frowned. "That's rather generous of you, Wirm."

"Yet it is true," said Wirm. "I am a man of my word, despite what some may say."

"Why are you even making that offer?" said Jenur.

Wirm's smiled widened once more. "Because I know you will not be able to defeat me."

With that, Wirm fired a smoke pillar at her. Jenur jumped out of the way just in time, but it turned out to be a distraction because suddenly Wirm was before her and she hadn't even seen him move. His body's stench—a mixture of swamp water and smoke that stirred the bad memories in her mind again—caused her to choke, giving Wirm the opportunity to smash one of his bronze knuckles into her face.

Getting punched in the face by Wirm was like getting hit by a large, heavy boulder. The blow sent her staggering, blood pouring from her nose, her whole world spinning. Her vision of the world was briefly replaced by the night Wirm beat her. It was like she was standing in the Grand Tiger's room again, rather than on the snowy beach of Urma.

But then she shook her head and her vision returned just in time for her to see Wirm's other fist coming at her. This time, she ducked, causing his fist to go flying past her. This left Wirm's stomach undefended, allowing her to jab at his stomach with her knife.

But before her blade could cut through his clothes and rip through his flesh, Wirm's body turned to smoke and she staggered directly through it. Jenur regained her balance just as Wirm's body rematerialized. As it did so, he whirled around and slammed the back of his left hand into the side of her face, once again blinding her. The blow knocked her flat off her feet and onto the cold, harsh snow.

The wet snow felt good on her broken nose, but Jenur didn't allow herself to lie there. She rolled just as one of Wirm's massive boots slammed down where her head had been and got to her feet as Wirm fired two pillars of smoke at her again.

The blood still flowing freely from her nose, Jenur managed to avoid the first pillar by moving to the right, but the second one struck her dead on in the chest. Her breasts burned from the smoke's heat and when the smoke cleared, she discovered that it had left a burnt, blackened hole in the chest of her coat, partly exposing her breasts to the unforgiving gelid wind that blew in just then.

She had little time to think about that, however, because Wirm was dashing at her again, his huge feet stomping through the snow like a giant through a village. Jenur tried to move, but her legs felt weak and her nose was still bleeding like a river. She merely managed a few inches back before Wirm was upon her like the tiger he was.

With his smile as chilling as ever, Wirm kicked Jenur in the gut. His boot hit with the force of a sledgehammer, knocking her over flat on her back. The fall jarred her, but she could do nothing to save herself because Wirm slammed his boot down on her stomach just then. A loud *crack* split the air, but whether it was something inside Jenur breaking or just her imagination, all she knew was that she was going to die.

"Stupid girl," said Wirm, panting as he wiped the sweat off his brow. "Foolish girl. Pathetic girl. You did not give me a good fight. All you did was run and dodge, run and dodge. If I had known how much trouble you would have caused me in the future, I would have killed you as a baby. At least then our fight might have been a little bit more challenging."

Jenur tried to raise her knife, but Wirm fired a thin stream of smoke from his left hand's index finger at her left hand. The smoke hit hot and burning, causing her to drop the knife and pull her now-burning hand close to her body.

"There will be no stabbing me," said Wirm. He cracked his knuckles. "But there will be plenty of me smashing you into pulp. And there will be no panamancer to put your face—or your body—back together after I am through with it."

He raised his gleaming bronze knuckles high, putting his hands together to form an even larger fist than the two of them separate. His smile was so wide now that it looked like the mouth of a fanged fish than that of a human being.

Jenur closed her eyes and did not wipe her bleeding nose. *I don't want to see my own death. I'd rather die not knowing a thing about what my corpse is going to look like.*

Then—without any warning at all—a loud explosion tore through the air. It was so loud that Jenur's eyes snapped open. Wirm had paused, looking over his shoulder, and Jenur raised her head just enough to see that the hut's roof had exploded. Flames and smoke rose from its innards, which were scattered by the start of yet another explosion.

The fire must have hit the fuel, Jenur thought.

But that thought was in her head for less than a second. With her left hand still burning from Wirm's smoke, Jenur reached over and grabbed her knife. In one smooth motion, Jenur jabbed the knife into the side of Wirm's boot, driving it directly into his ankle as far and as hard as she could.

Wirm howled in pure pain, jumping off her and jumping around on one foot as he reached for Jenur's knife. Jenur unsteadily got to her feet as quickly as she could, almost falling over once but soon succeeding. Wirm had hopped away from her now, still grabbing his leg, but Jenur didn't try to attack him. Instead, she jammed her hand down her pocket, found some pepper powder pellets, and without hesitation hurled them directly at Wirm's face.

Because Wirm was so distracted by the knife jammed in his foot, the pellets hit him directly in the eyes. He yelled in pain again and actually fell over this time, landing on his back and rolling in the snow as he reached for the knife again and again, but could not reach it due to the shortness of his arms.

For a single second, Jenur considered finishing it right here and now. With Wirm in so much pain, with his guard down completely, it would have been easy for Jenur to finish him now. The old bastard deserved to die for everything that he'd done to her and she was in the perfect position to do it.

But that single second thought disappeared entirely when Jenur shivered from the cold air and felt her broken nose throbbing and bleeding. She cast her eyes toward the hut, the flames leaping out and the smoke curling up into the sky, and knew that she had to get out of here right away.

While Wirm continued to groan and curse, Jenur turned and ran. Her destination was the village Yurima, the only settlement on Urma. She knew some people there, people who would hopefully take her in and heal her.

And if they would not, Jenur would simply catch a ride on a ship heading south. Because it was clear that she could no longer live in Urma, or for that matter, anywhere else, in peace, although that didn't stop her from running away just the same, trying not to look back at Wirm or the burning hut in which Dad's body had been buried.

Chapter Four

MALOCK SAT ON THE wooden, finely-crafted bench outside of Father's room in the atikan, his head in his hands and his mind full of worry. He barely took notice of the glowing rocks embedded in the ceiling that provided light for him to see by, nor did he give much thought to the polished marble floor upon which his bench stood. He didn't even notice the Burn of Grinf making his face hurt again. He just kept glancing up at the clock on the wall opposite him, the only object on the walls of the hallway, which told him that it had been ten minutes since the panamancers had taken Father into the room on his right, even though it felt more like ten hours.

Malock leaned toward the door, straining to hear what was going on behind it. All he heard were the mutterings of the Ranian panamancers and their wooden shoes clacking against the marble floor. But he didn't hear Father move or make any noise, not even once.

What is going on in there? Malock thought. *Why haven't they come out yet? Is Father all right? Is he—?*

He just sunk his head into his hands again. He should have known that Father would have collapsed. Although Father was a strong man and always took illness in stride, he was getting older and thus more susceptible to disease. Friyu had always been there to keep Father healthy, which made Malock feel like an idiot for not protesting Father's decision to have Friyu stay home when she should have come with them.

Friyu would know what to do, I bet, Malock thought. *She's been our panamancer for years and knows our health better than we do.*

What made this wait worse was the sheer aloneness Malock experienced as he sat there. None of the other delegates had come by to see how he and Father were doing. Their servants who had come with them from Carnag had stopped by, but Malock had ordered them to return to the ship so it wouldn't be neglected in this time of tragedy. He now wished he hadn't.

Just then, the door to Father's room opened and a woman stepped out of it. She was one of the panamancers, a native from Nikon if her red hair was any indication. She closed the door slowly and then turned to look at Malock. She seemed to be in her late thirties, not much older than Malock, but she gave off an air of experience that made her seem older than him by a couple of decades at least.

Malock stood up. "How is my father? Will he be okay? Do you know what kind of disease he's come down with?"

The panamancer shook her head grimly. "I am sorry, Your Majesty, but we do not know why your father collapsed, nor what illness he has come down with. We've used all of the usual spells to heal fainting, but he is not getting any better."

Malock felt his heart fall. "Not getting any better? At all?"

"At all," said the panamancer, nodding. "I just came out to ask you a few questions about your father's health."

"He's never done anything like this before," said Malock. "My father has always suffered from back problems, but he's never outright collapsed like this. He's always been healthy for his age and anytime he did come down with a disease, Friyu, our panamancer, would nurse him back to health with no problems whatsoever."

The panamancer listened with her hand on her chin and a frown on her face. "Was your father like this on the voyage from Carnag? We think he may have gotten seasick, but we're not sure."

Malock almost said no, but then he thought about it. Father had spent a lot of time in his cabin on board the *Grinf's Hammer*, complaining about his stomach and rarely attending meals, instead having his servants bring his meals up to his room. Father had even looked pale and sweaty, though not to the same extent as he had earlier, so Malock didn't think much of it at the time because Father hadn't thrown up or anything and had managed to get off the ship just fine when they docked at Rane.

Then he nodded and said, "He was rather sick on our ship while we were heading here, but nothing like this."

"That is not good," said the panamancer. "Does he usually get seasick like that?"

"No," said Malock. "Now that I think about it, it is awfully strange how Father was so sick. He is usually very good on the seas, rarely complaining or anything."

"He must have caught some sort of disease, then," said the panamancer. "Possibly from one of the other delegates, though it was probably unintentional."

"But you will be able to save him, yes?" said Malock, putting his hands together. "Even if you don't know what the disease is?"

The panamancer shrugged. "If we don't know what it is or what caused it, then we ... well, it will be a lot harder for us to heal. I was going to go to the medical library on the first floor to research the symptoms of your father's disease. It's possible he may have been inflicted with a rare disease none of us know or recognize."

"Please hurry," said Malock. "Do you need any help searching the books? Because I can—"

"No, sorry," said the panamancer, cutting him off abruptly. "Only resident panamancers have access to the medical library. Atikan rules, you understand. You'll just have to sit here and wait."

Malock sighed, but sat back down on the bench anyway as the panamancer walked past him, her robes flowing behind her. He watched her go, his hands on his knees, until she turned down the corner at the end of the hall and disappeared entirely.

Leaning back against the bench's back, Malock looked at the door to Father's room. He could still hear the voices of the other panamancers, blocked by the stone door and walls, as well as their footsteps as they walked around the room. Occasionally, a bright flash of light would show through the crack under the door, which told him that they were still using their magic on Father, despite what the panamancer had said earlier about not knowing what they were up against.

I cannot do this, Malock thought, shaking his head. *Sitting here, worrying incessantly about something I can't control, and wondering if Father will even make it. I need to take a walk. If the panamancers make any progress or something happens, I'm sure they'll let me know.*

Standing up, Malock walked down the hall in the same direction that the panamancer from earlier had taken. He walked past the doors on both sides of the hallway until he reached the stairs, which took him down to the atikan's lobby, a wide-open room with chairs scattered here and there, along with desks and books for people who were waiting to hear the status of their friends or family to read, although the lobby was void of everyone except for the secretary who sat at the desk, but she didn't look up at him as he walked by because she seemed to be busy with some kind of paperwork that he didn't stop to inquire about. A large statue of Atikos, Goddess of Healing and Steel, dominated the center of the lobby, depicting the goddess as a beautiful woman with a caring face who carried a bottle of medicine in one hand while wearing a dress of steel over her plump body. He ignored it as he passed.

Pushing open the doors, Malock stood for a moment and looked at his surroundings. The Ranian atikan had been built on top of a hill, not far from the Northern Agora, where the Meeting Hall was held, which loomed above Malock like a gigantic turtle shell. A freshly-swept stone path lead down from the atikan to the main road, which led to the buildings where the delegates slept and lived during the Northern Summit, as it usually lasted a week. A massive gate—carved with the symbols of every nation in the Northern Isles—guarded the way into the Northern Agora, although it was currently open, with two Ranian guards standing on either side, shields and spears at the ready.

Malock didn't know if the rest of the delegates were still inside the Northern Agora or not, but he didn't want to go there anyway. No doubt the other delegates were eager to hear about Father's current status, but seeing as there was nothing to report except that Father was likely going to die sooner rather than later, Malock saw no reason to go and inform them about it.

Instead, Malock walked down the path and turned to the left, walking toward the walled Garden of the Gods that was located not very far from the atikan. The Garden of the Gods was a garden that had been built by a team of botamancers and lithomancers around fifty years ago, designed to allow the delegates a calm, slow atmosphere in which to relax and reflect on their goals for the Northern Summit during breaks. It was not a place Malock had visited very often, mostly because he never had reason to, but today he thought that its calm layout and atmosphere might help him worry less about Father.

Unlike the Northern Agora, the Garden of the Gods had no gate and therefore no guards. Upon passing through the walls, Malock found himself standing at a fork. He looked down both paths, seeing only green plants and statues of the gods either way. His eyes lingered on the statue of Grinf down the right path, his face burning before he broke his gaze and went down the left path instead.

As Malock walked down the path, he recalled that the Garden of the Gods, like every other structure on Rane, had been built as a team effort by all of the nations that attended the Northern Summit.

Father had once told him that, when the Garden was complete, each nation had sent a statue of their nation's god or gods to be placed in the Garden. As a result, there were almost as many statues of the gods as there were plants, hence why it was named the Garden of the Gods.

Why am I thinking about the history of this stupid Garden? Malock thought. *Who cares? It's not like it will help Father.*

With his arms folded behind his back, Malock walked down the narrow stone path with no particular destination in mind. He just followed the path wherever it twisted or turned, whether it went over a bridge that crossed a thin, shallow stream or if it went under a couple of Nikon hanging hands that required he duck his head briefly to avoid getting his hair tangled in the trees' branches. There were not many insects or animals here, which was good because Malock was not in any mood to have to fight off wildlife.

Finally, Malock reached the end of the Garden, the very back, which was a platform that jutted out over the sea below. With polished metal railings and firm steel beams supporting it, Malock had no trouble with walking out on the platform and looking over the Crystal Sea, which crashed against the beach underneath it. He just looked out over the sea for a moment, hoping to feel his anxiety go down, but realizing that all it did was go up as he thought about Father and what he was going through.

What am I going to tell Mother when I get home? Malock thought. *I guess I will only have to worry about that when I find out what is going to happen to Father.*

Then Malock heard the scratching of straw against stone and looked over his shoulder. A short, bald-headed man, wearing the gray robes of the Ranian sweepers, was quietly sweeping the path that Malock had just walked on. The sweeper, who must have been on duty, didn't even seem to notice Malock. He had his head down as he brought the broom back and forth across the stone pavement, although there wasn't much to sweep that Malock could see.

Just a sweeper, Malock thought, turning his head back to the sea, which glittered from the sunlight overhead. *But did he have to start sweeping now? Why can't he go away and leave me alone?*

"Prince Tojas Malock of Carnag?" said a slightly high-pitched voice behind him.

Malock looked over his shoulder again and saw that the sweeper was now only a few feet behind him. The sweeper had an oddly wide smile, almost monkey-like in its length, and he smelled of wet animal fur for some reason. Malock hadn't heard the sweeper walk up behind him, but he supposed that he must have just been distracted or maybe the sweeper could move lightly, seeing as the sweeper did not wear any heavy shoes or boots on his feet.

"Yes, that is me," said Malock, turning around to face him. "Who are you?"

"Just a humble sweeper, trying to make this place as beautiful as it should be," said the sweeper, leaning against his broom. He kept shifting his feet, like he wasn't used to wearing shoes. "It's difficult because this is such a big Garden and everyone else is off-duty. Nonetheless, I am very much honored to work here, in this Garden, where I can see the gods themselves all the time, or their statues, at least."

Malock looked to the left. A statue of Hollech stood not far from him, depicting the horse-headed God of Deception, Thieves, and Horses riding atop a horse. It didn't make him feel particularly at home, especially when he remembered his past experiences with the gods.

The sweeper must have seen Malock frowning because he said, "What's the matter, Prince Malock? Eat something that didn't agree with you?"

"No," said Malock, shaking his head. "I guess you haven't heard about my father."

The sweeper frowned, almost exactly on cue. "You mean King Halock, the King of Carnag? What has happened to him? Is he okay?"

"He's ill," said Malock. "Deadly ill. So ill that the panamancers here don't even know what's killing him. Combine that with his old age and I'm afraid he might just die."

The sweeper wiped the sweat off his forehead with the sleeve of his shirt. "Oh my. That is quite serious. My sincerest condolences. I pray to all of the gods within this fair Garden that your father, the King of Carnag, makes a swift and speedy recovery."

Malock cocked his head. "You're rather eloquent for a mere garden worker."

The sweeper chuckled. "Oh, I have had practice. My father always taught me that speaking eloquently is a sign of education and wealth. Therefore, I base my speech off the speech of those on a much higher rung in society than I am." Then his grin widened and he said, "Oh, and it is also fun to do."

Something about the sweeper's grin made Malock feel off. He scratched the back of his neck as he said, "Well, I suppose there's nothing wrong with that. Better than peppering your language with all manner of foul curses, as the poor tend to do."

Leaning against his broom even more, the sweeper said, "Foul cursing is not the exclusive domain of the poor, Prince Malock. In my time here on Rane, I've heard many very rich, highly successful, and extremely powerful individuals use the dirtiest words you can imagine, including many that I've never even heard of. May I let you in on a little secret of mine?"

Malock, not knowing where this was going, nodded.

The sweeper leaned in and whispered, "Sometimes, to teach them to act more like the royalty they are than the lowlifes they are not, I put mud, scorpions, itchy plants, and anything else I can find in their beds so that when they wake up in the morning, they are covered in sores and stings and mud and all kinds of other nasty things. Sadly, it only makes them curse even more, but I still find it amusing just the same."

"So you're the dirt-bedder," said Malock. "I've heard of that happening to many delegates here, but I didn't know you were the one behind it."

The sweeper shrugged. "Are you angry at me? Are you going to tell the Northern Summit Committee to kick me out? I would probably deserve it … if you could prove it, that is."

Malock looked at the sweeper uncertainly. "Just who are you? You aren't a normal sweeper, are you?"

"What do you mean?" said the sweeper. "Of course I'm a normal sweeper. I've worked here for over ten years. I hail from the island of Friana, where I originally worked as a bartender for twelve years before I got sick of scrubbing the barf from the drunks off the floorboards and applied for a job as a sweeper here."

"Then how come you haven't told me your name?" said Malock. "I don't buy the whole 'your father taught you how to speak eloquently' excuse, either. You're hiding something."

"Me?" said the sweeper, putting a hand on his chest. "I would never hide anything from you, Prince Malock. I could get fired if I did that. I'm just an average sweeper, that's all. See?"

The sweeper began sweeping the ground with his broom, sending thin dust clouds up into the air. Malock folded his arms across his chest, glaring hard at the sweeper's false innocent expression.

"Then tell me your name," said Malock. "Or I will drag you up to the Northern Summit Committee's headquarters and tell them how you tried to trick me for reasons I do not know but which I am sure are far from benevolent."

At that, the sweeper ceased his sweeping and stepped back. "Well, then, Prince Malock, friend of Skimif, I guess you'll just have to catch me."

Before Malock could react, the sweeper dropped his broom, turned, and ran back into the Garden. The sweeper moved fast, much faster than Malock thought a human could even run, and just as Malock started after him, the sweeper disappeared into the fronds and branches of the Garden, his gray cloak disappearing from view.

"Hold it!" Malock said, running directly after him. "Stop! Who are you? What do you want?"

But there was no answer except for the wind blowing through the Garden just then and sending the branches swaying. Malock crashed through the brush, accidentally ripping his red robes as he did so, hoping to catch the sweeper, but upon passing through the branches, he saw no sign of the mysterious sweeper at all. He looked in every direction, but it seemed like the sweeper had vanished into thin air completely. No footprints or broken branches to indicate which direction that the sweeper had escaped to. When he listened as hard as he could, he heard nothing except for the sounds of insects buzzing through the air, the swaying of the branches over head, and his own breathing.

How did he do that? Malock thought. *He couldn't have just up and vanished. He was just a mortal. Right?*

Then again, 'just a mortal' couldn't have disappeared like that. Whoever this sweeper was, Malock hoped he was nothing more than a prankster of some sort. Of course, the sweeper had given him very few details for Malock to work off of, and what few details he did give to Malock were probably not true.

Just as Malock decided to go deeper into the Garden, thinking that maybe the sweeper somehow knew his way around here well enough that he could travel around the Garden without being seen or heard, an unfamiliar voice back on the path called out, "Prince Malock? Where are you?"

Brushing the twigs and leaves off his shoulders, Malock turned and walked out of the mess of trees and branches back onto the main stone path. A young woman, wearing the gray uniform of a sweeper, was standing on the platform that jutted out over the sea, looking out at the waves below. She seemed to think that he was down there, which Malock thought was silly, but with the way she leaned over the railing, it was clear he needed to announce his presence.

"I'm here," said Malock, loud enough that the woman started and turned to look at him. "What's the news? Did something important happen while I was away?"

The woman nodded, but she didn't look happy. "Yes, sir, but you won't like it. You won't like it at all."

Deep down, Malock thought he knew what she had come to tell him, but he didn't want to say it aloud in case he was wrong. He hoped his ominous feelings were just that, but somehow he felt that they were based in reality.

Nonetheless, Malock brushed his hair back with his hand and said, without any hint of worry in his voice, "Get to the point, sweeper. I'm not a fan of wasting time, especially when there is important news to be told."

The woman looked up at him. Although her skin was rough and dark, probably from working in the Garden, her eyes were a clear, stunning blue, full of worry and sadness.

"Your father, King Halock of Carnag ..." The woman bit her lower lip, like she couldn't continue. "He's ... Prince Malock, I am sorry to have to be the one to inform you of this, but your father is dead."

Chapter Five

PANTING, HER BODY SHAKING from the sheer cold, her bloody nose drying in the biting wind, Jenur ran down the vague path that led from her and Dad's (*Better not think about Dad, otherwise I won't make it*) hut to Yurima. While Yurima was within walking distance, it seemed like a thousand miles away to Jenur in her weakened state. She wrapped her arms tightly around her body, covering her burnt chest and keeping her breasts from freezing in the wind. Her movements felt sluggish, like she was running with thick mud clods clinging to the bottom of her feet. Additionally, she kept glancing over her shoulder, expecting any minute now to see Wirm or Kura or both coming after her. Thankfully, neither of them did, but Jenur knew it was only a matter of time before the two Dark Tigers recovered, regrouped, and restarted the hunt after her.

Just ... gotta ... make it to Xira's house, Jenur thought. *She'll heal me. She knows some panamancy. She likes me. Told me that she was just like me when she was my age, actually. She'll understand. She won't sell me out or turn me away.*

Xira was one of the hundred or so villagers of Yurima. How old she was, exactly, Jenur didn't know; in fact, Jenur didn't even know if Xira had a last name, mostly because everyone—even those unrelated to her—just called her Grandma or, if they were feeling less formal, Xira. All Jenur knew was that Xira had lived on Urma longer than almost anyone else and had been one of the first to welcome Jenur and Dad when they had come here months ago. Jenur had not spent much time with Xira, seeing as she and Quro had made a point of keeping to themselves while on Urma so as not to attract the attention of the Dark Tigers (a move, she realized, that didn't quite work out), but on the few occasions that Jenur had spoken with Xira, the old woman had always been kind and polite to her.

Jenur staggered up the incline, which under normal circumstances was not very difficult but today was like climbing a mountain. It didn't help that there was snow on the ground, which, while not as deep or thick as it was on other days, made it harder for her to run or move fast without slipping up. She had to watch her feet while at the same time watching her back. This slowed her progress considerably.

Nor was the sheer pain she experienced helping matters. Her nose had dried up, but it still stung in the gelid weather and her chest still burned from the smoke Wirm had hit her with earlier. Still, she knew that she just had to keep moving, had to keep walking, and eventually she would get there.

Assuming, of course, that I don't lose consciousness first, Jenur thought. *Because I'm pretty sure I'm on the verge of falling unconscious.*

Still she trudged on, trudged on and on, keeping her head down and trying not to let the freezing cold weather get to her. Anytime she felt like slowing down, she would just remind herself that Wirm and Kura were probably still alive and probably coming after her, which would prompt her to keep going.

Of course, she almost broke down more than once when she remembered Quro and how he was dead.

To keep the swelling down on her nose, Jenur scooped up some snow and held it up to her face. The ice felt prickly against her nose, but it did lessen the pain, despite feeling intensely cold against her hand. Not only that, but holding the snow against her nose forced her to move one of her arms away from her chest, thus exposing the skin showing through her ripped jacket to the cold. She thus had to force her other arm to cover more than it normally was able to, although as her arms were rather skinny, it didn't work very well, in spite of her coat's thick sleeves.

Finally, after a long while, Jenur spotted a wooden sign in the distance. She soon came upon it and stopped to read the sign, which was old and damp and partially covered in a slight sheet of ice and read:

YURIMA

POP. 101

Jenur could not help but smile at the sign, despite the snow covering her face and her body feeling like it was about to fall apart. She looked out beyond the sign and saw the tiny village of Yurima below. There were perhaps a dozen or so small houses—huts, really, not much larger than Jenur's and Dad's—along with one storefront, a few old docks at which a few fishing boats were docked, and a well in the center of the town where the inhabitants drew their drinking water. She didn't see anyone out, aside from a fishing boat just off the shore, though from what she could see, the fisherman in the boat appeared to be taking a nap because he wasn't sitting up or moving. Her eyes fixed on the hut lying in the northern part, which was where Xira lived. Her eyes also briefly swept over the boats docked at the docks, but she didn't see any boats that shouldn't have been there.

No surprise, Jenur thought as she walked past the sign and went down to the village. *Wirm and Kura wouldn't just leave their boat where anyone could see it. That's not how the Dark Tigers operate. They always work in the shadows.*

Hope rising within her, Jenur walked down the hill, keeping to the path that was partially obscured by snow. She wasn't bothered by the fact that no one seemed to be out in the streets. It was a cold day and most of Urma's inhabitants preferred to stay indoors on days like today. Especially with a mountain of gray clouds coming this way. No doubt a storm was about to start, which made Jenur wonder why the fisherman out on the sea was not making his way back to the shore. When the pain in her nose flared, however, she forgot all about the fisherman and his odd lack of concern over the incoming storm and simply picked up speed until she was within the town itself.

Yurima was quiet. Granted, it was a small town—the smallest Jenur had ever been to, in fact, although that did not make it a bad town by any means—but the utter, absolute silence seemed ominous and unusual. Her boots scraped against the icy, snow-covered street as she looked to her left and right. The huts' windows were closed, the doors appeared to be locked, and little Darek—a small boy of about five who was the youngest child in Urma—had apparently left his favorite toy wooden sword outside. Jenur stopped to stare at the sword for a moment, a sense of unease creeping up her spine the longer she stared at it.

Darek would never leave his toy sword outside like this, Jenur thought. *That's his favorite—and only, actually—toy. At the very least, his mother would have moved it out of the way so no one would trip on it. What's going on here?*

Shaking her head, Jenur kept walking. She supposed it was none of her business. Darek's mother had always been rather overprotective of her one and only son. Maybe she had sensed the storm coming and had dragged him into the house to wait it out, perhaps reasoning that it was better for his toy sword to be stuck in the cold than her son. Of course, the biggest flaw with that theory was that it would not have been difficult for Darek or his mother to take the sword inside with them too, as it was not very large or heavy, but Jenur decided it made more sense than any other theory, at least at the moment.

That was when Jenur heard it. A low sob, coming from within one of the huts; Darek's hut, to be precise. Jenur stopped and listened to the sound. It sounded like the sob of a child—possibly Darek—but if that was the case, then why was Darek sobbing? And why wasn't his mother or one of the other adults in the village comforting him? For that matter, what could make the perpetually cheery Darek sob?

Though Jenur knew that she needed to get to Xira right away in order to get her nose fixed before the injury became too serious, she turned and walked up to the tiny hut that Darek and his mother called home, picking up Darek's toy sword as she did so in order to give it back to him. She would stop by just long enough to see what

Darek was sobbing about. Besides, if Jenur remembered correctly, Darek's mother had worked as a doctor's assistant before moving out here. She might be able to help Jenur until they could have Xira come over and check out her nose.

Jenur knocked on the wooden door of the hut. "Darek? Is that you? Are you—"

"Go away!" Darek's shrill voice sounded, so loud that Jenur jumped. "Don't hurt me like you did mama!"

Jenur realized that her voice must have sounded unfamiliar to Darek due to her broken nose. But what astounded her most was the pain and fear in Darek's voice, which she had never heard in his voice before.

"Darek, it's me, Jenur," said Jenur, stepping up to the door again. "Jenur Takren. Remember me? I live in that hut with my dad a few miles outside of town."

"J-Jenur?" said Darek's voice on the other side, trembling and uncertain. "You're not hurt?"

Jenur shook her head. "I am, but I'll be okay. What about your mama? Is she okay? Are you all right?"

That must not have been the right question to ask because Darek just wailed again. He screamed so loudly that he sounded like he was dying.

"Darek!" said Jenur. "What's the matter? Can you let me inside?"

"No!" Darek shouted. "You don't want to see what happened to mama."

"But I can't help you if I can't come inside," said Jenur. "Would you please let me in? Please? I just want to help you, Darek. All right?"

Darek went disturbingly quiet for a few seconds. Then he spoke again, but his voice was smaller now, hoarse from the screaming, with a hint of fear in it.

"O-Okay," said Darek. "I'll get the door."

A moment later, the doorknob turned and the door opened inward. As the door opened, the light from the sun behind Jenur showed her what was inside. And it made her stomach sick.

Standing in the doorway was little Darek, his chubby face stained with tears and his left eye bruised. His black hair was as messy as a wild garden and his clothes had dark red stains on them that looked like blood, although Darek himself didn't seem to have any wounds or injuries aside from his black eye.

But just beyond Darek, lying in the middle of the hut, was a short, middle-aged woman with the same hair color as Darek. She looked almost normal, like she was taking a nap; well, except for her throat, which had been sliced open and ripped out. Her head lay in a pool of the blood that had gushed from her throat and, based on its dryness, it had been like that for quite a while.

Jenur dropped the toy sword, fell to her knees and cupped Darek's face in her hand, looking over his tiny body while trying not to feel sick or scared.

"Darek, what happened to your mother?" said Jenur. "And what happened to you? Are you injured? Why hasn't anyone come by to check up on you? Who hurt you?"

Darek sniffled, wiping away one of the tears rolling down his face. "Bad people came. They killed mama and hit me."

"Bad people?" said Jenur. "What kind of bad people? What did they look like? Did they give you any names?"

Darek sniffled again. "N-No. They wore cat masks."

Jenur felt her heart sink to the pit of her stomach. "Cat masks? Like, with big teeth and stripes?"

Darek nodded, but didn't say anything. He just ran up to Jenur and hugged her and began sobbing into her chest. Jenur wrapped her free arm around him and held him close, while her mind raced as she processed what he had told her.

"And everyone else?" said Jenur. "What happened to the other people in the village? Are they dead, too?"

Darek didn't respond. He just kept sobbing and saying, "Mama's dead, mama's dead, mama's dead," over and over again. He did, however, nod once, which told Jenur all she needed to know.

Those bastards, Jenur thought. *Wirm must have known or suspected that the Yurimans would have protected me and Dad if he and Kura failed to kill one or both of us. He and Kura must have killed every other person in this village just to make sure I wouldn't have any help. Surprised he spared Darek, considering how much he hates children. Must not have thought him to be a threat.*

To a certain extent, Jenur was not surprised at Wirm's brutality. Generally, Wirm preferred to kill subtly and one at a time, but there had been a few times in the past in which Wirm had decided a scorched earth tactic was the best way to go about completing a mission. Once, he had approved of a plan by a certain Tiger (whose name Jenur could not remember) to bury an entire town underneath a lava flow. The Tiger had been aiming to kill just one person—a priest of Senva who had been annoying a local king by publicly criticizing the king's policies and attitudes toward his people—but Wirm had thought the plan a good one anyway, as he felt it would help cement the reputation of the Tigers as a group who were willing to do whatever it took to finish the job.

But that didn't make Jenur feel any better at all. If Darek was telling the truth about everyone being dead, then that meant Xira was dead, too—which meant Jenur would have to figure out something else fast. Though she didn't hear Wirm or Kura coming, she had no doubt in her mind that the two of them were already on their way over and would be here soon.

And once they get here, they'll find a frightened little boy and an equally frightened young woman, Jenur thought. *Both of whom are completely defenseless, of course.*

She couldn't express those thoughts to Darek, though, without frightening the boy even more than he already was. She would need to be strong for him because she was the only adult left.

But what am I supposed to do? Jenur thought, averting her eyes from the corpse of Darek's mother. *There's nowhere left to run to on this island. The best chance we have of surviving is taking a boat. Yet even that might not work; after all, Wirm and Kura have a boat, too, and could easily track us down if they had to.*

Of course, staying here was not much of an option, either. It seemed like no matter what Jenur chose to do, the Dark Tigers would catch them. Maybe not immediately, but she figured that she and Darek could put off their deaths—and she had no doubt that Wirm would kill Darek, too, seeing as she was protecting the boy—for only a few minutes longer. After that ... well, Jenur didn't even want to think about it.

"All right, Darek," said Jenur, patting him on the back. "It's okay, it's okay. We'll get out of here and go somewhere else, where the bad people can't get us."

Darek was still sobbing into her chest. Seeing him like this only made Jenur angrier than ever at the Dark Tigers, but there was nothing she could do to fight Wirm or Kura now. What Jenur needed to do was exactly what she had told Darek: Get out of there. Go somewhere else. *Anywhere* else.

Maybe Carnag, Jenur thought. *Malock will probably take us in.*

Of course, the problem with that was that Carnag was thousands of miles away, well to the south of the Great Berg and Urma. While Jenur did have some sailing experience, she didn't think she could make it all the way to Carnag using one of the tiny fishing boats docked in Yurima's port. Especially with a small child like Darek. They wouldn't have time to pack the necessary food, clothing, water, and other things to help them reach Carnag. In all likelihood, they would end up starving or dying of thirst out at sea. And that was assuming that they weren't sunk by a storm or attacked by pirates or sprang a leak or any of the other thousands of different things that could sink a massive battleship and utterly destroy a tiny fishing boat.

Jenur looked over her shoulder. The storm clouds from before were now directly overhead and a powerful wind was blowing through. No doubt a blizzard would begin to rage, which meant that she and Darek couldn't leave, at least not yet. They would have to spend the night in Urma. Jenur might have been willing to risk the sea by herself in this dangerous weather, but when she looked at Darek and heard his sobbing, she knew she would have to wait.

"Darek, we can't leave just yet," said Jenur, speaking in as soothing a tone as she could. "There's a storm coming, a really big one from the look of those clouds, and—"

"But I don't want to stay here!" Darek said, his voice slightly muffled by her coat. "Not when mama is dead."

Jenur glanced at Darek's mother's corpse. Her skin was pale as the snow outside and the blood had congealed, its stench filling Jenur's nostrils and making her sick.

"You're right," said Jenur. "We can't stay here, not with this corpse. We should go to one of the storage buildings, where the food is kept. We'll be safer there."

Darek didn't object to that. He just buried his head deeper into Jenur's coat and muttered something she couldn't hear. Relieved that he was going to come willingly, Jenur stood up, lifting him with her other hand while still holding the snow against her nose, and left to go find the nearest storage building they could hide in even as the wind howled and the temperature dropped like a rock.

Chapter Six

MALOCK SAT ALONE IN the room where Father had breathed his last. His eyes were on Father's corpse, which was still and peaceful. Father's eyes were closed, his lips formed a line, and his beard was tangled and gray. His skin was cold to the touch, which Malock had discovered when he had brushed his fingers against Father's skin earlier. A plain, white shroud covered Father's body up to his neck. It had covered Father's face earlier, but Malock had pulled it down so he could see Father's face better.

Father can't be dead, Malock thought, but deep down, he knew it was true. Here was Father's corpse, lying on the bed before him, as still as a rock and as cold as ice. To deny that would be to deny reality, and Malock wasn't one to deny reality even when it was vicious, cruel, and unfair.

Malock had sat in here for a few hours, but it was only recently that he had been allowed to mourn Father alone. Nearly all of the other delegates had come to pay their condolences to Father. Even the Nikons, never a close ally of Carnag, had come by to inform Malock that they were sorry of Father's passing and that they hoped that Father had been granted a beautiful place in the afterlife by the gods. Additionally, several of the crew members of the *Grinf's Hammer* had visited as well, offering to move Father onto the ship so they could take his body back to Carnag and give it the proper burial that it deserved.

But Malock had denied that request, at least for the moment. He knew it was silly to do so, as there was no reason to let Father's body lay here. His excuse was that the body needed to be prepared for the voyage home, which was partly true, as the panamancers had not yet spread the proper incense over the corpse.

His real reason for the delay, however, was that he still could not really believe it. While Father had been getting on in years, Malock had expected Father to live much longer than he did. At the very least, he had not expected Father to die of a disease like this. He had thought Father would die of old age back home, but he supposed that that was not to be Father's fate.

Speaking of the disease, the panamancers still couldn't tell Malock what it was. The head panamancer—the red-headed woman from earlier, whose name was Kirja Amane, who was also a member of the Northern Summit Committee—had told him that, despite her research, she had found no reference or description of the disease in any of the books in the medical library so far. Of the few diseases that did resemble it, none of the spells that usually worked on those diseases worked on this one. This was another reason Malock had decided not to leave just yet. He wanted to give the panamancers time to study Father's corpse and figure out what the disease was, although he first wanted time alone with Father's body before he would allow them to do that.

I can't believe that Father is dead, Malock thought. *What will Mother do now? What will I do?*

Thinking of Mother made him even more depressed. He had told some of the servants from the ship to send a gray ghost to Mother informing her of Father's death. There was a mage on board who could use his magic to send a message to Mother, but still Malock didn't know what Mother would do or say.

She'll probably break down completely, Malock thought. *I'm barely keeping it together myself.*

At that moment, there was a knock at the door. Malock looked up from his chair on the other side of the table on which Father's shrouded body lay. At first, he wanted to say, "Whoever you are, I'm not interested in talking," but then he realized that actually, yes, he did need to talk to someone, if only to take his mind off the depressing thoughts that were trying to invade his mind.

So he said instead, "Who is it?"

"It is I," said a familiar voice. "King Fabadi of Shika. May I come in and pay my respects to Halock?"

Malock stood up and pulled the shroud over Father's face. Back on Carnag, it was considered impolite for people outside of the family to see the deceased's face, even if that person was a friend. It was fine for non-family members to see the deceased's body while covered with a shroud, but they could not actually see the body itself. This was because it was considered bad luck to see the corpse of someone outside of your family, unless you were a panamancer, grave keeper, or mortician.

Then Malock said to the door, "Come in."

The door opened and King Fabadi entered. His eyes darted between Father and Malock for a moment before he gently shut the door closed behind him. His expression was grim and he hardly looked like the confident orator that he had earlier.

"My condolences, Tojas," said Fabadi, putting his hand over his chest. "Though your father and I never got along very well, I still respected him for who he was and what he stood for. I appreciated how he always treated me with respect during the Shikan-Carnagian negotiations. I still remember how he and his wife comforted me when Raya died."

Malock nodded. "Your condolences are accepted, King Fabadi. I am sure Father would have appreciated them, too, if he was still alive."

"Indeed, he would have," said Fabadi. He looked down at the shrouded corpse for a while before saying, "Does Markinia know of this yet?"

"No," said Malock, shaking his head. "I sent a messenger to tell her, but I doubt she's gotten the message yet."

"She will be devastated," said Fabadi. "I have no doubts about that. When my own wife died ... it was worse than when my daughter died. It was why I never remarried."

His voice cracked when he said that, but not quite as much as it could have. Perhaps Fabadi had gotten over his wife's death.

Nonetheless, Malock said, "I was very young when your wife died and I don't remember hearing much about it, except when my parents discussed it once. May I ask how it happened or—?"

Fabadi looked up. "She died in childbirth giving birth to Raya. I had the best panamancers and midwives on Shika tending to her while she gave birth, but despite that, she still died, and almost took Raya with her as well. It was a miracle of Nimiko that Raya didn't die."

"Oh," said Malock. Now he understood why Fabadi seemed so stricken about Raya's death. "I didn't know that was how it happened. I'm sorry to hear that."

Fabadi waved his concerns off. "It's none of your concern. That was twenty years ago. Today we are going to mourn your father, not talk about my own losses, of which you have heard plenty about already, I'm sure."

Malock folded his arms behind his back and looked down at Father's shroud. His throat became constricted, but he still managed to say, "We still don't know how or why Father died. It's a complete mystery."

"I am surprised that Skimif let it happen," said Fabadi.

Malock snapped his head back up at Fabadi. "What?"

"I said, I am surprised that Skimif let this happen," said Fabadi. "You spent so much time defending Skimif from my accusations earlier that I thought maybe Skimif was a friend of yours. Evidently, I was mistaken."

"Skimif doesn't have anything to do with this," said Malock. "Nor do any of the southern gods or anything else you spoke about earlier."

"But Skimif is the God of Martir, is he not?" said Fabadi. "Yet he has not done much to make the world a better, safer place for us mortals, now has he? In fact, I'd say that he has done very little to make anything better. I wonder why that is."

"It's because that kind of change doesn't happen in a day, Fabadi," said Malock. "Can't we talk about this later?"

"Actually, no, we can't," said Fabadi. He stepped forward, his eyes focused directly on Malock's, and said, "Because I was hoping that you and I could discuss this issue in private."

"Is that the whole reason you chose to come here?" said Malock, leaning back in disgust. "Do you honestly not care about my father at all?"

"A person can have multiple reasons for doing something," said Fabadi. "I did want to pay my respects to Halock because I did respect him for his actions and personality. I also came because I wished to speak with you in private about Skimif and the southern gods. I see no contradiction between those two desires."

"I'm not in the mood for political blathering," said Malock. "When Raya died, were *you* in the mood to talk politics with someone else?"

Malock realized a little too late that he shouldn't have said that. Fabadi's mouth contorted into a fierce scowl and he stepped forward again, this time much more menacingly. He looked quite ready to hit Malock over the head with his scepter.

But then Fabadi shook his head and said, "When Raya died, I wanted to punish her killer, who you defended and supported on the basis of her word alone. I only wish to offer you support in this time of need, should you ever decide to go after Halock's killer."

"Father's killer?" said Malock. "What are you talking about?

Father died of a natural disease. I doubt anyone killed him."

"Can you be so sure?" said Fabadi. "Your father has made many enemies in his day, I am sure, just as all of us rulers have. You yourself no doubt have some people who would want to see your head on a platter and your body thrown to the sharks. It seems far too convenient that Halock should die so soon after you return home."

"Convenient for who?" said Malock. "Are you saying Father was poisoned?"

"Perhaps," said Fabadi. "There are many undetectable poisons in the world. Perhaps Halock ate or drank something laced with one such poison and it ended up killing him. Who knows?"

"You don't have any proof of that claim," said Malock. "Speculation, that's all it is. The only way Father could have been poisoned is if one of our servants on the *Grinf's Justice* intentionally poisoned him, and I can assure you that there is not a single man or woman on board that ship who would ever even dream of doing such a thing."

Fabadi stroked his chin, his scowl turning into a more thoughtful expression. "Then someone on Rane must have done it."

"One of the other delegates?" said Malock. "Granted, I know that some of them probably don't care about Father's death, but I hardly think any of them would pick this moment to kill Father. The Northern Summit, after all, is supposed to be a time for the nations to come together, not a time for the political backstabbing that we usually do."

"Did I say that it was one of the delegates or a servant of them?" said Fabadi. "No, I didn't. Stop putting words into my mouth. It's an uncouth habit."

"Then who could have done it?" said Malock. "Someone on the Northern Summit Committee?"

"Clearly not," said Fabadi. "The Northern Summit Committee is not made up of assassins, nor are any of their members loyal to one nation over any of the others. No, I think the culprit—if there is one —is someone else."

"If not the delegates or the Committee members, then who do you think could have done it?" said Malock. "And that's assuming, of course, that Father was even assassinated, a claim which you still haven't offered me any proof of, by the way."

"Tell me, Tojas," said Fabadi. "You went to the southern seas once, yes? You met the southern gods or at least some of them, correct?"

Malock nodded. "Yes. Why do you ask?"

"Has it ever occurred to you that some of those southern gods may have had a servant of theirs poison Halock somehow?" said Fabadi. "If that is true, then doesn't that, to a certain extent, make it Skimif's fault, since he was the one who allowed the southern gods to travel beyond the Dividing Line more than they usually do?"

"Again, just baseless conjecture," said Malock. "Where is your proof? It sounds to me like you're trying to make this whole affair into something bigger than it really is."

Fabadi held up his hands. "All I am saying is that there is usually a lot more going on than meets the eye when it comes to these gods. I just want to make sure you have considered all of the possibilities, and that if you agree, that we may be able to work out something between

Shika and Carnag."

"Assuming you can ever prove that to me, then yes, maybe we can," said Malock. "But until then, I will see you at the next round of Shikan-Carnagian negotiations."

Fabadi raised an eyebrow. "Are you telling me to leave?"

Malock pointed at the door and said, "I'm telling you that I wish to spend more time alone with my father and that I'm not interested in listening to more of your conspiracies."

"Fine," said Fabadi. "I've said my part. If you ever change your mind, you know how to get in touch with me. May the gods bless you and help you and your mother and your nation as you grieve Halock's tragic passing."

With that, Fabadi turned and left the room, leaving Malock all by himself. He did not look back once as he left, nor did he say anything as he closed the door behind him quietly and carefully.

Malock sank back into the wooden chair underneath him and sighed. He then looked at Father's shrouded, still form and, despite what he said earlier, he wondered if Fabadi's words had some truth to them.

And if they do, Malock thought, *then I need to investigate this immediately. Perhaps I could contact Skimif somehow and ask him if he knows.*

Then again, Malock had not spoken with Skimif in a long time. He didn't even know how to get in contact with the newly-ascended God of Martir. For all he knew, Skimif was too busy fulfilling his duties as the God of Martir to have any time for Malock, which would explain why Skimif had been silent so far.

Once I get back to Martir and have Father's body buried, then I will find a way to contact Skimif, Malock thought. *Until then, I must put this thought out of my mind and worry only about what I do know, which is that I and my mother and the rest of Carnag will have a hard road ahead of us without Father's guidance.*

Chapter Seven

JENUR AND DAREK SAT together in the dark, freezing storage building amid boxes and crates full of food like black fish and spicy potatoes, extra clothing, a variety of fishing equipment, and anything else the inhabitants of Yurima might have needed in their day-to-day lives. Boxes, most marked with the name 'WARAM SUPPLY CO.' painted on the side in faded red paint, were stacked neatly on top of each other, while massive crates surrounded them like armed sentinels. Through the wooden walls, the roaring of the blizzard could be heard, while thick white snowflakes shot past the windows.

Despite that, Jenur didn't feel safe at all. While the blizzard would likely keep Wirm and Kura at bay for now, there was no telling how long it would last. Once it passed, the two Dark Tigers would be on the move again. Likely they would stop in Yurima to search for her and they would probably find her, too, even if it would take them a while.

Therefore, Jenur planned for her and Darek to make an escape the minute the blizzard died down. There was nowhere else on Urma to run to, so they would simply take one of the fishing boats and try to row as far from Urma as they could.

Assuming the bay doesn't freeze over during the blizzard, Jenur thought. *Assuming Wirm and Kura don't decide to brave the blizzard rather than take cover somewhere safe. Assuming the blizzard doesn't end up freezing the door and trapping Darek and me inside here, thus giving Wirm and Kura more time to find us.*

She glanced at Darek as she thought that. The little boy was sitting on her lap, inside her coat, as a way to keep him warm. He was nibbling on a chunk of bread Jenur had found in one of the crates. His face was stained with tears and he looked like he was about to cry any minute now, but it had been a couple of hours since he had stopped sobbing. Jenur had asked him if he was okay, but Darek didn't seem to be in the mood to talk.

No wonder, Jenur thought. *He probably saw Wirm kill his mother right before his eyes. I can barely imagine what he must be going through right now. He's probably completely devastated.*

Jenur's nose tingled just a little, but she had managed to find some bandages and medial supplies among the crates, allowing her to bandage her nose as best as she could. It was a temporary fix and Jenur would probably need to see a panamancer soon—not to mention the bandage made her nose feel much heavier than usual and forced her to breathe primarily through her mouth—but for now, it would have to do.

As they sat there, cuddling together, sharing the warmth between their bodies, trying not to freeze to death, Jenur's mind wandered over to the thought of who had hired Wirm and Kura in the first place.

How could anyone know where Dad and I were? Jenur thought. *Only a handful of people even know we're here and none of them would ever hire assassins to kill us.*

It couldn't have been Malock or Rint. Nor could it have been Skimif, who was probably too busy with his new duties as God of Martir to give much thought to what Jenur was doing. All three of them were her friends. The only possible explanation she could come up with was that one of those three had let slip her location to someone who wanted Jenur dead.

The only question was, who?

Someone out there wants me dead, Jenur thought. *And it's not just Wirm and Kura, either. Someone much worse than either of them, I bet. Whoever it was must have promised Wirm a lot of money to go after me, seeing as he never leaves Ruwa or personally takes missions anymore.*

Her first thought was that it must have been Ramufa the Nimble-Fingered. A freelance thief, guard, and the gods-know-what-else, Ramufa had framed Jenur for the murder of Princess Raya Kabadi a few months back. Jenur had never gotten the chance to get back at Ramufa, but she knew that he didn't care much for her life.

Then again, if Ramufa wanted me dead, I think he'd have done it himself, Jenur thought. *Besides, he doesn't even know where I am. Must be someone else.*

No matter how much Jenur racked her brain, she could not guess who might have hired Wirm and Kura to kill her. Whoever their client was, he somehow had access to knowledge that only a handful of people were privy to.

Could it be ... a god or goddess? Jenur thought. *The gods probably have all sorts of ways to know about us. Seeing as I am in the Great Berg, Xocion probably knows I'm here. He is the God of Ice, after all.*

But that made no sense, either. Jenur had never even met Xocion, much less done anything to make him her enemy. What purpose could Xocion have for sending two assassins after her? Especially if she was in his domain, where he could easily kill her himself with an avalanche or a blizzard or something else?

Then again, I was the one who came up with the idea of killing Bifor Kamon all those months back, Jenur thought. *But Bifor was only pretending to be a Xocionian. So Xocion probably has nothing to do with it.*

The way Jenur saw it, this whole situation had many questions but no answers at all. And there was a good chance that Jenur would not live long enough to find out the answers to those questions. Once the blizzard ended, Wirm and Kura would be on their way here and that would be the end of her and Darek, no matter if they tried to take a boat or not.

At that moment, above the roar of the blizzard and the creaking of the storage building, a loud *bump* echoed. Darek almost screamed, but Jenur put her hand over his mouth and whispered, in a harsher than usual voice, "Shush! Do you want to be heard by the bad people?"

Darek shook his head, but Jenur didn't lower her hand from his mouth. She just peeked above the nearest crate as best as she could, but she didn't see anything. Her first thought was that one of the boxes had fallen over, even though she didn't see any fallen boxes, but the next moment she heard that *bump* sound again and she realized that the sound was coming from the door. Someone or something on the other side was trying to get in, but since the door was locked, they had to try to break it down to enter.

Another *bump* and the door pushed inward before snapping back to its normal shape. It was a tough, thick door, but with the repeated *bumps* from the outside, Jenur realized it was only a matter of time before whoever was out there would get in.

Darek, showing surprising strength for such a small boy, grabbed Jenur's hand and ripped it off his mouth. But when he spoke, it was in a softer voice, which told Jenur that he was listening.

"Who's out there?" Darek asked, his voice almost a hiss he was trying to speak so quietly.

"No idea," said Jenur, keeping her voice low as well. "Could be one of the bad people or could be a friend or could be someone else we don't know."

"If it's a bad person, can we run away?" Darek said.

Jenur did a cursory look around the room. There was only one door, the exit, and the windows were too high up for Jenur to climb up to. Technically, she could make the climb herself by stacking a bunch of boxes and crates on top of each other to give her a boost, but as long as she was with Darek, that method of escape seemed impractical and dangerous.

"I don't think we can, Darek," said Jenur. "If this person turns out to be one of the bad people, we'll have to fight."

Tears rose up in Darek's eyes and his lower lip started trembling, prompting Jenur to hold him closer and say, in as soothing a voice as she could muster, "It's okay, it's okay, Darek, we'll be all right. I can fight the bad person and protect you. Just keep as quiet as you can so I can get the element of surprise on him, okay?"

Darek sniffled, but thankfully he didn't cry. He was a brave little boy, much braver than Jenur had been at that age for sure.

"Good boy," said Jenur. "Now I want you to sit here as quiet as you can while I look for something to defend us with, okay? Here, you can even have my coat to keep yourself warm."

Jenur raised Darek off her lap and put him on the cold, hard floor. She then slipped out of her coat and covered him with it like a blanket. Standing up, Jenur had to suppress a shiver as the bitingly cold air nipped at her upper body, despite the layers of thick shirts she wore. It was like being clawed at by a lion, but Jenur didn't show any fear. She just began moving through the storage building, peaking into boxes or crates, looking for anything that could work as a weapon even as the *bumps* at the door grew louder and more insistent with each passing minute.

In particular, Jenur was looking for a knife, as that was the kind of weapon she was most used to. Frustratingly enough, Jenur couldn't find even a butter knife with which to arm herself. She did, however, find a fishing line and a variety of sharp hooks inside a box full of fishing supplies.

Her first instinct was to ignore the line and hooks and keep looking, but then a sharp *snap* caused her head to whip towards the door. The lock had been broken. Whoever it was would now be here within seconds.

Deciding that beggars couldn't be choosers, Jenur snatched up the line and hooks and immediately ducked behind a crate to give her time to tie them together. She heard the door creaking open, causing the volume of the blizzard to increase to an almost unbearable loudness, and then heard thick, heavy boots walking across the floor. Whoever it was must have been too tired to talk because they did not say anything, although going by the sound of the door closing, it appeared that they were planning to wait out the blizzard here, too.

Jenur decided to peek around the side of the crate. After all, she would need to find out who had broken in, which would determine her next move.

So, carefully avoiding getting the hooks in her hands, Jenur stuck her head around the side of the crate. Not her whole head; just her eyes in order to prevent herself from being spotted.

A large man sat against the door, a parka pulled down over his head and his arms wrapped around his body. He was breathing hard and seemed close to falling asleep. Jenur had never seen the man before. He clearly wasn't from Urma or Yurima, but he wasn't a Dark Tiger, either. He looked almost harmless, but Jenur wasn't going to take any chances.

She pulled her head back behind the crate and, removing her thick gloves to allow her fingers to move freely, began looping the fishing line through the hooks. Within seconds, Jenur had created a necklace of sorts that she could easily kill a person with. The idea was to take the necklace and wrap it around the neck of the victim. The hooks would then dig into the victim's throat, piercing it and killing the victim. It was a tactic Jenur had used a few times as a Dark Tiger, but it was always one of her least favorite tactics because it was often messy and sometimes even failed. Yet it was the only weapon she had on her right now, so she would have to make do.

Slipping her gloves back over her hands, Jenur peeked out from behind the crate again. The parka man's chin was on his chest, like he was asleep.

Jenur pulled the hook necklace taut to make sure it would not break and then looked at the man again.

Still he slept.

Maybe I should spare him, Jenur thought. *He's clearly not a Dark Tiger or any other enemy. Still, I can't take any chances. For all I know, he could be even worse than the Tigers. He might be a serial killer or maybe a wanted criminal or something else. For Darek's sake, I can't let this man live.*

Keeping as silent as possible, Jenur stood up and doubled over. She held the hook necklace in her hands and began creeping toward the parka-hooded man. He was as still as a layer of dust on a chair and didn't seem to hear or notice Jenur at all.

He must be very tired, Jenur thought as she inched toward him, making as little noise as possible. *He probably won't even feel the hooks ripping through his throa—*

Without warning, a long, wooden wand appeared mere inches before Jenur's face, its tip glowing with energy. Jenur froze immediately, her eyes screwing up as she attempted to look at the wand tip before her.

"Nice try," rumbled a voice from inside the parka of the man. He wasn't looking up at her at all; instead, his right arm had extended, as rigid as a support beam, with the wand gripped firmly in his hand. "But you really aren't as stealthy as you think you are, beautiful."

Jenur bit her lower lip. Her heart was beating madly and she was sure that the man, whoever he was, was going to blast her face off and then go and kill Darek while he was at it.

Then the man turned his head toward her. He had sleet on his thick eyebrows, but it was his green eyes—same shade as a field of tall grass on a hot summer day—that took away her breath. His nose was blue, but despite that, he didn't look as cold as Jenur felt.

"Aren't as beautiful, either, beautiful," said the man. "What happened to your nose? Got into a fight with someone or did you just trip and break it on the ground?"

Jenur just scowled. "I don't need to tell you anything."

The man chuckled, his wand arm never wavering. "Guess that's your gods-given right as a human being, but if you keep playing hard to get, well, I may just have to blow that less-than-pretty face right off your head."

"Jenur?" said Darek from the back of the storage building. "Jenur, what's—"

"Shut up, Darek!" Jenur snapped, without taking her eyes off the wand before her.

But it was too late. The man glanced in the direction of Darek's voice and said, "Is there a little boy in here? You don't look old enough to be a mother, beautiful."

"He's not my son," Jenur said. "He's a friend whose life I am trying to keep safe."

The man stroked his chin with his free hand. "What happened to

97

his real mother, then? Did you steal him from her? Based on that boy's voice, I'd guess he's about five, which is awfully old to steal, since most sterile mothers tend to steal babies when they're not even a year old yet."

"His mother is ..." Jenur remembered Darek's mother's corpse. "She's dead. Killed by a murderer."

"Oh," said the man. "A murderer, eh? That explains the corpses I saw in town. Only reason I came in here was because I didn't want to keep warm in the same house as a dead person. As a Diogian, I think it's bad luck to be in the same house as a corpse unless that corpse is buried under the house's foundations."

"That doesn't sound better to me," said Jenur.

The man frowned. "You're right. Houses shouldn't be built on the graves of the dead. But since you're so smart, beautiful, I'm sure you get my point."

Jenur scowled. "Stop calling me beautiful. I have a real name, you know."

"Then why don't you tell it to me?" said the man. "I mean, I could easily force it from you via telepathy, since I know some telemancy despite that not being my specialty, but I tend to subscribe to the Telemancy Rules of Ethics, which state that anyone who reads another person's minds without their consent is pretty much scum."

"Tell me your name first," said Jenur. "And where you came from. You're clearly not a native Yuriman."

"And you're clearly not from around here, either, beautiful," said the man. "Thought you were Shikan at first, since you've got pale skin, but I think you're probably Ruwan now that I see you have very dark hair. You even act like a Ruwan. Yeah, I see that hook necklace. Only Ruwan girls would think of killing a stranger like that."

Jenur didn't let go of the hook necklace, although as she didn't think she'd get to use it, she lowered her hands. "Where are you from, then?"

The man smiled. "The great nation of Nikos, duh. Can't you tell? You should go there sometime. Great place. Lots of good food and music."

"How do I know you're telling the truth?" said Jenur. "You might be a serial killer for all I know."

"My friends do call me a lady killer, but I've never taken the life of another human being before and would never think of doing that," said the man. He cracked a grin. "Unless that human being wanted to tear my throat apart with a hook necklace, but I can trust you wouldn't do that, right?"

"As long as you don't blast my face apart with that wand of yours," said Jenur. "Or try to harm Darek in any way. Because if you did try that, I'd rend you limb from limb."

The man chuckled. "You've got venom, beautiful, and I like girls with venom. Makes it interesting."

"Interesting?" said Jenur. "Is that what Nikons say when someone threatens to rend them limb from limb?"

"That's what *I* say," said the man. Then he frowned and stroked his chin again. "Then again, maybe that's why I got in so much trouble at the Academy. Couldn't always tell the difference between the girls who wanted me and the girls who wanted to kill me. Huh."

"Are you just going to keep rambling?" said Jenur. "How's about this: You lower your wand and I lower my hook necklace. We agree not to attack each other. Maybe we'll talk or something, learn about each other."

"Eh, my arm was getting tired anyway," said the man as he lowered his wand from Jenur's face. "Last time I held up my arm that long was when I came face-to-face with an angry aquarian who looked like a shark. Damn fish would've ate my face off if my friends hadn't saved me."

Jenur stepped backwards, but she didn't raise her hook necklace. She eyed the man, who now held his wand near his feet, though its glow had gone out. His green eyes continued to glitter from within the parka, but he didn't seem threatening at all.

Just then, Darek appeared from around one of the crates. He looked absolutely terrified, clutching Jenur's jacket as tightly as he could. He froze for a moment when he saw the man, but when he noticed Jenur, he ran over to her and into her legs, clutching them tightly as he buried his head into her knees.

"That the kid?" said the man. "Scared little thing, ain't he?"

Jenur patted Darek on the head as she glared at the man. "He thought you were going to kill us."

The man chuckled. "Well then, that would certainly make me scared if I were his age."

"Oh, and everyone he's ever known is dead," said Jenur. "So forgive him if he doesn't exactly trust you."

The man wrapped his arms around his body. "*Everyone* is dead?"

"As far as I know, yes," said Jenur. "Darek and I are the only survivors. Well, technically Darek is the *only* survivor, seeing as I don't actually live in town."

"Well, geez, I saw a few bodies and thought maybe that only a few people had died, but everyone?" said the man. "That's messed up. Did some kind of disease or animal or something come through?"

Jenur's fist clamped down around the hook necklace. "If by 'animal' you mean 'two of the worst Dark Tigers ever,' then yes, I guess you could say that a couple of wild beasts slaughtered everyone."

"Dark Tigers?" said the man. He jumped to his feet, holding his wand like a sword. "Shit, I didn't know they were here. Shit, shit, shit."

He briefly turned around, opened the door, and peeked out into the blizzard, only to get a face full of snow that forced him to shut the door again. He slumped against the door, his green eyes bugged and contrasting sharply with the snow covering his face.

"What are you so freaked out about?" said Jenur. "Did someone hire the Dark Tigers to take you down?"

The man shook his head. "Of course not. Yeah, some girls I knew in my Academy days kept threatening to hire the Dark Tigers to make me shut up, but that was all in good fun. Nah, the Dark Tigers want me for different reasons, I can assure you."

Jenur raised an eyebrow. "I've never known the Dark Tigers to go after anyone. We—I mean, they never went after anyone unless they were paid to."

"That's the official policy, but let me tell you, Nijok Wirm has vendettas of his own and he ain't above sending his men after his own enemies when he wants," said the man. "Some things are worth more than money, you know?"

"I suppose you aren't going to tell me what they want you for, then," said Jenur.

"Nope," said the man. "Let's just say it was an accident and that, despite my best efforts to apologize, they don't quite see it that way. The Dark Tigers ain't a forgiving bunch."

Jenur nodded. "You're telling me. Well, if you aren't going to tell me that, then could you at least tell me your name?"

"Fair enough," said the man. "The name's Braim Kotogs. I'm a necromancer by trade, but a lover by design. And your name is ...?"

"Jenur," said Jenur. "Jenur Takren. And this is Darek."

Darek didn't look at Braim. He just clung as tightly to Jenur as he could, shivering and shuddering in the cold.

Braim stroked his chin. "Jenur Takren, eh? Feel like I've heard that name somewhere before. Maybe I knew a girl with your name back in the Academy. If so, she wasn't nearly as pretty as you."

"Enough with the small talk," said Jenur. "What are you doing here? Where did you come from?"

"Let's see," said Braim. He leaned forward, like he was going to share a secret, and said, in a whisper of a voice, "I'm on a top secret mission for the Magical Superior of North Academy. Supposed to be investigating some weird surges of magical energy the Superior sensed happening around Urma. Know anything about that?"

Jenur shook her head. "I'm not a mage, so I don't know anything about it."

Braim frowned. "Damn. Was hoping all I'd need to do was ask a few of the natives if they heard or saw anything strange, but I guess I'll have to do some groundwork. After, of course, this blizzard is over."

"After the blizzard passes, we have to get out of here," said Jenur. "The two Dark Tigers I mentioned earlier are still alive. I don't know how far they are from us now, but once the storm passes, I have no doubt that they'll head directly for Yurima. They'll kill us if they can find us."

"By Diog's name, beautiful, why didn't you mention that before?" said Braim, putting his hands on his head. "I thought you said that the Dark Tigers had already come through here."

"They did, but they'll be back," said Jenur. "They want to kill me. And I guess, when they see you, they'll want to kill you, too."

Braim slammed his fist against the ground. "Damn. Why do they want you dead, anyway? Someone hire them?"

Jenur hesitated. While Braim didn't seem like a threat—in fact, he seemed more like a joke—Jenur still didn't know him all that well. He could have been lying to her for all she knew, though when she looked into his eyes, she didn't see any deception at all. He seemed totally honest.

So Jenur said, "Sort of. I mean, someone did point them in my direction, but to my knowledge, the Dark Tigers aren't being paid. They're just going after me because they hate me."

"Looks like we got something in common, then," said Braim. "Both of us pissed off the Dark Tigers. By the way, beautiful, what did you do to piss 'em off?"

Jenur pursed her lips. She glanced at Darek, who still seemed too afraid to look at Braim, and thought about how Darek might react if he learned that she used to be one of the 'bad guys,' as she had called the Dark Tigers.

So Jenur said to Braim, "It's my secret, just like your reason for pissing them off."

Braim nodded. "Fair enough. I won't ask you what you did and you won't ask me what I did. That's another thing we have in common. We keep secrets like this."

Kind of wish I didn't have anything in common with you, Jenur thought, but aloud she said, "Earlier you mentioned something about 'magical energies' or something around here. What did you mean?"

"Technically, I'm not supposed to say," said Braim. "But since you're obviously not the source of the disturbances, it won't hurt to tell you. Granted, the Magical Superior might get angry, but honestly he gets angry about everything I do. Can't please everyone, am I right?"

He said that as if he expected Jenur to agree, which she supposed she did, though she wasn't sure why she was so reluctant to. Maybe it was his tone.

"Anyway," said Braim. "So you know the North Academy is near here, right? Best and oldest mage school in the entire Northern Isles? Said to have been founded by the first ever mage?"

"Uh, yes," said Jenur. "I've heard about it, but I didn't know it was near here. Who in their right mind would build a school in the Great Berg?"

"It's pretty safe and remote," said Braim. "Not many people live near the Great Berg. The founder of the school didn't want outsiders to have easy access to it, since he believed that you can't have any distractions when it comes to learning magic. He also believed that only the most serious students were worth teaching. Figured anyone who made the trek all the way to the Great Berg was probably serious about learning magic or maybe blessed by the gods. Either way, if you made it up here by yourself, then you were guaranteed a spot."

"Who was the founder?" said Jenur. "He sounds like a harsh man."

"That's just the thing," said Braim. "No one knows. We don't have any pictures of him or drawings, no names anywhere, nothing. Pretty freaky, right?"

"But then how do you know that he's the founder?" said Jenur. "How do you even know that he's a he?"

"There's only one clue to his identity," said Braim. "We've got an old journal that details the construction of the original Academy buildings, though we still don't know who wrote it. The text is really faded and written in a language no one speaks, reads, or writes in anymore. We think it was written by the founder, but it could just as easily have been written by the construction crew who built it, so what do we know?"

"Get on with it," said Jenur. "I'm not interested in a history lesson."

"Got it," said Braim, nodding. "Well, you see, the Magical Superior sensed a massive surge of magical energy near here. Normally, that isn't unusual, 'cause there are a lot of students who train around here, but this was bigger—far bigger than any human or aquarian mage could ever hope to do. God-level, actually."

Jenur gulped. "God-level? You mean there's a god somewhere nearby?"

"Yeah," said Braim. "Again, wouldn't be that strange, 'cause the Great Berg is Xocion's domain and sometimes other gods and goddesses show up, too. Only difference was that this energy surge didn't feel quite like a normal one to the Superior. I told him it was probably nothing, but the man told me to go and check it out anyway."

"Didn't he know that this blizzard was about to come through?" said Jenur. "It wasn't exactly a secret."

"I know," said Braim. "I told him there was this huge blizzard about to blow through, but as usual the Superior told me that I was a big boy and could take care of myself. Guess he forgot that I happen to specialize in telemancy and necromancy, *not* pagomancy. He's a smart guy, but I sometimes wonder if his old age is getting to him."

"Sounds like a great boss," said Jenur.

Braim snorted. "Beautiful, he's what I call a pain in the ass. But I still respect him. Just don't tell him I said that. Okay?"

Seeing as Jenur didn't think she'd be running into the Magical Superior anytime soon, she nodded.

"Great," said Braim, slapping his hands together. "Guess we're stuck together for a while. At least until the storm blows over."

"You've got to get us out of here," said Jenur. "The Dark Tigers are still out there. When the storm passes, they'll kill us all."

"Yeah, you said that already," said Braim, tapping the side of his head. "Ain't deaf yet, unlike the Superior. But sure, I'll take you two away from here, though we'll have to go directly back to the Academy and there's a rule that says that non-mages aren't allowed in the Academy, but I'm sure the Superior will make an exception. He's a nice guy."

"But you just said he was a pain in the ass," said Jenur.

"He's a nice pain in the ass," said Braim. Then he frowned. "That came out wrong."

Darek giggled a little, which was the first time Jenur had heard him make any positive noises in quite a while. Braim seemed to notice, too, because he said, in what he evidently thought was a kind voice, "Like that, little guy?"

But then Darek just tightened his grip on Jenur's legs and buried his face deeper into her knees, causing Jenur to look up at him and shrug.

"Never been good with kids anyway," Braim muttered, looking down at his own knees.

Jenur patted Darek on the head and said to Braim, "So how far is the Academy from here?"

"Not allowed to say," said Braim. "Remember, only mages are allowed to know that kind of information. All I'll say is that it isn't far and that we should hopefully be able to make it back pretty quickly."

"Will the Dark Tigers be able to follow us?" said Jenur. "Could they find it?"

"Nope," said Braim. "Even if they made a point of following us, the Academy is enchanted to make it impossible for anyone who lacks permission to step on Academy grounds to enter. You two will be fine, since I'm giving you permission to enter."

"That's good," said Jenur. "I'm just worried that Nijok Wirm might—"

"Hold on," said Braim. "Did you say Nijok Wirm? The Grand

Tiger himself? *He's* here?"

Braim had jumped to his feet and looked like a trapped cat.

"Yes," said Jenur. "He and one other, a female aquarian named Kura. They tried to kill me."

"By the gods," said Braim. "You know what? I really don't want to know what you did to them now. If Wirm himself is here, then you must have done something *spectacularly* bad to piss them off. Wirm never leaves Ruwa for anything. I'm almost curious to know what you did, but honestly, I'm pretty happy remaining ignorant."

"Yeah, I know," said Jenur. She gestured at her bandaged nose and said, "Got this from Wirm. I only managed to wound him, but I know he's still alive. Wirm isn't the kind of guy to give up even when you stab him in the foot with a knife."

"You stabbed him in the foot?" said Braim. "Great. I bet Wirm isn't even waiting for the blizzard to die down. He's probably trudging through the snow thinking of all the ways he can kill you right now. Just my luck that I had to run into the girl who pissed off the leader of the Dark Tigers."

"Can't you teleport us?" said Jenur. "You're a mage, right?"

"Not *that* kind of mage," said Braim, shaking his head. "I was never good at teleporting. If I tried to teleport all three of us now, we'd probably all turn inside out. Granted, that would mean the Dark Tigers couldn't kill us, but since we want to survive, I think that wouldn't be very fun, now would it?"

"Do you have a boat?" said Jenur.

"Yep," said Braim. "Not a big one, but I think all three of us ought to be able to fit in it pretty well. If not, you can always sit on my lap, Jenur. I won't mind. Honest."

Jenur rolled her eyes. "We're stuck in a village full of corpses in the middle of a blizzard, with the world's most deadly assassin after both of us, and you think this is the perfect opportunity to flirt."

"It's my philosophy that one should never waste a perfectly good opportunity to flirt," said Braim. "Never know which breath will be your last, right? Better make 'em count."

"I think there are better ways to make your words count than by flirting," said Jenur.

Braim shrugged. "Let's agree to disagree. Anyway, is it me or does the storm sound like it's dying down?"

Jenur listened. Braim was right. The wind didn't sound as loud as it had earlier and the snow through the windows looked thinner. Braim peeked through the door again and stuck his arm out before pulling it back in.

"Looks like it is," said Braim. "I think we'll be able to leave in the next few minutes. I'll lead, so you two just stay close to me and follow, all right?"

"All right," said Jenur. She looked down at Darek and said, "Darek, did you hear what Braim said? He's going to take us away from the bad guys."

Darek looked up at Jenur, his eyes starting to tear up. "What about mama?"

"We ..." Jenur bit her lower lip before continuing. "We can't do anything about her right now. We're going to leave her body here, along with everyone else's bodies. Maybe later, when the bad guys leave, we can come back and bury them."

"We most definitely will have to," said Braim. "The Diogian Creed says that all corpses have to be given the proper burial. Corpses that aren't buried are a slap in the face to Diog, the God of the Grave."

Who cares what some stupid god thinks? Jenur thought, but aloud she said, "Yeah, I guess so."

Braim closed the door and leaned against it again. "Remember: The minute the storm dies down, we leave immediately. So you two get ready to go on my signal."

Jenur nodded as she grabbed her coat off of Darek's body and put it back on her own body. As she did so, she couldn't help but hope that the blizzard had killed Wirm and Kura. She didn't see how either of them could have survived it, but she also knew that the Dark Tigers were not easy to kill. All she could hope was that by the time Wirm and Kura arrived, she, Darek, and Braim would be long gone.

Chapter Eight

Y URIMA LOOKED LIKE A completely different place after the blizzard. The roofs were covered with layers and layers of white snow, the light of the sun overhead reflecting off the snow and hurting Jenur's eyes whenever she looked at them. Not to mention that the snow had covered the streets so deeply that it was impossible to move at a pace faster than a quick waddle. In fact, the snow was so deep that Jenur had to carry Darek with her, since he was too small to walk through it himself.

Braim led the way, waving his wand and forcing the snow to move out of their path. He had explained that, while he was no pagomancer, he knew enough to be able to manipulate snow. Still, it was clear that ice magic wasn't his specialty because sometimes the snow failed to move or he only moved about half as much as he had intended. It was almost embarrassing how bad he was at it, but Jenur knew better than to say that aloud. She was so tired from the events of the day that she just wanted to get to Braim's boat and get out of the village before Wirm and Kura arrived.

Speaking of Wirm and Kura, Jenur had not seen either of them since she, Darek, and Braim had left the storage building. She was comforted by the fact that the snow was probably slowing down the two Dark Tigers' progress, but again, she didn't relax or slow her pace. She knew better than to let her guard down when the two Dark Tigers who hated her the most were nearby. She didn't see either of them hiding in the houses or on the rooftops, but just because she couldn't see them didn't mean they weren't there.

Just have to keep calm, Jenur, Jenur thought as she redoubled her grip on Darek, who was clinging to her as tightly as ever. *For Darek's sake, you have to keep your cool.*

Easier said than done. Every time her nose throbbed with pain, she was reminded of Wirm's fist slamming into her nose and shattering it like glass. And every time she remembered that, her heart raced and she wanted to pick up her pace, but Braim seemed content to move at his current pace, so Jenur would just have to mentally goad Braim on and hope that he could hear her thoughts.

Finally, Jenur, Darek, and Braim left the village's limits and ended up on Yurima Beach. Like the village, Yurima Beach was covered in snow, but it was not nearly as thick and was quickly being swept away by the ocean waves that slid across the sand. The fishing boat Jenur had seen earlier was nowhere to be seen on the ocean's surface, which in all probability meant that it had been sunk beneath the waves. She wondered who had been in it at the time.

A single dock was all that made up Yurima's 'port.' A few fishing boats—devoid of anything except some rope and nets—were tied to the dock, but it was the boat tied at the very end of the dock that caught Jenur's interest.

The boat looked nothing like any boat Jenur had ever seen. It had a clear glass dome covering the cockpit, which was currently covered in snow and ice. Its bow was shaped like a chisel, while a large, box-shaped motor stood at its stern. A large pile of snow had gathered in the center of the boat. As Braim had said, the boat did indeed look big enough for all three of them, though when Jenur looked at it, she wondered how such a tiny thing could possibly survive going out onto the ocean.

"Here we are," said Braim, gesturing at the boat as they walked across the dock. "I call her the *Floating Bubble*. 'Cause her dome looks like a bubble, doesn't it?"

"It does," said Darek. It was the first time he'd spoken since they'd left the storage building. "Will it pop?"

"'Course it won't," said Braim. "This baby is reinforced Kaian glass. Add just a touch of reinforcement magic and it would take the strength of a full-grown adult baba raga just to crack it."

"Is the rest of the boat just as sturdy?" Jenur asked.

"Yep," said Braim. "Weak boats don't last long out here. Gotta design 'em nice and sturdy. Only problem is, the ice and snow and stuff is covering it."

They had by now reached the boat. Braim waved his wand over the dome and the ice and snow began to melt. Soon the layers had melted completely, leaving behind a glistening glass dome that was as clear as the water around World's End. With another wave of his wand, the snow inside the boat floated up into the air and threw itself into the ocean with a small splash.

Braim then stepped aside and said to Jenur, "Ladies first."

Jenur ignored him as she stepped into the boat, which shook under her foot, but she managed to get onto it with little trouble. She and Darek sat down under the dome, while Braim climbed in and took up a spot at the stern, where the motor was.

"Uh oh," said Braim as he examined the motor. "Looks like this thing's frozen over, too."

"You mean you didn't insulate it?" said Jenur. "Seems like a pretty shortsighted thing of you to do."

Braim tossed an irritated look over his shoulder. "It was insulated, beautiful. That's why I was surprised to find it frozen. Guess that blizzard must have been worse than I thought."

"Just hurry, will you?" said Jenur. "Wirm and Kura could be here any minute. The longer we delay, the more time they have to get here."

"Calm down," said Braim, tapping the motor with his wand. "You said you wounded both of them, didn't you? With all of this snow, it'd be pretty difficult for them to get here. Besides, I still don't know just which parts of the engine are frozen. But yeah, I'll be quick anyway."

Darek cuddled up closer to Jenur and Jenur put her arm around him as Braim flipped open the lid of the motor and began looking through it. She could sense Darek's tenseness, which was no surprise, as he was just as frightened of the Dark Tigers as she was. She kept glancing over her shoulder through the dome to the dock and beyond that, to Yurima itself, but the town seemed as silent and still as usual.

That's the thing about the Dark Tigers, though, Jenur thought. *They only show themselves when it's too late to stop them.*

Braim suddenly stopped looking through the motor. "Uh oh."

"Uh oh?" Jenur repeated. "What do you mean, 'uh oh'?"

Braim looked over his shoulder at her again, a frightened expression on his face. "The fuel is completely frozen. As is the wiring and the motor itself."

"So?" said Jenur. "Just heat it up and melt it. Not that big a problem, right?"

"Actually, it's a huge problem," said Braim. "See, the fuel is very sensitive to heat. If I tried to use a heat spell on it, there's a good chance the fuel would blow up in my face and sink the boat. Which wouldn't, y'know, be good."

"What?" said Jenur. "But you must know how to use fire magic to avoid that sort of thing, don't you?"

"Like I said, I specialize in telemancy and necromancy," said Braim. "Sure, I know a thing or two about pyromancy, but last time I tried to do this sort of thing, I ended up blowing up half of the East Dormitory and set fire to the Superior's favorite robes."

"Isn't there anything you can do?" said Jenur. "Don't you have any magical powers that can move the boat or something? Like, maybe some hydromancy or something?"

"Not much of an hydromancer, either, to be honest," said Braim with a shrug. "I mean, I could fill a cup of water for you, but beyond that, my hydromancy sucks."

"Damn it," Jenur said. "Isn't there *anything* else you can do? Anything else at all?"

"Not to worry," said Braim. "I can send a message back to the Academy asking for help. The Superior will probably send someone to come and get us. Just hope it isn't Irliza. She'd never let me live this down."

"I don't care who saves us," said Jenur. "How long will it take for them to get here?"

Braim tapped his chin as he looked out over the cold ocean and said, "Depending on the waves, the wind, and a bunch of other factors, I'd say it shouldn't take 'em half an hour, possibly less. If they send someone who can teleport, it would only take them a few minutes at most."

"Then send them a message asking for a teleporter," Jenur said. "*Now.*"

"Okay, okay, hold your horses," said Braim, holding up his hands defensively. "Here we go."

Braim turned to the port and held up his wand before him. A long, gray line of smoke poured out of the wand's tip and in a few seconds, a large, shapeless smoke cloud stood before Braim, floating above the water.

"All right," said Braim. "To the Magical Superior: This is Braim Kotogs. My boat's engine, motor, and even the fuel have completely frozen over and I am stuck here. Furthermore, I am stuck here with two survivors from the village of Yurima, which appears to have suffered an attack by the Dark Tigers in which nearly all of its inhabitants were killed. The two Dark Tigers are still active, according to one of the survivors, and could be here any minute. Nijok Wirm is one of the two Dark Tigers. Send help as soon as possible, preferably a teleporter."

As soon as Braim finished speaking those words, the cloud began shape-shifting until it looked almost exactly like Braim. The only difference was that it was completely gray, its form immaterial. It then opened its mouth and repeated Braim's message in his voice word-for-word before it turned and zoomed away into the sky. It soon disappeared from view when it flew past an iceberg floating nearby.

"What was that?" said Jenur as Braim leaned against the engine, his arms folded across his chest.

"Hm?" said Braim. "What was what?"

"Smoky you," Darek piped up. "Was he your brother?"

Braim laughed. "No, no. It was a gray ghost. It's the primary method of long-distance communication between mages who are too far for any other forms of communication to be practical. Every mage can do it."

"So do you know how long it will take for the Magical Superior to respond?" said Jenur.

"Not sure," said Braim. "Depends on how fast the ghost gets to the Academy. The Superior isn't the kind of guy to delay whenever his students or faculty are in trouble, though, so he'll probably send someone the minute he gets the message."

"But you said that could take half an hour," said Jenur, "depending on whether the person he sends can teleport or not."

"True," said Braim. "But what are you so worried about? I don't see Wirm or Kura anywhere. I bet they're probably still digging themselves out of the snow. By the time those idiots get here, we'll all be safely behind the walls of the Aca—"

A dull, yet threatening, *thud* interrupted Braim and caused Jenur to look over her shoulder. The bubble dome of the *Floating Bubble* was cracked for some reason, and through the clear Kaian glass, Jenur spotted two figures standing on Yurima Beach. From a distance it was hard to make out any distinguishing features on them, but the identities of the two figures was no mystery, especially when Jenur noticed that a long, thick metal dart had pierced the Kaian glass. The dart had just missed her head by inches. Considering how far away the two Dark Tigers were from them, Jenur was surprised they had been that accurate.

"By the gods," said Braim. "They're here already?"

Darek squeaked and buried his face deeper into Jenur's chest. Jenur held him as comfortingly as she could, but her deepest instincts were goading her to run and never look back. Especially when she saw the two figures making their way to the dock; if they did that, then there truly was no hope of escape for them.

"Stay here, you two," said Braim as he stepped out of the boat. "I'll keep those two busy. Or rather, the village of Yurima will keep them busy."

Before Jenur could ask him what he meant by that, Braim twirled his wand through the air three times and then pointed it directly at Yurima. A deep, dark presence filled the air around Jenur, like smoke, but she could not see it. She sensed it coming from Braim, who continued to aim rigidly at the village.

By now, Wirm and Kura were almost at the dock. They were still too far away for Jenur to distinguish them, but she thought she saw wisps of smoke trailing like a cape in the wind behind one of them. She wasn't sure how Wirm could still run, considering she had stabbed him in the foot, but she banished the thought from her mind as she watched them draw closer and closer to the dock.

But just as Wirm and Kura reached it, the roofs of the huts in Yurima exploded. Dozens of figures leaped out of the small buildings, hurtling through the air like rag dolls tossed about by a child. The figures crashed onto the dock, blocking Wirm and Kura's route, before they rose from their tangled mess of limbs and bodies and rose to their full height. The two Dark Tigers backed off from the dock as the figures began walking toward them, though their movements were slow, awkward, and jerky.

"What the hell is going on there?" said Jenur. "What are those things?"

The sweat running down Braim's face told Jenur that, whatever he was doing, it was far more difficult than it appeared. "Didn't I tell you? I said the village of Yurima was going to keep them busy."

"Village of—?" said Jenur before it dawned on her exactly what Braim was doing. "By the gods. That's insane. And a little morally questionable."

"I'm a necromancer," said Braim, without looking at her. "Everyone says we're insane and morally questionable. But it's like the Records of Diog always say: 'The dead make excellent shields.'"

Jenur could not help but watch as the Yuriman corpses advanced on Wirm and Kura. A few of the corpses went down, perhaps from a blow to the head by one of the Tigers, but the vast majority of them just kept advancing, forcing the Tigers to retreat further and further up the Beach. It was times like these that made Jenur wish she knew a little magic herself, but since that would require dedicating her life to a particular god or goddess and she was, at best, apathetic towards the gods, she decided that she could do without magic for now.

"See? It's working just fine," said Braim. "I doubt the corpses will be able to kill or even harm those two, but they should at the very least delay them until our rescuer arrives, whoever that might be."

Indeed, Braim's words seemed to be correct. The corpses continued to advance, while the Dark Tigers continued to retreat. For a moment, Jenur thought that maybe they would be able to get away after all.

But then one of the Dark Tigers—it had to be Wirm because Kura couldn't do that—transformed into a massive smoke cloud. The cloud then shot over the heads of the corpses, skittering over their scalps as a few of the taller ones swiped at it, and crashed on the dock. The smoke cloud rolled into a ball, but as it rolled, its form became more and more clear until the ball had completely transformed back into Nijok Wirm himself.

As Wirm rolled to his feet, his trajectory making him slide across the icy surface of the dock, Braim aimed his wand at him, but the Grand Tiger hurled something small, sharp, and shiny through the air. The small object struck Braim's wand hand, causing the necromancer to curse as he dropped the wand onto the deck. A sharp, metal throwing star stood out of Braim's hand like an ugly sticker, making him swear like a sailor under his breath.

But Braim didn't get much time to swear. Wirm was still advancing, throwing star after star at Braim. Braim managed to dodge a few of them, but one struck his left knee and another sliced through his shoulder, causing him to stagger backwards from the blows. He was so distracted by the throwing stars that he didn't seem to notice that he was about to fall backwards into the ocean.

"Braim, watch out!" Jenur shouted.

She shouted too late. Braim's right foot slipped off the back of the pier and he fell back first into the water with a splash. Jenur and Darek both watched as Braim struggled to swim, but his heavy clothes must have been weighing him down because his head soon disappeared beneath the water, only a small collection of bubbles floating up to the surface. Seconds later, the bubbles vanished.

"Braim!" Jenur almost screamed, even though she knew there was no use in screaming for him. "No!"

Darek was crying now, wailing at the top of his lungs, but at the moment Jenur didn't know what to say to comfort him. She reached out towards the spot where Braim had disappeared, but then a massive hand wrapped around her arm and hauled her out of the boat. Darek screamed behind her, called out for her, but Jenur could not stop Wirm from pulling her out of the boat.

The Grand Tiger slammed Jenur down onto the pier and slammed his boot against her chest. His boot had crushed her breasts, causing Jenur to gasp in pain as Wirm looked down on her.

Wirm looked like he had slept out in the cold all night. His skin was blue as the sea, a bandage had been wrapped around his foot (though it was not the foot he was using to pin Jenur down), and he looked like he had had a bad day and was just about done with it.

"There you are, you little witch," said Wirm, his low voice somehow audible above Darek's crying. "Thought you could get away from me, did you? Of course you did. You were always arrogant, always uppity. Just like your father."

Wirm drew a long, jagged knife from his belt. Jenur instinctively reached for her own, but then Wirm fired another blast of smoke at her hand. The smoke burned like fire, forcing her to retract it and hold it up against her chest.

"See this knife?" said Wirm, waving it in front of her face. "This was the knife I stole from my father, the knife I used to kill my first paid target. Can you see the blood on it? I haven't washed it since."

Jenur did see what appeared to be dried blood on the blade, but she didn't focus on it too deeply because she was distracted by Braim's death, Darek's crying, and Wirm's boot intensifying the pain from the burns on her chest. Her eyes nonetheless followed the blade as Wirm waved it through the air.

"I haven't used it even once since that day," said Wirm. "But you are such a special nuisance that I decided that I needed my lucky knife if I was going to make sure you were dead. I didn't use it earlier because I underestimated you, but no more. You will die, just like all of those Yurimans did."

"Darek," Jenur coughed. "What about Darek?"

"The little boy?" said Wirm, glancing at Darek, who was still crying. "I hate screaming children. You don't even know the things your father promised to do for me so I wouldn't kill you when you screamed like that as a child. I'll slit his throat and toss his body into the ocean, or perhaps burn it with his mother's."

At that, Darek's scream increased in volume and intensity, so loud that Jenur could barely hear her own thoughts. She wanted to comfort him, to tell Darek that it was all going to be all right, but she was in no position to comfort anyone, not even herself.

Wirm, on the other hand, didn't seem to notice Darek's shrieks of terror at all. He spun the knife in his hand, an animal-like grin of savage pleasure on his lips, and then brought the knife directly toward Jenur's face.

Before the blade could cut through Jenur's skull, another hand appeared out of nowhere and caught Wirm's arm. Shocked, Jenur looked to her left and saw a middle-aged woman standing there, a woman with thick, beefy arms and similar winter clothes like the kind Braim had worn, except rather than being white, they were as black as volcanic ash.

"What the hell?" said Wirm, looking into the woman's eyes. "Who in all of the Northern Isles are you, old witch?"

"Just a lady who can't stand seeing a man beat on an innocent little girl," said the woman. "I see your own parents didn't teach you any manners, did they?"

Wirm growled, but before he could do anything, the woman raised her other hand and pointed a wand—similar to Braim's, but longer and thinner—directly at Wirm's face.

"Guess you have to learn them the hard way," said the woman.

A blast of fire exploded from the wand tip, hitting Wirm directly in the face. Wirm howled in pain and anger as he staggered backward, but the mysterious newcomer gave him no time to recover. She slashed her wand like a sword, sending an arc of electricity at him that sent Wirm flying off the pier.

Too shocked to move, Jenur watched as Wirm flew through the air until he landed—with a loud *splash*—into the cold water and sank like a stone. He didn't rise again.

"Good riddance," said the woman as she lowered her wand. "There are enough idiots in this world anyway. Don't see any reason to have more."

Then the woman looked down at Jenur and smiled. "You all right, girlie?"

Jenur shook her head. "N-No. Who are—"

"Call me Irliza," said the woman. "Got Braim's message. The Magical Superior sent me to save you guys because he knows that Braim and I are best friends."

There was something distinctly sarcastic about the way she said 'best friends,' but Jenur didn't think to question it.

She just said, "Well, you're too late. Braim is—"

"He's fine," said the woman. "Already teleported him back to the Academy. He's being watched over by the panamancers. I just came back for you and that little boy there."

Irliza nodded at Darek, who was still crying and screaming. Despite Wirm being gone, Darek seemed to be crying harder than ever. It made Jenur wonder just how long a boy his age could cry and if she ever cried that long herself when she was that young.

"But enough talk," said Irliza. "I see that jerk's friend is still alive. That means it's time for us to get the hell out of here."

Jenur raised her head just high enough to see that all of the corpses lay in a pile Yurima Beach, probably because Braim wasn't around to direct them anymore. Kura was climbing over them, but it would probably be a while before she got to them.

"All right," said Irliza. "You two, just grab on. Have either of you teleported before, per chance?"

Jenur shook her head, while Darek just howled as he always did.

"I'll take that as a no," said Irliza. "Well, as long as you remember to hold on and not to scream or throw up, you should be just fine."

Jenur had no idea what that meant, but as she was still in no mood to ask questions, she just reached out for Darek's hand. To her relief, Darek took her hand and held it tightly. He seemed to have stopped crying now, merely sniffling and hiccuping heavily.

"All right," said Irliza. "Here we go."

Irliza waved her wand through the air even as Kura's voice rang out over the pier: "Jenur!"

But it was too late for Kura to do anything. Soon everything around Jenur faded; the pier under her, the freezing air, the thin sheet of ice under her body, and the sight of Kura running at them.

Then Jenur felt herself spinning around and she could see nothing except for blurry colors that made her sick to her stomach. She still clung to Darek and Irliza as tightly as she could, but she could feel her grip slipping little by little as she continued to spin. It almost made her panic as she wondered what would happen if she let go of Irliza mid-teleport.

A moment later, Jenur felt her feet hit solid ground, her world stopped spinning, and Irliza announced, "We're here!"

But Jenur didn't get to see where 'here' was. She saw a massive red structure standing before her, caught glimpses of what looked like ice walls in the distance, but then it seemed like all of the injuries and pain she had received while fighting Wirm and Kura came back all at once.

The pain overwhelming her, Jenur immediately collapsed onto

the grass beneath her. Her world rapidly going dark around her, the last things Jenur heard were Darek calling her name and Irliza calling for help.

Chapter Nine

One week later ...

THE BRIGHT, SUNNY DAY seemed like a slap in the face to Malock. He squinted up at the sun, which shone with an effusiveness that was entirely inappropriate on the day of Father's funeral. He wished that the God of the Sun would tone it down. There was nothing happy or bright about today.

Skimif ought to be doing something about it, Malock thought. *Surely he must know what's happening today. Or is my father's funeral too insignificant in the grand scheme of things for him to care?*

Those bitter thoughts had plagued Malock's head all week as he and Mother went through the funeral preparations with a Diogian priest and undertaker named Droman Kein. Any time he had a moment by himself in which to think, Malock would always look up at the sky and wonder what Skimif was doing or if Skimif even knew about Father's death. Considering that Skimif had not spoken to Malock at all since his ascension, it seemed unlikely that he did.

Then again, it wasn't like he and Father had been best friends while Father lived, Malock thought. *It had been Father and Mother who had ordered the Justice Enforcers to try to arrest him while he was a mortal. Perhaps it's for the best that he's not here today.*

"Tojas?" said Mother, breaking him out of his thoughts. "Are you paying attention?"

Malock shook his head and looked at Mother. Instead of her usual red dress, Mother today wore a charcoal black mourning dress that had the hammer of Grinf stitched into its chest area. Her graying hair had been prepared with elaborate curls by her hair stylist and the perfume wafting off her body—possibly Grinf's Smoke, which was her favorite perfume and one quite appropriate for the funeral— made her seem all the more older than she appeared. Especially when he looked into her eyes and saw the pain and sadness within. In her hands she held a red handkerchief, which she dabbed her eyes with.

"Sorry, Mother," said Malock. "I was ... distracted."

Mother nodded. "I understand, Tojas. We ... we all have been a little distracted these days, haven't we?"

Malock nodded. "We have."

They were standing in the Carnagian Royal Cemetery, which was located not far from Carnag Hall. Rows upon rows of tombstones— most large and elaborate—ran from one end of the Cemetery to another, each representing one of Malock's deceased ancestors. The oldest ones were chipped and cracked, the names and dates faded from centuries of exposure to the elements, while the newest—the tombstone belonging to Malock's grandfather, King Arlox Hal—still looked as new as the day that it had been erected so many years ago, though some plants were steadily creeping up its side.

Malock and Mother did not stand alone in the Cemetery. The

various Carnagian nobles, as well as visitors from other islands, all stood around the grave in which Father's coffin would be buried. All of them wore their best clothes for this event; crimson robes for the men, blood-red dresses for the women. Most Malock recognized, such as Darfna Enux the playwright and the famous Grinfian monk and public debater, Yamaru Domaha. All of the guests had already given Malock their condolences. King Fabadi himself was present among them, garbed in a Grinfian cloak that looked to have been tailored for just this occasion, though Malock had done his best to avoid the King of Shika, as Fabadi still seemed to believe in his assassination theory, despite the lack of evidence supporting it.

Not that the guests were the only people here. At least a dozen Justice Enforcers—including the gold-collared elite ones—patrolled the outer edges and entrances of the Cemetery. Neither Malock nor Mother expected any danger or trouble to befall the funeral, but Father, despite his greatness, had earned himself more than a few enemies over his lifetime. Better to be safe than sorry was always an important aspect of Father's philosophy, anyway. He likely would have wanted it to be this way.

There were no commoners among the guests. Occasionally, Malock would spot one such person at the gates to the Cemetery, but they were nearly always turned away by the Justice Enforcers. Father had been beloved by many of the commoners—a fact Malock had had confirmed on his way to the Cemetery earlier today when several commoners stood on the sidewalks of Port Blasan and wept and gave their condolences to Malock and Mother. Still, there were just too many people who wanted to come and the Cemetery, as large as it was, simply did not have enough room for everyone. That didn't stop the commoners from coming to the gates or, in the case of one particularly devoted man, trying to climb the walls of the Cemetery and bypass the gates entirely.

Father's casket had not yet been brought out. His body was being prepared for burial by Droman Kein in the little grave keeper's lodge located up the main path into the Cemetery. Kein had promised to be quick, but he had said that about ten minutes ago and Malock was starting to think that Kein's old age must have been getting to him because Kein had not sent his assistant to explain his delay.

Maybe that's for the best, Malock thought. *Do I actually want to see my father's body right away?*

Mother sniffed, causing Malock to put an arm around her shoulders. He could not help but recall how she had reacted when he had returned home with Father's corpse a week ago. She had wept for the entire night over Father's corpse, not letting anyone comfort her, not even Malock. The next day, however, she had returned to her usual self just in time for her and Malock to work with Kein to begin the funeral preparations.

Still, it was easy to tell that Mother had not recovered entirely from the shock of seeing her husband dead. Malock had heard from some of Mother's maids that Mother still cried about Father at night and would often require a lot of comforting from said maids before she would be willing to go back to sleep. Once, two days after Father's corpse was returned to Carnag, Mother had awoken with a scream and claimed to have seen Father's corpse hanging from the ceiling of her room, a thought that had scared her so deeply that it had required the combined efforts of the royal hypnomancer and the royal oneiromancer to keep her asleep and to keep her dreams from becoming nightmares.

Today, Mother was as stable as she always was, but every now and then Malock would notice that she was not entirely well and so would find a way to comfort her as best as he could. Part of him was wondering how she would react when Father's corpse was actually brought out and lowered into the grave, but he chose not to worry about that because he doubted he'd react much better than Mother would.

"Glad those damn Heathens aren't here to mess things up," one of the nobles, speaking in what he obviously thought was a whisper, said to the other noble standing next to him. "They'd have a field day with this, I'm sure."

His friend glanced nervously up at the sky. "Are you sure you want to talk about them like this? You know, with Skimif being in charge of everything now?"

Malock pretended that he was not listening to them, but with so little else to distract him, he listened to their conversation anyway.

"Eh, who cares about Skimif?" the first noble muttered. "He's not done much to make this world different that I can see. He's probably got bigger things to worry about than anything we might say."

"I don't know," said the second noble. "The Heathens have been getting rowdier since Skimif's ascension. Didn't you hear? Rumor has it that the Heathens are planning to overthrow several nations and plunge all of the Northern Isles into chaos."

"Idiot," said the first noble. "The Heathens aren't even half a shadow of their former selves. I have heard—from a far more reliable source than 'rumor'—that the Heathens have been losing members every day since Skimif's ascension. Pretty soon, they'll be nothing more than a footnote in history, if even that."

"If you say so," said the second noble. "But I still wonder whether Prince Malock will allow the movement to continue to operate with Carnagian borders. They're too dangerous."

"Of course he will," the first noble responded. "Prince Malock is a known Heathen sympathizer. I see no reason he'd stop them now. He lacks the guts to do it anyway."

Malock cleared his throat loudly at that, causing the two nobles to start and look around. Malock didn't say anything, nor did he even look at them, but a brief glance told him that the two nobles had shut up now.

Good, Malock thought. *Out of everything I've gone through over the past week, I am not in any mood to hear a bunch of idiot nobles criticize me for things I haven't even done yet.*

Still, Malock knew there was some truth to their words. Ever since Skimif had ascended to godhood, the Brotherhood of Heathens was stagnant, at best, and dying off at worse. At least, that was the impression that Malock had received from Aqur, the leader of the Brotherhood, when he had spoken to her briefly upon returning to Carnag a while ago, though he had been so busy over the past two months since Skimif's ascension that he had not had time to sit down and talk with Aqur about the Brotherhood's status in-depth. Though he still considered himself a member, Malock didn't even know where the new Heathen headquarters was, as the old one had been burned down in Skimif's fight with Grinf two months ago.

But to Malock's knowledge, the Heathens were not planning any sort of uprising at all. True, Aqur was always more willing to fight for the Brotherhood than Skimif had been, but so far, she had kept the Heathens under the radar. In fact, Malock hadn't even heard of any public demonstrations from the Heathens yet.

I just wonder what Aqur is planning, Malock thought. *Is she still waiting for orders from Skimif or is there something else going on that I don't know of?*

As a matter of fact, Malock had considered sending Aqur an invitation to the funeral, but he had refrained from doing so, partly because he knew that none of the other guests would appreciate having the leader of a hated social movement in their midst, but partly because he knew that Aqur would never accept it. Unlike the other Heathens, Aqur had never treated Malock with much respect or kindness. She had always tolerated him because Skimif had accepted him; otherwise, he was quite sure that she would have put a bullet in his head and discarded his body in a back alley somewhere in Port Blasan (which she had more or less threatened to do to him the first time Malock had met her).

I wonder if that's why she hasn't spoken to me much since Skimif's ascension, Malock thought. *Maybe this is her way of saying that I am no longer welcomed within the movement. Wonder if the rest of the Brotherhood agrees with that.*

Malock's thoughts were interrupted when Kein's servant—a young boy whose name escaped Malock at the moment—dashed out of Kein's grave keeper's lodge and ran down the path to the open grave, where all of the guests stood. The grave-keeper-in-training ran past the guests and came to a stop before Malock and Mother, his round face covered with sweat from all of the running he had done.

"Master Kein is on his way with the body of King Halock," said the assistant, huffing and puffing. "He sent me to tell you that he has performed all of the usual preparations and that Diog has told him that King Halock's grave is in accordance with the Rites of Diog, as described in the Records of Diog, the Book of Burial Preparation, Chapter Four, verses nine through eighteen."

He recited all of that like he had spent a very long time memorizing it and meant to put it all to use whether he needed to or not.

To which Malock said, "Thank you for informing us. We appreciate all of the work and effort that Kein has put into preparing Father's body for burial. It is more than we can repay."

The assistant nodded. "No need to repay us anything, Your Majesty. The work itself is pay enough. There is no more noble work than preparing the body of a great man to pass into the next life, as Master Kein always says."

"That is a noble sentiment," said Malock. "You may now return to your master."

The assistant bowed and was off, heading back to Kein's lodge. Less than a minute after the assistant slipped through the front door of Kein's lodge, the door opened again. A large, heavy wooden casket —lined with gold Grinfian hammers that jingled and jangled like bells —floated out, followed by a middle-aged, barrel-chested man who wore dirt-brown robes, holding a wand before him, directing the casket's passage through the air.

The guests moved aside to allow Master Droman Kein to float the casket past them. Malock felt his heart wrench at the sight of Father's coffin, while Mother dabbed her eyes again and made a suffocating sound, like she had suppressed a cry. The guests' reactions ranged from the silent tears of Darfna Enux to the quiet but annoyed expression of King Fabadi. No one said a word as Kein carefully lay the coffin into the freshly-dug grave.

Then Kein stepped back from the grave, lowering his wand as a priestess of Grinf brushed past him. The priest was Yoram Vinri, the new Head Priestess, who had taken on the role shortly after the old Head Priest had been kicked out. Malock had not spoken with her much, but from what he knew of her, she was far more honest than her predecessor had been, which was also why Malock and Mother had chosen her to give the eulogy for the funeral.

Priestess Vinri took a spot before the grave. In her right hand, she held a piece of paper, which had her speech on it, and in her left, she held a wand. All eyes were on the Priestess as she lifted up the paper, scanned it briefly, and then lowered it.

"Gathered friends, guests, and family of King Todar Halock, Son of King Arlox Hal, Grandson of King Iryu the Second Most Just, Father of Prince Tojas Malock, Husband of Queen Jinaria Markinia, Defender of Grinf's Courts, King of Carnag, and Carnag's Diplomat," Vinri began. "We have gathered today to mourn the death of this great man, who in his life accomplished much, from building more boot factories in the northwestern provinces to setting the foundation for future peace negotiations between Carnag and Shika.

His sudden, tragic death will be remembered generations from now, but so will his grand life, which, while perhaps not as eventful as that of his grandfather King Iryu, was nonetheless a life worth living."

Malock felt tears beginning to form in his eyes, but he brushed them away. Mother, however, had stopped dabbing the tears in her eyes and was now silently crying. Malock just hugged her tighter, while the other guests continued to listen to Vinri's speech.

"One of the defining features of King Halock's life was his desire to serve our patron Grinf with all his heart and soul," said Vinri. "He listened to the Priesthood, instituted laws to ensure justice was served, and showed no sympathy to the criminals and crooks who would terrorize the innocent citizens of Carnag. Once, not long before his death, he even came face-to-face with Grinf himself, an honor that even King Iryu the Second Most Just was never granted in this life."

At that, the Burn of Grinf—which Malock had received as punishment from Grinf not long ago—flared on Malock's face, forcing him to rub it to get it to stop. None of the other guests paid him any attention, mostly because they seemed awed by the fact that Father had actually met Grinf once.

I wonder if they would be so awed if I told them that Grinf had punished me during that same meeting, Malock thought. *They certainly wouldn't be quite as eager to hear about it, that's for sure.*

"There is an anecdote that Prince Malock and Queen Markinia shared with me that I think illustrates King Halock's best qualities," said Vinri. "Once, ten years ago, King Halock was walking along the streets of Port Blasan, with his bodyguards by his side. He stopped and spoke with many of the commoners, business owners and merchants, factory workers and street cleaners, mages and priests, in order to understand fully just what was going on in their lives and how he, as King of Carnag, could help."

Malock remembered this story well, since he had been there to witness it. He kept quiet, however, and simply listened along with everyone else.

"But then King Halock saw an innocent old woman being robbed by an evil criminal," Vinri continued. "Without waiting for his bodyguards to act or to call the Justice Enforcers, King Halock charged the criminal himself. He took down the criminal easily and returned the lady's stolen goods back to her. He even personally marched the criminal to prison, where he handed the criminal over to the prison warden to be punished as they saw fit. This is a wondrous example of King Halock's innate sense of justice and compassion for those who cannot defend themselves, an example that will sadly never be repeated now that King Halock is no longer with us."

Mother somehow managed to retain her composure, despite the flood of tears coming out of her eyes. Malock, too, could no longer hide or hold back his tears, and he didn't want to, either. Through blurry eyes Malock watched as Vinri folded up the speech and tucked it into her robe pockets.

"I was asked to make this eulogy quick," said Vinri. "And so I have. It is now time to complete the burial process in accordance with the Ordinances of Grinf and the Records of Diog."

Droman Kein walked up to the grave until he was at her side. Vinri nodded at Kein, who raised his wand and fired a large blast of fire at the coffin in the ground below.

The minute the flames touched the coffin, the fire completely filled the pit; in fact, it flew upwards, forcing the guests and Vinri and Kein to step back to avoid getting burned. The flames soon got under control, however, and didn't go beyond the edges of the grave, simply burning brightly under the watchful and tearful eyes of the various gathered guests.

Mother buried her face in Malock's chest, openly weeping now. Malock held her tighter than ever, looking at the burning grave, while several of the guests had bowed their heads in prayer. On the other side of the pit, King Fabadi still stood, the fire reflecting in his old silver eyes, his expression as stiff as ever.

This is it, Malock thought. *Father is gone for good now. We— Mother and I and all of Carnag—are on our own now.*

Just then, Malock felt someone touch his left shoulder. Puzzled, Malock looked over his shoulder and saw Banika Koiro, his former first mate and current Captain of the Justice Enforcers who patrolled and protected the Cemetery, standing there. Her golden captain's helmet was under her left arm, revealing her curly blonde hair. As always, her expression was hard to read, but based on the way she stood, Malock figured something was wrong.

"What is it?" Malock muttered, low enough that only Banika could hear him. "Can't you see we're a little busy?"

"I apologize for the interruption, Your Majesty," said Banika, her voice as low as his. "Under ordinary circumstances I would have waited until the fire was done burning before coming to you, but this is too urgent to leave for later."

"What is too urgent?" said Malock.

Banika leaned in closer, her eyes scanning the various guests still gathered around the grave. "One of my Enforcers was found dead in the southwest corner of the Cemetery."

Shock shook Malock's form, but he kept a calm expression. "What?"

"One of my Enforcers was found dead in the southwest corner of the Cemetery," said Banika, repeating herself clearly. "There are no signs of a struggle on his part. From what I could tell, he died of a heart attack."

Malock's eyes widened and he briefly glanced around the Cemetery before replying in a quick whisper, "Died of a heart attack? Where is the body? Is it still here?"

"I had my men move it," Banika said. "The others are searching the Cemetery for the killer even as we speak."

Another quick glance around the Cemetery told Malock that Banika was correct. Some of the Enforcers were peering around the tombstones, sometimes even poking them with their swords or spears.

"When did this happen?" Malock muttered. "And why didn't you inform me of this the minute it happened?"

"I didn't want to interrupt the ceremony," said Banika. "I thought we might be able to catch the killer before anyone knew what happened."

"Clearly, you didn't," said Malock, trying and failing to keep the annoyance out of his voice. "Are there any clues at all as to who had killed him?"

"None we could find," said Banika. "It's almost like he saw

something that scared him to death. Literally, in this case."

"You don't have *any* idea who killed him?" Malock said above the crackle of the flames of the burning grave, though not loudly enough that anyone but Banika could hear him.

"None whatsoever," said Banika. "We don't know how any killers could have gotten inside. All of the exits are under heavy scrutiny by some of our best gatekeepers, while the more magically talented among us have cast magical barriers around the Cemetery very similar to the Protection around Carnag Hall."

"So we're dealing with a killer who can bypass our best mages, kill Enforcers without having to lay a finger on them, and disappear without a trace," Malock said. "Wonderful."

"We don't think the killer is quite as dangerous as you make him or her out to be," said Banika. "We suspect that the killer is one of the guests."

Malock quickly glanced at the guests, none of whom seemed to have noticed Banika's arrival. They were all too busy staring at the flames.

"One of the guests?" said Malock. "Impossible. Certainly not all of the guests here are saints, but that doesn't mean any of them are killers."

"It is the only reasonable explanation we have so far," said Banika. "How else could a killer have gotten in undetected and kill one of our men without notice? The only problem is that we don't know who it could be, which is why I chose to inform you of this, despite our current ignorance of the killer's identity."

"How am I supposed to know who did it?" Malock said. "As I

said, none of these guests are killers or even inclined to do so. An uninvited guest must have somehow slipped past the defenses."

"I must disagree, Your Majesty," said Banika. "No one could have gotten past our defenses without permission from you or Queen Markinia. One of your guests is a killer, but we don't know who and we don't know how to go about finding out who the killer is."

Malock pursed his lips. He looked at the guests again. While he wasn't exactly fond of some of them, such as Darfna Enux, he didn't think of any of them as being potential killers. Otherwise, neither he nor Mother would ever have invited any of them to the funeral.

And what purpose could any of them have for killing an innocent man? Malock thought. *Perhaps more importantly, who else are they planning to kill?*

"Banika," Malock said. "Keep searching the Cemetery. Look inside Kein's lodge if you must. If there is a killer around here, then he or she must be apprehended right away."

"But if that killer is among your guests, then I must stay here and protect you, sir," said Banika. "I have a feeling that the killer may be aiming for you or Queen Markinia."

"And you still don't have any proof that any of my guests are killers," said Malock. "I am your Prince. What I say goes. I thought you understood that, Banika."

Banika, for once, frowned. "But—"

"Just do it," Malock said, his whisper almost turning into a hiss. "If you find anything, be sure to report directly to me. No need to cause a panic among the guests by announcing that there is a killer somewhere in the Cemetery."

Banika looked very much like she wanted to disobey, but her better nature got the best of her and she nodded. "As you command, Your Majesty."

With that, Banika walked away from Malock, donning her gold helmet as she did so. Malock watched her go, then turned his attention back to the fiery grave. Mother was still sobbing in his chest and didn't seem to have noticed his conversation with Banika, which was for the best as he didn't want to burden her with the knowledge that there might have been a killer among the guests.

But Malock did observe his guests more closely. None of them acted suspiciously or questionable in the slightest. He had been serious when he had told Banika that he didn't think any of them could be killers, but at the same time, doubt began to invade his mind as he considered Banika's arguments in favor of the killer hiding somewhere among the hundred or so guests that stood around the grave.

It wouldn't be very difficult for a killer to hide among us, Malock thought. *They would just need to make sure not to draw attention to themselves. They likely only killed that Enforcer because he stumbled upon them, which means that their real target is still alive, though who it could be, I'm not sure.*

Now Malock was starting to wish that he'd brought his sword with him. At this point, any weapon would have been better than no weapon at all. If Banika was telling the truth, then it was logical to assume that the killer was after either him or Mother. True, there were some other high-profile guests here tonight, such as King Fabadi, but somehow he doubted the killer would have infiltrated the funeral of the King of Carnag to kill the King of Shika.

His eyes darted from face to face, but the only expressions anyone wore were ones of mourning. None of them looked guilty or like they were hiding something. That made him feel a little better before he realized that any professional killer would know how to hide their feelings or thoughts from others so that they would not be easily captured. Especially now that the Enforcers knew that there was a killer in the Cemetery, which would undoubtedly force the killer to be cautious about hiding his or her real identity.

I need some way of figuring out the killer's identity, Malock thought. *The only question is, how do I do that? Not like I can just go up to everyone and say, 'Hey, has anyone here killed a Justice Enforcer within the last five minutes or so?'*

That was when Malock noticed Kein's assistant standing next to his master. The assistant boy had his hands behind his back, his sad expression matching Kein's almost exactly. Malock had not noticed the assistant boy arrive, which he almost dismissed as nothing more than the assistant being quiet.

Then the assistant boy glanced at Malock. Unless Malock's eyes were deceiving him, the boy shot him a quick grin. It happened so fast that Malock wasn't sure the boy had actually done it, but he never got the chance to confirm it because at that moment, the flames rising from the grave grew larger, rising up well above the lip of the grave and lashing through the air like fiery whips.

"What's going on?" said one of the guests, the first noble from earlier. "Grave-keeper?"

Kein raised his wand, saying as he did so, "Oh, it's nothing too

serious. The flames sometimes get bigger than expected. Just let me
—"

One of the flames suddenly jumped out at Kein and struck his wand hand. The grave-keeper yelped in pain, dropping his wand and staggering backwards as the flames started lashing wildly through the air, almost hitting several of the guests and forcing everyone to scatter to avoid being burned.

One such flame went directly for Malock, forcing him to push Mother to the ground to avoid getting scorched. He himself then fell, just barely avoiding getting his face burned off. The flame went back into the grave, but another came at him too fast for him to dodge.

Then Banika Koiro jumped in front of him and held up her shield. The fire slammed into the shield, making the shield glow with the heat, but Banika managed to hold it back, despite the obvious toll it was taking on her body.

"Your Majesty, run!" Banika said, her voice strained. "Both of you, get out of here. We Justice Enforcers will take care of this!"

Malock didn't hesitate. He got to his feet and grabbed Mother's hand, pulling her up off the grass as the flame continued to push against Banika's shield. Mother was clearly in shock, but she managed to follow Malock anyway as he pulled her along behind her. They ran as fast as they could, while the other members of the Justice Enforcers dashed past them, probably going to help Banika fight off the flames.

Malock's destination was the nearest exit out of the Cemetery, which just so happened to be the western gate. Several of the other guests were also making their way to the western gate, while others had made mad dashes for the other exits. A few of the guests had tripped and fallen, but Malock spared them no help. Somehow he knew that the flames were after him and Mother and to stop for even a moment would be to seal their own deaths.

The western gate had been abandoned by its gatekeepers, which didn't bother Malock as that would just make it easier for him and Mother to escape. Unfortunately, due to Mother's age, it was impossible for them to run quite as fast as Malock would have liked, which made him more frustrated than anything else.

Just as they were about to exit through the western gate, the gate slammed shut of its own accord, causing Malock, Mother, and the handful of other guests who had joined them to skid to a halt before it. Malock let go of Mother's hand and grabbed the gate and shook it in an attempt to open it, but it was no use. The gate, for whatever reason, stood strong and rigid, despite the fact that it was not chained.

Frustrated, Malock whirled around just as Mother, who seemed to have gotten her voice back, said, "Tojas, what in the world is going on here? How did Kein lose control of the fire and why did the gates close shut?"

"I, too, would like to know that," said King Fabadi, who stood with the other guests just behind Mother. "But I am afraid, Jinaria, that we will not get to know that until much later. For now, we have to escape."

"But how?" said Darfna Enux, running his hands through his hair as he glanced back at Halock's grave, where almost all of the Justice Enforcers on duty today were battling the flames. "The gates are all closed. Don't you see?"

For once, Darfna was right. From Malock's position in front of the west gate, he could see that the other gates leading out of the Royal Cemetery had been closed off. Some of the other guests, like he had, were fighting to open the gates, while others just stood, anxiously looking between the ever-growing fire and its battle with the Enforcers and the locked gates that kept them penned in like rats.

"We'll be able to get out of this," said Malock. "We just have to be careful. We—"

At that moment, a rock hurled out of nowhere and hit his chest. It didn't hurt, but it did cause him to look around until he spotted Kein's assistant standing not far away from him and the guests.

Actually, the assistant boy wasn't standing at all. He was crouching on top of a tombstone, an older one based on the faded writing and cracked face, like a vulture ready to devour its prey. The boy held a bag of rocks in his right hand, while his left hand gripped another one like a precious diamond that the boy didn't want to lose.

"What are you doing?" said Malock, dusting off the spot where the rock had hit him. "You're Kein's assistant, aren't you? How did Kein lose control of the fire?"

The little boy grinned mischievously as he lobbed the rock up and down in his left hand. "Kein never lost control of the fire. He's much too good for that."

"Then he did it on purpose," said Fabadi, throwing an angry look over towards the fire. "But why?"

"I didn't say he did it on purpose," said the boy. "He just never guessed that someone more powerful than him was in this Cemetery or that that person had been looking for this exact moment in which to take advantage of his lack of imagination."

Something about the boy's smile and voice made Malock uneasy. "Just who are you, young boy?"

"Young boy?" the assistant said with a chuckle. "Oh, I guess it makes sense. My body certainly looks boyish, doesn't it? Let me fix that and show you what I actually am."

The boy's dark skin began melting off his face, causing Mother to shriek and stumbled backwards, while Malock, Fabadi, and the others just watched, unable to take their eyes off the disturbing sight. It wasn't just the boy's skin that melted, but his clothes, too, like a giant block of ice slowly melting in a hot summer sun.

But rather than revealing bone and blood, a new form now crouched on the tombstone. The boy wasn't a boy at all anymore, but a young girl, perhaps six-years-old. Her skin was far paler than the boy's had been, far too pale to be human, and her black hair stood up on its ends. She wore a gray skirt, blue leggings, pink shoes, and a bright green top. The chaotic mess of clothing would have offended Malock if he hadn't seen far worse things in his life. She dropped her bag of rocks, as if she did not need it anymore.

"Who ... who are you?" said Malock. "No, scratch that. *What* are you?"

The little girl giggled. "In your ugly, orderly mortal tongue, I believe you would call me the Chaotic Goddess."

"A southern goddess?" said Fabadi. "I knew it. Sent here by Skimif?"

"Yes," said the Chaotic Goddess. "Skimif has never liked you mortals very much and so sent me to teach you all a lesson."

"I knew it," said Fabadi. He looked at Malock and said, "Didn't I tell you? It's true. Skimif has betrayed us. His power has gone to his head. He—"

"You're jumping to conclusions," Malock snapped. "Are you so naïve as to believe her word, without any proof offered on her part? The southern gods are consummate liars. There's no reason to believe her just because what she said happens to agree with your crackpot conspiracy theories."

"I am not a liar," the Chaotic Goddess said, crossing her arms and pouting, looking more like the little girl she resembled than the goddess that she was. "I just like to have fun. And watching you mortals run around in panic, trying to avoid getting your faces melted like cheese, is a lot of fun, even though eating you would be even more fun."

Malock gritted his teeth. "I don't know what game you're playing, but it has to stop. Skimif would never order any god to harm us. That's not who Skimif is."

"You want proof?" said the Chaotic Goddess. She pulled out a scroll from her top and began reading from it. "*Dear Chaotic Goddess —that's me—I, Skimif, the new God of Martir, order you to go and crash the funeral of King Todar Halock of Carnag, who has recently passed away due to an illness that not even I had foreseen. This I want you to do because I am aware that many mortals fear me and are planning to reject me in favor of continuing to worship the northern gods, which just cannot do. Do not kill any mortals, as per the Treaty, but feel free to shake them up a little. Signed, Skimif.*"

"You could have written that yourself," said Malock.

"Read it yourself," said the Chaotic Goddess, folding and

throwing the letter at Malock.

Malock caught the letter, unfolded it, and scanned its contents. The handwriting was extremely similar to Skimif's; in fact, Malock honestly couldn't tell if it was forged or not. He knew those strokes and lines better than anyone here.

Yet he still looked up at the Chaotic Goddess and said, "This can't have been written by him. This just can't have been."

"But it is," said the Chaotic Goddess with a chilling smile. "The handwriting is the same as Skimif's. You can't possibly deny it."

"See? She has given you irrefutable proof," said Fabadi. He looked up at the sky and shook his fist. "Damn you, Skimif! I knew the Powers made a mistake by making you the God of Martir! I knew it!"

"I don't understand," said Mother. "What is going on here? Tojas, what is Fabadi going on about Skimif and the Powers? What does he mean?"

Malock crumpled the letter in his hand as he said, "It's just something we discussed at the last Northern Summit. I forgot to tell you about in the wake of Father's death."

"No wonder," said Fabadi. "But it doesn't matter. Everyone will know Skimif's true nature now. Once I leave this Cemetery, I will go back to Shika and make sure to send as many messengers to as many islands as I can, to let everyone know that our world, indeed our very way of life, is in danger."

"Sounds like a lot of fun," said the Chaotic Goddess. "Unfortunately, I can't let any of you leave, at least not right away."

Fabadi's triumphant smile fell. "What?"

"I want to have a little bit more fun with you all before I let you go," said the Chaotic Goddess. "Now the Treaty says we southern gods can't kill or harm mortals, but it doesn't say we can't have fun with them. It just means I need to be a little creative about how I do it. That's all."

"I don't like your use of the word 'creative,'" said Malock. "For that matter, I don't much like you, either."

"It would be more fun if you did," said the Chaotic Goddess. "But it's okay. I've been meaning to get more involved in the lives of mortals, so—"

Without warning, Banika Koiro ran up to them. Her shield and armor were blackened by the flames, but she otherwise didn't appear hurt. And without even stopping to ask what was going on or who the little girl was, Banika swung her sword directly at the Chaotic Goddess's neck.

Malock almost called out to Banika, asking her to stop, but much to his shock, Banika's sword connected, tearing through the Chaotic Goddess's neck like a knife through cloth. The Chaotic Goddess's head flew off her body and landed on the ground, rolling along until it stopped at Mother's feet. The Goddess's body, on the other hand, fell forward onto the grave in front of the tombstone, blood slightly leaking out of the stump.

"Oh my," said Mother, stepping away from the head. "Oh ... oh my."

"Wow," said Malock, looking at Banika with new found respect. "Great job. What happened to the flames?"

"The others have them under control," said Banika as she sheathed her sword. "When I saw that our assailant was a southern goddess, I realized that no one could be harmed or killed by the flames, which is why I left my men to save you."

"You killed a goddess," said Darfna. His eyes were wide and constantly darting between the Chaotic Goddess's head and her body. "An honest-to-goodness goddess."

Banika shrugged. "I wasn't even sure I would be able to harm her. I've never harmed a goddess before, much less killed one."

"And you still haven't today."

It took Malock a moment to realize that that voice had come from the Chaotic Goddess's severed head. The head rotated on the ground, a scowl on its face as its eyes focused on them all. When Mother saw it move, she just outright collapsed, her large red dress making it look like she lay in a pool of blood. Malock would have gone to comfort her, but with the Chaotic Goddess's apparently still functioning head between him and her, he was uncertain he could make it.

"The head is talking," said Darfna. He looked up at the others and said, "Even I couldn't make this stuff up."

"That's because I wasn't actually beheaded," said the Chaotic Goddess. "Or did you forget that we gods can't be killed by mortals? I only let you, ugly lady, think you killed me because I thought it would be fun to see your reactions to a talking head."

Banika drew her sword again, but as soon as she did, the Chaotic Goddess's body jumped up to its feet and touched the sword's blade with one finger. As soon as the finger rubbed against the blade, the metal turned into a floppy, rubbery substance, causing the blade to flop uselessly in Banika's hands.

"But I still don't like that sword," said the Chaotic Goddess's head. "It's no fun when you are trying to kill me."

"Is fun all you ever think about?" said Fabadi. "You southern gods truly do have your priorities in the wrong order."

"I like fun because chaos is fun," said the Chaotic Goddess's head. "To prove it, why don't I change the colors of your robes?"

The Chaotic Goddess's body snapped its fingers and suddenly King Fabadi's white robes were replaced with the brightest, most garish pink Malock had ever seen in his life. Fabadi gasped when he saw his own robes and said to the Chaotic Goddess's head, "Change them back. Now."

"No," said the Chaotic Goddess's head, like a small child disobeying her parents. "I think the pink looks good on you."

Fabadi stomped his foot and cursed in Shikan, but he didn't do anything, probably because he couldn't do anything against her. Although it was hard to take his anger so seriously while he wore such an outrageous color.

Malock folded his arms across his chest and said, "Is this the best you've got? All you've done so far is turn Fabadi's robes into the ugliest color you could think of and turn Banika's sword into a rubber toy. After the death of that one Enforcer and the complete and utter disrespect you've shown Father's grave, this all seems like a complete downgrade, if you ask me."

"That's because the Treaty says I can't harm or kill you mortals," said the Chaotic Goddess's head with a pout. "At least, I can't do it here in the Northern Isles. But just because I can't do anything like that, doesn't mean my servants can't."

"Your servants?" said Fabadi. "I thought you were working alone.

Who would ever serve you?"

"When did I say I was working alone?" said the Chaotic Goddess's head. "If I was working alone, that one silly Enforcer who almost ruined the surprise would still be alive. No, I've got one of my servants here and she's more than willing to do what I tell her to, especially if it's fun."

"Wait, are you saying one of the Enforcers is dead?" said Fabadi in shock. "When did that—"

A low hum buzzed through the air, cutting Fabadi off. The source of the hum was unknown for a moment before Malock looked up and saw a strange, birdlike creature swooping down from the sky, the hum buzzing from its throat. Its talons were aimed directly for Fabadi's throat, but the King of Shika managed to duck just in time to avoid having his throat torn out by the bird-creature, which flew back up into the air after it missed.

The creature soared overhead, its black plumage making it stand out against the white clouds in the sky above. As it flew, Malock got a better look at its body shape. It was vaguely humanoid, but instead of arms, the creature had two gigantic wings, with a long tail feather that billowed behind it like a robe.

"What is that?" said Darfna, who held his hands over his head, as if that would be enough to keep him safe from the creature's talons.

"A Bird Child," said the Chaotic Goddess's head with a chuckle. "They normally live on World's End, but I brought this one with me because she's quite loyal. She doesn't mind seeing new places, either, unlike some of her fellow Bird Children."

The Bird Child swooped and chirped. Her golden eyes were

scanning the mortals below, as if she was trying to figure out the best way to kill them all. Once again, Malock wished that he had had his own sword on him, as he was not interested in having his own throat torn out.

Then the Bird Child suddenly swooped down, but not toward Malock or Fabadi. Instead, she went for Mother, who was still lying unconscious on the ground. Malock was too far away to protect her, so he could only watch in horror as the Bird Child's talons came closer and closer to Mother's prone form.

But then a shield—Banika's shield, which Malock recognized due to its blackened color—spun through the air like a disk and struck the Bird Child in the back. The Bird Child went flying over Mother, crash-landing into the ground and rolling along it, getting its feathers all dirty and messed up.

Malock looked at Banika, who still held her throwing arm out. For once, Banika looked angry. Her eyes were narrowed, her breathing was harder than normal, and the way she gripped her sword told Malock that she was not afraid to use it, even though it was practically useless now.

"Hey," said the Chaotic Goddess's head. "That wasn't nice. Or fun. It wasn't even chaotic. How dare you."

Banika ignored the Chaotic Goddess's admonishments. She ran past the Chaotic Goddess's head, past Mother, until she reached the Bird Child. The Bird Child was just barely recovering from her crash, but she didn't have time to do even that, because Banika grabbed the Bird Child and pinned her to the ground, twisting one of her wings behind her back in a rather painful, unnatural direction.

The Bird Child snapped and hummed, but Banika said, "Try anything and you'll be the only one-winged Bird Child in the world."

The Chaotic Goddess's head laughed. "You think that will scare her? Blue-bird, please teach this silly mortal a lesson in respecting her physical superiors."

Without warning, the Bird Child's twisted wing snapped back, knocking Banika off. Before Banika could react, the Bird Child was on top of her, snapping at Banika's neck with her beak. Banika, however, managed to hold the Bird Child back, but she had to use both of her hands to do it and it was clear that she would not hold much longer unless someone intervened and saved her.

So Malock, without thinking, ran toward Banika and the Bird Child as fast as he could in his funeral robes, dropping Skimif's crumpled letter as he did so. The Bird Child kept snapping at Banika's face and throat, actually snipping off a part of her skin, but that was as far as she got. Malock grabbed the Bird Child by her shoulders and hurled her off Banika. The Bird Child stumbled through the dirt again, but immediately got to her feet and flew off into the sky, well out of Malock's reach.

"Thanks," said Banika as Malock helped her up. "But you didn't have to do that, Your Majesty."

"It's fine," said Malock. Then he looked up into the sky and saw the Bird Child coming at them again. "Duck!"

The two hit the ground as the Bird Child swooped past them, the tips of her talons skirting the backs of their clothing. As soon as the Bird Child flew back up into the sky, Malock and Banika got to their feet. Banika picked up her shield, while Malock said, "Any ideas for how we can beat it?"

"My plan was to just keep hitting it until it dropped dead or unconscious," said Banika. "Though considering how strong it is, I am starting to doubt that plan."

"We need the rest of your squad," said Malock, looking back to Father's grave. "Where are they—oh."

The rest of Banika's squad still stood around the grave, but they were unable to leave it because a ring of fire surrounded them, cutting off every exit. Some of the Enforcers were clearly trying to use their own pyromancy to control the flames, but they were just as clearly failing, for the flames did not move or die down at all. Droman Kein and Priestess Vinri were also stuck inside the ring of fire with the Enforcers and were having just as much luck in escaping, based on the way the flames refused to obey their feeble wand waves.

The Chaotic Goddess's head rolled across the ground until it stopped at the feet of her body. The Goddess's body picked up the head and reattached it securely on her neck while the Bird Child landed beside her, the Child's beak snapping at the other funeral guests, who by now had retreated a good deal from the fight.

Cracking her neck, the Chaotic Goddess said, "This fight is getting boring. I was hoping that my Child would be able to kill you at least one of you quickly, but that is obviously not going to be happening anytime soon."

"But you have us out-powered," said Malock. "What's to stop you from crushing us?"

The Chaotic Goddess brushed the dirt out of her hair as she said, "Well, yeah, sure I could crush you. I could turn the dirt beneath your feet into mud, which would let my little birdie kill you easier. But like I said, this fight is getting boring. I hoped it would be over quick, but if it's gonna last this long, then I'm out of here. Maybe we'll go find some other mortals to mess with."

Then Fabadi stepped forward before anyone else could speak. His robes were as pink as ever, but he seemed to have gotten over them by now, because his eyes were focused solely on the Chaotic Goddess, like he was trying to find the best spot to attack her.

"Are you returning to Skimif?" said Fabadi. "He sent you, didn't he?"

Fabadi threw a quick glance at Malock as he said that, as if daring Malock to contradict him. Considering that Skimif's letter—slightly crumpled, but still readable—lay on the ground for all to see, with Skimif's handwriting as readable as ever, Malock kept quiet.

"Yes, I am," said the Chaotic Goddess. "He probably has something else for me to do, something a lot more fun than messing with you mortals."

"Then I have a message for him that I want you to deliver," said Fabadi. "Are you listening?"

The Chaotic Goddess was picking her ear, but she nodded and said, "I'm no messenger, so make it quick."

Fabadi looked the Chaotic Goddess straight in the eyes and said, "Tell your master this: Though he may now be the God of Martir and may hold authority that even the gods themselves cannot challenge, that does not mean that we mortals will bow down and worship him or even honor him. Let him know that Shika and many other nations will stand against him, no matter what he does."

"Mortals won't worship him and Shika and a bunch of other islands will stand against him," said the Chaotic Goddess, though she didn't sound like she cared. "Okay. Got it."

Fabadi frowned. "You mean, you aren't going to laugh at my threat?"

"What's there to laugh at?" said the Chaotic Goddess. "You don't scare me. I'm a goddess, and with Skimif on my side, I'm practically untouchable. It's actually kind of funny, seeing you act all big and tough. You're nothing more than a flimsy old man whose life on this world, I bet, is not going to last much longer."

"But you will deliver the message nonetheless?" said Fabadi. "You will let him know what we think?"

"What *he* thinks," Malock said. He looked at Fabadi with distrustful eyes. "Carnag never said it would fight against Skimif."

Fabadi returned the distrustful look, but before he could say anything, the Chaotic Goddess clapped her hands together and said, "Well, I'll be sure to let Skimif know all of this. Don't know what he will do, but I'm sure he'll come up with something painful and fun. Maybe he'll even let me help. Sure would be more fun than watching him do something."

With that, the Chaotic Goddess hopped onto the back of the Bird Child. Grabbing onto the Bird Child's neck, the Chaotic Goddess waved at Malock and the others, saying as she did so, "Bye, bye! It was fun messing with you! Hopefully we'll see each other again very soon."

Then the Chaotic Goddess patted the Bird Child on the head and, with a flap of her wings, she soared into the air. The Bird Child flew so fast that the Chaotic Goddess almost went flying off, but she clung tightly to her neck feathers and a few seconds later, both the Bird Child and the Chaotic Goddess had vanished into the deep blue sky.

Chapter Ten

TELL ME MORE ABOUT your childhood, Jenur," said a calm voice. "Or if you'd prefer, you can tell me about your feelings instead."

Jenur awoke with a start at the sound of the voice. She sat up in the bed, the silk red blankets falling off her upper body and onto her lap, panting and sweating from the heat. She wiped her damp hair off her forehead and for a moment had no idea where she was. It seemed like she was sitting inside an oak-paneled study, with a large, polished wooden desk standing on the opposite wall and shelves and shelves of books—with pink, yellow, green, bright red, and a variety of other unusual colors for book spines—lining the walls. The ceiling was decorated with a mural that seemed to depict the entire Northern Pantheon. She only recognized it for what it was because she noted that the artist's depiction of Kano, Goddess of the Sea, Sand, and Art, was spot on.

"Jenur, are you awake? Are you listening to me?"

Jenur looked to her right and saw a short, chubby man with a long gray beard sitting on a chair next to her bed. He had tired-looking blue eyes, with heavy bags underneath them. In his hands he held a notepad and a pen, with which he seemed to have been writing something. Most unusual, he wore a rainbow, which covered his body like a mage's robe.

"Who ... who are you?" said Jenur. She blinked. "Where am I? What happened?"

"I see your subconscious is doing just fine," said the man. He jotted something down on his notepad. "But of course, that is to be expected. The subconscious is one of the few parts of the human mind that cannot be harmed except by the gods. Even telemancers can't hurt it, though Eyurna keeps telling me that she has learned how to influence it."

"Who's Eyurna?" said Jenur. "What do you mean, 'my subconscious is doing just fine'?"

The man lifted his round spectacles, as if trying to see Jenur more clearly. "Tell me, Jenur Takren, what was the last memory you had before waking up here?"

Jenur frowned. "I don't see—"

"Just answer the question," the man said in a polite, yet quite firm, tone of voice. "Then I'll explain where you are and what happened."

Jenur was under the impression that this man, although obviously well-mannered and meek, could be a lot more firm than he appeared. Best not to mess with him too much, she decided.

So Jenur fished around in her memory for what she remembered last. It was hard because her memories seemed confused and mixed up. It was like looking into a bucket full of mixed together paint, making it impossible for her to distinguish where one color started and where another ended.

"I don't remember much," Jenur admitted. "I do remember the feelings."

"Then describe your feelings to me," said the man. He held up his notepad and pen and looked at her expectantly.

"Pain," said Jenur. "And fear and exhaustion. Of the worst kind imaginable. You don't even want to know."

"Yes," said the man, nodding as he took notes. "Being attacked by the Grand Tiger of the Dark Tigers and seeing an entire village full of corpses—among everything else Braim has told us about—would certainly cause you to feel all of those emotions, and likely far more that you can't even describe."

Hearing the man mention Nijok Wirm suddenly caused the back of Jenur's head to ache. Before she knew it, she remembered everything that had happened before she woke up. Kura attacking her in the valley, Wirm killing Dad and attacking her just outside of their home, discovering Darek and the slaughtered Yurimans, meeting Braim ... all of it came rushing back so quickly that she only barely understood what she was seeing.

Jenur put her hands over her eyes, saying, "Make it stop! Make it stop! These memories ... they're too painful."

"Sadly, Jenur Takren, I am not a memormancer," said the man. "Otherwise, I would help, but you must deal with the memories yourself."

Jenur wanted to say, *Gee, thanks,* but since the memories were still rushing through her mind like a boulder rolling down a hill, she just focused on gaining control of the memories.

Thankfully, it didn't take her long to do that. Soon the rush of memories slowed down to a trickle and even sooner the trickle became nothing. Her head still hurt, but she no longer had to worry about her out-of-control memories.

Lowering her hands from her face, Jenur looked at the man again. "I got control of my memories. They aren't going to bother me anymore."

"Wonderful," said the man. "I suppose I don't need to ask you what you remember. You probably remember it all now, don't you?"

"Down to the last detail," said Jenur. "And that confuses me because I didn't know I could remember so much."

"My brother—who is a memormancer, by the way—always used to tell me that people remember things more clearly when those events are associated with strong emotions," said the man. "Now of course, not being a memormancer myself, I can't say how true that is, but it does make a certain amount of sense, doesn't it?"

"I guess," said Jenur. "You still haven't told me your name or where the hell we are. And I don't trust nameless people."

"My name is Noharf Ximin," said the man. "And your body is currently resting inside the medical ward of North Academy. It has been there for the past week and has shown little-to-no signs of movement, which is why I was called in to check on your subconscious to make sure you were not dead or dying."

"My body? My subconscious?" said Jenur. "I know you mages don't exactly speak normal, but is it really so difficult to say, '*You* are currently resting inside the medical ward of North Academy'? Makes me sound like some kind of strange creature when you talk about my body like it's separate from me."

Noharf tapped his chin with his pen. "Hmm, I see you aren't aware of where we actually are. You see, Jenur Takren—"

"Just call me Jenur," said Jenur. "You don't need to use my last name all the time."

Noharf hesitated, then continued, "You see, Jenur, right now, you are actually dreaming this entire experience. None of it is real. It is all a creation of your subconscious, as most dreams tend to be. I am the only thing here that was not created by your subconscious."

Jenur blinked. "Pull the other one."

"It's not a joke," said Noharf, putting his pen and paper down on his lap. "As I said, you've been unconscious for a week, in a coma, actually. The panamancers have been working hard to heal your wounds and make sure you don't die, but they've seen such little movement from your body that they had to call me in to make sure you were not in any trouble."

"What are you, then?" said Jenur.

"An oneiromancer," said Noharf. "A practitioner of dream magic, in other words. Not to brag, but I am considered one of the best, which is why the Magical Superior invited me to teach here at North Academy."

Noharf looked quite proud about that.

"So we made it after all," said Jenur. Then she started. "What about Darek? And Braim?"

"Both are fine," said Noharf. "Braim is still recovering from the blows the Grand Tiger dealt him, but he's going to make it. As for little Darek, he's been put under Irliza's care, since she's so good with kids. He is suffering from no injuries that we can find, though he has been rather quieter than usual for a boy his age."

"He saw his mother get killed right before his eyes," said Jenur. "And probably heard the rest of his neighbors get killed, too. I'm surprised he hasn't just collapsed completely."

"We have been trying to get one of our telemancers to search his mind to see if there is any lasting mental damage," said Noharf. "Unfortunately, Darek has rejected every single offer we've made to search. He doesn't trust any of us, except for Irliza, and she's no telemancer, sadly."

"No wonder," said Jenur. "He doesn't know any of you. I'm surprised he even trusts Irliza. I guess it's because she was the one who saved us."

"No doubt about that," Noharf agreed. "Though he's been quiet, he has asked about you every day and has visited you just as often. He really seems to care about you."

Jenur nodded. "Well, I did save his life. I'm the only person he really knows around here."

"Are you family?" said Noharf. "Because you two look similar."

"No," said Jenur, shaking her head. "We're not. We just happened to live on the same island. That's all."

"I see," said Noharf. "Well, I think it's time for you to wake up, then, if you are ready. Just be warned that you may not feel like your usual self when you awake."

"I don't care," said Jenur. "Sleeping for a week is more than enough time for anyone to rest, in my opinion."

"All right," said Noharf. He placed his pen on his notepad and held out his hand. "Now take my hand. I'll end this dream and when we awake, we'll both be in the medical ward of the Academy."

"Okay," said Jenur. Then she looked around the dream room with a frown. "Why am I dreaming of this place? I've never even been here before."

"I do not know," said Noharf. "Dreams are often a product of our subconscious, which usually carries a variety of images and memories we rarely have direct access to. Perhaps this room is in fact an amalgam of various places you have been to or seen in your life."

Jenur looked at him. "You're the oneiromancer. Shouldn't you be able to explain this to me?"

Noharf shrugged. "Oneiromancy is not an exact magic. Dreams are as individual as we humans are, which means that I cannot interpret yours like I could mine or Braim's because I don't know you very well."

"You mean there isn't like a book of dream interpretation you can read that explains what all of this means?" said Jenur, gesturing at the bookshelves and mural. "None at all?"

"Such books do exist," said Noharf. "And I own more than a few myself. But they aren't comprehensive, again because individuals do not have the same dreams or see the same images in their dreams."

"Aw," said Jenur. "Are you sure you can't interpret any of this?"

Noharf sighed and said, "If I had to make a guess, I'd say that this is your subconscious's way of keeping you safe. After all of the excitement and terror you've been through, this room is meant to represent the security you so desperately desire."

"Oh," said Jenur. "I was hoping it would be a bit more interesting than that."

"The only part I don't understand," Noharf continued, like Jenur hadn't said a word, "is the mural of the gods on the ceiling. It's an unusual sign, one I've never quite seen before. Usually, only one god appears in a person's dream, and that one god is usually the god that the person worships. Yet here you have a mural depicting almost every god in the Northern Pantheon. I wonder why that is."

"I don't know," said Jenur. "And at this point, I don't really care. I would just like to wake up now. We can figure it out later."

"If you insist," said Noharf. "Now like I said, just grab my hand. I'll take it from there."

Jenur grabbed Noharf's outstretched hand, which was soft and warm. As soon as her fingers wrapped around his, Jenur felt like she was being lifted up out of her bed. For a moment, the entire room disappeared, replaced by an empty blackness that almost made her panic, but her panic died down when Noharf squeezed her hand reassuringly.

Then a new room slowly came into view. First she saw the ceiling: pure white tiles, with bulbs of bright light hanging from chains like snakes hanging from tree branches. Then she saw the curtains around here, which were just as white as the tiles on the ceiling, partly pulled back.

A second later, Jenur felt a thin, yet warm, blanket covering her whole body. She raised her head just enough to see the blanket, which was white like everything else in the room. She seemed to be laying on a bed of some sort, a very small one, with little room in which to move around.

Then she heard someone grunt to her left and she turned her head to look. Noharf sat in a chair by her bed, his hand still gripping hers. He looked exactly like how he had in her dream, including the rainbow robes that Jenur had thought looked very tacky when she first saw them. His eyes were initially closed, but then they flickered open and he looked at Jenur.

"How are you feeling now?" said Noharf. "Anything hurt?"

Jenur shook her head. "Feel a little stiff, but that's probably because I've been in bed for a week. Otherwise, I feel just fine."

"Then the panamancers did their job well," said Noharf. "I imagine you'll make a speedy recovery, unless something else happens, although I doubt anything will."

Jenur took her hand out of Noharf's and felt her nose. It was indeed whole again, feeling just like how it had felt before Wirm had broken it. Her hands didn't burn anymore, nor did her chest. She felt as good as new, aside from the stiffness, which she figured she could get rid of by moving around a lot.

"Morning, beautiful," said a voice behind Noharf, causing Jenur to crane her neck to peer around the oneiromancer.

Lying in the bed next to hers, his face just visible through the gap in the curtains, was Braim Kotogs. At first, Jenur didn't know it was him because he wasn't wearing his parka, but she knew those green eyes anywhere, as well as that smile she always disliked. His face was slightly paler than usual, but aside from that, he looked far better than he had when she had last seen him.

Noharf moved out of Jenur's line of sight and said, "Ah, Braim.

You're awake. I thought you were asleep."

"I was," said Braim. "But then I decided I wanted to be the first person to welcome Jenur back to the world of the living. It's way more exciting than being out cold for a week, ain't it?"

Jenur rubbed her forehead, which for some reason was starting to hurt. "Actually, I kind of wish I was back in a coma."

"Now that's just rude," said Braim, though he didn't sound annoyed. "If it wasn't for me, you and Darek would be like the rest of the Yurimans. But it's okay. I only do good deeds for their own reward, not for the rewards or praise or anything like that."

Noharf frowned. "Then why have I heard that you've spent the last three weeks demanding the Magical Superior raise your pay? I would think that teaching the next generation of mages would be sufficient reward in itself."

"That's different," said Braim, brandishing his wand and shaking it like a finger. "Teaching is a job. Saving the lives of a beautiful woman and a cute kid is the right thing to do."

Jenur rolled her eyes and decided to try sitting up. Much to her surprise, she actually succeeded, despite her stiff body. She realized that she was no longer wearing her thick winter coat and boots. Instead, she wore a thin, linen gown, same shade of white as the entire medical wing seemed to be, with a pair of thick wool socks covering her feet. She knew she had socks on because she could feel them keeping her toes warm.

"You might not want to move," said Noharf. "Even if you're feeling just fine, you still—"

"I was asleep for a week," said Jenur, stretching her arms. "I think that's more than enough time to rest, to be honest. I want to get up and walk around the place. I want to see Darek."

"Too bad," said Braim. "You just missed the little guy. He was here an hour ago hoping to see you, but left when the doctor told him that you weren't awake yet. He'll probably be ecstatic to see you, though."

"That's why I want to go and see him myself," said Jenur. "I also want to learn more about the Academy so I know where I am. Maybe someone could give me a tour or something."

"Perhaps later," said Noharf. "As I said, you probably still need to rest a little longer. Your body—"

"You're an oneiromancer, right?" said Jenur, interrupting him. "Not a panamancer. So what do you know about my health or my body? Why not just let me decide how I feel?"

Noharf stroked his chin, but in an agitated way. "I am just trying to show that I am concerned for you, Jenur. Not trying to restrict you or anything."

"Can't argue with beautiful, Noharf," said Braim. "She can be as stubborn as a zinyu when she wants to be. Better let her try. Won't hurt anyone but her."

"I will have to speak to Eyurna," said Noharf. "She's the head of the medical ward, after all. She should get to decide whether Jenur gets to walk around or not."

"Then where is she?" said Jenur. "If she's the head, why wasn't she here monitoring you to make sure you weren't going to harm me accidentally?"

"One of our students came in around the same time I arrived to check on you," said Noharf. "The student had botched a spell—not sure what spell, since all I saw was a third eye and burnt skin—and had botched it badly enough that Eyurna had to take care of him personally. But don't worry, I will go get her and see if she has time to come see you."

Noharf stood up from his chair to his full height, which wasn't very impressive. He walked beyond Jenur's line of sight, going through her curtains as his shoes scuffed against the stone floor.

When Noharf left, Jenur lay back down in her bed. Her brief burst of energy from before was slowly ebbing away and she was starting to feel tired again. Her body wanted to rest, but her mind wanted to get up and walk around and find out everything that had happened over the last week.

"The Dark Tigers haven't been seen since Irliza blasted Wirm," said Braim, causing Jenur to look at him.

"What?" said Jenur.

"Those two Dark Tigers," Braim repeated. "No one has reported seeing them since we got here."

Jenur remembered seeing Irliza blast Wirm into the icy waters around Urma, prompting her to say, "So is Wirm dead?"

"No bodies have been found, either," said Braim. "The Superior sent a couple of people back to Urma to find them, but neither Wirm nor Kura were anywhere to be seen. They did find the corpses of all of the Yurimans, though, and buried them and burned down the whole village while they were at it."

Jenur grimaced. "Did they have to burn the whole thing down? Was that really necessary?"

"Totally," said Braim. "The Records of Diog state that, if an entire town or village is slaughtered, then the whole place needs to be buried to the ground to ensure that no souls are left behind. Otherwise, the souls of the dead haunt the place and it becomes a ghost town. Trust me, even as a Diogian, ghost towns are not places you want to be."

"Did anyone tell Darek that?" said Jenur.

Braim shook his head. "Nah. The poor guy's been through enough as is. If we told him that his entire town has been completely decimated, that there's not even one building left standing there ... well, I think he'd be completely crushed."

Jenur nodded, but then started. "What about my Dad? You remember me mentioning him, don't you?"

"Yeah, I do," said Braim. Braim looked down at his pillow. "They checked out your house and found that the entire thing was already in ashes. Your dad's corpse was nowhere to be found. They think it might have been destroyed in the fire."

Suddenly, Jenur didn't want to get up at all. She could feel the tears starting to well in her eyes, but she didn't let them flow, not yet.

"Did they find anything?" said Jenur. "Anything at all? Even just a small trinket that might have belonged to him?"

"Nope," said Braim. "All they found was a large pile of ash and a some burnt wood that might as well have been ash. Pretty depressing sight, according to one of the guys."

The tears began flowing down her face now, but Jenur wiped them away and tried to act like she wasn't crying. "Oh. Well, I guess that makes sense. Wirm isn't the kind of guy who does anything by half-measures. He goes all out when he wants to kill someone. No doubt he would have done the same to me, if he'd caught me."

"No doubt," said Braim. "Thankfully, he doesn't know how to get in here and probably never will. The North Academy is one of the few places that the Dark Tigers have never set foot in. Ever."

Still wiping the tears from her face, Jenur said, "Ever?"

"Ever," Braim confirmed. "The Magical Superior has made sure that no murderers or thieves or anyone else like that could ever take even one step on these hollowed grounds. It's one of the reasons Wirm never took on any assignments that required assassinating someone in the Academy. He knew he couldn't do it."

Sniffling, Jenur said, "Wait, how do you know Wirm didn't accept any Academy-based assignments?"

"Oh, er, uh," said Braim, looking away suddenly. "I just ... well, no one has ever been assassinated here by the Dark Tigers. Granted, we've had some threats from the Silent Knives, but the Dark Tigers have never ever been here. It's just a fact."

Braim was obviously lying directly to Jenur's face, but she didn't see any point in interrogating him. All she wanted to do was curl up into a ball and cry. With Dad dead, what else *could* she do?

"So we're safe here," said Braim. "Completely and totally safe. The North Academy is one of the most secure places in the entire Northern Isles. Some say it's even more secure than Rock Isle, but considering Rock Isle is full of the world's most dangerous criminals, I tend to think that is an exaggeration."

"I wouldn't be so sure," said Jenur. "Wirm is smart, much smarter than any of us. I bet he's looking for a way in right now, even as we speak."

"Then he'll fail," said Braim. "Remember, North Academy is inaccessible to anyone who doesn't have permission from Academy faculty. Seeing as we're all pretty anti-Dark Tiger around here, I can't see anyone agreeing to let the leader of the Dark Tigers inside. And even if Wirm somehow got past that particular limitation, there's a bunch of other defenses that would stop him before he even set one foot on campus."

"Like?" said Jenur.

Braim chuckled darkly. "Trust me, you don't want to know all of the nasty surprises the founder of this place devised to keep out unwanted guests. For that matter, you don't want to know all of the new nasty surprises that the Magical Superior has installed since he started running the place. Let's just say that Wirm had better stay out of the water if he wants to keep both of his legs."

Though intellectually Jenur knew she should probably be concerned that a school—even if it was a mage school—apparently had the same kind of defenses that most small nations employed, emotionally she was too drained from mourning Dad to care. She just looked back up at the bland, featureless ceiling, her mind's eye replaying the explosion that had torn apart the roof of her house over and over until she thought she could draw a picture of it if she had to.

Why did Dad have to die? Jenur thought. *First Kinker, now Dad. It's like everyone I love has to die at some point. I wonder who I'm going to lose next.*

At that moment, a silhouette passed by her curtains and the next moment, a tall woman with hawkish eyes was staring down on her.

The woman wore the white medical robes of a panamancer, but unlike other panamancers Jenur had known in her life, this one gave off an aura of impatience and annoyance, as if she was in a great hurry and didn't have time to waste focusing on Jenur.

"Noharf told me you were awake," said the woman. "I see he was correct. He also told me that you claimed not to be hurt or injured and that you wanted to walk around the Academy."

"That I do," said Jenur. It was hard not to feel intimidated by this woman, but since Jenur had faced far worse than an impolite doctor, she didn't let the intimidation get to her. "I'm just a little stiff is all."

"You were badly injured when Irliza brought you here," said the woman. "Worse than Braim or the little boy. It's a miracle you survived as long as you did. Most people in your old condition would have succumbed to the pain long ago, but you kept going. I'm impressed."

You don't even know the half of it, Jenur thought, but she said aloud, "It's not a big deal. I've been in worse condition."

"Since my assistants and I healed you, I suppose it would be all right for you to get up and walk around for a bit," the woman said. "We will have to get you some suitable clothing, however, because in your current gown you'd freeze to the bone if we let you walk around. I will be back in a moment with some appropriate clothing."

And just like that, the woman left, leaving Jenur feeling more than a bit confused.

"That was Eyurna," said Braim. "Head of the medical ward. She's actually really nice, but she can be a bit formal and curt."

"Got the formal part," said Jenur. "By the way—I almost forgot to ask—how are you doing?"

"I'm doing all right," said Braim with a shrug. "The ice water was freezing and getting stabbed by those throwing stars was hardly what I'd call a good time, but Eyurna and the other nurses worked their magic and I'm pretty much as good as new. Only reason I'm still here is because they're not convinced I'm better yet, even though I've told them that I'm fine."

"Well, you *were* knocked off into the water," said Jenur. "The freezing, ice-cold ocean water around Urma. With throwing stars in your body. I'm surprised you didn't freeze to death."

"Irliza saved me," said Braim. "She sensed I was underwater and teleported me here. She's the only reason I'm still alive."

"She's the only reason any of us are still alive," said Jenur. "Wirm would have killed all three of us if Irliza hadn't shown up and beat him."

"Yeah," said Braim, nodding. Then he leaned forward slightly, an eager grin on his face. "Irliza didn't tell me how she beat Wirm. Said it wasn't important, but you saw what she did, right? Was it glorious? Was it amazing?"

Jenur nodded. "Both. She shot him in the face with a fire blast and then followed it up with an arc of electricity. He fell in the water and didn't rise again."

Braim chuckled and clapped his hands together. "That's even better than what I imagined. Only wish I could have been there to see it myself."

Stretching her arms again, Jenur said, "Would have been even better if she had actually killed Wirm, but I guess we can't have everything we want, huh?"

"You bet it would have been better if she had killed him," said Braim. "That bastard has lived way too long. But hey, maybe he actually did die and his body was swept away by an ocean current or dragged off by some sea creature. That could be why they didn't find his corpse."

Although Jenur found herself hoping that Braim's theory was correct, deep down, she knew better than to agree. Back in her Dark Tiger days, she had once been told a story by one of the senior Dark Tigers about Wirm's younger days. Supposedly, Wirm had been hired by a young king in some distant land to assassinate a potential threat to the young king's rule, but when Wirm arrived, he was ambushed and savagely beaten to a pulp by a group of the young king's soldiers. As it turned out, the young king held a grudge against Wirm because Wirm had killed the king's father and had made up the story about the threat to his rule in order to lure Wirm away from Ruwa.

Then the soldiers dumped Wirm's broken body into a deep pit full of poisonous water snakes. But, the story continued, Wirm somehow escaped the pit, hunted down and killed each soldier who had participated in the beating over a three month period, and then ended the whole thing by killing the young king himself.

Granted, Jenur didn't know if that story was true, but it fit with what she knew of Wirm. He had an impossibly strong will, one that almost rivaled that of the gods themselves, and once he decided to kill someone, he would hound that person to the ends of the earth and back if he had to.

And what a coincidence, there are two people he hates currently inside the Academy, Jenur thought. *Me, and Braim. If Wirm is still alive at all, he's no doubt trying to figure out how to get past the Academy's defenses. If I worshiped the gods, I would pray to them to keep us safe.*

Chapter Eleven

After the Chaotic Goddess left, the funeral was canceled early, before the flames in Father's grave—which had returned to their regular size and nature, since the Chaotic Goddess was no longer influencing them with her strange magic—died. This was because almost all of the guests were traumatized by the events, even though no one had been hurt. Most of the guests especially wanted to leave after it was revealed that one of the Justice Enforcers had been killed without any of them knowing it. Frankly, Malock didn't try to stop them from leaving, as he understood their fear.

That was also why he and Mother were immediately transported from the Royal Cemetery back to Carnag Hall much faster than they normally would have gone. Not only that, but they were escorted by a much larger squad of Justice Enforcers than usual, with Banika leading the squad. Not that Malock was complaining. While he didn't think he or Mother was in any immediate danger, a quick glance at Mother—who was visibly shaking and trembling in the carriage during the entire trip back to Carnag Hall—told him that she needed the illusion of safety far more than he did.

Now Malock was back in the Throne Room of Carnag Hall, kneeling before Mother's throne. Father's throne, made of ruby and gold, was vacant and Malock did not feel comfortable with sitting in it. Especially with the huge bronze statue of Grinf looming behind the thrones, a statue he normally didn't like even in the best of circumstances, but which today he hated with a burning passion, a passion spurred on by the Burn of Grinf on his face causing his face to feel like it was on fire.

They were the only two inside the Throne Room at the moment. Mother's eyes were bloodshot from all of the crying she had done recently, and she trembled in her throne every now and then, but the matter which they were to discuss was not one that required their servants to be present.

"With the passing of your father, the nation of Carnag is without a ruler," said Mother as she wiped the sweat off her brow with her handkerchief.

"But there is still you," said Malock. "You're still the Queen of Carnag. I am certain you can rule alone, Mother. You are a strong woman."

Mother shook her head. "Oh, Malock, I am not strong at all. For years, I have depended largely on Halock to lead the nation. I have helped, that is true, but Carnag is what it is primarily because of his work, not because of what I did. Carnag needs a king more than anything."

"But does it have to be me?" said Malock. "I have no experience in leading a nation. Yes, Father and you have both taught me a great deal about what it means to be a ruler, but there is a big difference between being taught how to do something and actually doing the thing. I don't think it would be right of me to take Father's crown right now."

"But it is written in the Royal Laws that you must," said Mother. "You remember, don't you? Should your father die, you are to become the King of Carnag immediately or as soon as possible."

"I know what the Royal Laws state," said Malock. "I spent three years studying them as a youth. I just don't think I'm ready for the throne. That's all."

Mother put a hand over her heart, her eyes stricken. "It doesn't matter what you think. You may only go against the Royal Laws if Grinf himself has given you a command or law that contradicts them. Has Grinf given you such a command or law?"

Malock gritted his teeth. "No, Mother, Grinf hasn't spoken to me since the day he gave me this."

Malock pointed at his face, which chose that exact moment to burn. "And I am pretty sure that this is not a law or a command."

"Then you have no grounds on which to shun your duty," said Mother. "The people will expect you to take the throne soon. They will be highly disappointed if you don't."

Malock glanced at Father's throne. "I am surprised that you are so eager to replace Father so soon after his death."

"I am simply a believer in the Royal Laws," said Mother. "Besides, you won't be Halock's replacement. You will be the next King of Carnag. There is a large difference that I am sad to see you apparently do not understand."

"I understand it well enough," said Malock. "I also understand that making me King would be a mistake at this point. Once I am older, I will agree to it, but as it currently is, I do not believe I am qualified for it."

Mother laughed. It was the first time he had heard her laugh since she had learned of Father's death, but it wasn't a mirthful laugh. It was a cynical, bitter one that cut to Malock's heart like a surgeon's blade.

"Tojas, Tojas, Tojas," said Mother. "You are thirty-years-old, almost thirty-one. Your father took the throne when he was in his mid-twenties and he did just fine. Besides, you will have me to help you and guide you if you need it. You need not do the job alone."

"I know," said Malock. "It's just ... that is Father's throne and I don't want to disrespect his memory by sitting on his Throne with my inexperience, even though I know that it is technically mine now."

"You will not be disrespecting anything, Tojas," said Mother. "You will simply be fulfilling your duty as the Crown Prince of Carnag. No need to be reluctant."

Malock scratched the back of his neck. "It's just that the idea of becoming King ... I can hardly imagine it. I always thought it would be a long time before I ever became King, and yet here is my chance to take it. It is so abrupt."

"Again, why won't you?" said Mother. "The Royal Laws state that you must."

Malock looked Mother in the eye. "I guess what I am afraid of is pressure from the people to do things I would rather not do."

Mother frowned. "What are you talking about? What would the

people pressure you to do that you do not want to do?"

Malock looked away from Mother, instead focusing on the steps before the thrones. "They may want me to stand against Skimif."

Mother's frown was replaced by a scowl. "Don't you dare mention the name of that blasphemer in this building. I know you were—"

"Are," Malock corrected, though Mother didn't seem to hear him.

"—part of his little movement and are very sympathetic towards it, but that does not mean that mean you can just talk about him wherever and whenever you like," Mother said. "He is a no-good troublemaker and blasphemer of the gods."

"Mother, he *is* a god now," said Malock. "Remember? He is actually above all of the other gods. I wouldn't call the god of the whole world a 'no-good troublemaker' or a 'blasphemer of the gods.'"

"I know, I know, Tojas," said Mother. "But he is still who he always has been, is he not? I respect all of the gods, but how can I respect this god? How can I respect the god who spent his last remaining days as a mortal blaspheming Grinf and all of the other gods? Are you afraid that he will smite me or punish me in some way for choosing not to respect him?"

"No," said Malock, shaking his head. "I just think you're being unfair to him. I know Skimif, or knew him before his ascension, at least, and I know he's a good guy who would never harm anyone."

"But I was told that the Chaotic Goddess was sent by him to scare us," said Mother. "She even gave you a letter in Skimif's handwriting, did she not?"

Malock felt the pockets of his funeral robes, in which he had stashed Skimif's letter. "Yes, she did, but doesn't it seem strange that the God of Martir would send orders to the other gods via paper and ink? I think this paper is forged, but I don't know how or by who or for what reason."

"That's because Skimif really *is* behind it," said Mother. "He is using his new power to establish a totalitarian rule over everyone on Martir. If the people want you, as the King of Carnag, to stand against him, then that just shows that the people are reasonable."

"It shows that the people are misinformed," said Malock. "And that I, as the next King, must not allow them to sway the decisions I make regarding the future of our nation. Mother, you sound just like Fabadi and I don't like that."

"Has it ever occurred to you that it may be because Fabadi is right?" said Mother. "Fabadi and I have not always gotten along due to the cultural differences between Carnag and Shika, but if he does indeed stand against Skimif, then I believe he is right and that we should support him."

"That is the decision I will make when I become King," said Malock. "Remember, Mother, that the King always holds more authority than the Queen. It says so in the Royal Laws."

Mother huffed. "Oh, so now you are okay with being King? Earlier, you claimed that you didn't want anything to do with it."

Malock sighed. His knees were getting tired from all of the kneeling, but he didn't stand up, mostly because he still respected Mother. "I am still reluctant to wear the crown, but if becoming King would allow me to avoid dragging Carnag into a conflict that I believe is wrong, then I will gladly abandon the title of 'Prince' and don the title of 'King.'"

Mother frowned. "You are only saying this because you and Skimif were friends."

"And?" said Malock. "You were the one pushing me to become King. Are you now going to try to stop, or at least discourage, me?"

"No," said Mother, shaking her head. "I would never think, even for a moment, to prevent you from becoming King. It is your royal inheritance, duty, and destiny. I am not like some mother queens who, when faced with their son ascending to the throne, do whatever they can to stop that from happening so they can keep political power to themselves."

"Then what?" said Malock. "What are you trying to accomplish? Make me feel guilty for not wanting to get involved in something that we can't even be certain is true?"

"I have only one question to ask you, Tojas," said Mother. "You keep insisting that Skimif is innocent, that he is not responsible for what the Chaotic Goddess did or for any of the other things I have heard the southern gods doing in the Northern Isles. You say he is your friend."

"That's because he is," said Malock. "I don't see why that is so hard for you to under—"

"Then why has he not spoken to you since his ascension?" said Mother. "Why has he been so silent? Surely, if he is the friend you claim he is, then it would make sense for him to talk to you at some point, yes?"

"That's because he's busy," said Malock. "He just ascended a couple of months ago. No doubt he's still adjusting to being the God of Martir. I doubt it's an easy task."

"Maybe," said Mother. "Or maybe, now that he is the ultimate god, he doesn't see you as his friend or equal anymore. He doesn't bother to explain or defend himself because he doesn't see the need to explain or defend himself to us mortals who can't defeat him."

"You're wrong," said Malock, but even he could sense the uncertainty in his words. "Skimif is still a good man. Even with his new-found power, I doubt he has let any of it go to his head."

"Do you have any proof of that claim?" said Mother. "I see no proof. I have only seen my beloved husband's grave defiled by someone who claims to have been sent by Skimif to do that, and with proof to back up her claim."

"Mother, I don't think you're thinking rationally about this," said Malock. "With Father's death, your emotions are out of whack and are affecting your critical thinking faculties. Maybe you should go to the Grinfian Monastery and mourn Father in solitude for as long as it takes for you to get over it while I lead Carnag from here."

"I am thinking quite rationally about this, Tojas," said Mother, but her hands shook in her lap. "I do not need to grieve Halock in solitude when I have done enough of that over the past week. With Skimif running the world and the southern gods on the loose, I do not believe that I, as Queen of Carnag, have the right to take any amount of time off from my duties."

Mother said this with such anger in her voice, with her hands shaking and her eyes flashing, that Malock was almost intimidated by her. Which was unusual because Malock was rarely intimidated by Mother; at least, he had not felt intimidated by her anger since he was a small child. He would have to be careful about how he worded his next few sentences.

"Mother, maybe we should talk about this later," said Malock. "I can see you're getting worked up about it, and in your old age, you really can't let yourself get too worked up over anything, otherwise you might hurt yourself. Why don't we schedule my coronation and talk about this after I am King?"

Mother slammed her fist down on the arm of her throne, though the sight was less impressive than it might have been because she was not very physically imposing. "I am *not* getting worked up over anything. I am simply acknowledging the seriousness of our current situation, Tojas, which I do not believe that you understand."

"Mother, I am just as incensed at the Chaotic Goddess's inappropriate behavior at the funeral as you are," said Malock. "I just think it is wrong to blame Skimif for it when we don't have much proof that he was behind it."

"No proof, of course, except for that letter she gave you," said Mother. "The letter written in Skimif's handwriting, the letter that, I have been told, you yourself confirmed was written in Skimif's handwriting. My son, are you really so quick to defend your 'friend' that you are willing to deny the reality of Skimif's true nature before you?"

The crumpled up letter in Malock's pocket felt heavier than normal, but he didn't pull it out and look at it or show it to Mother. He had already read and reread the letter dozens of times on the way home from the funeral. He could recite the entire letter from memory now, if he had to, without omitting any of the words written upon it.

Despite that, Malock said, "It is probably forged. The southern gods are liars and deceivers. The Chaotic Goddess most likely forged it to justify her actions. I know the southern gods, Mother, and this is exactly the kind of behavior that they would engage in if they thought they could get away with it."

"But you have no proof of that claim, Tojas," said Mother. "It is your own desire to defend your friend, rather than embrace the truth, that is leading you to say such things. Maybe you were right. Maybe you aren't ready to don the noble mantle of King, to step into your father's shoes and do what he did."

Malock stood up. "Or maybe, Mother, you are the one who isn't willing to embrace the truth. I know how much you and Father hated Skimif when he was the leader of the Brotherhood of Heathens. Has it occurred to you that your own biases might be affecting your judgment?"

"I am not some silly girl, swayed by whatever little feelings happen to flit through my heart," said Mother. "And I haven't been a silly girl since I gave birth to you, my son. Do not accuse me of such shallowness."

"Then you should know that I am not swayed by my feelings, either," said Malock. "Maybe I lack the decades of experience you have, but that does not mean I cannot make wise or intelligent decisions based in reason and truth rather than bias or emotion."

Mother chuckled sadly. "Tojas, I know you mean well, but I know you well enough to know that you are very much a man of passion. You likely will not overcome that passion until you are much older and have more experience."

Malock sighed. "You know what, Mother? I am done discussing this. I've decided that I do in fact want to be the King of Carnag. Since it's pretty clear that neither of us can persuade the other right now, I think we should drop the matter of Skimif at least until after my coronation. How does that sound?"

To his relief, Mother nodded, though it was obviously with great reluctance. "I suppose so. The last thing Carnag needs is for the Royal Family to be divided. I hope that you at least take the time to consider what I said, rather than rejecting it immediately."

"I will consider it when I can, Mother," Malock said. "Now if you will excuse me, I am going to inform the Royal Event Organizer of my coronation so he can begin planning the event."

"Tell him not to plan it too far off," said Mother. "It's never wise for Carnag to be without a king for too long, you know."

"Yes, I do," said Malock.

With that, Malock turned and began walking across the Throne Room, his boots clicking against the stone floor underneath. As he walked, he could not deny that Mother's arguments—and the letter in his pocket—weighed far more heavily on his heart that he had let on.

Chapter Twelve

EYURNA RETURNED WITH NEW clothes for Jenur very soon. To Jenur's delight, Eyurna had brought back Jenur's old winter clothes, which had apparently been repaired and washed. Eyurna said that they had used their magic to repair the hole in the chest, which Jenur was more than grateful for. She had suspected that she might be forced to wear mage's robes around the Academy, but was thankful that she was not. She had never liked mage's robes and didn't think she would be able to move around in them very well, at least not easily.

After getting dressed in her old clothes, Jenur felt a lot better. Granted, she was still slightly stiff, but she didn't let that limit her. She decided she would get rid of the stiffness by walking around and working it off. Besides, she was concerned about Darek and wanted to see him again just to be sure he was okay.

Braim, too, had recovered enough to walk around. Unlike Jenur, however, Braim was given mage robes to wear. They were rather different from most mage robes Jenur had seen, however. They looked thicker and appeared to be made out of wool or some other material suited for the colder climate. Additionally, they were a dark gray, so dark that it was almost black. The robes conformed to Braim's body better than most mage robes Jenur had seen, probably to keep his body heat in better.

"There we go," said Braim, patting his robes. "Much better than that parka I had to wear." He looked at Jenur and grimaced. "Why would you want to wear that? You'd look much better in some mage's robes, I bet."

"I'm not a mage," said Jenur, adjusting her coat to make it fit comfortably. "And I happen to think that most mage robes look ridiculous."

"They only look ridiculous because you haven't given them a chance," said Braim. "But I guess it would be inappropriate for a non-mage to wear mage robes. Even if they would look better on you than those other clothes."

Jenur decided to ignore Braim's comments about her fashion choices for the rest of the day. She had much better things to worry about than what he thought.

Now that she was no longer in her bed, Jenur got a better look at the medical ward in which she had spent the last week. As she had noticed before, the walls, floor, and ceiling were all completely white. There were about two or three dozen beds, each covered with a curtain like the one that had shrouded Jenur's bed. The room smelled sterile, with a slight tinge of vomit, like someone had just thrown up. Indeed, at that moment Jenur heard vomiting sounds from behind one of the curtained beds, causing Eyurna to groan and say, "I will be back in a moment."

The panamancer disappeared behind the curtains of one of the beds. A loud moan of pain emitted from behind the curtained bed, followed by some low mutterings from Eyurna that Jenur couldn't understand. Then there was a brief flash of light and the next moment Eyurna returned, tucking her wand away into her belt as she did so.

"A sick student?" said Jenur.

Eyurna nodded. "Very sick. He ate some bad food, or so he says. He's been in here for about a day. I just cleaned up his vomit and cast a spell that should calm his stomach and put him to sleep for a couple of hours."

"Was it Hetha again?" said Braim, glancing at the bed. "That kid's always getting sick."

"Yes, it's him," said Eyurna. "This time, I think he's telling the truth about his illness, rather than looking for another excuse to avoid doing his training."

"I don't understand why the Superior hasn't just kicked him out already," said Braim. "What does the Superior see in him that the rest of us don't?"

"This is all a very interesting discussion," Jenur interrupted. "But I really would like to go see Darek now. Do you know where he is?"

"He's with Irliza," said Eyurna. "Let's see, at this time of day, Irliza is probably with her students in the sports field. Braim, would you please take Jenur to Irliza and Darek? I have to stay here and keep an eye on the patients."

Braim rolled his shoulders. "Sure thing, Ey. I'll give Jenur the grand tour of the Arcanium while we're at it. Doesn't that sound fun,

Jen?"

"Please don't call me 'Jen,'" said Jenur. "We're not that close."

Braim wagged a finger at her. "Not that close *yet*."

"Not that close *period*," Jenur responded.

"Why do I have a feeling that I will be seeing one or both of you back in here by the end of the day?" said Eyurna.

"Because your feeling is wrong," said Braim. "Because by the end of the day, we'll be best friends. Right, Jen?"

"What did I say about not calling me that?" said Jenur.

Braim just chuckled and walked past her, gesturing for her to follow as he said, "Not that close *yet*."

Jenur sighed, thanked Eyurna for taking care of her while she was unconscious, and followed Braim down the center of the room. Braim didn't even look back to see if she was following, but he must have heard her footsteps because he said, "It shouldn't take us long to get to the sports field from here. Unless we decide to take a few detours, that is."

Jenur caught up with him just as they reached the double doors, which were closed. "No detours."

Laying one hand on the doorknob, Braim looked at her and frowned. "But detours are a lot of fun. Besides, it's not like you *have* to be there right away or anything, right? Irliza's taken good care of Darek so far. I'm sure he won't mind staying with Irliza for a few more minutes. Or hours."

Jenur didn't change her expression. She just looked Braim hard in the eyes and said, enunciating each word clearly, "No. Detours."

"Fine, fine," said Braim as he turned the knob and pulled the door open. "Your loss. There's a lot of interesting stuff around here that you can't see anywhere else, not even in the other mage schools."

"I don't care to see any of it right now," said Jenur. "You're going to show me the way to where Darek is and you're going to do it fast."

"All right," said Braim. He stepped aside and gestured at the open door. "Ladies first."

Jenur rolled her eyes, but walked through the door anyway, with Braim following and closing it behind them.

Jenur found herself standing in a long, stone hallway, stretching in both directions dozens of feet, with a bunch of doors on each side that no doubt led to many different rooms. The hall was lit by more of those strange bright light orbs hanging from the ceiling, but there was not much to look at. There was no one else in the hall today, not even any of the faculty.

"Where is everyone?" Jenur asked as Braim began walking to the right.

"In class," said Braim. "This is the time of day when teachers and students are all in their classrooms, trying to learn various spells and how to serve their chosen gods better."

Jenur began following Braim and caught up with him quickly enough. "Is Irliza in one of these rooms?"

"Nah," said Braim. "Actually, quite a few teachers don't like these rooms. Too cramped. Not enough room to practice spells or avoid the dangerous spells students occasionally lose control of. Most of these teachers tend to teach outside somewhere on the campus grounds, though today I think most of the teachers are inside. Irliza tends to prefer teaching outside."

"All right," said Jenur. "So where are we currently?"

"The main campus building," said Braim. He tapped the stone floor with his shoe as they walked. "We call it the Arcanium. Oldest building on campus. These stones were probably laid by the founder himself when he founded this place all those years ago. We're basically walking on history."

Jenur glanced at the floor as they walked. "History isn't all that interesting, is it?"

"Oh, it is," said Braim. "You just haven't seen the whole place yet. It's easily one of the most beautiful buildings in the entire Northern Isles. Wait until you see the floating rooms."

"Floating rooms?" said Jenur. "What are those?"

"I don't want to spoil it, but I'll tell you anyway," said Braim as they reached the end of the hall and turned to the left. "Some of the rooms in this building aren't actually connected to it. They float right up against the side of the building, with nothing suspending them at all. They're mostly on the upper floors and were probably designed by the founder himself."

"Upper floors?" said Jenur. "Just how big is this building?"

"Five stories tall," said Braim. "With a basement. We're on the ground floor right now."

"Five stories tall?" said Jenur. "You must have a lot of students."

"Actually, there's probably less than a hundred on campus total this year," said Braim as they walked down another hallway that was at least as long as the last. "There's only about a dozen teachers, not counting the Superior."

"That seems awfully small," said Jenur.

"It's always been this small," said Braim. "Didn't I tell you that we only let in students who look for us? They have to make it here themselves to show their seriousness in wanting to become real mages. That's how I did it, that's how every other student or faculty member here did it, and it's worked pretty well so far. After all, our students tend to be better at magic than students from the bigger schools."

Jenur nodded. "I remember you mentioning that to me earlier. But why is the building so big if you have so few students?"

"No idea," said Braim with a shrug. "The founder built it that way, but the book he left doesn't say why. Methinks the founder thought he would have a ton more students than actually would come. Guess he thought most people would love traveling to the coldest place on the planet in the slim hopes of being accepted into the most intense mage school in all of the Northern Isles."

"So you don't accept everyone who makes it here?" said Jenur.

"Yeah," said Braim. "Sometimes we send people back if they clearly don't care. There was this one guy who came here about two weeks back who offered the Superior half his personal fortune—which was quite large, about as large as the treasury of a small country—in exchange for attending here. The Superior's not a big fan of money, though, so he said no and the rich guy left whining like a kid."

"So motives matter, then," said Jenur.

"To an extent, yeah," said Braim. "That guy was clearly not interested in learning magic for its own sake. He probably just wanted to attend to be able to brag to his friends. Loser probably wouldn't have lasted even a week if the Superior had accepted him."

"Sounds like it," said Jenur.

Eventually, the two reached the end of the hall and emerged into what Braim called the 'lobby.' It was a huge, wide-open room, with a marble statue of some unknown person standing in the center of a fountain that shot crystal clear water into the air, which splashed down into the fountain itself. The entrance to another hallway stretched directly from where Jenur and Braim had just exited, which probably led to another part of the building. The front doors were large and made of a thick crystal, but they were currently closed shut. As far as Jenur could see, there were no other people in the lobby except for her and Braim.

But the lobby itself wasn't what caught her attention. It was the two hundred or so paintings hanging on the wall at the very back of the lobby, closer to Jenur and Braim than to the front doors. All of the paintings had golden frames, reflecting the lighting from the orbs hanging from the ceiling and making for a dazzling appearance, though from a distance, it was impossible for Jenur to make out the individuals in the paintings.

"What's that?" said Jenur, pointing at the wall of paintings.

"That is the Wall of Mastery," said Braim, nodding at the paintings. "Each one of those paintings is a portrait of the best students we've ever had. While all of our students are great, these two hundred are the best of the best, which is why we've chosen to honor them with their own paintings that will last forever."

Jenur looked at Braim questioningly. "Forever?"

"I'm being literal," said Braim. "These paintings were drawn by the great magical artist Kinum, current head of the Northern Artists. Then the Superior himself cast an anti-aging spell on the paintings, making them immune to rot and fading. The paintings are supposed to inspire other students to strive to achieve the heights of greatness that these guys did."

"Interesting," said Jenur. "So you've only had two hundred students worthy of being on the wall?"

"Yep," said Braim. "When I say 'the best,' I mean *the* best. Loads of these students even put us teachers to shame, but most of them didn't return to teach. They went on to do other things, like answering the summons of the gods or following their own passions. Some are even well-known, though most don't care about fame or fortune."

"I see," said Jenur. "How long has it been since the last one graduated?"

"The last one graduated about ten years ago," said Braim. "I was actually in the same class as him, but I decided to stay after graduation, whereas he left because he claimed that the Academy was no longer intellectually stimulating to his brain anymore. Don't know where he is nowadays."

"What was his name?" said Jenur.

"Bifor Kamon," said Braim.

Jenur's eyes widened. She immediately walked over to the Wall of Mastery, Braim following behind her with a look of concern and confusion on his face.

"Hey, Jen, what are you doing?" said Braim. "Where are you going? I thought you wanted to go see Darek."

"I do," said Jenur. "But I just need to check something, just to make sure that the Bifor you mentioned is the Bifor I'm thinking of."

"You've met Bif?" said Braim. "How's he doing nowadays?"

Blown into pieces, Jenur thought, but somehow she didn't think Braim would take that news very well, considering how much he seemed to respect Bifor. Besides, she wanted to make sure that this Bifor Kamon was not the same Bifor Kamon that she knew, the one who had been a fanatical Tinkarian who had tried to assassinate Prince Malock—and the entire crew of the *Iron Wind*—on their first voyage to World's End so many months ago.

Upon reaching the Wall of Mastery, Jenur began scanning the paintings for Bifor's familiar face. She hoped she would not recognize any of them, but much to her chagrin, it didn't take her long to find Bifor's painting.

There was no doubt about it: The cruel, haughty, large face staring out from her was undoubtedly the same Bifor Kamon she had known not long ago. He was missing the large scar that ran from his crown down the side of his face to his chin, and he looked a lot younger, but there was no mistaking those intellectual eyes or the arrogance with which he held himself. He also wore green mage robes in this painting, rather than the more practical sailor's uniform he had worn as a member of the crew of the *Iron Wind*. Below his painting, his name was written in an elegant script colored gold.

"That's him," said Braim, pointing at Bifor's painting needlessly. "The man himself. He was always smarter than the rest of us, always studying his books and practicing his magic. There were even rumors that he might take over as the next Magical Superior after our current Superior retires, but Bifor and I were friends and he never once told me that he'd like that job. He always thought I'd be better at it, actually."

Jenur scowled as she looked at the painting. She wanted to rip it off its spot on the wall, throw it on the floor, and stomp on it with all her might. She had not thought about Bifor in a long time, but seeing him again—even if it was just a harmless painting—caused her anger to shoot up her spine like a lightning bolt.

"He was a master in all areas of magic, but he always said Tinkar was his favorite god," Braim continued. "He kept talking about how important it was for us mages to study the future, to know our own fates, so we could make the best decisions now. Gotta admit, he always freaked me out whenever he started talking about that stuff. Never been much interested in it, since dictamancy has always been a fairly esoteric magical discipline and most dictamancers either get depressed or go insane after a while."

Or were insane to begin with, Jenur thought.

But aloud, she said, "So Bifor never got into trouble or anything?"

Braim chuckled. "Nah. He was always the good one, much better behaved than I ever was. Unlike me, he took his studies seriously, though he had this annoying habit of constantly debating with the teachers in class. Normally that sort of behavior would get you punished or reprimanded, but he was so good that the teachers rarely got angry at him. Lucky bastard."

He said 'lucky bastard' as a term of endearment, although Jenur would have dropped the 'lucky' and just gone with 'bastard' to describe Bifor.

"Where did he come from?" said Jenur.

"Some obscure little island no one knows about," said Braim. "I think he said he came from Zinza. Said it's part of the Friana Archipelago, not far from Ruwa. Pretty amazing he made it to the Great Berg all the way from there, considering he came from a dirt poor family, but he did, and he did it better than anyone else, which is why he got accepted into the Academy."

Not far from Ruwa, Jenur thought. *I thought he'd actually came from the depths of darkness, but I guess even the evilest people have to come from somewhere.*

"Hey, Jen?" said Braim. "I know you don't like me calling you that—at least not yet—but why have you balled your fists and look like you're about to start punching people?"

Jenur looked down at her hands. She had indeed balled them into fists; in fact, she had balled them so tightly that her knuckles were starting to turn white. She relaxed her hands, but deep down, she continued to seethe.

"It's nothing," said Jenur. "It's just that I knew Bifor Kamon a while ago. We worked on the same ship."

Braim frowned in confusion. "Bifor was a sailor? Huh. I didn't think he was the kind who enjoyed that kind of work. Thought for sure he'd find a way to become the adviser of a king or something. He always seemed destined for greatness."

"Yeah, he thought he was pretty great," said Jenur. "Always pissed me off."

Braim didn't seem to catch the anger in her voice because he chuckled and said, "Know what you mean. Bif always had a way of pissing everyone else off, especially the faculty, with his annoying habit of correcting us or showing off his knowledge and skills. Still, everyone knew he was the best, which is why he was tolerated for as long as he was."

"Doesn't surprise me in the least," said Jenur. "Knowing him, I bet he even tried to teach a class once."

"He did, actually," said Braim. "I was even in it. It was a class about the history of magic and the teacher was running late, but Bifor didn't want to waste time waiting. So he started telling us about these Tinkarian cults he studied in his free time and probably would have given us homework if the teacher hadn't come in and dismissed the class when she realized that there was no time left in which to teach us."

"Did he ever come back to the Academy after leaving?" said Jenur.

"Unfortunately, no," said Braim with a sigh. "He didn't even send us any letters. How's he doing nowadays, anyway?"

"He's dead," said Jenur.

Braim did a double-take. "What? How did he die?"

Jenur did not feel like explaining that Bifor had been blown into smithereens by a cannon, nor did she feel like explaining the complicated series of events that led up to Bifor's death. For that matter, she didn't want to explain that she had partially helped kill Bifor. She had a feeling that Braim might not like her as much if she admitted to that, even if she explained that Bifor was nothing more than a sociopathic fanatic who didn't see anything wrong with murdering the entire crew of a ship on the orders of a god.

So Jenur said, "He got blown up by a ship cannon several months back. Wasn't much left of him except for his wand."

Braim put a hand over his mouth. "Whoa. I never thought he'd die like that. Always assumed he was going to outlive everyone else and die studying some obscure book about the history of arcanian mages or something."

"That probably would have been a better way for him to go," said Jenur, although in reality, she was thinking, *The bastard deserved nothing less than what he got.*

"Wish I would have known," said Braim. "Could have at least visited his funeral to pay my respects. We were great friends in our student days, even though his know-it-all attitude always pissed me off."

"There wasn't a funeral," said Jenur. "There wasn't anything to bury and it happened out at sea, well away from land."

"That's even sadder," said Braim. "I'll have to tell the Superior about this. The Superior always respected Bifor. We'll have to do something to acknowledge his death, even though it happened a while ago."

"You don't have to," said Jenur, turning to face Braim. "You know Bifor. He wasn't the kind who cared about rituals or anything. You'd better honor his memory by teaching students and encouraging them to become as ... as great as him one day."

Jenur said the word 'great' with supreme reluctance, but Braim didn't seem to catch that. He just nodded and said, "You know what? You're probably right. Still, I'm gonna miss him. I was hoping to invite him back one of these days, for old time's sake, but I guess I can't do that anymore, now can I?"

Jenur thought about Bifor aiming his wand at Prince Malock and the aquarian woman Vashnas and said, "It was probably for the best.

I doubt he would have accepted the invite. He left the Academy for a reason, didn't he?"

"Guess so," said Braim. "Still, I can't even remember the last thing I said to Bifor, since the last time I saw him was ten years ago."

"Whatever it was, I'm sure it was good," said Jenur, deciding that she didn't want to talk about Bifor anymore. "Anyway, we're wasting time standing around here talking about Bifor. Just take me to Darek, all right?"

"Okay," said Braim. "But Jenur ... I appreciate you telling me about Bifor. I probably would never have known about his fate otherwise, so thanks."

Jenur smiled, but it was a fake smile. *If only you knew the truth, Braim. If only you knew.*

Upon exiting the Arcanium, Jenur got her first good look at the commons area. She recalled seeing a little bit of it when she first arrived, but she had collapsed soon after and therefore only vaguely remembered some colors and shapes, if even that much.

The first thing she noticed was the cold air. It came as something of a shock, as she hadn't realized just how warm the Arcanium had been. It was a sharp reminder that she was still in the Great Berg and that, somewhere not far away from her current position, what little was left of Dad's body was still lying in the smoking ruins of their home back on Urma.

Then she noticed that the commons area had no snow on it at all. In fact, the grass was bright green, like it was the middle of summer, rather than the dead of winter in the Great Berg. Smooth, clean stone paths ran through the commons area, connecting the dozens of buildings that made up the entire campus.

The buildings appeared to be dorm buildings, as they did not look big enough to hold full classrooms. They were made of a kind of red brick that Jenur had never seen before and, like the grass, lacked any snow or ice whatsoever. Each of these buildings on the right hand side of the commons looked exactly the same: Two stories, with four windows in the front (two on each floor), though the windows lacked glass and they had no doors at all, which seemed like an odd design choice to Jenur.

On the left side of the commons were another set of buildings, but unlike the buildings on the right side, these ones were all as different from one another as they could be. One had to be at least three stories high, with a large entrance that fifty people could easily slip through without trouble. A statue of some god holding a large book in hand, opened somewhere in the middle, stood in front of it, which told Jenur that that had to be a library, for only libraries had statues of the God of Reading set outside before them.

Beside the library stood a slightly smaller building, though what it was for, Jenur didn't know. It was square, shaped almost exactly like a box, but a tower stood out of the box, the tip of which went just above the library. It reminded her of the Tower of Giants she had once seen in Shika during her time as a Dark Tiger, even had a similar pointed tip. She wondered if the builder of that tower had taken inspiration from the Tower of Giants.

All of this was built in the middle of what appeared to be a gigantic, bowl-shaped canyon. The canyon wasn't made of rock, however. The massive, white walls that reflected the light of the sun overhead were clearly made of ice. They did not look huge from a distance, but Jenur knew they had to be enormous for her to be able to see them at the size that she did.

"This is the commons area," said Braim, gesturing around the general area. "Pretty cool, huh?"

"Are those ice walls in the distance?" said Jenur.

"Uh huh," said Braim, nodding. "The founder of this place built it in the center of this massive ice canyon. We're basically right up against the Great Berg itself."

"Has anyone ever tried to scale those walls?" said Jenur.

"Oh, sure," said Braim. "It's one of the challenges you have to pass if you want to become a student here. Gotta climb them yourself, without any magic, and if you do, you are guaranteed a spot as a student."

"How tall are those walls?" said Jenur.

"Bigger than the Tower of Giants on Shika," said Braim. "I know it *sounds* harsh, but honestly, we're very selective here. We don't accept just anyone, after all. You gotta prove you're willing to do whatever it takes to be an Academy mage."

"So there are no other ways in or out of here at all?" said Jenur.

"Actually, there are loads of ways in and out of here," said Braim. "But only we Academy mages know where they are or how to access them. Potential threats, like the Dark Tigers, have never made it past those walls. Not even once."

"Not even once?" said Jenur. "But all they have to do is climb them, don't they? What's to stop someone from getting the right climbing gear and scaling the walls' face without any of you knowing?"

"Magic," said Braim simply. "The kind of spells that would make your skin crawl if you knew what they did to people. I won't get more specific than that."

Jenur frowned. "How do you tell the difference between someone trying to get in who genuinely wants to become a student versus someone who has other reasons for wanting to get in?"

"Only the Magical Superior knows," said Braim with a shrug. "He keeps tabs on the walls at all times. He can sense whether someone wishes to become a mage or if they're just trying to get in for other reasons."

"Oh," said Jenur. "Got it."

Braim patted her on the shoulder. "It's all right. Like I said before, Wirm can't get in here. He may think he's all that, but neither he nor any of his Dark Tigers have ever stepped foot in this place before, and never will as long as the Superior keeps them out. You and Darek— and everyone else, for that matter—are all right."

Jenur shrugged off his hand. "Saying stuff like that is bad luck."

"Not if it's based on fact," said Braim. "But what are we doing, worrying about something that will never happen in a million years? Let's go find Irliza and Darek. After that, we can all go get lunch together. It's about lunchtime and I haven't eaten anything since breakfast."

Jenur nodded and started following Braim down the steps of the Arcanium to the commons area. She glanced over her shoulder at the building they had just left and almost started at its sheer size. As soon as they reached the bottom of the steps, Jenur turned to get a better look at the place as a whole.

The Arcanium easily dwarfed the library. Braim must have been downplaying its size when he said it was a mere five stories. It had to be at least six, maybe seven, and, as he had said, certain rooms jutted out of the side, floating seemingly of their own accord. Two towers stood up out of the top of the building, though the left one slightly leaned inward, like someone had pushed it into that position. Like every other building on campus, the Arcanium was made of that same red brick and had no ice or snow on it. Above the Arcanium's entrance was a frieze that seemed to feature every single god in the Northern Pantheon, based on the few that Jenur recognized. Just above the frieze was some writing, but it was too far away for Jenur to read, not helped by the fact that it appeared to be written in a language she didn't know.

"Beautiful, isn't it?" said Braim. "I mean, not as beautiful as you, obviously, but still a pretty dang impressive building, if I do say so myself."

"What is that red brick that all of these buildings seemed to be built out of?" said Jenur. "I've never seen it."

"Heatstone," said Braim. "Usually, you find this stuff in the Volcanic Isles well to the south of here, but apparently the entire campus is sitting on top of a massive deposit of the stuff. In addition to some heat spells cast by our kairomancers, it's why you don't see much snow or ice anywhere and why we always have enough building material on hand to do repairs if we need to."

"Oh," said Jenur. "Don't they ever get too hot?"

"Not really," said Braim. "This heatstone is different from the kind you see at the Volcanic Isles. Because it's so close to the Great Berg, it's not as hot as it could be. As a result, the temperature in the Academy is pretty temperate year round unless one of our resident kairomancers decide to change it."

"That's awfully convenient," said Jenur. "Maybe the founder was a miner who discovered the heatstone here and thought this would make a great spot for a mage school."

"Who knows?" said Braim. "All I know is that it makes this damn place bearable. Even then, there are days where I wonder what the founder was thinking, building a school in one of the least habitable places on Martir. He was probably crazy."

Jenur looked away from the Arcanium and said, "Enough talk. I want to see Darek now."

"All right," said Braim. "Then let's move."

Braim suddenly took off at a far brisker pace than Jenur had ever seen him move. She tried to keep up, but because her joints were still stiff from the recovery, she was always at least a few steps behind him, much to her frustration. She knew it wasn't a race, but she really wanted to see Darek, mostly to assuage her own irrational fears that he was in some kind of danger, even though he wasn't.

"Irliza should be somewhere around here," said Braim. "But where—"

A column of flame shot up into the air from behind one of the dorms, followed by someone screaming and then someone else swearing loudly.

"There she is," said Braim. "Something must have gone wrong. As usual."

"As usual?" said Jenur. "What, is Irliza a bad teacher or something?"

"Nah," said Braim, shaking his head as he changed course to one of the dorms. "It's just that Irliza has some new students and they aren't very good at controlling their magic yet. I just hope that no one got their hair burned off this time."

"What if Darek was the one who got hurt?" said Jenur.

"Doubt it," said Braim. "Irliza isn't that irresponsible. She's probably keeping Darek out of the way so he doesn't get himself hurt or anything. He's probably fine."

Hope you're right, Jenur thought.

Jenur and Braim jogged around the dorm building until they reached the back of it. Then they came to a stop, allowing Jenur to see just what had happened. She was surprised at what she saw.

The area behind the dorm building was actually a steep incline, leading down to what looked like a sports field with twin goalposts—with huge nets in between them—standing at either end. Lists rose up from the ground on the far right side of the field, facing Jenur and Braim, while a tall referee's chair literally floated in front of the lists. The lists themselves appeared to be made out of heatstone and looked like they could seat two or three hundred people at most.

But that wasn't what caught Jenur's attention. In the center of the sports field was a big, blackened patch of earth, wisps of smoke arising from it like the tentacles of a squid. A dozen or so people were gathered near the blackened patch of earth, probably Academy students based on the uniform red-and-black robes they wore. They looked like they had just finished running away from something, for a few were obviously panting and others were sitting on the grass looking exhausted.

Not all of them were standing away from the patch, however. A young man—maybe in his twenties, Jenur wasn't sure—was cowering before a shouting middle-aged woman with beefy arms that Jenur had no trouble recognizing as Irliza. Irliza no longer wore the charcoal black winter clothes she had worn when Jenur had first seen her; instead, she had donned charcoal black mage's robes that looked similar to what Braim currently wore. Irliza's loud voice echoed throughout the open field, but it was hard to make out what she was saying, since her voice got lost in the open air, although her angry tone was obvious even from a distance.

"Knew it," said Braim. "Well, we'd best get on down there quick before Irliza becomes too angry. You don't want to see her when she gets super angry, trust me."

But Jenur wasn't quite ready to go down there yet. She was looking for Darek, but couldn't find him anywhere until she spotted a small child standing next to Irliza. There was no way that little guy could be anyone else, since as far as she knew there were no other children Darek's age in the Academy. Unlike the student being yelled at, Darek didn't look scared or frightened at all, though from her current position it was hard to tell for sure what his expression was.

So Jenur once more followed Braim, this time down the incline to the sports field. Several of the students seemed to notice Jenur and Braim because they looked at the two as they approached, but no one came up to them or spoke to them or anything. Perhaps they were afraid of Irliza overhearing them talking to someone without her permission or maybe the students were too freaked out by whatever happened to speak. As they ran by the students, Jenur noticed that they had quite the diverse age group, with one student who looked to be as young as her all the way to another student who had to be in his early forties at least.

As Jenur and Braim drew closer to Irliza, Darek, and the student, Irliza's shouting became more and more coherent. It sounded like the student—whose name must have been Arnyum, based on how often Irliza called him that—had somehow botched a pyromancy spell and nearly killed everyone, but Jenur paid little attention to it because her focus was almost entirely on Darek, who didn't seem to have noticed her or Braim yet.

"And furthermore," Irliza said, waving her wand through the air, sparks of electricity shooting from it as she did so, "you should have *known* you aren't capable of controlling a Pyro Pillar yet, you daft idiot, but obviously you were trying to impress the girls, which again is something you should *know* you don't need to do, but I guess you're so driven by passion that you can't—"

"Hey, Irliza!" said Braim, raising his voice to be heard over Irliza's shouting. "What's up?"

Irliza ceased shouting immediately and looked at Braim. Darek also looked at Braim, but then his eyes immediately fell on Jenur. Jenur smiled at Darek, but oddly, the little boy just hid further behind Irliza.

Doesn't he recognize me? Jenur thought as she and Braim slowed to a stop a few feet from Irliza, Darek, and Arnyum.

"Braim, Jenur!" said Irliza, her tone going from annoyed to delighted in an instant. "Glad to see both of you are walking around again. I didn't think Eyurna was going to let either of you out of the medical ward for at least another week."

Braim chuckled. "I managed to convince her I won't die if I get some exercise in. Say, what happened here?"

Irliza's smile turned to a frown as she gestured at the student. "Oh, I was just teaching this class some advanced pyromancy when Arnyum here tried to use a spell he knows he's not allowed to use yet. Almost killed the entire class with his foolishness."

Arnyum didn't say anything, but based on his sheepish expression, it was clear that Irliza's story was the truth.

"So I've been yelling at him hoping to get him understand the stupidity of his decision to try this," said Irliza. She looked at Arnyum and said, "Do you understand what you did wrong now?"

Arnyum nodded, but didn't say anything or look at any of them. He seemed too ashamed of himself to say anything.

"Good," said Irliza. "Now go and tell the rest of the class that class is dismissed and you can all go get lunch now. But I want you to come back here as soon as you are done eating to fix this, okay?"

"Yes, teacher," said Arnyum, bowing respectfully. "I'll be sure to do it."

With that, Arnyum went to rejoin his fellow students, though it was with a rather dejected slouch. Jenur didn't pay much attention to his departure, however, because she was still trying to look at Darek, who by now had hid behind Irliza so much that he was almost completely hidden behind her robes.

"Oy," said Braim as Arnyum walked away. "Hate teaching pyromancy. So many things can go wrong that it's amazing this kind of stuff doesn't happen more often."

"It's because of their inexperience and lack of loyalty to Grinf," said Irliza. "I've got a Xocionian, a Ghatmosian, a Mican, and a bunch of others, but only one Grinfian. That's the main reason this stuff happens like this."

"Why do you teach them pyromancy at all, then?" said Jenur.

"Because it's important for mages to understand *all* aspects of magic," said Irliza. "A whole understanding of magic is what sets North Academy apart from all of the other mage schools, even though most of our students end up specializing anyway."

Jenur saw no reason to argue with that, so she instead bent down to get a better look at Darek and said, "Hey, Darek. It's me, Jenur. Why don't you come out and give me a hug?"

Darek peeked out from behind Irliza's robes, but for whatever reason, he didn't look like he wanted to come out at all. He just stared at Jenur in horror before pulling his face behind Irliza's robes again.

Jenur felt her heart sinking, but she tried to keep a positive attitude. She looked up at Irliza and asked, "What's wrong with Darek? Why does he seem afraid of me? He knows me. Right, Darek?"

Darek just let out a little whimper, while Irliza scratched the back of her head as she said, "Well, you see, I told him that the reason Nijok Wirm and that other Dark Tiger killed his mother and his fellow villagers is because they were after you. Now he thinks that if he stays with you, Wirm will kill him, too."

Jenur frowned and tried to look around Irliza's robes at Darek. "Darek, is that true?"

Darek didn't reply. He just moved around Irliza so Jenur couldn't see him even when she looked around the mage's robes. So Jenur stood back up to her full height, feeling even worse than she had when Wirm had broken her nose.

"But I thought he came to see me every day," said Jenur. She looked at Braim. "Didn't you tell me that?"

Braim shrugged, looking a little sheepish. "Well ... I *might* have bent the truth just a little to make you feel better. Just a little, you understand."

"I didn't mean to scare him or anything," said Irliza. "It's just that he wanted to know why the Dark Tigers did what they did and so I told him based on what Braim had told me. Sorry."

Jenur ignored Irliza's explanation. She tried to look at Darek again, saying, "Darek, it's not my fault that the Dark Tigers want to kill me. I mean, the Dark Tigers can't even get in here because of the defenses around it. Even if they do find a way in, I'll protect you no matter what."

"No," said Darek, his voice slightly muffled because he had put his face in Irliza's robes. "Go away. I won't die like mommy if you stay away from me."

"Hey, kid," said Braim, his tone sharper than usual. "Your mother's death wasn't Jenur's fault. It was Wirm's fault. Jenur had nothing to do with it."

"No," said Darek. "I don't want to see Jenur ever again. I want to stay with Irly."

"Irly?" said Jenur, looking at Irliza.

Irliza shrugged. "It's what he calls me. I don't mind it."

Jenur looked back down at Irliza's legs again, though she could not see Darek. "Come on, Darek, you know I care about you. Like Braim said, it was the Dark Tigers' fault. They're the ones you should be afraid of, not me."

"But the Tigers wouldn't have killed mommy if they hadn't wanted to kill you," said Darek. "Go away!"

Jenur found it hard to argue Darek's point, but she still had to get him to trust her. She just needed to think of a way to do it, though the more she racked her brain for a solution, the harder it became for her to come up with one.

Then an idea came to her, prompting Jenur to say, "Well, if you don't come with me, who will take you out of this place?"

"I'm never going to leave ever," said Darek. "I'm gonna stay here and become a mage."

Jenur looked at Irliza in disbelief. "Did you know that he wanted to do that?"

"Well, he always did seem very interested in our magic," said Irliza. "And I did let him play with my wand once. But I didn't think he actually planned on staying here."

"Would you let him?" said Jenur.

"That's up to the Superior," said Irliza. "Though I must say, it would be unusual because children aren't allowed to stay in the Academy, even the children of teachers or students. I have a hard time imagining the Superior letting him stay."

"I'll be good," said Darek, peeking out from behind Irliza and looking up at her, his eyes wide with fear. "I promise I won't cause any trouble or anything. I'm a good boy."

"I know you are, Darek, but like I said, it's the Superior's decision," said Irliza. "I don't have the authority to decide whether you get to stay here or not."

"Has the Superior said anything about Jenur or Darek recently?" said Braim.

"No, he has not," said Irliza. "The Superior has been quieter than usual this week. Some of the other teachers and I have tried to speak with him, but he's shunned contact with everyone. The last thing he told us was that he agreed to let Jenur and Darek stay here for as long as they need to, but after that, they must go."

"Why?" said Braim. "I know the Superior hardly shows every card in his hand, but he's never shunned contact with everyone."

"That is what troubles the rest of us," said Irliza as she pocketed her wand. "There's a lot of speculation about what the Superior is doing. Some think he's come down with some kind of terrible disease, while others think he received a message from the gods that he cannot share with anyone."

"That's not good," said Braim. "Last time the Superior did this, it was because he discovered that the end of the world was going to happen. Sure, the end of the world actually didn't happen, but it almost did."

Jenur looked at Braim in surprise. "You guys knew about the end of the world, too?"

"Of course," said Braim. "It wasn't exactly a secret, you know, especially when Skimif came to power."

"It was a dark time," said Irliza. "Many of our students left when the knowledge became well-known, mostly because they didn't think there was any point in continuing their magical education if everything was going to end."

"And not a single one of those cowardly bums returned when it turned out that the world was going to continue as usual," said Braim with a huff, folding his arms across his chest. "Good riddance, I say. We don't need fakers like that wasting our time learning stuff they aren't prepared to dedicate their whole lives to."

It had never occurred to Jenur to think about how the knowledge of the end would have affected other people. Seeing Braim and Irliza's expressions, she could tell that it must have indeed been a dark time for them, maybe the darkest time for the Academy ever.

But that was past and right now she needed to convince Darek to trust her. Jenur had no desire to stay in the Academy. Sure, it was safe here, so safe that even Nijok Wirm could not enter, but Jenur had no interest in becoming a mage. Becoming a mage would require that Jenur pledge allegiance to one god or another and she did not worship or want to worship any god. All she wanted to do was live a normal life and she wanted Darek to live a normal life, too, if only to make up for his mother's death.

Then again, can we leave? Jenur thought. *Wirm is probably dead, but it's just as likely that he's still alive, maybe licking his wounds, but alive nonetheless. Even if he isn't, the rest of the Dark Tigers certainly are and once they find out that he's dead and I'm still alive, they'll probably drop everything else they're doing just to kill me. And if Darek is with me, they'll probably kill him, too. We can't live a normal life.*

It was a difficult situation, and honestly, she couldn't see any way out of it. The only possible way that she and Darek could have a normal life outside of the Academy would be if the Dark Tigers were to disband or give up their insane desire to kill her. Since neither seemed likely to happen anytime soon, that meant Jenur found herself in quite the pickle.

As far as Jenur could tell, she and Darek needed help. Her first thought was to go to Malock and ask him to protect her and Darek, which he would undoubtedly agree to do, since he and Jenur were good friends. And since he was the Prince of Carnag, he most likely had access to all kinds of different protection methods that would keep Jenur and Darek safe from the Dark Tigers.

No, not really, Jenur thought. *The Dark Tigers specialize in killing royalty. I wouldn't be surprised if they knew exactly how to get past all of the Carnagian Royal Family's security. If Darek and I went to Carnag, we'd be safe only for a time. We need a better solution.*

Then an idea occurred to her. She looked at Braim and said, "Where is the Magical Superior? Where does he live, exactly?"

"In the left tower of the Arcanium," said Braim. He pointed back up the hill toward the tower that peeked out above the top of the nearby dorm building. "It's his living quarters and study. Why do you ask?"

"I want to speak with him," said Jenur. "That's why."

"Speak with him?" said Irliza. "About what?"

"About helping me and Darek," said Jenur. "Right now, the only reason we're alive is because the Dark Tigers don't yet know how to get past the Academy's defenses. We can't stay here forever, so I thought I'd speak to the Superior and see if he might know of somewhere we could go to be safe."

"Weren't you listening to what I just said?" said Irliza. "The Superior doesn't want to talk to anyone. Besides, no one is allowed to go up to his study without first being summoned by him. Not even Braim is allowed to do that, and he's the Superior's pupil."

"What's he going to do to me if I come uninvited?" said Jenur. "Blast me into smithereens? The worst he can do is say no, right?"

Braim started tugging at the sleeves of his robes, nervously glancing between Jenur and the top of the tower on the other side of the dorm building. "It's just not done. Ever. I mean, I can't even remember the last time someone just went up to the Superior's study and talked with him without being summoned by him first."

"That's because it's never happened before," said Irliza. "The Superior has always made it clear that *he* is the one who calls, not any of us. Certainly not non-mages like Jenur here."

"He sounds like a swell guy," said Jenur. "But I don't care if it is or isn't done. I am going to go up there and bang on his front door until he either lets me in or kicks me out of the Academy."

"You can't be serious," said Irliza.

"I am," said Jenur. "I'm just not nervous or frightened because I've run into far, far worse than a powerful mage before. There's nothing he can say or do to scare me."

"It's just not a smart move," said Braim. "You don't know what will happen or what he'll do. He's made it very clear that he doesn't want anyone to enter his study uninvited."

"Then I'll just go by myself," said Jenur. "Neither of you need to come with me. Just give me the directions to the Superior's study and I'll find it myself. That way, no one has to get into trouble except for me."

Braim scratched his arm. "Well ... I guess we can do that. But I'm coming with you anyway. The Superior might be more willing to talk if he knows I'm with you, since I'm his pupil."

"I would say that both of you should stay away from the Superior unless summoned, but it's clear to me that neither of you will listen to me," said Irliza. "Darek, do you want to go with them?"

"No," said Darek from behind her. "I want to stay with you right now."

"All right, then," said Jenur. She turned to Braim. "Lead the way to the Superior's study, then."

Chapter Thirteen

AFTER SENDING A LETTER to the Royal Event Organizer to inform him of the upcoming coronation, Malock retired to his room. He was tired from the events of the day and wanted to take a nap before dinner, which would be sometime within the next two hours. He ordered his servants not to bother him until dinner and closed the door to his room to ensure his privacy. Without changing his clothes, Malock kicked off his boots and walked over to his comfortable red bed. Pushing aside the curtains, Malock fell onto the bed and pulled the blankets over his body. His feet ached from all of the running he had done today and all he wanted to do was rest.

Just as he closed his eyes, he heard something nearby, like a shoe scrapping against the floor of his room. Irritated, Malock sat up and peered through the curtains surrounding his bed. He thought it might have been a mouse, but he didn't see anything out of the ordinary in his room. Everything looked perfectly normal, causing him to shut the curtains and fall back onto his bed.

I must be hearing things, Malock thought. *After everything that happened today, it's no wonder if I am. A quick nap ought to cure my overactive imagination of that little problem.*

His pillow was so soft that he wanted to sink into it, but his concentration was once again broken by the sound of something scrapping against the floor. This time, it was slightly louder, as if the thing was closer to his bed.

By the gods, Malock thought. *You know what? I'll just ignore it. It's just my imagination, my tired imagination that needs a good rest from all of the craziness that happened today. Once I do that, then I'll get up and have some of that delicious dinner that the kitchen has no doubt prepared for me.*

That was when Malock heard the unmistakable *click* of a gun's hammer, causing him to snap his head to the right. The barrel of a pistol was aimed directly at his face, so close that Malock could smell the gunpowder wafting out of it. He wanted to scream, but knew that if he did, it would probably be the very last thing he ever did in his life.

Instead, he raised his eyes to see who held the gun. Standing at the side of his bed, pushing aside the curtains, was an aquarian woman with a green bandana tied around her head. She had a jellyfish-like head, but the expression of pure hatred on her face was nonetheless obvious.

"A-Aqur?" said Malock, not moving an inch from under his blankets. "What ... what are you doing here? Why are you pointing that gun at my face? Is this a joke or something? How did you even get in here?"

Aqur's scowl became even more pronounced. "I bribed one of the teichomancers to let me past the Protection. He also gave me a map of

Carnag Hall's layout, complete with servant passages, so it was easy for me to sneak in and hide in your room until you returned from your father's funeral."

"You mean you were here for *hours*?" said Malock. "That must have gotten boring very quickly."

"Not really," said Aqur. "I spent the last few hours imagining what your face would look like when I pointed my gun in your face. It looks even uglier than I thought it would, to be honest."

"Why are you aiming your gun at my face?" said Malock, starting to feel sick the longer he smelled the gunpowder. "You aren't going to shoot me, are you?"

Aqur tilted her head to the side. Her green eyes literally glowed in the dimness of Malock's bed, which didn't make Malock feel any safer about his current situation. "Of course I am. Why else would I break into this place and wait for hours in your closet until you returned from the funeral?"

Malock gaped. "But ... I thought we were friends or at least allies within the Brotherhood. Aren't all Heathens brothers and sisters? Isn't that what Skimif always used to say?"

Aqur's face twisted with anger. She pulled her gun out of his face (much to Malock's relief) and then grabbed him by his shirt collar and hauled him up to his knees until his face was level with hers. She smelled like the streets, like she hadn't bathed in a long time.

"Don't mention that traitor's name to me," Aqur growled. "Or I'll do far worse than simply putting a bullet in your brain."

Malock gulped. He had always known Aqur to be highly volatile and, at least to an extent, crazy; in fact, the first time he had met her, she had threatened to do to him then what she was planning to do to him now. He had never thought, however, that Aqur would actually go ahead with that threat.

"T-Traitor?" said Malock. "Are you talking about Skimif?"

"Who else?" said Aqur, saying the words with such ferocity that spittle flew from her mouth onto Malock's face. "If he was here right now, I'd put a bullet in his head, too. And hang his body from the top of Carnag Hall as a lesson for anyone who would dare to betray the Brotherhood."

"That would be difficult for you to do," said Malock, "because Skimif is the God of Martir and I doubt something as simple as a bullet could kill or even wound him."

"Do you think I'm stupid?" said Aqur, shaking Malock as she said that. "I suppose you do. I know how you humans think about us aquarians, so it's no surprise to see such obvious bigotry from you."

Malock felt something press against his chest and, looking down, he saw Aqur's gun pressed directly against his heart. Her tentacle was on the trigger, but so far it didn't seem like she was going to pull it just yet.

"I don't hate aquarians at all," said Malock, sweat running down his face as he looked back up at Aqur's face. "In fact, on my first voyage to World's End, I was in a relationship with an aquarian. Her name was Vashnas. Ever heard of her?"

"No, I haven't," said Aqur. "I have, however, heard of certain humans enslaving certain aquarians and using them for all kinds of devious purposes, but that's not the point. The point is, Skimif—and you—are nothing more than traitors to the Brotherhood's cause. And traitors deserve to be punished."

Aqur dragged Malock out of his bed and tossed him on the floor. Malock landed on the floor hard, but before he could get up, Aqur pinned him down with her right foot and aimed her gun at his forehead again. At that moment, the Burn of Grinf started to hurt his face, but Malock paid it no attention as he looked up into Aqur's face.

"But I don't understand," said Malock, holding up his hands. "What did Skimif and I do to make us traitors?"

"You mean you honestly don't know?" said Aqur. "This just proves how out of touch you royals are with the rest of us. I knew it was a mistake right from the start to let you join, but that damn idiot and traitor Skimif decided otherwise."

"P-Please explain," said Malock. "I've never intended to betray anyone, much less my fellow Heathens."

Aqur's gun trembled in her grasp, but she said, "You and Skimif are traitors because you abandoned us."

"Abandoned you?" said Malock. "What do you mean?"

"Don't play dumb with me," said Aqur. "You remember what Skimif always said, don't you? *Someday soon, in the future, the gods' reign will end and it will be we mortals who control the world ... The gods' days are numbered ... A new age is upon us ...* what a joke. A big, fat, fucking joke."

"Oh," said Malock. "I see now. You're upset that the gods are still around."

"No, I'm upset that I didn't get to become a goddess," said Aqur, her sarcasm as obvious as an incoming hurricane. "Of course I'm upset that the gods are still around. Every last member of the

Brotherhood—at least, those who are still with us—is angry that Skimif lied to and betrayed us."

"But Skimif didn't mean to," said Malock. "He honestly believed the Day of the Gods was coming. He was just mistaken, that's all."

"Mistaken?" Aqur said with a snort. "Yeah, right. 'Mistaken' is what you say when someone says it's going to be sunny all week but then rains all week. I don't know how you can be mistaken about something as big as the Day of the Gods."

"Even so, isn't this better than the world ending?" said Malock. "If Skimif and I had not convinced the Powers to spare us, then everyone—god and mortal alike—would be dead now."

"So it was *you* who did that," said Aqur. Her gun hand shook. "I imagine you must have convinced the Powers to make Skimif a god so you or maybe Carnag could have Skimif's favor. When are you going to tear down that statue of Grinf in the throne room and replace it with a statue of Skimif, I wonder?"

"I don't worship Skimif and have no desire to do so," said Malock. "I did that because it was the only way to convince the Powers to spare us. I'm sorry if that upsets you, but it's the truth."

Aqur stomped down on Malock's chest, causing him to gasp for air as she said, "Liar. I know you royals well. Always lying, always sneaking, always having an agenda. Isn't that how politics works? You wanted Carnag, or maybe just yourself, to be favored over every other nation in the world. You thought Skimif would grant you that favor, though with your father's recent death, I guess that didn't exactly work out the way you planned, now did it?"

"That's ... not ... true," said Malock. "I wasn't thinking of politics at all when Skimif and I were trying to save this world so ungrateful people like you could keep living. We had purely altruistic motives for doing what we did."

Aqur chuckled. "No one has 'purely' altruistic motives for anything they do, Malock. Please don't delude yourself. It's embarrassing."

"The point still stands," said Malock. "At the very least, you can't accuse me and Skimif of being up to any wrongdoing."

"But I can accuse you of betraying the Brotherhood's ideals," said Aqur. "The message was that we mortals would be free of the gods. For the first time ever, the mortals would answer to no one but themselves. That was the promise. Skimif repeated that idea every day and every night, like a magical chant. Then he went and became a god himself; and not just any old god, but the king of the gods, even."

Through she was clearly angry, more than once during her mini-speech Aqur's voice almost broke. It was like she was trying very hard not to cry, but Malock didn't dare point that out because, while she may have been on the verge of tears, she was also on the verge of blowing his brains out.

"I'm sorry that Skimif's promise never became true," said Malock. "But that's no reason—"

"Furthermore," Aqur continued, almost like Malock hadn't said anything, "the Brotherhood itself ... it's dying, Malock. Every day, we lose more members. They know the promise of a new era was a lie. They don't announce their leaving, but they just go and never come back or send letters or anything. Even Ower has left. Stupid kid."

Aqur's lips trembled, but she continued. "The Brotherhood took a major blow when Princess Raya was killed so many months ago, mostly on the Shikan side of things, but even then, under Skimif's leadership, the future still looked bright for us. For a while there, I was truly convinced that not even the gods themselves could stop us.

"But then news of Skimif's ascension swept through the Northern Isles like a tidal wave. Heathens—fakers—began leaving one by one at first, but now they're leaving in droves and I am fairly certain that, by the end of the year, there will be no more Brotherhood of Heathens at all. All because of Skimif's lies."

She spoke quickly, like she had been thinking about all of this for a long time now and wanted to get it out as fast as she could. Not that Malock was in any mood to stop her. He knew better than to interrupt someone who was aiming a gun at him.

"I've tried to convince them to stay, but even I can't think of any reason why they should," said Aqur. "The Brotherhood doesn't offer them anything they can't get elsewhere, and for a far less severe price. They go back to their friends and families and jobs and pretend like they never dreamed of bigger things, never saw that new era that Skimif always promised us."

Then she shook her head and continued speaking in a much quieter voice. "There are only a few of us left now, less than a dozen, I think, and shrinking. I don't know what else to do. I only know that I still believe in that dream of a new era, a godless era, even though it seems more like a delusion than a reality now."

"Aqur," said Malock, his voice as low as hers. "I am sorry to hear about that. I wish I could have done something to help, but it's too late now. Killing me won't bring the Brotherhood back."

Aqur sniffed and wiped the tears out of her eyes, but her aim never wavered. "Maybe not. But it will force Skimif to pay attention to me. He'll have to come down from his high seat and talk to me. Explain to me why he lied and deceived the entire Brotherhood from the very start. It's the only way I know that I can talk to him."

"Killing me will only tarnish the Brotherhood's reputation even more, even if it does force Skimif to talk to you," said Malock. "Please, Aqur. Think about what you're going to do. Is this really what you want the Brotherhood to be remembered as? An organization that kills its 'traitors'? How does that make you any better than or different from the Dark Tigers or any other lawless group like that?"

"Stop talking," said Aqur. "Stop it. I know what I want—what I *need*—to do and I don't need your moralizing to confuse me."

"I'm not moralizing," said Malock. "I'm just trying to convince you that this isn't the best way to go about helping the Brotherhood. Do you really want to go down in history as the murderer of Prince Tojas Malock?"

Aqur's lips trembled and so did her gun hand. "Who cares what history remembers me as? That's for history to decide, not me. I will do what I think is right."

"What you think is right is not always so," said Malock. "Please, Aqur. Just take a moment and think. Ask yourself if this is truly the best way to deal with your problems."

He wasn't sure if his words were having any effect on Aqur. She looked like she was starting to listen to his words, but she still aimed her gun at him. Her tentacle was still on the trigger. One pull on the trigger would be all she would need to do to end Malock's life here and now.

Then Aqur lowered her gun. She blinked back the tears in her eyes and said, "Damn you. You and your logic. You're right. Killing you wouldn't help me or the Brotherhood at all. It would make me feel better, but it wouldn't get us anywhere. Damn you."

Malock gulped. "I'm glad to see you came to that conclusion, Aqur. I knew there was a reasonable person somewhere in that emotionally-charged mind of yours and—"

"But that doesn't mean I have to live long enough to see the Brotherhood die," said Aqur.

Without warning, before Malock could even realize what was going on, Aqur shoved the barrel of her gun into her mouth and pulled the trigger. An explosion followed, with her brains and blood exploding out of the back of her head as she fell over backwards onto the floor. The gun clattered out of her hand when her body crashed onto the floor, blood quickly pooling out of the back of her skull.

Malock sat up abruptly. "Aqur!"

At that exact moment, the door to his room burst open and half a dozen servants stumbled through the doorway. They must have heard the gunshot go off because the lead one, whose name was Orel, said, "Prince Malock! What in Grinf's Most Just Name is—? By the gods!"

Orel and the other servants were looking at Aqur's corpse, their mouths agape at the blood and brains all over the floor. One of the servants even looked sick, his face turning green the longer he stared at Aqur.

"What happened, sir?" said Orel, looking at Malock. "Who is this woman? And where did she come from?"

Malock tried to speak, but the shock just made him stutter and mumble. He couldn't tear his gaze away from Aqur's corpse, even with the pool of blood growing ever larger around her head.

"He is in shock," said Orel. "Quickly, someone get Friyu to ensure that His Majesty is not harmed. And send for the kathamancers as well to clean up the mess and to remove the body."

While the other servants dashed off to fulfill Orel's orders, Malock just sat there and stared at Aqur's body, still trying to figure out just what had happened and wondering if he was, in some small way, responsible for it.

Chapter Fourteen

THE STAIRWAY LEADING UP to the Superior's study was narrow and confining. Not only that, but unlike the rest of the Arcanium, the walls didn't seem to be made of heatstone because the stairway was extremely cold, so cold that Jenur had to hug herself to keep in as much warmth as she could. Braim didn't seem to mind the cold, though he still looked nervous the higher they walked. He had not said a word to her since agreeing to take her up to the Magical Superior's study, which Jenur didn't mind because he usually said dumb things anyway. It was only disconcerting when he refused to look at her or make eye contact with her, like he thought she had some kind of disease or something, though it was more likely just his way of showing his nerves.

The stairway was also quite dark, forcing Braim to light up the tip of his wand so they could see where they were going. It was like walking inside a deep well, except without the water and mold. She wondered if the founder had designed this stairway this way or if maybe the Superior had cast some spells to make it seem this way in order to discourage unwanted guests from coming in uninvited.

The light from Braim's wand revealed to her what looked like paintings on the walls. Some looked like mages, others resembled gods like Kano and Tinkar, and still others were strange symbols that might have been an ancient language that no one read or spoke anymore. When Jenur had asked about them, Braim explained that the paintings had been painted by the previous Magical Superior, who had used his magic to decorate the hallway with images of mages from his time and the gods, as well as write secret messages in his own code that no one had yet been able to crack.

"Why would he do that?" Jenur had asked.

"Because he was also an artist in addition to being a Superior," Braim had said. "These paintings also have magical properties. The Superior can hear us through them, at least if he's listening to them at the moment. But don't worry. They won't attack us or anything."

Jenur wasn't sure why Braim had said that, since she had not been afraid that the gold-framed paintings would jump off the walls and try to harm them. But now she eyed the paintings with a wary eye. How much could the Superior hear through the paintings and how much could he not? Did he even know why they were coming up or was that yet a mystery to him?

Whatever he may or may not know doesn't really matter in the end, Jenur thought. *What matters is that Braim and I will talk to him and get him to listen to us, whether he wants to or not.*

Of course, Jenur didn't really know what to expect from the Superior. Braim had told her that the Superior was an old man and a master mage, as well as a master academic and intellectual, but beyond that he seemed reluctant to talk about the Superior. Most likely he was nervous about the idea of them going up to talk to the Superior uninvited, which made Jenur nervous, too, despite herself.

We've made it up this far without trouble, Jenur thought. *He hasn't tried to use his magic to get rid of us or anything. Maybe he actually does want to talk with us or maybe he's sleeping and doesn't know that we're coming up here to see him.*

"How much farther up do we need to go?" said Jenur. Her voice seemed louder in the stairway.

"Not much farther now," said Braim. "You know, I'm surprised we've been making as much progress as we have."

"Why?" said Jenur. "Is it because you and I are still recovering somewhat from our injuries?"

"Nah," said Braim, shaking his head. "It's because sometimes, whenever the Superior doesn't want anyone to come up and see him, he'll cast an illusion in which the uninvited guest keeps walking and walking up without making any real progress. An endless staircase, so to speak."

"Whoa," said Jenur. "That sounds ... excessive."

"It's really freaky," said Braim. "But don't worry. It lasts only until the uninvited guest gives up and goes back down the stairs. Leaves no long-lasting damage; well, okay, it does leave the more naïve ones thinking that the endless staircase is real, but besides that, it's totally harmless."

"How do you know that the Superior hasn't put us inside some other illusion?" said Jenur. She glanced at the walls and said, "Maybe not an endless staircase, but something else?"

"Don't worry," said Braim. "I'd know if we were in an illusion.

Psychimancy isn't my specialty, but I'm familiar enough with the basics of illusion-casting to be able to tell when I'm in one or not. Trust me, this is all real."

"All right," said Jenur. "But if the Superior is so powerful, what's to stop him from casting an illusion even you can't recognize?"

"Jenur, that's just paranoia speaking," said Braim. "You seem to think that the Superior just likes to mess with us. That's hardly the truth. He's just very stern and strict."

Braim then gestured at the stairway. "And hey, he hasn't tried to confuse us yet, so maybe he does want to talk with us."

"I hope so," said Jenur. "Because I don't want to have climbed this stairwell just to find out that I will have to climb back down it."

"Same here," said Braim, nodding. "Though we could always teleport back down, if you want."

"Why didn't we just teleport up?" said Jenur.

"Because the Superior cast a spell around his tower to keep people from doing that," said Braim. "He's nice, but he doesn't really like people just appearing inside his study without his permission or knowledge. Especially if he is in contact with the gods."

"So the Superior talks to the gods?" said Jenur. "How often does he do that?"

"Pretty often," said Braim. "Almost every day. And he never talks to the same god twice. Makes him really lucky, privileged even. Most mortals never get to speak to even one god in their whole life, much less a different god every day. He really is special."

"What kind of magic does he specialize in?" said Jenur, glancing at a painting of the god Tinkar to her left. "Every mage I've seen specializes in some kind of magic, so what's his specialty?"

Braim shook his head. "The Superior is different. Unlike the rest of us, he doesn't specialize in one area over any other. The reason he is the Superior is because he is an arcanian, a master mage who is proficient in almost every area of magic. That's why the gods talk to him and that's why he's the head of the school."

"Wow," said Jenur. "Now I'm no mage, but I thought that magic works best only when you are loyal to one or two gods. Does the Superior worship every god equally?"

Braim chuckled. "Nah. That would be impossible. Every god has different worship preferences, so trying to please them all is basically impossible. Nah, the Superior figured out another way, but he's refused to share it with the rest of us."

"Why?" said Jenur. "Wouldn't sharing this knowledge actually help everyone, make all of the other mages stronger?"

Braim glanced over his shoulder at her, though with the light before him, his face was covered in darkness. "It's tradition, Jen. It's a tradition passed down from Superior to pupil ever since the founding of North Academy. The Superior says that it would be too dangerous if everyone knew it because not everyone is capable of using that knowledge for good."

Jenur frowned. "Sounds like someone is trying to keep all of the best stuff to himself."

Braim stopped and turned to face her. Jenur was forced to stop as well, looking up into Braim's face, which was illuminated by the wand light. He looked at her with such anger in his eyes that Jenur almost wanted to run away.

"Don't say something like that about the Superior ever again," said Braim. "You don't know him. He has good reason for keeping that secret strictly within tradition. Besides, I've seen enough bad mages in my time to understand that that kind of knowledge would probably cause more harm than good if it became common knowledge."

Though Braim made no moves to harm her, Jenur didn't think it would be wise of her to continue to argue with a mage who could control the dead.

So she said, "I'm sorry. I just don't think that keeping information from the general public is always a wise thing."

Braim huffed, turned around, and continued walking up the stairwell, saying, "You may be beautiful, but you have a lot to learn about the way things work around here."

His sharp, cold tone stung Jenur like a wasp. She supposed it was because Braim had always treated her rather jovially, so to see him act that way toward her surprised her greatly. She wondered if Braim was offended.

He probably doesn't hate me, Jenur thought as she resumed walking after him. *I imagine he'll go back to his usual goofy self soon enough.*

A few seconds later, the two of them finally arrived before the door to the Superior's chamber. It was the strangest door Jenur had ever seen, and she had seen quite a few strange things in her life up to this point.

Firstly, it was bright purple. This was in stark contrast with the bleak gray stone that the interior of the tower was built from. It was so bright that it even shined in Braim's wand light, forcing Jenur to squint to avoid damaging her vision.

But that was hardly the weirdest part. Two eyeballs had been built into the door, located just above Jenur's head. At first, they appeared to be mere decorations, but as soon as Braim held up his wand, the eyeballs swiveled downward to focus on them. The eyeballs looked so real, like someone had taken out the eyeballs of an actual human being and stuffed them into the door. Their irises were blue, same shade as the sky on a summer afternoon.

"'Sup, buddy," said Braim to the door. "It's me, Braim Kotogs, and one of our visitors, Jenur Takren. We're here to speak with the Magical Superior, if that's okay with him."

The eyeballs shifted from Braim to Jenur and back again. When they focused on Jenur, Jenur felt something like a hot wave go down her body, causing her to shudder. She looked at Braim, who hadn't shuddered at all, making her wonder if that was because he was used to that feeling or if the eyes hadn't scanned him the way they had scanned her.

"I know this isn't exactly normal procedure, but Jenur here really wants to talk to the Superior," said Braim. "I tried to stop her, but she's too stubborn to listen to reason. She's the kind of girl who learns best by doing than by listening to reasonable people."

Jenur glared at Braim, while the eyeballs continued to look at him, though it was hard to know what the eyeballs might have been thinking, if they were thinking anything at all. Or maybe it was the Superior they were actually talking to. That seemed far more likely to her. After all, how else was the Superior supposed to know who was out there and who wasn't if he didn't look through the eyes?

Then the eyes rolled upwards until they had completely turned around, leaving only the plain white backs of the eyes showing.

"Um," said Jenur. "Is that a good thing or a bad thing?"

Braim shrugged. "I don't know. I've been teaching here for ten years, been the Superior's pupil for five, and I still don't understand those eyeballs all the time. But I have a hunch the Superior doesn't want to talk with us, so—"

Just then, the door cracked open, the movement so minute that Jenur almost missed it. Braim noticed it first, however, because he actually started, almost dropping his wand, though he redoubled his grip on it before he lost it.

"Guess I was wrong," said Braim, the surprise in his voice obvious. "I'll go in first, since I'm his pupil and all."

Jenur stepped aside to allow Braim to enter. He pulled open the door and slipped inside. Jenur hesitated for a moment before following, wondering what she would see and why the Superior had agreed to speak with them.

Upon entering the Superior's study, Jenur felt something like a heavy cloud fall on her shoulders. Her mind became fuzzier and she suddenly felt very tired, like she needed to take a nap. She yawned widely, despite herself, but shook her head and tried to get over the dizziness. Not only that, but there was a strong, smoky scent in the air, yet Jenur did not see a fire place or cigar or anything else to indicate the smoke's source.

The Superior's study was much larger than Jenur had thought it would be. It was shaped somewhat like a dome, with tall, slanting walls made of the same heatstone as the rest of the Arcanium. At least, Jenur thought that they were made of heatstone. Each wall was colored differently: Red, blue, green, and yellow, all stretched up to the center of the ceiling, where they converged in a vortex of color.

Bookshelves lined the walls, but rather than being straight and tall, the shelves stretched up with the walls, curling upwards yet somehow preventing the books from falling out. This was especially impressive considering that most of the books were thick and probably heavy, though it made Jenur wonder how the Superior could get a book that he wanted off the shelves.

Then again, if he designed the shelves to be like that, then it probably isn't too much trouble for him to cast a spell to get any book he wants, Jenur thought.

Another thing Jenur noticed was a table in the center of the room. On top of the wooden table were what looked like hundreds of small stone statues. At first glance she didn't know what they were statues of, but when she looked at them more closely, she realized that each statue represented a different northern god or goddess. They actually looked more like figurines than tiny statues, which made Jenur wonder why the most powerful mage in the world apparently still played with toys.

In the very back of the room was a bunch of curtains, with the same colors as the walls, obscuring the back wall. Jenur didn't see the Superior, so she assumed that he had to be behind those curtains. Of course, she didn't actually hear or see him, but as she didn't see him anywhere else in the room, she figured that that was where he had to be.

Braim didn't stop to look at everything like she did. He just kept walking towards the back wall, without even looking over his shoulder to see if Jenur was following. Jenur hurried to catch up with him, but something about those curtains in the back made her walk less freely than Braim. She felt like she had to be silent, as though she had stepped into a monastery of Amaren Monks.

The closer they drew to the curtains, the more tired Jenur felt. Her eyes started to droop and her movements became a lot more sluggish, while Braim walked with his usual briskness. He didn't seem even to notice her sluggishness. She wondered if this was the result of some kind of spell the Superior had cast, though Braim had not mentioned any such spell to her before.

Maybe it's a spell that only affects non-mages or something, Jenur thought.

Soon, they reached the curtains and Braim got down on one knee. He gestured for Jenur to do the same, which she did, largely because she was too tired to keep standing. She put her hands on her knee as Braim smiled at her compliance.

Then Braim looked at the curtains. "Magical Superior, it's me, Braim Kotogs, your pupil. And this is Jenur Takren, one of the newcomers. She would like to talk with you about getting out of the Academy."

Jenur didn't know if she should say anything or not, so she didn't. She just tried her best to stay awake, but again that same heavy feeling of tiredness just fell over her whole body. She wished there was a pillow or something that she could rest her head on.

The curtain stood still. There was no sign that anyone was even behind it, yet something told Jenur to stay put. Then a voice came from behind the curtain, an old voice that reminded Jenur of the ruins of Castle Ruwai back on her home island of Ruwa: dark, foreboding, with a slight hint of mystery.

"Kotogs," said the voice. "I already knew you and Jenur Takren were on your way up here. Knew it before even you did."

"Well, that's just fine," said Braim. "Are you going to help Jen, then?"

Jenur shot him an irritated look at the use of that abbreviation, but the Superior—that was who the voice had to belong to—continued to speak.

"She may speak with me," said the Superior's voice. "For a short time. I am rather busy and I would rather not waste any time speaking to a non-mage about such trivial matters."

Braim nodded at Jenur as if encouraging her to speak. Jenur was still tired, but she managed to say, "It sure would be easier to talk with you if you would come out from behind those curtains. I hate talking to people I can't see."

"Very well," said the Superior. "If that will make the conversation more pleasant, then so be it."

The curtains suddenly pulled back. Sitting cross-legged on a pile of blankets and pillows in the same colors as the walls, with a dozen open books scattered around him in varying stages of completion, was an old man who had to be at least a century old. His skin was dry and tight, his hands were thin and bony, and his mage's robes—which were colored auburn—only loosely fit him. A long, wooden wand—

more like a staff than a wand—lay across his lap, carved with a bunch of different words that Jenur couldn't read, as they appeared to be written in languages she didn't know.

The man had no hair, either on his head or on his face. It was impossible to tell what his skin color might have once been, for it was as gray as a storm cloud and was thin, revealing veins under his skin that made him look sickly. Nonetheless, the Superior gave off an aura of pure magical power that Jenur could not deny, so she knew better than to mess with him.

"Greetings," said the Magical Superior, his strong voice contrasting with his thin frame. "Call me the Magical Superior."

Jenur hesitated. "Is that your real name or—?"

"I discarded my old name decades ago after my master passed on the title of Superior to me," said the Magical Superior. "A necessary sacrifice, for the Magical Superior must devote himself fully to magic and the gods in order to be effective, which means abandoning all ties I have had with my past life. I have no attachments to distract me from my mission."

"Okay," said Jenur. "That's nice. Well, Magical Superior, I was wondering if you could help me and Darek with our current predicament."

The Magical Superior scratched his chin thoughtfully. "Go on."

Jenur found the Superior a hard read, so she just said, "Well, you know that Darek and I are on the run from the Dark Tigers."

The Superior frowned. "You mean Wirm and his band of killers."

"Yes, exactly," said Jenur, nodding. "Do you know him?"

The Magical Superior's face was impassive. "In another life. But please go on. I am listening."

Wirm never told me that he knew the Magical Superior, Jenur thought. *What is going on here?*

Aloud, Jenur said, "See, I don't think Wirm is actually dead. I know Irliza blasted his face with fire and threw him into the water, but I also know that Wirm has a reputation for surviving even the most gruesome of fates. I was once a Dark Tiger, you know."

"I know," said the Magical Superior. "And I know every other secret you have not told me."

Jenur gaped. "But ... how ...?"

The Magical Superior gestured at his books. "Your mind is an open book, Jenur Takren, adoptive daughter of Quro the Thinker. You clearly never learned how to protect it from mental intruders."

Jenur's face burned with embarrassment as she wondered what else the Superior now knew about her. Braim didn't say anything, but somehow she knew that he was in agreement with the Superior.

"Apologies," said the Magical Superior. "I did not mean to offend or embarrass you. My telepathy is constantly active and you are so ill-equipped to block mental intruders that I ended up reading most of your thoughts. I will refrain from doing so for the remainder of this conversation."

Without warning, that heavy, sleepy feeling that had fallen over Jenur evaporated and she felt wide awake once more. She realized it must have been the Superior's telepathy that had almost caused her to doze off. Which she found odd, as she didn't know that telepathy could do that.

Shaking her head, Jenur said, "Thanks. Anyway, I was wondering if you could help Darek and me find a place we could stay. We don't plan to stay here at the Academy forever. This is a nice place, but—"

"But it is no place for non-mages," the Magical Superior interrupted. "Correct?"

"Exactly," said Jenur. "So I thought you might be able to point us to another place we could go."

"A reasonable request, as they come," said the Magical Superior, stroking his chin. "But I am afraid I can be of no help to you, Jenur Takren, or to your little friend, Darek. Ultimately, even my powers are limited by the will of the gods."

"What?" said Jenur, leaning forward, ignoring Braim's alarmed look he was giving her. "What do you mean, 'even my powers are limited by the will of the gods'? What are you talking about?"

The Magical Superior looked away. "I have said too much. I should never have let either of you beyond the door. I should have cast the endless staircase illusion and sent you both home. May the gods forgive me."

"What are you babbling about?" said Jenur. "For the most powerful, intelligent mage in the world, you're not making a lick of sense right now."

"Master, I agree with Jen," said Braim. "You're really worrying us."

The Magical Superior kept looking away, but he did speak to them. "I cannot help you. I am not allowed to help you. It is beyond my power. Please do not force me to disobey the gods."

"In the name of the entire Northern Pantheon," said Braim, "*what* are you talking about, Superior? Did the gods tell you not to help Jenur and Darek?"

The Magical Superior nodded once.

"But why?" said Jenur. "Why would the gods ever do that? And why would you ever listen to them? What's going on?"

"I ..." the Magical Superior seemed to struggle to find the words. "I ..."

"What?" said Jenur, leaning forward even more. "What?"

The Magical Superior looked at Jenur and Braim directly. His eyes were ablaze with worry and his entire body seemed to shake with fear.

"Run," said the Magical Superior. "Both of you. Run, and never return to this place."

"Run?" said Jenur. "Run from who? Run from what?"

"Run from me," said a hauntingly familiar voice behind Jenur, one she had thought she would never hear again.

Jenur didn't even think. She jumped to the side, pushing Braim away from her as she did so, as a large, jagged knife thrust into the spot where she had been kneeling previously. Jenur rolled several feet away until she reached her hands and knees, panting as she looked with horror upon the massive man who now stood before her.

Nijok Wirm, Grand Tiger of the Dark Tigers, stood up as he flipped the gleaming knife in his hand. His face was burned, burned so badly that parts of his skull showed through, but somehow he didn't seem at all affected by the pain he had to be experiencing. His clothes were blackened, probably from Irliza's lightning bolt from earlier, but all that did was contribute to his fierce look. His bronze knuckles were as shiny as ever.

Jenur's courage drained away from her. Once more, she flash

backed to the day when Wirm had beaten her for her laziness, but this time it was interspersed with scenes from just a week ago, when she had fought Wirm. Her every instinct was telling her to run like hell, but she somehow managed to stay where she was.

"Jenur Takren," said Wirm, his insidious smile sending chills up her spine. "So glad to see you. How was your stay in my brother's school?"

"Your brother's—?" said Jenur. She glanced at the Magical Superior. "You mean you're Wirm's brother?"

"His older brother," said the Magical Superior, who had not moved an inch from his spot on his pillow. "But it has been years since we went our separate ways. I never thought I would live long enough to see him again."

"Nor did I you, younger brother" said Wirm. "But I suppose that Tinkar had a different fate in mind for both of us."

Through the gap in Wirm's legs, Jenur saw Braim recovering from her shoving him aside. He was aiming his wand at Wirm, hot energy swirling at the tip, but then Wirm whirled around and hurled a throwing star at Braim. The knife stabbed straight through Braim's wand hand, causing him to cry out in pain as he dropped his wand and curled into a fetal position, clutching his wand hand as it bled profusely.

"No son of mine will kill me," said Wirm. "Or perhaps it would be more appropriate to say, no *former* son of mine."

"You're no father," Braim said through gritted teeth. "You were never my father, even if you did sleep with my mother. Bastard."

"I could care less about what you think, broken child," said Wirm, turning away from Braim. "I will deal with you once I have slain Jenur. For now, be a good child and keep quiet while your father does what he needs to do."

"Braim is your son?" said Jenur. "What?"

"He didn't tell you?" said Wirm. "I would think any true son of mine would be proud to be the son of the Grand Tiger, but I suppose that is what happens when you sleep with a whore who could care less about your profession."

Based on the look of sheer hatred that Braim was giving Wirm, Jenur understood why Braim had not wanted to tell her about his relationship to Wirm. Still, it boggled her mind to know that Braim was the son of one of the most ruthless mortals she had ever known. The two were as different as night and day.

"Master," Braim said, looking at the Superior. "Why don't you stop him? He's pure evil."

The Magical Superior just looked down at his legs. "Because Lord Xocion told me not to interfere with Wirm's mission. It is against the will of the gods to do so."

"Why would the gods—?" Jenur shook her head. "Doesn't matter. I hate those bastards almost as much as I hate Wirm."

"So I am worse than a god?" said Wirm. "What an honor. Though to be honest, I do not know anything about what the gods may have to do with this situation. I do appreciate, however, that they have ordered my older brother to let me do as I please. It will make this kill that much easier."

Jenur's eyes briefly scanned the room. "Where's Kura?"

"I killed her," said Wirm, "after it became clear that she was more of a liability on this mission than an asset. I never liked her much anyway."

Jenur had never liked Kura much, either, but she still could not help but feel disgust at Wirm's boasting. "You're a monster, you know that?"

"I am a master," said Wirm. "But I suppose the distinction must be difficult to tell for someone as weak as you."

"How did you even get in here?" said Jenur. "Braim told me that no one can enter the Academy unless they first receive permission from the Superior."

Wirm chuckled. "Is not my presence proof that I have received permission? My brother told me that the gods ordered him to let me inside. He had no choice but to agree. A kinder older brother one cannot imagine."

"How long have you been here?" said Jenur.

"A few hours," said Wirm. "Brother and I were just catching up when you and my bastard son came in. Luckily, I was able to turn into smoke and hide in plain sight until I chose this exact moment to reveal myself."

"Why didn't you just kill me right away?" said Jenur. "I was in bed, completely unconscious, for a full week."

Wirm scowled and tossed a hateful glance at the Magical Superior. "I would have entered sooner, but my foolish brother resisted the gods' orders until just today. I admit that that surprises me, as my brother has always been more loyal to the gods than I have ever been."

"But how did you even survive?" said Jenur. "You were blasted in the face with fire and you fell in the freezing ocean. You should be dead."

"Under ordinary circumstances, I likely would have," said Wirm. "But someone rescued and healed me. I do not know who, but it does not matter. I will still crush you into a fine powder and scatter your powder over the surface of the Crystal Sea."

Jenur didn't dare take her eyes off Wirm to glance at the Magical Superior. She wanted to, but she knew that taking her eyes off Wirm even for a moment could give the Grand Tiger the opening he needed to kill her. Granted, she was unarmed at the moment, but that didn't mean she had to be stupid and let her guard down.

"Why don't we make this quick?" said Wirm. He cracked his knuckles. "I will beat you into a pulp that not even Quro would recognize. If he were still alive, that is."

The memory of the house exploding caused anger to shoot up in Jenur's very soul. She completely forgot her fear of Wirm, forgot that he was bigger and stronger and had more weapons than her and was far more experienced than she was. All she knew was that she wanted to kill Wirm, kill him where he stood, and she would do whatever it would take to do it.

Her anger must have been showing because Wirm smiled and said, "Oh, the kitten is getting ready to pounce. I wish I had some string to let you play with, but no matter. I will take your body and nail it on the front doors of the Den to show to the others just what happens when they choose to betray me."

Smoke began rising from Wirm's form, while the Magical Superior sat by and watched helplessly. Braim continued to moan in pain as the blood from his hand began to stain the sleeve of his jacket.

"Then bring it," said Jenur. "I'm not going to run anymore. I'm going to kill you, rip your head from your body, so you can't kill anyone else ever again."

Wirm's smile now looked ghostly in the smoke wafting around his form. "Brave words from a de-clawed, frightened little kitten. But I would expect no less from a former Dark Tiger. It is what I taught you, after all, and it is what has granted me the success I have today."

"It will also take away that success," said Jenur. "That success ... and your life."

Chapter Fifteen

MALOCK SAT AT HIS place at the dining table in the Great Dining Room, a blanket wrapped around his shoulders. He was staring at the table, Aqur's suicide replaying in his mind over and over again, playing the memory in such sharp detail that he thought he could now recite every little detail if he had to. The look of utter despair in Aqur's eyes as she placed the gun's barrel in her mouth ... the blood exploding from the back of her head, getting all over the floor of his room and staining his bed sheets ... the gooey bits of brain that were mixed with it ... the scent of aquarian blood filling his nostrils like a toxic fume ...

In my time, I've seen a lot of death, Malock thought. *But somehow, I don't think I'll ever quite forget this one.*

After his servants had burst into his room, Malock had been escorted out by Friyu and some of the other servants. Friyu had asked Malock a ton of questions about his health and Malock answered each question honestly and truthfully. No, he hadn't been harmed by Aqur, though he was in shock, which was why he sat at the dining table with the heavy red blanket draped over his shoulders like a cape.

Not only that, but Malock had been interrogated by Banika and some of the other Justice Enforcers who acted as the guards of Carnag Hall. They had wanted to know how Aqur had gotten past security. Malock had told them what Aqur had told him, though he knew it didn't help the Enforcers very much because no one knew who had sold that information to Aqur. Malock gave Banika permission to look through the servants' belongings to see if she could find any clues as to the traitor's identity, but he doubted she would find any.

But Malock didn't sit alone at the long, exquisitely decorated dining room table. Mother had come out of the Throne Room as soon as she heard the news and now sat right next to him, one of her arms around his shoulders, even though she normally sat the far left end of the table, which was where the Queen of Carnag traditionally sat. She had not said much since sitting next to him, but he did not need her to. He was content just to sit there and try to understand everything that had just happened.

I would never have thought of Aqur as one to kill herself, Malock thought. *She always seemed strong to me, much stronger than any of the other Heathens. Yet she went ahead and killed herself anyway. And Skimif did nothing about it.*

That last thought—*And Skimif did nothing about it*—echoed in his mind. Prior to Skimif's ascension, Skimif had been close friends with Aqur. In fact, Skimif had even made Aqur the deputy leader of the Brotherhood of Heathens and had once even admitted to Malock that Aqur could easily take over the Brotherhood if she wanted to. Why had Skimif not help Aqur? Why did he let her kill herself? Surely, as the God of Martir, he could have saved her or at least talked her out of it, couldn't he?

This went back to Skimif's absolute silence. Since Skimif's ascension, he had said nothing—absolutely nothing—to Malock or to anyone else. Malock originally had accepted that Skimif was just too busy to come and speak with Malock like they used to, but with Aqur's suicide, he was starting to wonder if Skimif was becoming every bit as apathetic as the gods themselves.

Maybe this isn't such a grand new era after all, Malock thought. *Maybe putting Skimif in charge wasn't such a good idea. Perhaps it would have been better to let the Powers destroy the world and be done with it.*

No. That was a silly thought. Existence beat nonexistence every day of the week, as far as Malock was concerned, but that didn't fix his concerns about Skimif. Would it really have been so terrible for Skimif to come down and talk to Aqur, at least? He could have saved her life, maybe even given her a new purpose.

Would she have believed him, though? Malock thought. *She was so convinced that the Day of the Gods wasn't coming that I think it would have been impossible even for Skimif to change her mind or give her a new reason to live.*

That made Malock wonder just what kind of life Aqur might have led prior to joining the Brotherhood. He knew very little about her past; in fact, he knew nothing at all when he thought about it. He had never asked Aqur about her beginnings or where she had come from or what she had done for a living. He didn't even know where she used to live. All he knew for sure was that she had been one of the first people to join the fledgling Brotherhood when Skimif first founded the movement, but when, where, and how the two met, Malock didn't know.

Guess I'll never know now, unless Skimif chooses to come down from his high seat and tell me, Malock thought. *But what are the chances of that happening?*

His thoughts were interrupted when Banika entered the dining room. Her expression, as usual, was unreadable, while she carried a bundle of robes in her hands.

"Banika?" said Mother as the Captain of the Justice Enforcers approached. "Did you find any clues as to who had sold that information to Aqur?"

"No, Your Majesty," said Banika, shaking her head. "Not yet. We still haven't checked the gardener's things, but we are beginning to doubt that there is any evidence to find. Whoever the traitor is, we think, probably already destroyed all of the evidence linking them to Aqur."

"Then get the psychimancers in," said Mother. "Have them read the minds of every servant. Surely the traitor would be thinking of Aqur, since her attack was very recent."

"Already did that, Your Majesty," said Banika. "Still no sign of the traitor. We've asked most of the servants if they had seen or heard any suspicious activity, but they all claim that they hadn't seen anything unusual while Aqur was in Carnag Hall."

"Keep searching," said Mother. "And don't forget to use the topomancers. Have them search for anyone who shouldn't be in places that they're not allowed to be in. If you catch anyone, be sure to tell Malock and me immediately."

"Yes, ma'am," said Banika, bowing her head. "Your will be done."

Malock looked up at the bundle of robes in Banika's hands. "Banika, what is in that bundle you've got there?"

"It's something we found on Aqur's corpse when we were searching it for any clues as to the traitor's identity," said Banika, raising the bundle. "We're not sure what it is. We thought you might know, Your Majesty, or would at least be interested in seeing it."

"Then show it to me," said Malock. "I've got nothing better to do."

"As you command," said Banika.

She began to unwrap the bundle. In just a few seconds, Banika held the robes in her right hand while carrying the object in her left.

Malock had never seen such an object before. It was shaped like a box, except as clear as crystal. It glowed very softly, almost imperceptibly, but appeared to be as light as air because Banika showed no strain in lifting it.

"Do you recognize this, Your Majesty?" said Banika.

Malock shook his head. "No. But it looks like magic to me. Have you shown it to any of the mages?"

"I did," said Banika. "I showed it to Friyu. She said it might be a magic-nullifying device. She thinks Aqur may have used it to get past the Protection, which is otherwise impossible without the express permission of someone from within Carnag Hall."

"Someone must have given it to her," said Malock. "The question is, who?"

"The answer to that mystery is still obscure, Your Majesty," said Banika. "But we are working hard on finding it out."

"Good," said Malock. "But may I have the cube, Banika? I would like to look at it more closely."

"Of course, Your Majesty," said Banika. She handed the cube to him. "Is that all you want?"

Turning the cube over in his hand, rubbing his fingers against its corners, Malock nodded and said, "Yes. You may leave and return to overseeing your squad."

Banika nodded again and said, "Yes, sir," before turning around and walking out of the dining hall, the back of her red armor disappearing beyond the open doorway.

Mother looked at the cube curiously. "Tojas, dear, why did you want to look at that? You don't know much about magic."

"I know, Mother," said Malock as he looked at the cube from every angle. "I just feel like there is something missing and that this cube is the final piece of the puzzle. I just don't know how to fit it in, that's all."

"In my opinion, Tojas, you are wasting time," said Mother. "What you should be doing—once you've recovered from the shock of Aqur's suicide, of course—is preparing for your coronation. I have already heard back from the Royal Event Organizer and he has given me about a dozen different ideas for how he'd like to do it, ideas he asked me to share with you so we can know what you'd like."

"Later, Mother," said Malock, his eyes on the cube. "Besides, I don't particularly care how we do it. I am more interested in figuring out the importance of this cube than anything."

"But it is your coronation," said Mother. "I would argue that it is far more important than that magical little cube—more like a toy, really—that you've got there."

"Mother, must we really argue about this now?" said Malock, looking at her. "I have more urgent things on my mind at the moment than my coronation, as important as that may be."

"Your coronation will be the most important event in your life," said Mother. "It's not every day that you become king, after all. Besides, what does looking at that little cube do for you? Nothing, since you're no mage and so don't understand things like magical objects."

Malock placed the cube down on the table and sighed. "I suppose you're right. It's just that I've had other things on my mind recently. I'm still trying to understand Aqur's suicide."

"I understand," said Mother. "But really, I think the world may well be better off without her. She was not very kind or friendly, based on what you have told me, and of course as a Heathen, that just made her—"

Malock glared at Mother. "Mother dear, would you please be so kind as to shut up? I'm not exactly in the mood to hear you bash Heathens, especially one who had killed herself literally twenty minutes ago."

Mother, thankfully, did not argue or shout back at him. She did look rather offended, however, but Malock paid no attention to that. Offending his mother seemed less important than making sure that Mother didn't insult a suicide victim, even if he had never gotten along very well with that suicide victim.

Then Mother said, under her breath, "Well, I guess Skimif didn't see fit to do anything about it, now did he?"

Malock didn't even look at her, mostly because he knew she was right. Looking at the cube, however, did give him an idea.

Maybe I should stop sitting around, waiting for Skimif to explain himself or talk to me, Malock thought. *Maybe I should go to him.*

Yet that thought seemed ridiculous to him. He didn't know how to contact Skimif. Having only been the God of Martir for a couple of months now, Skimif hadn't had time to build up a following of mortals who would devise all sorts of rituals and convoluted theologies to worship him. Malock wasn't sure that even prayer would work because he had no idea if Skimif even listened to prayers.

Someone somewhere must know something about contacting him, Malock thought. *The only question is, who? I doubt any of the Heathens have. Based on what Aqur told me, the Heathens have been just as ignored by Skimif as everyone. And I don't think any of the Grinfian Priests, Priestesses, or monks around here would know. I doubt there is a single mortal in the Northern Isles who could tell or show me how to do it.*

What Malock needed was someone who had experience in contacting gods. A servant of the gods, perhaps, but not just any old servant—a servant who had served the gods for many years and who would also be willing to help Malock find a way to contact Skimif. This servant would also need to know how to speak in the mortal language so Malock could speak to them. Ideally, the servant should know Malock and consider Malock a friend or at least not hate him.

I don't think there's any servant of the gods in all of Martir who fits those criteria exactly, Malock thought. *Except for ... oh. Hanarova.*

Malock didn't want to call in her. Hanarova was a katabans, a minor spirit who had served the gods for all her life. Specifically, she had served the Mechanical Goddess and still served her, to Malock's knowledge. Last time Malock had seen her was on World's End, shortly after Skimif's ascension. She had been returning to Stalf with the Mechanical Goddess, which was the last Malock ever thought he'd see of her.

Yet here I am, thinking of summoning her and asking for her help, Malock thought. *Sometimes, I hate fate.*

Hanarova—or 'Hana,' as she preferred to be called—was the only katabans Malock really knew. Granted, she had helped him get to World's End in time to stop the Powers from destroying the world, but she had also attempted at one point to feed him to some of the southern gods. So he felt his wariness of her was entirely justified.

But I can't just sit around here and let my distrust of her keep me from contacting Skimif, Malock thought. *She's the only option I have right now. But first, I'll need to contact her, and I think I know just the way to do it.*

"Mother," said Malock, looking at her. "I wish to go out into the Garden. I want to get some fresh air."

"Oh," said Mother, seemingly taken aback by his request. "Why, of course. Do you need any help?"

"No, I can go out there myself," said Malock. "But I would like to bring Friyu with me, just to make sure that I do not faint or anything. I am still in shock, after all."

"Of course, of course," said Mother. "I will send for Friyu right away. Do you want me to accompany you out there in the meantime or—?"

Malock stood up. "No, I can do it myself. Just make sure to send Friyu to the Garden."

"I will," said Mother.

Malock nodded and then began walking away to the Garden, trying to think of what he would say to Skimif once he would get to speak to his old friend.

A few minutes later, Malock stood in the Carnagian Royal Garden as the sun began to set in the west, casting a twilight over the Garden. The twilight made the Grinf's Eyes and the black dollops look eerie, but Malock did not feel particularly afraid here. The Royal Garden had always been a place of safety for him, though when he looked out over at the gazebo near the center of the Garden, he could not help but remember Princess Raya's assassination. He had held her in his arms as she died, getting blood all over his hands and clothes. It was like the assassination had happened yesterday, even though it had actually been several months ago.

Thinking of Raya caused him to think of Fabadi. King Fabadi's words from the funeral still rang in his mind, now more than ever: *Skimif has betrayed us. His power has gone to his head.*

I can't accept that, Malock thought. *Fabadi is wrong. The Chaotic Goddess was lying. The letter is fake. Skimif didn't order Jenur to assassinate Raya. Someone else is behind this.*

Despite telling himself that, Malock's doubts started to invade his mind. His hands in his pockets, he felt the letter, now little more than a crunched up ball of paper, and wondered just what was going on here.

For that matter, he wondered what Fabadi was doing right now. Last he heard, Fabadi had departed from Carnag as soon as the funeral was over and was probably on his way back to Shika even as Malock thought this. Fabadi had said he would send messengers to every nation in the Northern Isles to let everyone know of Skimif's alleged treachery. If that happened, Malock didn't even want to think about the repercussions.

I guess it's outside of my control now, Malock thought. *Once I speak with Skimif and find out the truth, then maybe things will start making sense.*

At that moment, Malock heard someone walking behind him. Turning around, Malock saw Friyu approaching, her hair as white as ever and her short wand in hand.

"Prince Malock," said Friyu, bowing as she approached him. "I received orders from Queen Markinia that I was to meet you out here in the Royal Garden, to keep an eye on your health while you were out here. I came as quickly as I could."

"Excellent," said Malock. "Now Friyu, do you know how to send gray ghosts?"

"Yes," said Friyu. "All mages do. It's a standard part of our education."

"Good," said Malock. "I need you to send a gray ghost to a certain someone I once knew. Can you do that?"

"Of course," said Friyu. "May I ask who you wish to send it to, Your Majesty?"

Malock shook his head. "You'll find out soon enough. For now, just conjure the ghost and I'll speak into it."

Without another word, Friyu flicked her wand, sending a cloud of gray smoke bursting from her wand tip. The formless gray cloud floated before Malock, coming up to his face.

Taking a deep breath, Malock spoke into the gray cloud, saying, "To Hanarova, servant of the Mechanical Goddess, on the island of Stalf: This is Prince Tojas Malock, Crown Prince of Carnag. I wish to speak with you personally as soon as possible. I require your help for an urgent task and I can offer you compensation for the work: money, jewelry, equipment, food, whatever you desire in exchange for your work. I know you are first and foremost a servant of the gods, but this task should not take very long to complete and I will reward you very handsomely for doing it if you agree to it."

Malock stopped speaking then. As soon as he did, the shapeless cloud began to shape-shift until he was looking at a perfect, albeit colorless, replica of himself. The gray ghost repeated his message verbatim before turning around and flying into the sky so fast Malock's eyes could barely keep up with it. In a moment the gray ghost was gone, leaving Malock and Friyu alone in the Garden.

"Your Majesty?" said Friyu, her voice slightly hesitant. "May I ask who this 'Hanarova' is?"

"An old friend," said Malock, "who lives very far from here. I don't know if she will respond or not, but I have to hope that she does."

"Well, if she lives far away, you can't expect her to respond very quickly, Your Majesty," said Friyu. "For that matter, you can't expect her to arrive here very fast, either. How far away is this 'Stalf' anyway?"

"Far enough for my tastes," said Malock. "Let's leave it at that."

"If you say so, Your Majesty," said Friyu. "But perhaps we should go back inside. It is getting dark out and with the nights as cold as they are—"

Friyu was interrupted when a large hole in the sky opened up with a loud, ear-ringing *bang*. Both Malock and the old panamancer jumped as something brightly-colored leaped out of the hole, somersaulted through the air, and landed on the ground perfectly. As soon as the new arrival landed, the hole in the sky closed shut with a *bang* that was just as loud as the last one had been.

Rubbing his ears, Malock looked at the new arrival, who was now stretching her arms and legs like she had been sitting down for a while. Her hair was longer than when Malock had last seen her, like she had grown it out, and she had abandoned her sailor's uniform for a new purple dress that resembled an upside down flower. But there was no denying the identity of the woman who now stood before Malock and Friyu.

"Hello, Hanarova," said Malock. "I didn't expect you to answer my ghost so quickly."

Hana finished stretching her arms and legs, then yawned. "Oh, the Mechanical Goddess is in the middle of her yearly upgrades where she basically takes everything apart and puts it back together better and stronger than ever. She said I was underfoot, so when I got your message, I decided it wouldn't hurt to respond to it right away, even though I normally never serve mortals."

"But ..." said Friyu, looking up at the spot in the sky where the hole had been. "How did you get here so fast? And without a ship or anything?"

"Took the ethereal," said Hana, cracking her neck. "It's the main method of transportation for us katabans. It's basically another layer of Martir, one usually inaccessible to mortals, except distance isn't nearly as big an issue there as it is here. I essentially ran all the way across the ethereal from Stalf to here."

"Katabans?" Friyu repeated, looking at Hana. "I thought katabans were only legend."

Hana looked at Malock with disappointment. "Malock, I am disappointed with you. I thought you were going to tell everyone about me when you got back. I suppose that's what I get for trusting a mortal man."

"I never—gah," said Malock, shaking his head. "Friyu, meet Hanarova. She's a katabans and katabans are real, but not necessarily always friendly or kind. Hanarova, meet Friyu, the panamancer of the Royal Family."

Friyu looked like she was about to faint, while Hana just waved at her and said, "Hi," before turning her attention back to Malock and saying, "So what did you summon me for, Mal? Did you just miss me? I didn't think we were very close friends, but I understand if you find mortals very boring after hanging out with—"

"I need to speak with Skimif," said Malock, interrupting her.

Hana raised an eyebrow, as if to say *How rude*, but when she spoke, she said, "You mean the big guy himself? Everyone's favorite king of the gods?"

She said the word 'favorite' like it was an insult.

"Yes, him," said Malock, nodding. "You're always serving the gods, aren't you? You know where the gods are, yes? So couldn't you take me to wherever Skimif is?"

Hana scratched the back of her head. "You're right. I do know how to contact most of the gods. I even know how to contact Skimif, though he hasn't actually hired me to do anything for him yet and the only news I've heard of him since the cancellation of the apocalypse is that he's been very busy trying to keep the other gods, northern and southern, in line."

"Then take me to him," said Malock. "I wish to speak with him in person. There have been a lot of things happening recently that make me wish to talk with him."

"But this goes against tradition," said Hana. "I know you aren't exactly big on the whole 'honoring the gods' thing, but usually, it is the *gods* who seek out the *mortals*, not the other way around. It's considered rude if a mortal demands that a god meets with them."

"You're right," said Malock. "But so what? Skimif is my friend. I'm sure he would be perfectly fine with me coming to see him. All I want to do is talk. I don't see how that is unreasonable."

Hanarova stroked her chin in thought. "Well, I guess I *could* take you to Skimif. I mean, if anyone gets in trouble for it, it will almost certainly be you. But I'm afraid that I'll have to charge you for it."

"Whatever you want," said Malock, rubbing his hands together eagerly. "I can give you money or clothes or land or whatever you katabans desire most. I could even give you one of the rare specimens of plants that grow in this Garden. Name your price."

Hana smiled in a way that Malock didn't like. "Name my price, huh? That's awfully generous of a prince like you. Most princes are usually pretty stingy with their wealth."

"Wealth is unimportant compared to the knowledge that I seek from Skimif," said Malock. "Again, just name your price and I will make sure you get it after I speak to Skimif."

Hana began playing with strands of her hair, obviously stalling. "Will it be the very first thing you do after speaking to Skimif?"

"The very first thing," said Malock. "Father—when he was alive —always taught me to honor my promises. Being a man of integrity, I would never think to betray my promises unless I was absolutely incapable of fulfilling them. Even then, I would find a way to do it."

"Well, in that case, listen up," said Hana. She leaned forward slightly and said, "I just want to make sure you understand what I'm going to ask for. All right?"

"Yes, definitely," said Malock, crossing his arms. "Could you just get on with it? I want to go talk with Skimif now and I can't do that if I'm standing here negotiating with you."

"All right, all right," said Hana with a giggle. "You mortals can get pretty uptight sometimes, you know that?"

"Not nearly as uptight as the gods," said Malock. "Can you just name your price now?"

"Sure," said Hana. She put her hands behind her back and said, "In return for taking you to Skimif, you promise to court me."

At that moment, Malock's face began burning, but he was so stunned by Hana's price that, for the first time since receiving the Burn of Grinf, he was not bothered by it.

"Excuse me?" said Malock. "I don't believe I heard you correctly.

Did you say you wished to be made part of my court? If so, that is an unusual request, but I believe I can grant—"

"No, you don't understand me," said Hana. She pointed at herself, then pointed at Malock slowly, as if he was an idiot. "I, Hanarova, want you, Prince Malock, to court me. As in, romance, potentially ending in marriage, which would eventually be consummated in—"

"Okay, I get it," said Malock, holding up his hands. "But you can't be serious."

"Why wouldn't I be?" said Hana. "Sure, you and I haven't always gotten along, but I think we could smooth over those differences over a few romantic dinners, don't you think?"

"But ... why?" said Malock. His brain felt like it was frying. "Why would you ever ... I mean, why?"

"I've grown fond of you, Mal," said Hanarova, smiling at him. "And I've been getting tired of serving the Mechanical Goddess and I think she's been getting tired of me. Sooner or later we'll have to go our separate ways and I've been meaning to settle down, though I admit I always thought it would be with a nice male katabans. I suppose a rich mortal male will have to do."

"I ..." Malock looked at Friyu for help. "Friyu, what do you think?"

Friyu rubbed her old knuckles together. "I think, Prince Malock, that you should always be careful with the promises you make. Like your father always was."

"You're unhelpful," said Malock. Then he looked at Hana and said, "Hana, I mean, we're not even the same species. I'm human and

269

you're katabans. I don't even know how that would work."

"We could find a way to make it work," said Hana. "All I have to do is keep this physical body of mine and I don't think the physical side of things should be much of a problem."

"Let's not get ahead of ourselves now," said Malock, tugging at his collar. "Are you sure there's not something else you might want? Say, half of the treasury in the Carnagian Royal Vault? Your own mansion somewhere in the Konez Isles, perhaps?"

"Nope," said Hana, shaking her head. "If I marry you, then I'll get the other half as well. Anyway, I could pretend to be human if you needed me to. I've studied you humans long enough to be able to mimic your behaviors and attitudes very well."

"But ..." Malock struggled in vain to come up with a good argument. "I know. You katabans don't age, right? People will notice if I get older while you stay the same."

"Not really," said Hana. "Our physical bodies do age, just at a slightly slower rate than mortal bodies. I can always say that I use a lot of makeup or perhaps have a personal geromancer who keeps me looking youthful."

"Are you absolutely sure that this is what you want?" said Malock. "Because, as Prince of Carnag, there are a ton of other things I can give you. Why, I could order one of the factories to manufacture special, one-of-a-kind boots, made specially for your feet, that you can't get anywhere else."

"Boots bore me," said Hana. "I'd much rather have you. And that is my final offer. Take it or leave it."

"But—"

"But hey, it's no big deal if you say no," said Hana with a shrug, turning around. "I mean, it's not like I'm the only way you could possibly score a meeting with Skimif. Nah, you're pretty smart. You'll figure out a way to talk to Skimif even without me. I'll just go back to Stalf and see if I can be more useful to the Mechanical Goddess. Or maybe I could look to see if the other gods need help."

"No, wait," said Malock, holding up one hand. "All right. After I speak to Skimif and find out what I wish to know, I'll ... court you."

Hana whirled around, her face alight with the widest smile Malock had ever seen on a woman's face. "Great! We can leave right away. We'll travel via the ethereal. Should be quick."

With dread creeping up his spine, Malock turned to Friyu and said, "Before we go, tell Mother I have gone to talk to Skimif."

"But Your Majesty," said Friyu, "how long will you be gone? Will you be back in time for your coronation?"

"Yes, I will," said Malock. "I don't intend to be gone long. I'll try to be back before morning."

"After our first night out together," Hana added.

Malock grimaced. "Yes, after that. Just make sure Mother knows I am safe and that I'll be back well before the Royal Event Organizer even sets one foot in Carnag Hall."

"Yes, Your Majesty," said Friyu, bowing her head. "If I may ask, what exactly are you going to ask Skimif about?"

Malock looked up at the sky. "A lot of things, Friyu, things which may very well affect the lives of every person not only on Carnag, but in all of the Northern Isles."

Chapter Sixteen

NIJOK WIRM HURLED A ball of smoke at Jenur. Jenur ducked to avoid the ball, which exploded against the bookshelf behind her, sending dozens of books falling to the floor as she rolled back to her feet.

Wirm didn't miss a beat. He drew a throwing star from his pocket and hurled it directly at Jenur with the speed of a bullet. Jenur tried to dodge this, but her body was still recovering from the coma, thus slowing her down, and allowing the star to cut through her right shoulder. Hot pain burned her shoulder as it bled, but she didn't let the pain get to her. She just ran away from Wirm, heading for the table, but before she could reach it, a cloud of smoke passed over her and the next moment Wirm stood before her, his knuckles held high above him.

"You cannot escape me, girl," said Wirm. "Die!"

He brought his fists down on her head, but Jenur jumped back to avoid getting hit. The Grand Tiger's fists smashed into the floor, actually cracking it. With his guard down, Jenur lashed out with a kick, striking the Grand Tiger directly in the nose with her foot and causing him to roar in pain as her boot smashed his nose.

As Wirm grabbed at his nose, his vision obscured by his tears and blood, Jenur brought the heel of her other boot up. She aimed for his face, but then Wirm suddenly caught her boot before it could hit him and grasped it with surprising firmness.

"Good ... good hit, girl," said Wirm, his voice somewhat distorted by his broken nose. "But not good enough."

He lifted her up by her leg and threw her against the far right wall. Jenur flew through the air, twisting and turning her body, trying to stop her trajectory, but then she slammed into the bookshelf and fell to the floor, stunned. The impact of her body crashing against the bookshelf caused books—heavy, thick tomes—to fall on her, smashing into her face and crushing her breasts under their heavy covers. One book fell on her bleeding shoulder, causing more blood to come out and even more pain to flow to her brain.

Gasping from the pain, trying to recover as quickly as she could, Jenur looked up in time to see Wirm running toward her, his massive feet causing the floor to shake. There was murder in his eyes, pure murder, and Jenur knew that she perhaps had only a few seconds left unless she did something.

So Jenur began pushing the books off her body, but she couldn't do it fast enough. The books were heavier than boulders, or so it seemed, and with her right shoulder still bleeding, she really only had her left hand to move the books with. She realized quickly enough that she wouldn't be able to escape, but that didn't stop her from trying.

Wirm was almost within arm's reach now, but before he reached her, a bolt of light struck Wirm in the side. The blow sent him staggering to his left, hitting him so hard that he actually fell flat onto his back, for a moment stunned by the blow.

Surprised, Jenur looked in the direction the bolt had come from and saw Braim standing in front of the Magical Superior. His right hand was still bleeding and useless, but his left hand was not, which was the hand in which he held his wand. He looked like he was in supreme pain, but he didn't seem at all likely to sit down and give up.

Wirm was recovering by now. He sat up, rubbing the side of his body where Braim had hit him, looking at his son with pure hatred in his eyes.

"So you decide to stand and fight me anyway?" said Wirm. "Perhaps you are less of a disappointment than I thought, my so-called 'son.'"

"You aren't my father," said Braim. "And I'm not your son. I'm going to kill you where you stand. The world will be a safer place without you."

Wirm sighed. "I was hoping to deal with you *after* I dealt with Jenur, but I suppose some people just cannot wait for their turn to die. That is appropriate for you, since you are a necromancer, after all."

"Die!" Braim shouted as he fired another light bolt at Wirm, but the bolt never hit Wirm because at that moment Wirm transformed into a cloud of smoke, allowing the light bolt to pass harmlessly through his form.

The cloud of smoke that was Wirm hovered over to Braim, crossing the distance between them in less than three seconds. Braim aimed his wand wildly, but without a clear target to hit, it didn't matter where he pointed the thing. The cloud descended over his body, becoming so thick and so gray that soon Braim was completely lost inside it.

"Braim!" Jenur shouted, but it was impossible to tell if Braim could hear her or not. "Braim! Are you still alive?" Braim!"

The only answer she received was the sound of someone hacking and coughing from within the cloud. It took her only a moment to realize that it was Braim who was hacking and coughing and he sounded like he was getting worse and worse with each passing second.

Wirm's trying to choke him, Jenur thought. *He's filling Braim's lungs with smoke. He'll be dead within minutes.*

The thought prompted Jenur to push the books off her body faster. All the while, Braim continued to hack and cough. An occasional burst of light would shine from within the cloud, but the smoke cloud didn't get thinner; in fact, it thickened, becoming almost as solid as a wall.

Just hang in there a little while longer, Braim, Jenur thought as she shoved the books off herself. *Just a little while longer and—*

As she pushed the last of the books off her body, Jenur sat up and realized that there was nothing she could do to save Braim. She had no magic which to use to blow away the smoke, nor could she run in there and try to save him herself. All she could do was get to her feet and stand there, watching as the gaps of time between Braim's hacking and wheezing grew longer and longer until, finally, Braim went silent. Something fell to the floor with a *clunk*, prompting the smoke to pass away, revealing a sight Jenur would never forget.

Braim had collapsed onto the floor. His clothes were blackened and distorted from the smoke. His face had burn marks all over it. His hand no longer bleed because the wound had been burnt shut. His body didn't move at all, though his fingers were still curled tightly around his wand.

Wirm's form rematerialized a few feet away from Braim. That same smile—that ugly, horrible, evil smile—was etched across Wirm's face, while the Magical Superior, who had still not moved from his spot, looked down at his dead pupil with horror in his eyes. The Magical Superior had both hands on his wand, but it was clear that that was merely a symbolic gesture.

"That is what happens to those who cross the path of the Grand Tiger," said Wirm, smoke trailing from his lips, "even if they are family, though to be honest, I never considered that fool my real son. His mother was a whore."

Jenur could barely believe her eyes. She wanted Braim to get up and continue fighting, but his body was so still and Wirm was so confident that she knew it was a fool's hope. No one could have survived something like that, not even a mage like Braim. Wirm was too professional to spare him.

"But do not worry, brother," said Wirm, glancing at the Magical Superior. "You may keep his body and give him a proper burial once I am finished with the kitten here. It does not matter one whit to me what you do or don't do with his body."

The Magical Superior looked up at his brother, his old frame trembling with anger. "You killed your own son, my nephew, my pupil, because he chose to stand against you."

Wirm smirked. "I have always been ruthless, brother. Don't you remember what I did to our teacher? Family means nothing to me if that same family has betrayed the ideals I stand for."

"What ideals *do* you stand for, brother?" said the Magical Superior. "I see no ideals. I only see the ruthless, animalistic behavior of a beast pretending to be a man."

Wirm chuckled. "What do I care? You can't harm me. The gods have protected me from you. It's rather funny when you think about it. You have spent your whole life devoted to the teachings of the gods while I have spent my whole life rejecting those same teachings, and yet it is I who the gods favor. Irony does not even begin to describe the situation."

"I do not always understand the gods," said the Magical Superior. "But there is one thing I *do* understand, and it is that you risk the wrath of the gods by murdering innocents."

"Brother, I have spent decades doing far worse things than killing a bastard son in cold blood," said Wirm, "and yet the gods have not so much as slapped my hand for it. I am not afraid of facing the consequences for my crimes when it is clear that the gods do not care to punish me."

"Your villainous behavior will catch up to you one of these days, Nijok," said the Magical Superior, his lips trembling. "And when it does, you will remember my words."

Wirm chuckled. "Moralize to me all you wish, brother, but without the action to back it up, I see no reason to fear your petty words. This is always how it has been, ever since we were children.

You were always the weaker child, completely incapable of doing anything other than threatening to tell mommy and daddy when I was doing something I wasn't supposed to. You have not changed one bit since then."

The Magical Superior lowered his eyes. "If the gods were not restraining me, you would not be so boastful."

Wirm's smile didn't wither. "And then I would kill you and no longer have to suffer the embarrassment of having a weakling such as you for a brother. Anyway, this is getting nowhere. I have a cat to skin and then I must return to Ruwa and make sure that the other Tigers have not burned down the Den in my absence."

Wirm turned away from the Magical Superior and looked at Jenur. He cracked his knuckles again as he said, "Now, kitten, it is time that I once and for all put an end to the pathetic existence you call a life. Because I am in a hurry, I shall take your life speedily. This way, you will not have to undergo a painful, drawn-out death and I will not have to waste my time killing you."

Jenur hands shook. "Maybe it's your own death that will be short, Wirm."

"Threatening me? Again?" said Wirm. "Please. You cannot even touch me. You are completely unarmed and know not a whit of magic. You are wounded. And then there are the emotional scars no doubt tearing at your psyche, probably making it impossible for you to concentrate on your own survival. The odds are against you."

"Maybe so," said Jenur. "But I've faced terrible odds before and survived. I'm not the weak little kitten you think I am."

"The kitten has fangs," said Wirm. "Or at least wants me to

believe that it does. But enough talking. Allow me to finish you once and for all."

Wirm's body began unraveling, turning into smoke, until soon his whole body was nothing more than a smoke cloud. Jenur took a fighting stance, even though she knew that it was fruitless. She couldn't hit smoke. In all likelihood, she would end up exactly like Braim, maybe even worse, because Wirm hated her so much.

I'll just have to go down fighting, Jenur thought. *I guess dying might not be so bad. I'll get to see Dad again, and maybe even Kinker, too.*

The smoke cloud hovered in the air, right above where Wirm had stood, for only a brief moment. Then it shot toward Jenur, hurtling through the air at a surprising speed. She could already smell its horrid scent, could already feel its heat burning her eyes, but Jenur stood her ground as firmly as a mountain.

Then, without warning, a large, purplish net of energy appeared behind the cloud of smoke. The net clamped down on the smoke cloud, wrapping around it so tightly that the cloud could not move an inch. The smoke cloud struggled against the net, but it was clear that the smoke could not escape no matter how hard it tried.

Before Jenur's startled eyes, the smoke cloud started to take a different shape. Slowly but surely, the smoke cloud grew arms, legs, and a head, and in another few seconds the cloud was gone, replaced once again by the formidable, though now highly confused-looking, body of Nijok Wirm.

"What the hell—?" said Wirm, looking down at his body. "What was that? Why am I back to my normal body? Brother?"

Wirm whirled around and Jenur, her body no longer rigid, looked around Wirm's form to see Braim holding his wand, aiming it directly at Wirm. Braim was still lying on the floor, but he had propped himself up with his right arm while holding up his left arm as straight as an arrow. Despite the obvious physical effort that that minor movement took, Braim was smiling like a madman.

"You," said Wirm, pointing at Braim. "What did you do? I thought you were dead."

Braim hacked and coughed like a congested engine. "Form lock spell. Useful for shape-shifters like you, you old bastard. Knew it would come in handy if I ever ran into you again."

Wirm punched his fist forward, obviously expecting to send a ball of smoke or something worse at Braim, but absolutely nothing happened. Wirm tried again and again, but the only thing he succeeded in doing was make himself look like a fool.

"Magic negation spell, too," Braim said. His voice was incredibly hoarse, barely audible, but somehow understandable. "You lose."

"You son of a whore," said Wirm. "I will kill you. I will rip you limb from limb. I will burn you into ashes and burn your ashes into ashes. I will desecrate your grave and dump the remains of your body into the toilet. I will—"

"Wouldn't waste your time cursing me," said Braim, a smile on his lips very much like Wirm's. "Might want to look behind you."

Jenur immediately took that as her cue. Scooping up the throwing star that Wirm had thrown at her, Jenur ran at Wirm as fast as she could, ignoring the pain flaring in her right shoulder.

Wirm turned, but far more slowly than he normally did, as

though his body was slower than it usually was. Instinctively, Wirm reached for one of his pockets, but Jenur didn't let his fingers so much as touch one of the flaps. She threw the throwing star, her aim straight and true, with all of the might she could muster, at Wirm's throat.

The star flew through the air, flashing in the light of the Superior's study, and lodged itself deep into Wirm's throat. Wirm's eyes widened, a gagging, choking sound emitted from his mouth like that of a dying beast, and he collapsed onto the floor like a rag doll. Blood trickled from his throat, slowly pooling around his still head. He twitched once or twice, but then he stopped entirely.

Panting, her right arm hurting like crazy, Jenur put her hands on her knees and wiped the sweat off her forehead. *It's over. Wirm is dead. Quro is avenged.*

She was so tired that she just wanted to fall down and sleep, but she didn't. Instead, she dragged herself over to where Braim now lay. She wasn't the only one to do that. The Magical Superior had gotten up from his pillows and was making his way over to Braim, his bare feet seemingly gliding across the surface of the study floor.

Both Jenur and the Magical Superior reached Braim at the same time. Not that it mattered, however, because Braim had fallen back down and didn't seem to be breathing at all.

"Braim," said Jenur. She looked up at the Magical Superior, who had bent over Braim with his wand in both hands. "Can you save him?"

"I will try," said the Magical Superior, his hands shaking as much as his voice. "But I cannot guarantee anything. My brother—no, the beast—must have damaged his lungs beyond repair. I am surprised Braim had enough strength for even a simple form-lock spell, much less a magic negation spell. Please steady my arms."

Jenur nodded and reached over for his arms. They were as thin as sticks, and felt like them when she wrapped her fingers around them. Nonetheless, she summoned the strength to still them, causing the Magical Superior to say, "Thank you," as he focused on Braim's body.

Blue lights emitted from the wand, bright orbs that trailed up and down Braim's body. Not being a panamancer, Jenur didn't know what those orbs did or were supposed to do. She just hoped that they would somehow heal Braim. She didn't know what she'd do if he died.

The Magical Superior's face was impassive. The best she could tell was that he was concentrating deeply, so deeply that Jenur almost held her own breath out of fear that her breathing might break his focus. The faint, bitter smell of smoke rose from Braim's corpse, making Jenur want to cough, but she held it in because she didn't want to make any unnecessary noise.

Then the blue orbs returned to the Magical Superior's wand and he sat back. Jenur, sensing that he wanted her to let go, did so, but leaned in a little to get a better look at his face, hoping to see some sign of good news in his expression.

But when the Magical Superior looked up at her, she saw only sadness and depression.

"I am so sorry, Jenur Takren," said the Magical Superior, tears starting to form in his own eyes. "But I am afraid that Braim is dead."

Chapter Seventeen

ENTERING THE ETHEREAL WAS one of the most unreal experiences Malock had ever felt in his entire life. And that was saying something, because Malock had experienced many strange things in his life.

Before they entered the ethereal, Hana had made sure Malock was holding her hand tight. She said it was important that they stick together while in the ethereal, mostly because she didn't want to lose her potential future 'husband,' but also because this was the first time she had ever taken a mortal into the ethereal and so she had no idea what might happen. She said that she didn't think Malock would get hurt or anything but that Malock ought to stick close to her anyway just to be safe.

When Malock agreed to that, Hana told him to take a step forward with her in unison to ensure that both of them made it into the ethereal together. After a few practice tries to make sure they were both in sync, they took exactly one step forward into the air around them.

That was when things got strange. Carnag Hall, the Protection reflecting the setting sun, the Royal Garden, the noises and sounds of Port Blasan ... all of that faded into nothingness, gradually replaced with a long, wide, seemingly endless white road that stretched out into what appeared to be a starry night sky for as far as the eye could see.

Malock gasped when he first set foot on the shiny white road. In the sky above and below the road, dozens of stars, constellations in the shapes of gods, stars colored red and blue and green and many other colors, shone almost like miniature suns. Large white islands were just off to the sides of the road, appearing to be made out of the same substance as the road itself. That was when it occurred to Malock that he had see this white material before. It was the same kind of stone that paved the streets of the Throne of the Gods, except far brighter.

Malock and Hana were not alone on the road. Dozens of other beings—probably other katabans—walked along the road, some moving forward, others walking in the opposite direction, but none of them stopped to look at Malock or Hana. The katabans did not look anything like any katabans Malock had ever seen before. All of them glowed pure white, glowing so brightly that it was impossible to look directly at them without hurting one's eyes. They resembled moving spheres of light.

Confused, Malock looked at Hana to ask her why this was when he almost jumped. One of those very same orbs was standing next to him, holding his hand exactly the same way that Hana had. The proximity of the orb's light forced him to look away, though it did nothing to quench his curiosity.

"Hana, what the hell is going on here?" said Malock, holding up his other hand to protect his vision. "Why are you glowing like that?"

Hana's voice chuckled from within the ball. "This? This is my true form, Mal. When katabans are on the ethereal, we are forced to travel in our true appearances."

Still not looking at her, Malock said, "But why?"

"It's quicker this way," said Hana. "Our mortal forms aren't practical for travel on the ethereal. These forms are, since they're much lighter and don't have things like feet and shoes to get in the way."

"I see," said Malock. "But what *is* the ethereal, anyway?"

"A layer underneath the world," said Hana. "Or above it. Not sure, to be honest, since I've never bothered to learn its exact location in relation to the rest of Martir. It's how we katabans can travel all over Martir so quickly. The ethereal is connected to every location on Martir. Even the gods sometimes use it."

"Does it go on forever?" said Malock, looking down the road as far as he could see.

"No," said Hana. "It loops around, actually. It may look like a long, straight road, but in reality it is closer to a circle. A really, really big circle."

Malock looked around the place with a frown on his face. "How do you navigate it? Everything looks the same to me."

"Your mortal eyes must be deceiving you, then, because everything looks quite different to me," said Hana. "Or maybe, because mortals were never supposed to use the ethereal, your eyes are showing you only what they can process. Who knows? More importantly, who cares?"

"Very well," said Malock. "I guess it doesn't matter what everything looks like to me. You can tell the difference between things, so you can just lead me to Skimif."

"Of course," said Hana. "Hold on tight. We're going to go fast."

Malock made sure to redouble his grip on Hana's hand, and just in time, because Hana zoomed forward at breakneck speed. Malock jerked along behind her, struggling to keep himself from stumbling over his feet just barely. He had always known Hana could move much faster than any mortal, but he hadn't expected her to run this fast in the ethereal. They swerved in and around the various other katabans, some of whom seemed to finally take notice of Malock if their stares were any indication (although as everyone looked like big balls of light to Malock, he wasn't even sure they were staring at him).

Then Malock saw something black coming at them from the corner of his eye. He tried to turn his head to see what it was, but then the thing slammed into them with enough strength to cause Malock to let go of Hana's hand involuntarily. He reached for her hand as they were separated, but she was still moving too fast and didn't seem to notice that he had let go.

Malock slammed into the shining white road of the ethereal, landing on his right shoulder and rolling with the impact. He accidentally knocked over the legs of another katabans, who began shouting at him in some language Malock didn't know, and kept rolling until he reached the edge of the road. Malock scrambled to find a handhold, anything to grab onto, but the road was perfectly smooth and in the next moment he fell off the edge into the abyss below.

But Malock didn't fall forever. All around him, the ethereal faded and morphed, just like how Carnag had changed into the ethereal when he had entered it. The shining white road vanished, along with the stars and katabans, and Malock landed on a hard stone floor flat on his back.

The air knocked out of his lungs from the impact, Malock gasped. His vision was fuzzy and his head was spinning. He did not think he had fallen very far, but he felt like he had been drop-kicked off the side of a building. His stomach grumbled, like he was about to throw up, but he held down his lunch as he shook his head and cleared his vision.

What happened? Malock thought. *Where am I? What attacked us?*

When Malock's vision finally cleared, he found himself staring up at a dark, cloudy sky through a large hole in an old stone ceiling. Thunder rumbled in the distance, while a cold, unfriendly breeze blew through the area, cutting through Malock's funeral robes like a knife. His teeth chattering, Malock slowly sat up to get a better look at his surroundings.

From what Malock could see, he was sitting in what appeared to be the ruins of a temple of sorts. Single stone pillars, made of a black stone he couldn't identify, rose from the earth to support a ceiling that no longer existed. Some of the walls still stood, with faded carvings on them that Malock couldn't see due to the bad lighting. The stone floor underneath him was cracked, but he could just barely make out, through the dust and dirt, what looked like paintings that might have once been beautiful works of art but which were now unrecognizable.

The oddest feature of all, however, was the horse-headed man sitting in the throne opposite him. Then Malock blinked and he realized that the 'man' was actually a statue, made of the same black rock that the rest of the ruins were made of. But it looked so real that Malock was afraid to touch it for fear of it coming to life and throttling him.

"Like Master Hollech's statue?" said a voice behind him, one Malock thought familiar but which he did not recognize right away. "Crafted by the Divine Carvers eons ago, back when Master Hollech was still considered a respectable name in mortal circles, it is truly a work of art, albeit not one appreciated by most mortals."

Malock whirled around and spotted a stout, bald-headed man with a wide, monkey-like smile standing not far from him. The man wore old brown robes, but his feet were completely bare. He looked like a homeless person, but something about his appearance told Malock that this man was no harmless beggar.

"Who are you?" said Malock. "And why am I in a temple that is obviously dedicated to Hollech?"

"*Was* dedicated to Hollech," the man corrected. "But I suppose it still is, in a way, because none of the other gods or their followers have tried to lay claim to it since it was abandoned so long ago. Not that Master Hollech would allow them to, of course."

Malock rubbed his eyes and looked more closely at the man. "Wait a minute. You look like the sweeper from Rane who I spoke to a week ago. The one in the Garden of the Gods."

"You remembered!" said the man in false excitement. "Oh, I am so honored. I thought that, in all of the excitement that followed your father's death, you would have forgotten about little old me. I have been told that I make an impression on people, so this makes sense."

"But I don't understand," said Malock. "What are you doing here? Who are you, really?"

"Call me Ramufa the Nimble-Fingered," said the man. "Master thief, freelancer on the side, and the protege of Master Hollech himself."

"Ramufa," Malock repeated. "I think Jenur told me about someone named Ramufa once."

"No surprise there," said Ramufa. "I was the one, after all, who killed Princess Raya, your potential wife-to-be, and framed Jenur for it. I can't see her forgetting me so easily after that."

"So *you're* the one who killed Raya," said Malock. "Once I return to Carnag, I'll be sure to place a bounty on your head and tell King Fabadi who really killed her."

"That will be completely unnecessary, Prince Tojas Malock," said a voice behind Malock, a voice that caused him to freeze. "Ramufa here already has at least six different bounties on his head from various nations for various crimes he has committed. There is no need to add another, in my humble opinion."

Malock slowly turned around, even though he didn't trust Ramufa at all. He lay his eyes on the stone statue of Hollech that had been sitting there, but which now was not a statue at all. A man sat there, a man wearing the same red and golden robes that Father had; in fact, the man *was* Father. His eyes glittered with malevolent intent and he sat with one leg brought over the other, but besides that, he looked almost exactly like Father.

"F-Father?" said Malock. "No way. You're dead."

Father frowned. "Saw right through me, did you? I suppose it makes sense that you did. I should have chosen a better disguise. Maybe I should have been Princess Raya. Or … what was his name? Kinker Dolan. Possibly even Vashnas."

Malock grit his teeth. He had never met this god before, but he soon figured out who it really was. "Drop the games, Hollech, God of Deception, Thieves, and Horses."

Father sighed, but soon his entire body began to melt off him. It was a disgusting, gut-wrenching sight, watching as Father's clothes, skin, and hair flowed down Hollech's body like lava, entering a couple of vents located near the throne like rainwater in a city after a storm. When the last of it had passed away, a new figure sat in Hollech's throne.

A strong, muscular man, wearing a dark coat that was the same shade of black as the stone throne in which he sat, reclined before Malock. His shoes appeared to be made of fine silk, like the kind worn by the Three Queens of Nikos. Yet it was his head that drew Malock's attention, because it was not the head of a man, but the head of a horse, complete with flowing mane, though his eyes were the eyes of a being far more intelligent—and infinitely more malevolent—than any horse could be.

"How did you know it was me?" said Hollech. "I thought for sure my disguise would have fooled you. Being the God of Deception, I know best how to deceive people, especially gullible mortals like you."

"Easy," said Malock. He gestured at the ruins. "This is your temple and Ramufa is your servant. I am no Hollechian myself, but even I can tell what kind of temple a god like you would inhabit. That, and there was a statue of yourself sitting in that throne, so I knew it had to be you pretending to be my father."

Hollech whinnied like a horse, which might have been his way of chuckling. "Very astute. I must have underestimated your cleverness. I will make sure not to do that again, no worries there."

Malock looked over his shoulder at Ramufa, who had not moved an inch from his original position, and then turned to look back at Hollech. "Did you bring me here?"

"Yes," said Hollech. "'Twas I who attacked you and my sister's servant as you were going on your merry little way to speak with Skimif. Normally I make a point of working through Ramufa or, on occasion, a particularly gullible katabans, but I thought this particular task far too important to hand over to a mere servant. When you want something done right, you must do it yourself, as I always say."

"Where are we?" said Malock. "I didn't know you had a temple. I was always told that Hollechians never had temples because people always vandalized them or tore them down."

Hollech spread his arms around. "It was not always that way, Prince Malock. Long ago—well before you were born, well before even your father was born—the rocky, mountainous island of Chinchia was home to the largest cult of Hollechians that history has ever seen. To honor me, they built this temple on the highest mountain on the island, Mount Holl. They worshiped me here by setting up elaborate deceptions to fool one another, including one memorable deception in which one Hollechian convinced his father that he was actually dead. Good times."

Hollech spoke of it like it had happened yesterday, though it had to have been at least a hundred years ago if the god was telling the truth.

"But alas, my followers have always been on rocky terms with the followers of my siblings," said Hollech, lowering his arms onto the arms of the throne. "The followers of my brother Delok, the God of the Sky, were highly offended that my temple had been built much closer to the sky than the temple they had built for Delok. So the Delokians got together and slaughtered all of my followers and ransacked this temple of mine. Not-so-good times."

"I've never heard of that story," said Malock. "How do I know you're not lying?"

"I don't expect you to believe it," said Hollech. "Besides, I haven't even finished it yet. Anyway, after the Delokians killed the last Hollechian, a terrible disease suddenly broke out among them and in less than a month after committing their unforgivable crime against my followers, all of the Delokians died out. To this day, Chinchia is completely uninhabited, shunned and avoided by every other nation in the Northern Isles because of the killer illness that has no cure."

"Did you spread the illness among the Delokians?" said Malock.

"Maybe," said Hollech. "Maybe not. I'll let you decide. The point is, I've since used Chinchia as my primary base of operations, because no one ever comes here—under the mistaken belief that that killer illness is still around—a deception I have always used to my advantage. I brought you here so you couldn't speak to Skimif."

"But why?" said Malock. "I still don't understand. Why don't you want me to speak to Skimif?"

Hollech steepled his fingers, which Malock now noticed looked less like human fingers and more like a weird combination of human fingers and horse hooves. "Because then you would mess up the plan that I and several of my siblings have been carefully orchestrating over the past two months. We have worked very hard, you know, planting false evidence to ensure that the mortals follow exactly the path we want them to follow, and I will not even think of allowing you to ruin it before I want it to be ruined."

"What plan?" said Malock. "I have no idea what's going on here at all. I didn't even know you had anything to do with ... well, whatever is going on here."

"That is precisely why I had to bring you here," said Hollech. "Ignorance is both a handy tool and a dangerous weapon, depending on how it was used. For a while I used the ignorance of easily-provoked mortals like Fabadi as a tool to instill fear and uncertainty in the minds of the Northern Isles' leaders, but you began to use your own ignorance as a weapon to find out what was going on when you asked Hanarova to take you to Skimif. So I had to break that weapon so it could not be used against me."

"Fabadi?" said Malock. "Wait, are you saying that you've been manipulating everyone?"

"Bingo," said Hollech, clapping his hands together, which sounded like an odd mixture between the sound of clapping human hands and galloping horse hooves. "You are just so smart, aren't you? Almost as smart as Ramufa."

Ramufa stepped out of the shadows on Hollech's right. Startled, Malock looked over his shoulder and saw that Ramufa was indeed no longer standing where he used to. That made Malock wonder just how fast Ramufa could move.

"But why have you been manipulating everyone, Hollech?" said Malock, turning back to face the god. "What do you hope to gain from instilling fear and uncertainty in everyone? Don't you realize what might happen because of you?"

"I know exactly what will happen if my plan goes off without a hitch," said Hollech. "Otherwise, I wouldn't be doing it. I expect to see mortals raging against the gods, against Skimif, and to show Skimif that we gods—both northern and southern—are not so easily bossed around by an upstart like him."

"Wait," said Malock. "Are you saying that you're trying to get us mortals to hate Skimif?"

"You finally figured it out," said Hollech, once more clapping his hands together. "Yes, yes, that is exactly what I hope to do. I hope to make every mortal on Martir fear Skimif, to think of him as a malicious tyrant who deceived the Powers themselves into giving him power far greater than even we gods possess. And this plan of mine is working splendidly, based on what Ramufa and the others have told me."

Malock shoved his hands into his robes and pulled out Skimif's letter. He held it up in front of Hollech, his arm trembling as he said, "Did you forge this letter?"

"Ramufa did, actually," said Hollech, patting Ramufa on the head. "He is a master forger, but I did make a few tweaks to make sure that no one would notice its falsehood. I'm glad to see my sister made sure you got it."

"You mean the Chaotic Goddess?" said Malock. "She's working with you?"

"Of course," said Hollech. "This is no one-god plan. I had to enlist the help of several of my siblings who were also unhappy with Skimif's ascension to pull it off. All of us share one thing in common: Our hatred of Skimif and our belief that he is completely undeserving of the power and authority which the Powers gave to him, a truth we hold to be self-evident."

"How many of you are there?" said Malock.

"Just the right amount," said Hollech. "And our plan is simple: Cause a lot of chaos, fear, and uncertainty, make sure it all appears to be the doing of Skimif and the southern gods, make sure to divide the mortals into those who support Skimif and those who not, and then kick back and enjoy the spectacle as mortals kill each other while Skimif helplessly watches on."

"That is utterly insane," said Malock. "You are crazy. A mad god, worse than any southern god I've ever met."

"Why would you say that?" said Hollech. "I would say it is an excellent plan that is working quite well so far. Wouldn't you say so, Ramufa?"

"Yes, Master," said Ramufa, nodding. "Aside from a few minor hiccups, the plan is the most devious plan I have ever heard Master Hollech create. It will truly set the standards for deceptive plans for the rest of the age."

"Of course it will," said Hollech. "I am the God of Deception, after all."

"It's not excellent because it's insane," said Malock. "You are deceiving us mortals to get us to kill each other. And for what reason? You hate Skimif because you don't like being bossed around? To me, you sound more like an undisciplined child than a god."

"You make our motivation sound so simplistic, but it is far deeper than that," said Hollech, shaking his head. "Believe me, as a northern god, I take no delight in watching mortals fight and kill each other. It truly pains my immortal heart to see that. I would rather all mortals unite under worship of us northern gods—specifically, me, but I am willing to share with my siblings—than war amongst each other, but I believe that in the long run, this will be completely necessary, in light of recent events."

"Are you saying that the ends justify the means?" said Malock. "That there is a greater good that we can only reach with short-term evil?"

"Exactly," said Hollech. "I am so glad you are catching on. I hate having to explain things, so the more you figure it out, the less explaining I have to do."

"This is still not right," said Malock. "The Powers gave Skimif his power not because he tricked them or anything, but because they had already been intending to make him a god and only made him the god of this world, rather than the new world they were planning to build on the ruins of this one, because I succeeded in convincing them to spare us."

"I am well aware of that," said Hollech. "But you know, unlike some of my siblings, I've never thought that the Powers were all-wise and all-knowing. I believed they could make mistakes, just like the rest of us, and in this instance, I believe they have made a huge mistake in giving a mortal so much power. What if Skimif becomes corrupt? What if he is incompetent?"

"He won't be and he isn't," said Malock. "But anyway, even if your plan works, how will this affect Skimif? He'll still be the God of Martir. At most, this will cause a slight disturbance in the world for a while, but I'm sure things will eventually settle down."

"True," said Hollech. "I admit that part of the fun comes from watching you mortals declare how you are going to stand against Skimif and the southern gods, how you are so totally unafraid of them, and so on. The Chaotic Goddess told me Fabadi's message and I must say that, while it was exactly what I was hoping for, it was also hilarious."

"I wish I could have been there to see it," said Ramufa. "Unfortunately, Master Hollech had me doing other things at the time. Was it funny?"

Malock thought back to Fabadi giving the Chaotic Goddess his message and shook his head. "No, it was not funny. It's even less humorous now that I know you all have been manipulating him."

"You must not have a very good sense of humor, then," said Hollech. "Typical of you mortals. Well, the point is, the mortals themselves don't need to be successful in overthrowing Skimif. The plan is to cause so much disruption and so much chaos under Skimif's rule that the Powers notice and come back to see what has happened. The Powers will discover that all of this is because of Skimif's incompetence, will strip him of his powers, and then restore the original egalitarian system that governed us gods in the old days."

"You want to bring the Powers back?" said Malock. "No way. Even if they do return, aren't you afraid they will find out that you and the other gods are the true culprits? What's to stop Skimif from telling them?"

"It will be very hard for Skimif to prove that," said Hollech. "Mostly because Skimif himself is too busy right now to stop us or get every little clue he needs to prove his case. Even if he succeeds, the Powers may well decide that he isn't competent enough to rule over us, and take away his powers anyway. It's a win-win situation no matter how you look at it."

"Unless the Powers don't return," said Malock. "They told me that they were busy creating their new world. I highly doubt that they are paying much attention to this one."

Hollech looked mildly surprised, but said, "I already knew that. But I also happen to know that the Powers have an agent in this world who keeps them informed of recent happenings. I have no idea who this agent is, but surely they will notice everything falling apart under Skimif's rule and then go and tell the Powers, which might eventually lead to the Powers' return."

"You're planning on a lot of things you can't control," said Malock. "What will you do if your plan fails?"

Hollech once more tapped the tips of his fingertips together, making that odd little clopping sound again. "Then I guess I will simply have to face the consequences for my actions. At the very least, I will have destroyed any hopes of Skimif building trust in the hearts of the mortals, which is good enough, I suppose."

"I cannot believe this," said Malock, slapping his forehead. "Wait, yes, I can. You gods have shown yourselves to be this petty before. I should not have expected the God of Deception to be that much better."

"I am flattered," said Hollech. "As I god, I always make sure to go out of my way to be as petty as possible. After all, ensuring that our world is not governed by a farmer with little-to-no experience in divine governance is rather petty, isn't it?"

Hollech said that with so much sarcasm that Malock thought he might better be called the God of Sarcasm than the God of Deception.

"What are you going to do with me?" said Malock. "Kill me? Or just leave me here until your little plan succeeds?"

"I would certainly enjoy seeing you die," said Hollech. "You have a history of showing blatant disrespect to the gods, northern and southern, and I think all of my siblings—save perhaps the Mechanical Goddess and Nimiko, though to be honest, none of us really like either of them since they helped you convince the Powers to ascend Skimif—would be quite happy if they knew you were dead."

"We could kill him just like his father," Ramufa suggested, rubbing his hands together eagerly. "Give him a terrible disease and watch him die."

"You know how my father died?" said Malock.

"Of course," said Ramufa. "I was there, after all, in the Garden of the Gods. I was the sweeper you spoke to. Master Hollech had sent me to ensure that King Halock, your father, died of the disease that we had given him."

Malock's eyes widened. "You killed my father?"

"Yes," said Hollech, nodding. "Well, technically, it wasn't I who did it. One of my siblings, the Diseased God, God of Illness, did it, since he's just as upset at Skimif's ascension as I am. All part of the plan, you see."

"Fabadi was right," said Malock. "Father *was* assassinated. You monsters."

"We thought it would help push you toward distrusting Skimif," said Hollech. "After all, I know how much you mortals care about your parents. I believed that if your father died of some kind of unknown disease under Skimif's watch, it might shake your confidence in your old friend, but I was apparently wrong about that."

Hearing Hollech speak so calmly about killing Father was more than Malock could handle. He bent over, grabbed a chunk of temple debris lying on the ground before him, and hurled it directly at Hollech with all of his might.

But then a hand appeared in the air, caught the debris chunk, and vanished. Shocked, Malock wondered where it went until Ramufa held up the chunk in his right hand.

"No throwing things," said Ramufa. "Didn't your father teach you that it's not polite to throw things, even at people you don't like?"

"I would guess not, Ramufa," said Hollech. "Prince Malock is certainly little more than an oversized child. And like a child, he often gets himself involved in things which he does not understand."

"I understand well enough what is going on here," said Malock.

"You're creating a false problem for the sole purpose of getting rid of someone you don't like. You're just a ... a politician, except worse because you're a god and gods are supposed to be better than mortal politicians."

"I would argue that mortal politicians are far more representative of us gods and our behavior than any priests or monks are," said Hollech. "But that is a debate for another day. Ramufa? Tell me how things are going in Shika."

"Very well, Master Hollech," said Ramufa. "King Fabadi has already sent messengers to every nation that participated in this year's Northern Summit. Not only that, but he's even scrambled the Shikan Army and Navy."

"Excellent," said Hollech. He returned his attention to Malock, a malicious grin on his equine lips. "Everything is going according to plan. I just need to keep this deception going on for a little while longer."

Malock shook his head. "You know what? I'm out of here. I'm not going to stand around here and listen to you and your sycophant of a servant brag about your evil plans. I'm going to find a way off this island, even if that means building my own raft, and I'll make sure everyone knows the truth."

"Can't have that," said Hollech. "I mean, I doubt you would ever find a way off this island yourself, because there isn't much you could use to construct even the simplest of rafts, but I know how resourceful you mortals can be, so to keep you busy, why don't we play a game?"

"A game?" said Malock. "Why not just smite me now? I'm a

human. You're a god. The Treaty doesn't prevent northern gods from killing mortals, does it?"

"No, it doesn't," said Hollech. "But unlike some of my other siblings, I find the 'smite everything' option to be terribly boring and not very creative besides. A game would be better."

"May I play as well, Master Hollech?" said Ramufa. "I know exactly what game you're talking about and I am very good at—"

But Hollech shook his head. "Sorry, Ramufa, but I would rather play this alone with the Prince. I want you to go to Shika and keep an eye on King Fabadi. Tell him that he has the full support of the northern gods in his quest to defend his world from Skimif's corrupt rule. Try to sneak in a reference to how Raya, if she were still alive, would approve of his plans."

"That is very good, Master," said Ramufa. "That last touch is especially nice."

"No, it's not," said Malock. "It's more manipulation."

"And that surprises you because ...?" said Hollech. "Surely you would have realized by now that manipulation is part of who I am and what I do. I guess it will take some time for that lesson to sink into that thick skull of yours."

"I shall depart right away, Master," said Ramufa with a quick bow. "I will return if there are any important developments."

"Good," said Hollech, though his eyes were solely on Malock as he said that. "Now be gone. I wish to start the game as soon as possible and I cannot do it so long as you are standing here like this."

"As you command, Master," said Ramufa.

With that, Ramufa took a step backwards into the shadows

behind Hollech's throne and vanished completely. Malock had never seen anyone move like that before, but he didn't question how Ramufa had accomplished it.

Hollech lowered his hands onto the arms of his throne. "Now that we are alone, Prince Malock, why don't you and I get this game started? It will be very fun, I can assure you."

Chapter Eighteen

SHORTLY AFTER THE MAGICAL Superior's pronouncement of Braim's death, he summoned half of the school faculty, including Eyurna and Noharf, to come and move both Braim and Wirm's bodies out of his study. The other teachers were shocked to discover that Braim was dead, even after the Magical Superior explained to them how he had died. To Jenur's surprise, the Superior didn't censor the truth or try to make himself look better. He told them exactly how it happened, exactly how he had been forced to sit by and watch, without the slightest hint of rationalizing his own position. He had also healed Jenur's shoulder with a simple wave of his wand, because it was a flesh wound that did not require much specialized knowledge on his part to fix.

Before the teachers removed the bodies, however, Jenur searched the pockets of Wirm's coat for any clues as to who had hired him to attempt to kill her. She knew it was unlikely that Wirm had any clues on him that would prove his client's identity, but it was the only way she could possibly find out who had known about her.

And if I can find out who the bastard was who sent Wirm after me, then maybe I can avenge Quro and Braim, Jenur thought. *Or at the very least learn how they found out where I was.*

Luck was on her side that day, because Jenur soon found a folded up, slightly damp letter in Wirm's top left pocket. It was in surprisingly good condition, despite having surely been dumped in the ocean water with Wirm a week ago.

She didn't look at it right away, however, until the teachers moved Wirm and Braim's corpses out of the Superior's study. Part of her wanted to follow them, but at the moment she felt that reading the letter was far more important than seeing what they were going to do with Braim and Wirm's bodies.

The Magical Superior was the only person still in the room with her. He was standing, leaning on his tall wand, looking at the paper in her hands with some interest.

"Are you going to stay here?" said the Magical Superior. "Or are you going to follow the teachers?"

"I'm going to read this letter," said Jenur as she unfolded it. "And find out just who hired Wirm to kill me in the first place. But if I may ask, what will you guys do with Wirm and Braim's bodies?"

"Braim will get a traditional Diogian burial," said the Magical Superior, "while Wirm's corpse will be dumped in the sea and left to the fishes. If he's lucky, the cold depths of the ocean will preserve his corpse."

The Magical Superior said that with such venom that Jenur almost felt afraid. He looked at the spot where Wirm's corpse had lain, which was as spotless as the rest of the floor since having Wirm's blood cleaned up.

"I'm sorry about killing your brother," said Jenur. "But I had to. He—"

"Why are you apologizing?" said the Magical Superior, looking at her in surprise. "Do you think my brother and I were close? We went our separate ways decades ago when it became clear that our differences in morality could not be reconciled. I will shed no tears for a brother of mine who wasted his life killing for money when he could have spent it using his intelligence to better the world."

Jenur sighed in relief. "Oh, that's good. I didn't really want to apologize for killing him anyway. He was a monster and the world is a better place without him."

"Indeed," said the Magical Superior, nodding. "He is a prime example of what happens when you walk the path of heathenism. Without the light of the gods guiding his path, he ended up following the road of murder and greed. I pity him."

Being a heathen herself—and having seen just how 'moral' the gods could be—Jenur didn't quite agree with that, but she saw no reason to get into an argument about morality with the most powerful mage on the planet. She had to read the letter.

So Jenur finished unfolding the letter and scanned its contents. She was annoyed to see that it was written in a language she couldn't understand. It looked like a bunch of squiggles and lines to her, though she had a feeling that she had seen this language somewhere before.

"What does it say?" said the Magical Superior.

"Not sure," said Jenur. "It's written in a language I can't read. Do you recognize it?"

She gave the letter to the Superior, who took it and examined it. His eyes widened the further he read, his jaw dropping as his eyes scanned down the page.

"What?" said Jenur. "Does it say who wrote it? What is it?"

The Magical Superior thrust the letter into Jenur's hands and stepped back. "It's written in Shikan, but it can't possibly have been written by who it says it was written. Just not possible."

"Why not?" said Jenur. "Who wrote it? Why do you look so freaked out?"

The Magical Superior put a hand on his forehead and looked up at the ceiling. "By the gods, I do not want anything to do with this. What will he do when he finds out that Wirm failed?"

"Just tell me who did it," said Jenur. "Cut the vague whining. Get on with it."

"You do not want to know," said the Magical Superior. "You really, really do not want to know."

"Actually, I do," said Jenur. "I want to know who it is so I can track down the idiot and give him what he's got coming to him."

"I understand what you want to do, Jenur, but if I were you, I would take Darek and run," said the Magical Superior. "Find someplace else to hide. This is a man who you do not—perhaps cannot—fight."

"I'll decide that for myself," said Jenur, "after you tell me who he is."

"Fine," said the Magical Superior. "I suppose you have a right to know, seeing as he's caused you so much sorrow over the last week."

"I'm listening," said Jenur as she folded her arms across her chest.

"Go on."

"The man who wrote that letter to Wirm, detailing your location and how much he would pay Wirm for killing you, is King Worxo Fabadi, the King of Shika," said the Magical Superior. "That is his signature at the bottom of that letter there."

Jenur immediately looked at the letter again. She still could not read it, but her eyes darted to the bottom of the letter anyway, where she saw the writer's signature.

"You must be mistaken," said Jenur. "You don't mean *the* King Fabadi, do you?"

"There is only one that I know of," said the Magical Superior. "And I have seen his signature before. That is no forgery. That is his genuine signature, written by his own hand."

Jenur looked at the letter again, mind spinning at the revelation. "But ... why would he ..."

"Why indeed?" said the Magical Superior. "I met Fabadi once, but I did not know he knew you. Did you once do something to harm him?"

"No," said Jenur, shaking her head. "No, I—oh."

"Oh?" said the Magical Superior. "What do you mean by that?"

"It's nothing," said Jenur, looking away, scratching the back of her head. "It's just ... I think I might know why he wants me dead."

"You do?" said the Magical Superior. "What is it?"

Jenur tossed him a scathing look. "Is that any of your business?"

The Magical Superior actually stepped back, as if he was afraid she was going to hurt him. "Uh, no. I suppose it isn't."

Jenur huffed and then went back to thinking about why Fabadi hated her. She had been framed by Ramufa, the servant of Hollech, for the murder of Princess Raya Kabadi many months ago. It had been a long time since Jenur had thought about it, but she remembered quite well how angry Fabadi had been with her, how he had demanded—quite harshly—that the Carnagian Royal Family hang Jenur for her 'crime' or at least give her over to the Shikans so they could properly punish her. The only reason Jenur had been spared was because Malock had believed her when she told him she was innocent, but up until now, Jenur had thought that Fabadi might have forgotten her.

Then again, Raya was his only daughter, Jenur thought. *And she didn't die very long ago, either. Expecting Fabadi to get over his daughter's death so quickly would be like asking me to get over Dad's death so soon.*

Yet that failed to explain how Fabadi had learned about her location. As far as Jenur knew, the only people in the whole world who knew where she and Dad had lived were Skimif, Malock, and Rint Dolan, an old man living on World's End. She didn't think any of those people would ever betray her or Dad by selling the location of their home to her enemies, yet there was no other explanation for how Fabadi had figured out where she was.

I need to talk to him, Jenur thought. *Someone else besides Malock, Skimif, and Rint must have known of my location. Someone who wanted me—probably still wants me—dead. The only question is, who could it be?*

Folding the letter up, Jenur said, "Magical Superior, could you teleport me to Shika?"

The Magical Superior raised one thin eyebrow. "Why? You will be walking straight into Fabadi's arms if you do so. He will probably order his Sun Guardians to kill you if he finds out you are there."

"It's all right," said Jenur. "I can protect myself. I still remember all of my moves from my days as a Dark Tiger. I'll be able to sneak around Castle Shika easily."

"Are you going to leave Darek here with us?" the Magical Superior questioned. "He will wonder where you went."

Jenur frowned when she remembered how Darek had quite shown a great distrust of her. On top of everything else that had happened recently, the memory weighed heavily on her heart, but she simply said, "I trust you guys to take care of Darek. Besides, I won't be gone forever. I'm just going to go there long enough to talk to Fabadi and ask him how he found me, maybe beat up the guy who told him where I was. That's all."

The Magical Superior sighed and said, "Well, I suppose I can help you get there. It's your life, not mine. But I still urge caution. King Fabadi is a clever king and he no doubt has many protections set up around his castle."

"Then teleport me as close to Castle Shika as you can," said Jenur. "Preferably directly inside the place. I'll figure it out from there."

"If you wish," said the Magical Superior. "Because Shika is so far to the south, I will have to use more power than usual when teleporting you. It will not hurt or anything, but you may feel a bit sick when you re-materialize on Shika."

"No problem," said Jenur. "I can handle feeling a little sick after everything I've been through."

"Very well," said the Magical Superior. "If you feel like going now, then please stand still. Don't make any sudden movements; otherwise, you might mess up the spell."

Jenur stood stock still as the Magical Superior gently touched her forehead with the tip of his wand. The tip grew hot, warming her cold forehead, as a reddish glow blinded her eyes. She had to close them so she wouldn't go blind permanently, but even with her eyes closed, she could see the glow through her eyelids, albeit not quite as bright as it was when her eyes were open.

Then the glow faded and Jenur's eyes snapped open. She blinked once or twice, wondering why the Magical Superior had stopped casting the spell, when she realized that the Superior was nowhere to be seen.

In fact, when Jenur looked around, she realized that she wasn't in the Superior's study anymore. Instead, she was standing inside a wide castle hallway, the walls, floor, and ceiling glowing softly all around her. A statue of Nimiko, the God of Light, stood off to the side, while a statue of some old Shikan king stood directly opposite the Nimiko statue underneath a window that showed a dark sky, confirming that it was indeed past sunset.

Though Jenur had never been to this part of the castle in particular, she had no trouble recognizing the hallway as being part of Castle Shika. She didn't see any people, which was fine by her, as she was in no mood to explain to any royal servants what she was doing here. She did, however, feel slightly queasy, although she managed to ignore it.

The Magical Superior must be incredibly powerful, Jenur thought.

I didn't even feel myself leave the study. No wonder he's considered the most powerful mage in the world. Good thing he's not a power-hungry tyrant; otherwise, I'd be frightened for the rest of the world.

The only problem she faced now was finding Fabadi's throne room. It was true that she had visited the castle before, but she had not been given a chance to explore it in any great depth. She figured she was just going to have to keep looking until she found it, but the problem with that was that she would be far more likely to run into some servant and thus lose the element of surprise that she needed.

There's gotta be a quicker and easier way to do this, Jenur thought. *Wonder if there's a map around here or something that I could use to find the throne room.*

Just as Jenur thought that, a cheery voice—whistling an unfamiliar tune to Jenur—floated down the hall from just around the corner, followed by the sound of leather boots scraping against the brightstone floor and the sloshing of water in a metal bucket. Alarmed, Jenur ducked behind the Nimiko statue just as a royal servant walked around the corner of the left end of the hall.

Keeping as quiet as possible, Jenur watched as the royal servant—a short, bald-headed middle-aged man she recognized as Jingus, having met him on her previous visit to the castle some months ago—walked down the hall, carrying a mop over his right shoulder and a bucket of soapy water in his left hand. He was the source of the whistling and he was surprisingly good at it, carrying the tune with a mastery Jenur wouldn't have expected from a man of his station.

Thankfully, even in the well-lit hallway, Jingus didn't seem to notice her. He just walked on by the statue of Nimiko, nodding at the statue as he passed as way of showing respect to the God of Shika, and then stopped and put his bucket on the floor. He then began to wipe the floor with the mop, still whistling his cheerful tune all the while.

Jenur almost tried to sneak away while he wasn't looking, but then she realized that this was her best chance to find the way to Fabadi's throne room. So she tiptoed out from behind Nimiko's statue as silently as she could, heading for Jingus, who with the volume of his whistling and the sloshing of the water in his bucket, likely couldn't hear her even if she were to walk normally.

As soon as she was close enough, Jenur put one hand on Jingus' shoulder and said, "Don't move or make a noise."

Jingus started, his mop clattering on the wet stone floor, but he didn't turn around to look at her. He must have sensed the threat in her voice, which was fine by her because she was in no mood to knock him out to make sure he didn't call for help. He did, however, tremble under her fingers.

"I'm not going to hurt you as long as you do what I ask," said Jenur. "Just give me directions to King Fabadi's throne room and you can go back to cleaning the floor of his castle like you were currently doing."

"W-Who are you?" said Jingus, his voice a terrified whisper. "An assassin?"

"No," said Jenur. "An actual assassin would have killed you by now. I just want to talk with your king. That's all."

"Your voice sounds familiar," said Jingus. "Where have I heard it before?"

"Nowhere," said Jenur. "You must be mistaking me for someone else. Now tell me where the throne room is or you'll 'accidentally' trip on the wet floor and crack your head open like an egg."

"Go back in the direction I came from," said Jingus, speaking fast. "Then go down a corridor, turn left, follow the hall, and you should eventually reach King Fabadi's throne room."

"Good," said Jenur. "Is he there right now?"

"No—"

Jenur increased the pressure on her grip. "Tell the truth."

"Yes," Jingus said, his voice higher than normal. "He's there. But he doesn't want any visitors."

"Why?" said Jenur.

"I-I don't know," said Jingus with a gulp. "But the other servants think King Fabadi is talking with an important guest, though I couldn't even begin to guess at the guest's identity, seeing as the King did not say if he was having any guests over tonight and I did not see any carriages arrive at the castle gates earlier today."

That's not good, Jenur thought, but she said aloud, "Any guards protecting the Throne Room?"

"N-No," said Jingus. "King Fabadi likes his conversations with his guests to be private. So whenever he has guests over in his throne room discussing important things, he sends his bodyguards away out of earshot. Th-That's why the other servants think King Fabadi has a guest."

That will make it a lot easier for me to get in there, then, Jenur thought. *I just wonder who the guest is. Maybe the person who told Fabadi where my house was?*

"So currently, King Fabadi is alone in his throne room with at least one guest?" said Jenur.

"Correct," said Jingus. "That's what the rumors say and all of the evidence seems to point to that."

"Any traps or spells I should be aware of?" said Jenur. "Perhaps cast by some Shikan mages to make sure no one can enter without Fabadi's knowledge?"

"No," said Jingus. "And that's the truth. King Fabadi's defensive spells are only active when he's alone. He has to turn them off whenever he has guests, so I imagine they are currently inactive, meaning it is safe to enter his throne room even if you weren't summoned by him."

"Good," said Jenur. "Is the door locked?"

"Most likely," said Jingus. "King Fabadi, as I've said, values his privacy above all else when he has a guest over. But I do have a key ring on me with the throne room key."

It took Jenur only a second to find the key ring hanging off of Jingus's belt and another second to identify and remove the throne room key from the ring: A golden key with a long shaft and sharp teeth.

Pocketing the key, Jenur said, "Thank you for being so cooperative. I am going to leave now, but don't turn around, don't even look over your shoulder, because if you do I swear to the gods that I will make sure you live to regret it. Understood?"

"Y-Yes," said Jingus, nodding, his voice quavering. "I understand completely. I have never understood anything better in my life."

"Good," said Jenur. "Now, it's time for me to go."

Chapter Nineteen

HOLLECH SHOOK HIS ARM and a handful of dice tumbled out of his coat sleeve into his equine hands. He closed his fist around the die blocks and held it up in front of Malock.

"Dice?" said Malock. "What are you going to do with a couple of dice?"

"Throw them at you to irritate you," said Hollech, his voice dripping with sarcasm. "No, actually, they are going to play an integral part of our game. It's a rather simple game, one which any mortal should be able to understand. Allow me to explain the rules, but I will be brief because I wish to start right away."

Malock shook his head and turned around. "I don't have to play this. I'm going to get out of this temple and find my way off this island. I have no need to humor a god like you."

"Are you so sure?" said Hollech. "Chinchia has been abandoned for decades. Even I don't know all of the many wild and dangerous creatures that roam the lands below this temple. Though I will say that I once heard the roar of something that might have been a dragon."

"I'd rather take my risks with a dragon than with you," said Malock as he started walking toward what he believed to be the exit.

Hollech sighed. "You really are a spoilsport, aren't you? Equina!"

As soon as the word left Hollech's mouth, the sound of clopping hooves entered Malock's ears and the next moment a huge black horse surged out of the darkness of a nearby wall. Startled, Malock stepped back as the horse stopped in front of him, snorting heavily through its nostrils and glaring at him with eyes as red as Malock's robes. It was easily the biggest horse Malock had ever seen, towering over him by two or three heads, with hind legs that looked strong enough to shatter rock.

"What is that?" said Malock.

"Equina," said Hollech. "My faithful horse. Ramufa is not the only servant I employ. As the God of Horses, every horse in Martir lives to obey me. When I speak, they listen, though Equina is a special case, as I have enchanted her to make her much larger, smarter, and stronger than her fellow equines."

Equina continued to snort and whinny, its long black tail whipping through the air like a rope.

"She won't hurt you," said Hollech. "At least, not if you stay and play. If you try to leave before the game is over ... well, let's just say that getting kicked in the head by Equina's hind legs, while an interesting sight to behold, would not be in your best interests."

Malock turned away from Equina, trying to ignore her rancid horse smell, and said, "All right, Hollech. I'll play your little game, and I'll beat it, too."

"You sound confident for a mortal who doesn't even know what the rules are yet," said Hollech. "I suppose that's to be expected. You mortals tend to be very confident in yourselves, even when you have no reason to be. Amuses me to no end, it does."

"Just tell me the rules," said Malock. "I'm getting impatient."

"Why of course, Your Majesty," said Hollech. "I would never think of wasting the oh-so-important time of the next King of Carnag. Unlike other gods, I always get straight to the point."

"Then get to it already," said Malock.

Hollech nodded. "The rules are simple. In this game, you and I take turns rolling a pair of dice. Whoever rolls the highest number in a turn receives ten points and whoever reaches one hundred points first is the winner."

"That *is* simple," said Malock. "Too simple. What are you hiding from me?"

Hollech put his other hand over his chest. "Me? Hiding something from you? Prince Tojas Malock, I expected better of you, accusing me of hiding something important. That's unfair and rather unprincely of you, dare I say unkingly, and—"

"You're the God of Deception," said Malock. "And Thieves and Horses. Forgive me if I take every word you say with a grain of salt."

"Maybe I do lie sometimes," Hollech admitted, "but this time, I am not. Those are the rules of this game, which is called 'decem dice,' created by my followers in this very temple all those years ago. It was a highly popular game in part due to its simple rules that anyone could understand."

"Let's assume I believe you," said Malock. "What is at stake? What will happen if I win and you lose or vice versa?"

"So glad you asked," said Hollech. "If you beat me, I will send you back home to Carnag completely unharmed. Not only that, but I will hand myself over to Skimif and tell him all about my plans."

"And if I lose?" said Malock.

"If you lose, Equina here will bash your skull in and turn your brain to jelly," said Hollech. "Then I fabricate the evidence to make it appear that Skimif or the southern gods are responsible for your death and your poor, hurting mother, now the sole leader of Carnag, joins King Fabadi's ever-growing coalition of anti-Skimif nations."

Malock looked over his shoulder at Equina. The horse stood still now, apparently watching the whole conversation, though whether Equina understood any of what was said, it was impossible to tell. All Malock knew was that he had no doubt in his mind that Equina's hooves—which appeared to be made out of steel—could easily kill him in one hit if she hit him directly.

"Now," said Hollech, "do you have any other questions or can we start playing now?"

Malock, seeing no way out of this, sighed in frustration and said, "All right. We can start playing. But don't throw a tantrum if I start beating you at your own game."

Hollech chuckled. "That certainly would be something because I have never lost this game even once in all of my eons of existence. But you can say that if you think it will boost your confidence. It will make your inevitable breakdown at your lost that much more amusing to watch."

"Who goes first?" Malock asked.

"The one who challenges the other player to the game is the one who goes first," said Hollech. "Because I challenged you, that means I get the first roll. Let's see what number I get."

Hollech threw the dice onto the floor. The dice rolled along the stone floor, bouncing off the ridges and cracks, until they stopped at Malock's feet. In the darkness of the ruined temple, it was almost impossible to see what the dice were, forcing Malock to bend over and look as closely as he could at the numbers on them.

"So?" said Hollech. "What are they?"

A flash of lightning overhead revealed the numbers to Malock. He looked up at Hollech and said, "Twelve and nine."

"Twelve and nine?" said Hollech. "That's good. That's very good. Your turn."

Malock picked up the dice and looked them over briefly. They had obviously been carved from stone, and rather crudely at that. Engraved in the blocks were numbers, one on each side of the block. They ranged from one to six, which made no sense to Malock because he had clearly seen the numbers twelve and nine of them. This made him suspicious.

"Did you rig the dice with magic?" said Malock, looking up sharply at Hollech.

"No," said Hollech, shaking his head. "If you are referring to the fact that the numbers are different from what you saw, it's part of the game. The dice are enchanted so that the numbers change with each throw of the dice. It makes the game that much more exciting, for you never know if you're going to get one or one hundred on the blocks."

"Seems like an easy way to cheat," said Malock. "A very easy way to cheat."

"There is no cheating involved, I can assure you," said Hollech. "I have no control over the numbers that the dice show. The spell generates completely random numbers. I am just as much at the mercy of the dice as you are. For this game, we are equals."

Malock didn't believe a word that came from the god's equine lips, but he had no way to prove that Hollech was lying and he couldn't just quit the game now, not with Equina behind him snorting and swishing her tail through the air. He would have to hope for the best.

So Malock tossed the dice onto the floor, just as Hollech had done. The dice rolled and clattered across the floor until they stopped at Hollech's feet. Hollech leaned over in his throne, peering at the dice with his small horse eyes, as Malock folded his arms across his chest and tapped his foot against the stone.

"So?" said Malock. "What are my numbers?"

Hollech looked up. "Six and three. Which means that I got twenty-one and you got nine, which means that I win this round and get ten points."

"No way," said Malock. "How do I know you're telling the truth?"

"See for yourself," said Hollech.

He gestured at the dice and they flew in the air toward Malock. The dice floated in midair in front of Malock, allowing him to see the numbers: six and three. Just as Hollech had said.

"See? I tell the truth," said Hollech. "Before I begin my second turn, let's keep a score to keep us honest."

Hollech pointed a finger at a nearby stone pillar, standing all by itself, and a beam of energy shot out from Hollech's finger and struck the pillar. With the precision of a master mason, Hollech carved the number ten into the pillar, with a zero directly underneath it.

"Current score: Me, ten, you, zero," said Hollech as he finished carving the scores into the pillar's surface. "But don't get too frustrated, Prince Malock. There are plenty of stories of decem dice players starting off badly and yet pulling a comeback victory in later rounds. Perhaps the same will happen to you if you are lucky."

"Just throw the damn dice," said Malock. "I'm getting sick of your voice."

Hollech chuckled as the dice flew back into his hand. "As you command, Your Majesty."

Another jerk of his fist and the dice soared from Hollech's hand. They clattered across the stone floor, just as they had done before, until once more they stopped at Malock's feet. As before, Malock bent down to examine the numbers as Hollech said, "What is my score?"

Malock had to squint to make it out, but he could not believe what he was seeing. He looked up at Hollech, completely dumbfounded, and said, "Twenty-six and fourteen."

"Really?" said Hollech. "Now *that* is what I call a good roll. Your turn."

Hollech reclined in his chair with a satisfied smirk, which looked strange on his horse face, as Malock closed his fist around the dice and stood up.

This is stupid, Malock thought, glancing at his closed fist. *And far, far too simple. What's Hollech got planned? What's he trying to do? Why would he play a game with me when he could just as easily kill me and frame Skimif or one of the southern gods for it? None of this makes sense.*

The best that he could figure, Hollech was stalling. The only question was, what was he stalling for?

Might as well keep playing, Malock thought. *Maybe I'll figure it out the more I play.*

Malock threw his dice, once again copying Hollech's movement. Another clatter across the stone floor and the dice stopped at Hollech's feet. As before, Hollech bent over in his throne, and said, in the same tone as before, "Oh my. A five and a four. That is not a good roll at all."

"A five and a four?" said Malock. "That can't be right."

"But it is," said Hollech. "Do you wish to look at the dice again?"

"No," said Malock, shaking his head. "I believe you."

"Good," said Hollech. "Let's see, that makes my score twenty and yours, once again, zero. Let me get that in stone real quick."

Like before, Hollech carved the number twenty into the pillar, right next to ten, while Malock got another zero.

"I am winning," said Hollech. "As usual."

Malock's hands balled into fists, mostly because he felt so helpless. Decem dice was clearly a luck-based game more than anything. It involved no skill at all. As far as Malock could tell, Hollech was only playing this game to torment Malock.

And it's working, Malock thought. *The bastard.*

Hollech picked up the dice from the floor and began rolling the dice between his fingers. "Let's see, let's see ... I think this game is starting to get a little boring. There's not much of a challenge to it, especially from a newcomer like you. We need to spice it up, make it far more interesting than a simple luck-based dice game."

"Here's an idea," said Malock. "We could just stop playing it entirely and end this whole madness while we're ahead."

"No," said Hollech, shaking his head. "I never quit a game I've started, even when it doesn't seem to be going in my favor. I mean, not that this game isn't going in my favor or anything, but I mean to say that I play every game to the end, no matter what."

Something about Hollech's tone seemed off to Malock. A slight sense of nervousness, perhaps? Or was it just Malock's imagination trying to make things seem better for Malock than they really were?

But why would Hollech be nervous? Malock thought. *He's clearly winning. And he's probably going to keep winning, considering that this game seems rigged. Either he's trying to make me let my guard down by pretending to be nervous or something is not going according to plan.*

Malock's thoughts were interrupted by the clattering of the dice thrown by Hollech. The dice, as usual, bumped against Malock's shoes, and once again, the numbers were too dark to read from a distance.

Hollech leaned forward in his throne, seemingly unconsciously, and said, "What numbers did I roll?"

Okay, he's definitely nervous about something, Malock thought as he bent down to get a better look at the dice. *Does it have something to do with the dice?*

It took Malock a moment due to the low lighting, but eventually he figured out what the numbers were. He looked up at Hollech and said, "Nine and eleven."

Hollech sat back in his chair, looking almost relieved. "Nine and eleven? Not bad. Let's see what you get."

Malock scooped up the die blocks in his hand. The dice had something to do with Hollech's nervousness, but Malock didn't understand why. A couple of crudely-carved pieces of enchanted stone, that's all they were. They couldn't hurt anyone, much less a god.

Unless it's not the dice themselves that Hollech is worried about, Malock thought, *but perhaps the numbers themselves make him nervous.*

Though that made even less sense. Hollech was currently winning. Sure, Malock might get lucky and win one or two rounds, but it was obvious that Hollech would win this match. No way would the god have chosen to play this game with Malock if he thought he was going to lose. Right?

Unless he underestimated my abilities, Malock thought, *or his own abilities at this game. That would explain his nervousness, though even then, it's not quite justified, since he's still doing much better than —*

A loud snorting sound behind Malock made him jump. He looked over his shoulder and saw Equina standing much closer to him than she had been previously. Her red eyes glared at him, like she was trying to communicate how much she wanted him dead.

"Equina says to hurry up and throw your dice already," said

TIMOTHY L. CEREPAKA

Hollech. "You can't control what numbers you get, after all, so standing around thinking won't do anything except waste time. Though of course, with your score the way it is, I can tell why you would want to delay the game."

"I'll throw, I'll throw," said Malock, turning his head back to face Hollech. "Hold your horses."

"Is that supposed to be a joke?" said Hollech, his eyes narrowing.

"No, it's a—never mind," said Malock with a sigh. "I'll just roll the dice."

At that moment, just as Malock rolled the dice, the Burn of Grinf flared up on his face again, causing him to reach up and rub his face as he always did. This time was particularly painful, causing his eyes to water from the pain as the dice rolled across the floor.

"Is my older brother's curse bothering you?" said Hollech's voice, smug and self-satisfied. "He once cursed a follower of mine with that same curse. I've never forgiven him for it, though to be honest I didn't think he'd ever do such a thing to one of his *own* followers."

Wiping the tears from his eyes to clear his vision, Malock said, "Just tell me what my numbers are."

"With pleasure," said Hollech, leaning forward in his throne once again to look at the dice at his feet. "Let's see ... eleven and twenty."

"Eleven and twenty?" said Malock. "Doesn't that mean I scored more than you?"

Hollech looked up. Malock expected to see an expression of anger or at least annoyance on the god's horse face, but instead, Hollech looked almost delighted. It was as if he was happy that he had lost this round, but that made no sense to Malock whatsoever.

"Indeed it does," said Hollech. "You are the winner of this round, which means you get your first ten points of the game."

As before, Hollech carved the number 'ten' into the pillar, just below Malock's two zeroes. He carved a 'zero' under his twenty, the first zero the god had gotten so far.

"Looks like luck was on your side in that match," said Hollech, bending over again to scoop up the dice. "Perhaps you'll win after all." Hollech did not look bothered by that notion as he said it.

After that, the odds suddenly became in Malock's favor. Hollech consistently rolled numbers in the single digits, whereas Malock kept rolling numbers in the mid-to-high double digits. Every time Hollech rolled a small pair of numbers, such as two and three, he cursed his luck, though his frustration at his apparent losses always seemed carefully acted to Malock. Malock's own joy at beating Hollech in every match, however, was genuine. His suspicions about the game being rigged had faded away almost entirely; at least, he now figured that if it was rigged, it was rigged in his favor.

Maybe Tinkar decided that he likes me now or something, Malock thought as Hollech rolled the lowest numbers either of them had rolled so far: a one and a two. *Either way, this match is mine.*

In fact, Malock was no longer even really afraid of Hollech or Equina anymore. He had almost forgotten about Hana, who he thought he did not need anymore. After all, he would just win this game and Hollech would hand himself over to Skimif and everything would work out in the end. It seemed too good to be true, but Malock didn't dare say that aloud, otherwise he would bring bad luck upon himself.

So Malock picked up the dice, but before rolling them, cast a quick glance at the score. Hollech's score stood at thirty, while Malock's was ninety. All Malock needed to do was score higher than a one and a two and the game would be his.

I guess Hollech didn't plan for what would happen if I actually started winning, Malock thought with a smirk. *Pretty good for a guy who hadn't played this game until just today.*

"Do you want to congratulate me now, Hollech?" said Malock as he raised his dice hand. "I mean, I won't stop you if you want to. It's pretty obvious that I'm going to win now. Maybe I'll ask Skimif not to punish you too harshly when you turn yourself in. He's a reasonable guy. I'm sure I can get him to lighten your sentence."

Hollech rested his head on his fist. "That is so merciful of you. Why, I am sure that your servants must call you Malock the Merciful. Maybe that is the name you will earn after your death. King Malock the Merciful."

Malock smiled. "I actually like that name quite a bit. Though to be honest, I don't feel like I've done much to earn that title yet."

Hollech shrugged. "Well, since you are about to win this, I'm sure you will have many decades in which to display your obvious mercy and generous nature to every boot-maker and judge in Carnag."

"You don't seem very annoyed by my inevitable victory," said Malock. "I would never have taken you to be a graceful loser, being a god and all."

"Not all of us gods throw tantrums every time things don't go our way exactly the way we imagined," said Hollech. "Unlike my brothers and sisters, I have some honor in me. If I lose, then I lose and that's that. Remember, thieves do have honor, and as the God of Thieves, I share that same honor with them."

Though Malock found nothing especially duplicitous about Hollech's words, a small voice in the back of Malock's head was trying to warn him not to roll that dice. Something bad would happen, even if this was the winning roll, but Malock wasn't sure what.

It must just be paranoia, Malock thought. *The gods are never this simple or easy to beat. Usually they skip games like this and just go straight to the killing. If Hollech's not grinding his teeth and threatening to turn me into a pony, it's because he's a graceful loser, just like I said.*

But somehow that didn't really fit in with what Malock knew of Hollech. Surely Hollech had to be angry that his carefully-constructed plan—which took a few months to put into action—was going to fall apart completely due to his losing a game of dice with a mortal. Malock had seen gods whose plans were wrecked or messed up and he knew from experience that they were never, ever happy or graceful about it.

Hollech is lying, Malock thought. *Makes sense. He's the God of Deception, after all. He's put on a show of being the graceful loser, but in reality, he's trying to distract me. The only question is, what is he trying to distract me from?*

Once again, Malock's eyes wandered over to the stone pillar where the score was kept. He had two zeroes, while Hollech had eight. Despite having never lost at this game, Hollech was taking his inevitable first loss in stride. Hollech's pride alone ought to have made him angry, yet he wasn't. In fact, he seemed almost eager, because he was leaning forward slightly in his throne, like he couldn't wait to see what numbers Malock rolled next.

There must be something else to this game than he's letting on, Malock thought. *Some rule I don't know about, maybe. A rule that would turn the odds in his favor, maybe a loophole that would give him the victory on a silver platter. But what is it?*

That was when it hit Malock like lightning. He looked at the scores, saw how far ahead he was of Hollech, then looked at Hollech himself. The god was smirking, a strange expression on his equine face, and now Malock understood exactly why Hollech had seemed so unconcerned about losing earlier.

"Come on, Prince Malock," said Hollech. "Just roll the dice. What do you have to lose?"

Malock held the dice up to his chest, now uncertain that he wanted to throw them at all. "My life."

"Your life?" said Hollech with a snort and a whinny. "You are going to win this. Your life will be perfectly fine. You have nothing to worry about. Just roll the die and win the game. You deserve it."

"No way," said Malock, shaking his head. "I know exactly what's up now, and I'm not falling for it."

"You're not?" said Hollech. "What do you mean? Didn't I already promise to you that I hadn't hid any of the rules from you? You mortals can be so paranoid sometimes, you know that?"

"It's not paranoia if it is based in reality," said Malock. "Because I've finally figured out the *real* rules of this game, not the fake ones you made up to trick me with."

"Oh?" said Hollech, resting his head on his fist again. "Tell me,

Prince Malock, just what these *real* rules are. I am quite interested in hearing about them, seeing as I have played by these particular rules in every game of decem dice that I've played over the last few centuries."

Malock pointed at the score pillar. "You're correct. You have played by these rules, which is no doubt why you've always won: Because you made them up."

"Made them up?" said Hollech. "Why would you say that?"

"Because only you know them," said Malock. "You said that the winner of decem dice is whoever reaches one hundred points first, yes?"

"Yes, I did," said Hollech. "I stand by that claim."

"So you stand by your lies," said Malock. "Not that I find that in the least surprising, but at least you admit it."

"You keep accusing me of lying," said Hollech, "yet you offer no proof. Nor have you bothered to explain what you think the rules *really* are."

"Allow me to state the rules, then," said Malock. "In decem dice, whoever reaches one hundred points first ... loses."

Hollech's eyes flickered over to the score pillar before returning to focus on Malock. "You mean to say that you think you are about to lose?"

"Yes," said Malock. "It's the only explanation that makes sense. It's why you are laid-back about losing. It's why you decided to play a game with me. You knew that my 'victory' would in fact be your victory. And since you're the God of Deception, you deceived me— just as, I am sure, you have deceived countless other individuals over the years—with the simplest lie you could come up with. Am I wrong?"

Hollech tapped his long nose. "You are much smarter than I originally gave you credit for, Prince Malock. Too smart for a mortal."

"I knew it," said Malock. "You were hoping I'd be dumb enough to roll the dice and 'win.' Good thing I figured it out before I made the worst mistake of my life."

"Don't be so happy so quickly," said Hollech. "The game is still not yet over. You must still roll the dice. If you refuse to, you will be considered to have forfeited the game and Equina here will knock your brains out."

Equina snorted and cantered along the stone floor, her hooves clopping against the stone loudly. Malock didn't look back over his shoulder to look at the horse, mostly because he knew Hollech was right.

But Malock didn't want to throw the dice. With that low number that Hollech had rolled, the odds were low—maybe even non-existent, if Hollech had indeed rigged the dice, as Malock suspected—that Malock would get a number lower than three. In all likelihood, this roll would be Malock's last.

Yet the alternative is to give up and get killed by a horse, Malock thought. *At least by rolling the dice, I have a chance, however microscopic, of turning this game around. Let's hope this works.*

Sending a brief prayer to Skimif, Malock rolled the dice.

Chapter Twenty

FINDING KING FABADI'S THRONE room was easy. All Jenur did was follow Jingus's directions to the throne room to the letter and she soon found herself standing before two massive stone doors. Like the rest of Castle Shika, they had been built out of brightstone, but they had also been carved with images of Nimiko, whose eyes had brilliant shining jewels embedded within. Oddly enough, the doors were cracked slightly; not enough for Jenur to enter, but enough for her to hear two voices floating through. Seemed like a security hazard to her, but she wasn't complaining.

Carefully, Jenur walked up to the doors and listened as hard as she could. She aimed her ear toward the crack in the door, trying to quiet her own breathing and heart in order to catch every word that was being said.

"...the northern gods support your every decision, King Fabadi," said a voice that Jenur knew she recognized, but which she couldn't place right away. "They are just as fed up with Skimif's corrupt rule as you and the other nations are."

"Even Nimiko?" said another voice, this one much older, which obviously was Fabadi's. "He has not spoken to me since Skimif's ascension, despite the Priests' efforts to communicate with him."

"Lord Nimiko certainly approves of your rebellion as well," said the other voice. "Master Hollech has every northern god on his side. You need not worry about that."

Master Hollech? Jenur thought. *There's only one creep I know of who calls Hollech 'master' and that's Ramufa. What in the world is he doing here and why the hell is King Fabadi talking with him?*

Then again, Fabadi had never known about Ramufa. He hadn't listened to Jenur when she had tried to explain to him that Raya had been killed by a servant of Hollech. That would explain why Fabadi wasn't currently murdering Ramufa, but that didn't explain what they were talking about.

What rebellion? What is so corrupt about Skimif's rule? Jenur thought. *Sounds like a lot of stuff has been happening since Dad and I went to the Great Berg, and honestly I am not sure I want to be involved in any of it.*

Still, Jenur had come this far, so she decided to stay where she was and listen to as much as she could before acting. Maybe Fabadi and Ramufa's conversation would enlighten her. Besides, she needed time to figure out the best way to enter the throne room, as she doubted that Ramufa or Fabadi would take very well to her barging through the doors and demanding to speak with Fabadi right now.

"That is good to hear," said Fabadi. "I was worried that we Shikans had somehow lost Nimiko's favor."

"Oh, no, you are still very much Nimiko's favorite nation," said Ramufa. "It's just that Skimif is determined to sever the close bond between the northern gods and the mortals, so he has given the northern gods so much work for them to do that they just don't have time to answer every prayer they receive, even from their own followers. It is a sad state, let me tell you."

"Indeed," said Fabadi, his voice tinged with bitterness. "And it will just become sadder once Skimif decides to take action against us or nullifies the Treaty to allow the southern gods to harm us mortals. Yet we must continue fighting on, no matter what."

"Brave words, Your Majesty," said Ramufa. "Even if this rebellion fails, I am certain that you will be remembered in Shikan history as the most courageous out of all of Shika's many monarchs. Even the northern gods will remember your courage."

"History's opinion of me is irrelevant," said Fabadi. "I must do what is right and I believe that this is right. To cower before a tyrant and his thugs like Skimif and the southern gods would be to forfeit my right to the throne of Shika, a right I have fought for and proven time and again whenever anyone has ever doubted my rule."

"No doubt," said Ramufa. "By the way, have you heard from the Dark Tigers yet, regarding Gaharna Vicin, otherwise known as Jenur Takren?"

"Not yet," said Fabadi with a sigh. "The last message I received was a letter from Nijok Wirm, the leader of the Dark Tigers, detailing where to deliver the promised payment of fifty-thousand coins. That was a week ago. I thought I would hear from them much sooner, but I suppose the mission must have been more difficult than I thought."

Jenur almost gasped. *He offered them fifty-thousand coins? That's almost as much as the bounty that Garnal Gray had before her death.*

He really *wants me dead, doesn't he?*

"She can be a handful, no doubt," said Ramufa in agreement. "I have met the woman before. Though she looks young and naïve, she is in fact a calculating and clever killer, always at least five steps ahead of her enemy. It is a wonder that she was caught the first time so soon after killing Princess Raya."

"I am no Tinkarian, but I like to believe that Tinkar had fated that to happen," said Fabadi. Then his voice turned angry. "At least until Prince Malock—the woman-chasing fool—fell for the girl's feminine charms and not only spared her life, but let her escape as well. I wonder if she promised to sleep with him to get that."

Jenur blanched. *Sleep with Malock? Yeah, right. Where did he get that idea from?*

"No doubt she at least promised him sexual favors in exchange for her freedom," said Ramufa. "As I said, she is calculating and clever. She used Malock's weakness for beautiful women to avoid the execution she deserved."

"Just thinking about it makes my blood boil," said Fabadi. "Especially when you consider that it happened on Carnag, or 'Grinf's Courtroom,' as those barbaric boot-makers like to call it. Where was Grinf when my daughter was murdered in his backyard? Nimiko certainly would not have tolerated that if it had happened on Shika."

"Oh, I wouldn't be so quick to criticize Grinf, Your Majesty," said Ramufa. "He is as fed up with Skimif's rule as you are, after all. It is wise not to insult your allies."

"Be that as it may, I eagerly await the day when Wirm steps through these doors with Vicin's head in hand," said Fabadi. "It will be a day of celebration on par with the Festival of Sunlight, except it will last a full week and everyone shall be invited, rich, poor, and even foreigners."

"Sounds like a fun party," said Ramufa. "But what if you could celebrate it today, rather than wait for those lazy Dark Tigers to get around to delivering Vicin's head to you?"

"I would love to celebrate it today," said Fabadi. "The only problem is that Vicin is currently at the Great Berg, which is several weeks' journey away from Shika by ship. Even if Wirm is beheading her at this very moment, I will not learn of it until a month from now at the earliest."

"Not necessarily," said Ramufa. "It would appear that you have a visitor standing outside these very doors, listening to every word we are saying. Why don't I let her in?"

At that moment, Jenur felt a strong hand, with long fingers, wrap around her neck and tighten. Panicked, Jenur struggled to break its grip on her neck, but the hand gripped her so tightly that it was impossible.

Then everything around Jenur went completely dark and the next moment she found herself floating just a few inches off the floor in a room she didn't recognize. Then the hand let go of her and she collapsed to the ground, falling on her hands and knees onto the hard brightstone floor, causing her to cough and wheeze as she rubbed her aching neck.

"It cannot be," said Fabadi's voice, which was coming from directly before her. "Gaharna Vicin?"

Still gasping for air, Jenur looked up. Sitting directly in front of her, at the top of a small spiral staircase, was King Fabadi of Shika. He wore pure white royal robes, with the symbol of Nimiko—a stylized version of the sun—sewn into the chest area. His silver blonde hair seemed to disappear into his white crown, while his scepter, which lay across his lap, glowed dimly.

"It is indeed her," said Ramufa's voice, which came from above her.

Jenur had to crane her neck to look directly up at the ceiling. A large crystal chandelier hung from the ceiling, which Ramufa hung upside down from. His dirty brown robes had not fallen to obscure his creepy, smiling face because he had a simple rope belt tied around his waist, though Jenur wished he didn't because she really hadn't wanted to see that smile ever again.

"How did you get in here?" said Fabadi, grabbing his scepter and pointing at her accusingly. "I thought you were at the Great Berg. Wirm said he would kill you."

Her throat still hurting, Jenur managed to answer, in a hoarse voice, "Wirm's dead. Killed him myself."

"Impossible," said Fabadi. "There's no way you could have killed the greatest assassin in the entire Northern Isles."

"Well, I can and I did," said Jenur. "As for how I got here, that's none of your business."

"It is very much my business," said Fabadi. "But I see that you will not tell me how you got past my defenses, servants, and guards. At least, not without force on my part. Ramufa?"

Ramufa nodded and hid his hands in the folds of his robes. Before Jenur could do anything, Ramufa's hands—floating in midair

—appeared behind her and grabbed her arms. Ramufa's hands then twisted her arms behind her back, twisting them in such an unnatural position that she almost screamed from the pain. It felt like Ramufa was going to snap her arms straight off her shoulders like twigs.

"Now, tell me how you broke into the castle," said Fabadi, his voice low and threatening. "Or I will order Ramufa here to break your arms and toss you out the window."

Fabadi gestured at a tall window on the far right side of the room. "Considering that we are many hundreds of feet into the air, the fall would likely kill you or at least cripple you for life. Now speak."

Jenur gritted her teeth, but since she couldn't break Ramufa's grip on her, she said, "The Magical Superior, the head of North Academy, teleported me here after I killed Wirm. I came here to find out why you wanted to kill me."

"The Magical Superior?" said Fabadi. "I always knew I couldn't trust that man. Sending an assassin to kill me ... what a coward. Perhaps North Academy's days as the largest and best mage school are about to come to an end."

"He didn't send me to kill you," said Jenur, doing her best to keep her voice level despite the increasing pain from her unnaturally twisted arms. "Like I said, I just wanted to find out why you wanted me dead."

Fabadi looked at her in disbelief. "You mean you do not remember killing my daughter, Raya Kabadi? Are you honestly this dense or are you just trying to deceive me? It's not working, if that's your goal."

"But I didn't kill Raya," said Jenur. "It was—"

Pain unlike anything Jenur had experienced yet surged through her arms and shoulders as Ramufa twisted her arms even further. Nothing broke, but the pain was so terrible that Jenur groaned, almost screamed. Nor did the pain let up; if anything, it just got worse. Her mind became so clouded with pain that it was nigh impossible for her to think clearly enough to form a coherent sentence.

"I remember your original excuse," said Fabadi. "And I still find it less truthful than a Hollechian lie. There was no evidence of this other killer having killed my daughter. You were the one holding the bloody knife. You were the one with the invisibility clothes. And now you are the one who will face the justice you so richly deserve."

Through the pain, Jenur managed to say, "Please ... listen ... to me ..."

"There is no need to listen to a killer," said Fabadi. "I will avenge my daughter's death here and now. Ramufa, hold her steady."

"Of course, Your Majesty," said Ramufa, his voice full of glee. "I will make sure this wicked assassin doesn't move even one inch from her current position. I for one happen to believe in justice, despite not being a Grinfian, and so am happy to be an instrument in bringing justice to fruition."

Fabadi rose from his throne and began walking down the short spiral staircase upon which his throne sat. As he did so, he unsheathed a shiny golden sword from his scepter. It was a very thin sword, but a mere glance at it was enough to tell Jenur that the sword's blade was sharp enough to cut through skin and bone. Her skin and bone.

"What ... are you doing?" Jenur said, squeezing every word out with a supreme effort. "Aren't you going to ... aren't you going to get an executioner?"

"The executioner is asleep and would take far too long to prepare the proper execution methods even if he was awake," said Fabadi as he stepped off the bottom step of the spiral staircase and began walking over to Jenur. "No, I will execute you myself, in this very room at this very hour. It is only right that I do so."

Jenur heard something fall to the floor on her left and looked and saw Ramufa standing right next to her, the stink of his bare feet filling her nostrils and making her feel sick. He still held his arms in his robes, looking at her with such intense eagerness that Jenur wondered if he was getting off from this.

"Is she steady, Ramufa?" said Fabadi as he approached the two, holding the sword before him like a professional swordsman.

"She is," said Ramufa, nodding. "If she tries to move now, she'll break her arms. And that would be quite painful, wouldn't it, Jenur or Vicin or whatever you call yourself now?"

Jenur realized Ramufa was right. Her arms felt like they were about to snap from the sheer pressure Ramufa was applying to them. Granted, having broken arms was probably better than getting beheaded, but it would only put off her inevitable execution.

The sound of Fabadi's footsteps approaching was somehow even more frightening than seeing Fabadi prepare the golden sword for her execution, prompting Jenur to say, "Fabadi, you're making a mistake."

"I am not making any mistake," said Fabadi. His voice was full of hate. "I am only bringing justice where once none existed. But do not worry. I am not a bloodthirsty lunatic. I will make your death swift and merciful."

By now Fabadi had finally reached her. He stood above her, holding his sword, weighing it in his hand as if thinking about where to strike first. There was not a hint of mercy in his eyes.

"Please," said Jenur. "It was Ramufa. He killed Raya."

"Ramufa?" said Fabadi. His eyes flicked up at the freelancer before returning to Jenur. "He wasn't even there that night. Who are you going to blame next? Perhaps the Powers? Or maybe you are going to say it was your twin sister who happens to look exactly like you. I do not tolerate excuses."

"But it's true," said Jenur. She was on a roll and she wasn't going to stop until she got it all out. "Ramufa killed Raya and framed me for her death. He's the killer, not me."

"What bull hockey," said Ramufa, sounding genuinely offended. "I may not be the most saint-like figure in all of the Northern Isles, but even I am not stupid enough to assassinate the daughter of one of the most powerful kings in the world."

"It is pathetic how you refuse to take responsibility for your own actions," said Fabadi, shaking his head. "I suppose I shouldn't have expected anything better from a killer like you."

"It's true," said Jenur. "Ramufa did it. He's *not* on your side. I don't know what his game is, but it's—"

More pressure on her arms, forcing her to shut up and groan from the sheer pain.

"Shut up," said Ramufa, though sweat was rolling down his forehead now. "I wasn't there when Raya was killed. I didn't even know it happened. Stop lying."

"It may be worth breaking her arms if she's going to keep this pitiful attempt at deception up," said Fabadi. "But I must ask you not to do so because I wish to be the first to cause her body lasting damage. Afterward, though, you may do with her as you wish."

I need proof, Jenur thought, her mind racing. *Anything to cast Ramufa's innocence into even the slightest doubt. But how?*

She looked up at Fabadi, who was raising his sword now, his eyes glinting with triumph. Then she looked at Ramufa, who was smiling so widely that he almost appeared to be drooling.

"Please," said Jenur, her voice weaker than ever, as she looked back at Fabadi. "Don't do this. You'll regret it forever. This isn't how to avenge your daughter's death."

"Don't even try, little girl," said Ramufa, the excitement in his voice almost overwhelming. "King Fabadi already has his mind set. There is no changing it, just as there is no changing the fact that it was your knife that killed Princess Raya Kabadi."

Fabadi hesitated and looked at Ramufa in confusion. "I never told you how Vicin killed Raya."

Ramufa looked up at Fabadi quicker than he should have. "Oh, well, I heard about it from one of your servants."

Fabadi frowned. "The exact method of Raya's death was never released to the general public. Nor did I tell any of my servants."

Ramufa gulped. "Um, well, I guess I just made a very lucky guess."

"No guess," Jenur said, ignoring the pain in her arms. "Ramufa knows because he was there. He used his own knife to stab Raya. It wasn't me."

"There you go with that lie again," said Ramufa, kicking her face with his foot. "When will you learn that that lie will never convince anyone, much less the clever King Fabadi?"

But Fabadi's frown only grew more pronounced the more he thought about it. "Wait a minute ... Raya was too far away from Vicin for her to stab her."

"That's because she's an initiate of the Thief's Way," said Ramufa, his voice hurried, slightly stumbling over his words. "Like me. She used her powers to stab Raya without having to get up close to her."

Fabadi was clearly still thinking, however, because he said, "That can't be true, otherwise Vicin wouldn't have required the Magical Superior's help in getting here and she would have already killed me. Yet you are obviously a master of the Thief's Way, Ramufa."

Ramufa was sweating profusely now. "You don't actually believe her? I mean, it's obvious she is making up a story just to save her own life. I, on the other hand, have been nothing but truthful to you during the entire time we've known each other. I am an honest man."

"Honest men do not become initiates—much less masters—of the Thief's Way," said Fabadi. "Nor do honest men lie about how they attained the knowledge they possess ... knowledge they couldn't otherwise have if they were truthful from the get go."

Fabadi's voice shook with rage. His eyes burned with white-hot anger, so intimidating that he could have easily set a tree aflame with his vision alone. He held his sword firmly, however, not allowing it to shake even slightly in his hands.

"Your Majesty," said Ramufa, taking one step back. "Why would

I ever kill Raya? Have you asked yourself that? I held no hard feelings against her. She was never my enemy. But Skimif, he—"

"Raya was a Heathen," Jenur gasped. She was determined to get every word out before Ramufa could come up with some plausible defense, even if it meant losing the use of her arms. "A member of the Brotherhood of Heathens. Ramufa killed her because Hollech told him to because Hollech was afraid the Brotherhood would succeed in convincing the mortals to abandon the gods."

"Lies," Ramufa said. "Princess Raya Kabadi was the most devout follower of Nimiko that Shika has ever seen. Master Hollech would never, ever, ever ask me to assassinate as pious a woman as her. Do you believe this junk, King Fabadi?"

Fabadi lowered his sword. His face was hard to read, but Jenur could sense rage bubbling just beneath the surface. "I find her story hard to believe."

Ramufa sighed with relief. "I always knew you were a smart man, Fabadi, the smartest king in all of the Northern Isles, in fact. So why don't you—"

"But easier to believe than your own," said Fabadi.

In one smooth motion, Fabadi raised his sword and stabbed Ramufa directly in the chest. The sword stabbed straight through Ramufa's body, the tip of the golden blade actually poking through his back. Ramufa wore an expression of pure shock on his face; at the same time, Jenur felt the pressure on her arms lighten. A quick glance told her that Ramufa's hands had disappeared, allowing her to straighten her arms and massage them.

Fabadi pulled his blade out of Ramufa's chest, but he didn't just let Ramufa go. He slashed at Ramufa's face, cutting the Hollechian's nose straight off. Ramufa cried in pain and staggered backwards, but it was no use, because Fabadi, his eyes full of cold fury, advanced without hesitation on Ramufa.

"Fabadi!" Ramufa said, blood flowing freely from his nose-less face. "Please! I—"

Fabadi was in no mood to listen. Another slash of the sword and a chunk of Ramufa's face went flying. The blow sent Ramufa falling flat on his back, but he had no time to recover, because Fabadi was soon upon him. With the force of an enraged baba raga, Fabadi hacked and slashed at the defenseless Ramufa, completely ignoring Ramufa's pleas for mercy and forgiveness, every blow starting another cycle of screams of pain before being cut short by an even sharper blow.

Jenur had to look away, mostly because she couldn't take that kind of brutality. She had never thought that Fabadi could be so cruel, so merciless, and so she was thankful that she had not been the victim of Fabadi's rage. Still, she could hear every slash of Fabadi's sword as it cut through Ramufa's skin, heard every scream of pain from Ramufa, until eventually Ramufa ceased screaming and begging and the only sound was Fabadi's sword as it tore apart Ramufa's body.

This went on for what seemed like minutes until the sound stopped without warning. By now, Jenur's arms had recovered from the pain, but before she could get up, a pale, wrinkled hand extended itself before her face.

Looking up at the hand's owner, Jenur's stomach lurched. It was

346

King Fabadi. His once pure white robes were splattered with blood, Ramufa's blood, and they smelled like it, too. His sword looked more crimson than gold, with the blood dripping off its tip onto the floor. Fabadi looked less like a noble king and more like a serial killer now, though Jenur accepted his help nonetheless.

"How do you feel, Jenur?" said Fabadi as he helped her to her feet. "Anything broken?"

Jenur rolled her shoulders, but shook her head. She was careful to avoid looking at Ramufa's corpse. "No. I'm fine. You?"

"Just stained my robes," said Fabadi, gesturing at the blood. "But they will be easily washed. For now, I must apologize for my earlier behavior toward you."

Jenur scratched the back of her neck, doing her best to ignore the awful stench of blood coming from his clothes. "It's all right. I know you were acting that way because of Raya's death. I understand your loss."

Fabadi snorted. "How can you understand my loss? Have you ever lost a daughter?"

"No," said Jenur, shaking her head. "But I did just lose my father recently. He was killed by Wirm."

Fabadi gaped for a moment before closing his mouth. Then he said, "I am sorry. I didn't order Wirm to kill your father. I only wanted him to kill you. I didn't even know you had a father."

"It's fine," said Jenur, though it was hard to get the words out when she thought about Dad's death. "What's done is done. You didn't intend to kill my dad and I didn't kill your daughter. I'd say that makes us even, wouldn't you say?"

"If you wish to think of it that way," said Fabadi. He looked over at Ramufa's remains and said, "I should have known better than to listen to the words of a Hollechian. They never tell the truth. He told me what I wanted to hear, rather than the truth, and as a result, I almost killed an innocent woman. That would have been a true injustice."

"You sound like a Grinfian," said Jenur.

Fabadi shrugged. "Perhaps the peace negotiations with Carnag have been influencing my thinking. Whatever the reason, I now have much to think about. Ramufa told me about many other things besides you and I now wonder just how much of it was truth and how much of it wasn't."

"Like what?" said Jenur.

"He told me that Skimif was a corrupt, power-hungry tyrant who was trying to sever the link between the northern gods and us mortals," said Fabadi. "He told me that Skimif was using the southern gods to scare us mortals and keep us in line."

"I don't know Skimif very well, but that doesn't sound like him to me at all," said Jenur. "I was there after he ascended, when he gathered all of the gods together to tell them what he planned to do now that he is the God of Martir. He didn't mention anything about tyranny or using the southern gods to frighten mortals into submission."

"Somehow, I sense that your story is truer than the one Ramufa fed me," said Fabadi. "I will now have to send messengers to the other nations I asked to join me in my rebellion against Skimif. I will need to tell them that Skimif is not as bad as I was told and that it was all a tragic misunderstanding."

"Sounds like a good idea to me," said Jenur. "Though to be honest, I've been so busy up north that I don't really know everything that's been going on down here."

"I am glad you agree," said Fabadi. Then he hesitated. "What you said earlier ... about Raya being a Heathen. Was that the truth?"

"Yes," said Jenur, nodding. "Raya was indeed a Heathen. She and Skimif were friends."

To her surprise, Fabadi just chuckled. "Raya always was an independent-minded girl. I don't know for sure why she would join such a contemptible movement, but now that I know she and Skimif were friends, that casts even more doubt on Ramufa's story that Skimif had hired you to kill Raya."

"Yeah," said Jenur. "Actually, Raya's death was a pretty big blow against the Brotherhood, because she was one of the most high-profile members of the movement."

"Yes, I can see that now," said Fabadi. He stroked his chin. "Yes, I will have much to think about now. I will need to rethink much of my own behavior over the last couple of months. And I will need to apologize to Prince Malock."

"Malock?" said Jenur. "Why him?"

"Because he always believed in Skimif's innocence, while I irrationally disbelieved in it," said Fabadi. "I said some harsh things to him then, things that I fear may have done more to unravel the work I have achieved through the peace negotiations more than anything else. I just hope it is not too late."

"Knowing Malock, it's probably not," said Jenur. "Well, I better get going now."

"You're leaving?" Fabadi sounded disappointed.

Jenur nodded. "Well, yeah. I still have a lot of things to do up north, back in the Great Berg. Gotta bury Dad's remains, attend the funeral of a friend, make sure another friend of mine is okay, and whole host of other things I don't even want to think about right now."

"I see," said Fabadi. "I suppose I cannot force you to stay, but know this, Jenur Takren: You can always find a home here, in Castle Shika, should you ever need it."

He said that while looking her straight in the eyes. He had such intense eyes that Jenur almost looked away, but she kept eye contact with him anyway so as to not offend him (after seeing what he did to Ramufa, she decided she would rather be on his good side as much as possible).

"Thanks," said Jenur. "Now I just need to figure out a way back north."

"You can take my personal ship," said Fabadi. "The *Intellect's Journey*. I will tell the crew of that ship to take you directly back up north. You may take whatever supplies you need with you: food, water, clothes, medicine, anything."

"That's nice of you to offer," said Jenur. "I think I will accept it. I'm not interested in trying to convince the captain of some trade ship to take me all the way up north anyway."

"Good to hear," said Fabadi. He wiped some blood off his face and said, "Thank you. Thank you for showing me who really killed my daughter. I feared I would die before getting to avenge her death, but now, when death does come, I will at least be able to die in peace."

"You're welcome," said Jenur. "I'm just glad that this is all over. I can finally go back and live the normal life I've always wanted to."

"I wish you luck in that endeavor," said Fabadi. "May the light of Nimiko shine upon whatever path you walk."

Jenur nodded. "Why don't we get you cleaned up and then set up your ship? I would like to leave as soon as possible."

"Of course," said Fabadi. "I will summon my servants, not only to clean me and dispose of Ramufa's remains, but also to take you down to the harbor, where the *Intellect's Journey* is. I am sure that Captain Jakod will be up to the task of heading to the Great Berg. He has gone there before."

"Let's hope so," said Jenur.

While Fabadi began calling for his servants, Jenur looked up at the ceiling. She didn't understand everything that was going on and suspected that there was far more going on than she would ever know, but deep down, she decided it wasn't her concern. All she wanted to do was go back north and make sure Darek was safe, among everything else she needed to do.

Whatever Skimif is doing, whatever the gods are doing, probably doesn't have anything to do with me, Jenur thought. *They can handle it all on their own. I have my own problems to deal with.*

Chapter Twenty-One

TIME ITSELF SEEMED TO slow down as the dice rolled across the cracked, uneven stone floor. All of Malock's senses went into overdrive. The snorting of Equina behind him ... the cracking of the stone arms of Hollech's throne as the god's fingers dug into them ... the burning in Malock's face ... the stench of horse hair, both from Equina and Hollech ... and of course the clattering of the dice as they rolled, rolled seemingly forever, until they bumped against Hollech's shoes.

As he had so many times before, Hollech leaned over in his throne, his horse eyes fixated on the die blocks. Malock held his breath. All Hollech needed to do was declare Malock the 'winner' and it would all be over.

For what seemed like an eternity, Hollech merely gazed at the dice. With his face down, it was impossible to tell what the god was thinking or feeling. It was probably too dark for Hollech to tell what the numbers were, but Malock doubted it would be long before he found out and announced them.

Then Hollech slowly but surely sat upright. A terrible, wicked grin crossed his lips as he placed the tips of his fingers together.

"One hundred and ninety-nine," said Hollech. "Looks like you win, Prince Malock. Congratulations. Equina? Please give him his award."

Malock knew it was useless, but he whirled around anyway, deciding that he'd rather die seeing his own death coming at him, instead of going out without having seen it. Equina was already turning around, preparing her powerful back legs to smash Malock's face in.

This is it, Malock thought. *I'm dead. It's all over. Hollech wins.*

Equina then lashed out at Malock, her thick hooves coming directly at his face. There was no time to dodge. No time to do anything except wonder just how much the impact was going to hurt when it came or if he would feel anything at all.

Just as Equina's hooves were about to collide with Malock's forehead, they stopped. Malock started, staggering backwards away from Equina's hooves, yet the horse wasn't moving at all. It appeared to have been completely frozen in place, as though it were a statue rather than a living creature.

"What the—?" said Hollech behind Malock, his voice shocked. "Equina? What happened to Equina?"

"I told her to stop," said a powerful, yet familiar, voice that seemed to come from everywhere at once. "And she wisely chose to listen."

At that moment, a bright light expanded in the room, so bright that it chased away every last bit of darkness so that it appeared to be daytime. Malock turned to see the light, but it was so bright that he was forced to cover his eyes with his hands to avoid getting blinded. Even then, he could still see it through his hands, but eventually the light faded, allowing him to lower his hands and see who had arrived.

A large, muscular aquarian man with the head of a hammerhead shark stood in the center of the room, wearing white robes that shone with the light of the summer sun. His skin was as shiny as polished silver, while a golden scepter—far grander and more magnificent than any mortal scepter—was in his right hand. A smell like that of the Crystal Sea overwhelmed the horse stench that had permeated the area, allowing Malock to breathe far more easily than before.

Though at first glance the aquarian appeared mortal, Malock knew that the newcomer was the farthest thing.

Joy welled up in Malock as he said, "Skimif! What are you doing here?"

Skimif looked at Malock with his distant, godly eyes. "To save you, of course, and to punish Hollech."

Hollech had stood up from his throne by now. Sheer disbelief was etched across his equine features, as though he had not expected this to happen at all. His lips were moving, but no sound came from them, like he was trying to speak but had forgotten how.

"How did you even know I was here?" said Malock.

"Hanarova, the servant of the Mechanical Goddess, told me," said Skimif. "She came to my home and begged me to save her 'future husband.' By the way, do you know what she meant by that?"

"Long story short, I made a deal with Hana that I am very likely to regret sometime in the near future," said Malock.

"Ah," said Skimif. "Doesn't surprise me. You always did seem like the impulsive type."

"It was less due to my impulsiveness and more due to her dirty business dealing," Malock muttered. Then he said in a louder voice, "Well, I'm glad you're here anyway. I thought for sure I was going to die."

"You likely would have," said Skimif. "But we can talk later. For now, I must address Hollech."

Skimif turned around to face the God of Deception, Thieves, and Horses, who still stood in front of his throne like he was shackled to it.

Then Hollech shook his head and put on a far more confident face. "Lord Skimif! I didn't expect to see you here. Why, I was certain you—"

"Cut the crap, Hollech," said Skimif, actually causing Hollech to shut up. "Your deceptions cannot fool me. As the God of Martir, I can see right through your tricks and lies. I am not some easily fooled mortal, so I suggest sticking with the truth."

Hollech shrugged. "Well, at least I can say I tried. Though I have to wonder if an upstart like you even deserves the truth."

"I am no upstart, Hollech," said Skimif. "The Powers willingly gave me rule over Martir and all that lives within it, including you northern gods. That means I have full authority to punish you whenever you act out of line."

"Your authority is undeserved," said Hollech. His voice was harsher now, losing the smooth, controlled tone it had earlier. "I don't know how you did it, but you tricked the Powers into giving you more power than any mortal has the right to have. I am only attempting to return the world to its original balanced state."

"You can justify all of the chaos and terror you and your kind have wrought all you want, but in the end, you are wrong," said Skimif. "Nor can you fight back. I have incapacitated Xocion, the Chaotic Goddess, and every other god, northern or southern, who allied with you. When I confronted them, they gave up and explained to me that you were the mastermind behind their alliance. You are alone and you have lost."

"Those traitors," Hollech growled. "I knew I couldn't trust them. Every last one of them deserves to burn in the pits of flame for their treachery."

"Perhaps that is what they deserve, but since their repentance is genuine, I have spared them from their punishment," said Skimif. He held out a hand and said, "And if you, Hollech, do the same, I will not punish you either. I do not take any pleasure or joy in punishing anyone. Just apologize for what you've done and I will let you off the hook."

That seemed like an amazingly good deal to Malock, considering all that Hollech and his ilk had done, but Hollech balled his hands into fists and snorted, "No. To apologize for my plan would be to bow to you. I will never bow to illegitimate authority, no matter who may have conferred that authority upon you."

"You're not speaking rationally," said Skimif. "Think about it. If you'd just apologize, then you won't have to suffer the consequences."

"I apologize for nothing," said Hollech. "I do not regret any of it. It was all necessary for the greater good of disposing of a tyrant like you from your seat of power. I would have freed everyone, mortals and gods alike, from your rule, if I had succeeded."

"You mean you do not regret murdering King Halock?" said Skimif. "Or manipulating the leaders of the Northern Isles into preparing for war against me? You don't regret giving King Fabadi the knowledge of Jenur's location, which he used to send the Dark Tigers after her? You don't regret kidnapping Malock and deceiving him about the rules of the game you played until the very last moment? You stand by all of that?"

"All of that, and much more," said Hollech. He pointed a hoofed finger at Skimif and said, "You don't understand. In the long run, all of this would have been for the greater good. Once the war among the Northern Isles started, the Powers would have returned to fix their mistake."

"I doubt it," said Skimif. "If the Powers had returned, they would not have simply disposed of me. They would have destroyed Martir, all of it, including you. It was what they planned originally. Only by becoming the God of Martir and promising to do better did I convince the Powers to spare us."

"What?" said Hollech, tilting his head to the side. "No. You're lying."

Malock stepped beside Skimif. The God of Martir radiated immense power, but Malock managed to tolerate it. "He's right. I was there. The Powers made Skimif the God of Martir precisely so that he would make the world a better place. By trying to bring the Powers back, all you're doing is putting Martir in danger again."

Hollech ran a hand through his mane, but he said, "No. Both of you are trying to make me doubt my plan. I was in the right. I was always in the right, right from the start. You can't fool me. I am the God of Deception."

"Then surely you must be able to tell when someone is trying to deceive you," said Skimif. "Do you or do you not sense deceit in our words?"

Hollech grit his teeth. "I ... you ... I don't have to believe you if I don't want to."

"That is your right," said Skimif. "But that does not make it right."

"I don't care," said Hollech. He pointed at himself with his thumb and said, "I will take whatever punishment you have in store for me, Skimif of Tunya. I will gladly sacrifice myself for the cause. To prove, once and for all, that you are nothing more than a power-hungry tyrant who must be stopped before he can cause any lasting harm to Martir as a whole."

Skimif shook his hammerhead shark-like head. "I was hoping you might recant your ideals, but I can see now that that is never going to happen. I suppose that leaves me with only one choice: To banish you beyond the Void for one thousand years."

Hollech's defiant smile turned into a gape of horror. "Beyond the Void? For one thousand years?"

"Yes," said Skimif. "I wish to give you plenty of time to think about what you have done. I can't convince you right this moment that your plan was wrong right from conception, but maybe if you have time to think on it, you'll figure it out on your own."

Hollech's gape immediately transformed into a snarl. "Then do it.

I doubt it will do any good. I will never stop believing the truth. Besides, a thousand years isn't that long for a god. In a blink of an eye, it will all be over and I will return to Martir."

"That may be so," said Skimif. "But time does not work exactly the same out in the Void as it does here. Besides, I imagine that the many unknown dangers will make it seem much longer than a thousand years."

"I can handle whatever is out there," said Hollech. "I am a god, after all. I can take care of myself."

"Fine," said Skimif. "Now be gone."

Skimif flicked his outstretched wrist and Hollech vanished in an instant. It was almost like Hollech hadn't been there at all; in fact, for a moment Malock didn't believe his own eyes, thinking that maybe Hollech was still there and that something else had happened.

But then Skimif lowered his hand and said, "I wish I didn't have to do that."

Malock blinked. "Oh. So he actually is gone, then."

"For a thousand years, anyway," said Skimif. "In the meantime, I will have to monitor his three domains while he's away. I'm no fan of deception, thieves, or horses, but someone has to control them, otherwise the world would go mad."

As if to prove his point, Skimif gestured at Equina. The horse suddenly unfroze, but instead of attacking Malock, she whinnied, sounding a little confused, and then galloped away from both of them until she disappeared into the darkness of the temple ruins.

"Perhaps I should have sent Equina with him," said Skimif. "Hollech could use the company, I'm sure. Then again, the whole point of this punishment is to isolate him and force him to think about his actions. Though whether it will actually work, I don't know."

Malock scratched the back of his head. "Well, I'm glad you came and saved me, anyway. I thought for sure I was a goner there. I will have to thank Hana for going to get you when I go home."

Skimif nodded. "By the way, I heard you are going to become King of Carnag. Congratulations."

"Thanks," said Malock. Then he hesitated, and said, "Not to sound accusatory, but where were you during all of this? Why did you let Hollech and his crew of idiot gods almost get away with destroying everything? Why didn't you stop them right away?"

Skimif's shoulders slumped. For a moment, he looked less like the all-powerful God of Martir and more like the mortal leader of the Brotherhood of Heathens that Malock had met so many months ago. "Making the transition from mortal to god was more difficult than I expected, to be honest. I've had Nimiko and the Mechanical Goddess helping me, but I still don't know the fullest extent of my powers and I was hesitant to act without first gaining mastery of my abilities."

"How much of Hollech's plan did you know of beforehand?" said Malock. "Sounds to me like you knew quite a lot, including much I didn't know, back there."

"I knew about all of it," said Skimif. "I was aware of a group of gods that was not happy with my rule, even aware that they had made a plan, but somehow it never occurred to me that they could pose a serious threat to me or to the world. I guess I thought I was so strong that no god would ever even think of standing against me, but I guess that just goes to show you that the gods don't always have common sense."

"I'll say," said Malock. "But did you know about ... did you know they planned to kill Father?"

Skimif hesitated, then nodded. "Yes, I did."

"Why didn't you save him, then?" said Malock. He felt his heart starting to wrench. "Why didn't you heal him? You could do that, couldn't you? You're the God of Martir. You can do anything, can't you?"

Skimif lowered his head. "I am sorry, Malock, but like I said, I was still learning. I didn't feel confident enough in my abilities to try even a simple healing spell on your father. Besides, Hollech's allies were causing all sorts of trouble all over the place and I had to prioritize. Otherwise, I would have saved him."

Malock's heart felt hollow. Skimif's answer made sense, but somehow, it didn't feel satisfying. He thought for a moment that Skimif was trying to deceive him, but then he remembered that Skimif was an honest person, far more so than Hollech or any of the other gods. Skimif was simply telling him the truth.

Still, Malock turned away from Skimif and said, "It's fine. As a ruler myself, I understand the need to prioritize. Not every little problem that comes your way needs to or can be dealt with immediately, after all. I am sure there were far worse problems to deal with in the world than the death of your best friend's father."

"Malock, please don't talk like that to me," said Skimif. "Like I said, I would have saved him, but—"

"Speaking of best friends," said Malock, turning back to face

Skimif. "Aqur killed herself. Did you know that?"

Skimif showed no sign of shock. "Yes, I did."

"Why didn't you visit her?" said Malock. "And talk to her? She was clearly hurting and confused. She needed you, needed you more than anything else. She didn't know what to do with her life. She thought you had betrayed the Brotherhood, betrayed her."

Skimif looked away. "I ... I would have talked her out of it, but as I said, I had to prioritize. I didn't think Aqur would kill herself. I thought that, once I had everything under control, I could go and visit her and talk with her. But I guess I was too late."

Malock was struck by the pain in Skimif's voice. It was clear that Skimif regretted his decision as much as anyone, making Malock feel like slightly foolish for criticizing him so harshly.

So Malock said, "Skim, I'm sorry for the tone. I forgot how close you and Aqur were. Of course you wouldn't abandon her like that, not forever. You were her best friend."

"But not a very good one." Skimif scratched his left arm. "A good friend would have been by her side, explaining to her why I did what I did. Not stand by and watch as every minute she drew closer and closer to the edge of despair."

Skimif sounded close to the edge of despair himself. Malock put a hand on his friend's shoulder, but Skimif knocked it off.

"I'm fine," said Skimif, though he still didn't look at Malock. "I'll be all right. I'm the God of Martir, after all. Nothing can truly harm me forever, right?"

That was clear code for *I don't want to talk about this,* so Malock decided to change the subject.

"Well, I guess you can take me back home now," said Malock. "The coronation is still in the planning stages and it would not do for me to disappear just when I am needed most."

Skimif nodded. "All right. Back to Carnag you go, then. I'll teleport you there. That's one thing I have learned to control, at least. Grab my hand."

As Malock grabbed Skimif's open hand, he got a glimpse at Skimif's face. Skimif wore an expression of sadness, sadness and pain, and there was nothing Malock could do to make him feel better.

I guess he'll just have to deal with Aqur's suicide on his own, Malock thought as the ruins of Hollech's temple vanished around them, soon replaced by the Royal Garden. *I just hope that he has the strength with which to do it.*

Chapter Twenty-Two

One week later ...

JENUR TAKREN TOSSED THE last clump of mixed dirt and snow onto Dad's grave, then impaled the shovel into the earth and leaned against it. Despite the bone-chilling temperature of Urma, sweat ran down Jenur's neck and forehead and she was panting hard. She had never realized just how physically-demanding digging a grave was, though she supposed it was because she had chosen to do so in the worst possible weather. The sky was gray and cloudy. One of the Academy's kathamancers had predicted it would snow like crazy soon, possibly even cause a massive storm, but Jenur had figured she would have just enough time to dig out Dad's grave and bury what little remained of him.

As she sat there, Jenur remembered what had happened when she had returned to North Academy about a day ago. She had not expected it to take less than a week for the *Intellect's Journey* to arrive at the Great Berg, but Captain Jakod had taken seriously King Fabadi's order to go as fast as possible and so had managed to reach the edge of the Great Berg in a mere six days. They had run into one of the mages from the Academy, who was training on one of the various ice islands scattered around the edge of the Great Berg, who had agreed to take Jenur back to the Academy. That was fortunate, for beyond the edge of the Great Berg the waters became frozen and the *Intellect's Journey* had not been built for ramming through fields of thick ice.

Upon returning to the Academy itself, Jenur had been greeted by Irliza and Noharf. They told her that the entire school was mourning Braim and that Braim's funeral was to be the very next day, which Jenur thought was too fast, but she was under the impression that such speed was normal at the Academy. She supposed that they didn't want to spend too much time away from learning, which made sense, as it was a school, after all.

Braim's funeral had been different from all of the other funerals Jenur had ever attended. For one, it had been a Diogian funeral. Being followers of the God of the Grave, Diogians had very detailed, highly specific rules and guidelines for what constituted an acceptable funeral and what did not. One of the few students specializing in necromancy at the Academy had been placed in charge of it and what she came up with still stood out in Jenur's mind.

All of the students and faculty of the school—around one-hundred twenty or thirty overall—plus Jenur and Darek, had gathered outside in the cold weather, near the graveyard where the corpses of past Superiors were usually buried, but which also doubled as a general graveyard for any students or faculty who died at the school. It had been a disturbingly large graveyard, with hundreds of tombstones with the names of various students, teachers, and

Superiors on them.

Once all of the mourners were gathered, the funeral itself started. The Diogian student had brought out Braim's casket, a fairly simple wooden coffin with the symbol of Diog—a stylized tombstone—carved into it. Apparently, Braim himself had made his casket, as the Rules of Diog stated that Diogians had to build their own coffins prior to their death. That seemed slightly disturbing to Jenur, but the Diogian student had explained that it was a way of helping to remind Diogians that even they would die someday and that when they did, they needed to make sure that their coffin would be pleasing to Diog.

Yet that wasn't even the strangest part about the funeral. Instead of letting mourners walk up to the open casket and say their good byes, the Diogian student had used her necromancy abilities to reanimate Braim's corpse just long enough for everyone to say their last words to him. The reanimated corpse hadn't moved or anything. It had just sat up in its coffin, staring at them with Braim's cold, dead eyes. The only ones who seemed even remotely comforted by this strange 'rule' were the handful of Diogian students; everyone else had seemed just as put off by it as Jenur had.

Thankfully, that part of the funeral had passed quickly and Braim's corpse was then lain back down in the coffin, which had then been closed tightly. The Diogian student then covered the coffin with incense that smelled like sweet flowers, which she claimed was necessary to ensure that Diog would not turn away the coffin just because it didn't smell pleasing to him.

And then finally, the coffin had been lowered into the grave, which the Diogian student, with mud-splattered robes, had dug out herself. As the coffin was lowered into the grave, however, the Diogian student dropped a piece of paper into the grave, which landed gently on top of the coffin. This paper, she said, had Braim's name on it, which would help Diog to identify who was inside the coffin when he came by to check on it later.

After the coffin was lowered into the ground, the Diogian student then buried it herself. She said she had to do it in order to make sure that it was buried properly, and she did it rather quickly, filling the grave with a combination of a shovel and lithomancy to complete the task in about five minutes.

After the coffin was finally buried, the Magical Superior gave a short eulogy about Braim. Much to her surprise, the Superior gave the entire eulogy without breaking down or crying. She had expected he would, seeing as Braim had been his pupil, but somehow he kept his composure through the whole thing. Though she did notice how he shook whenever he glanced at Braim's tombstone, which had been designed by the lithomancer teacher.

When the funeral was over, Jenur had spent a couple of hours with Darek. The little boy seemed to have gotten over his distrust of her, probably because he had seen Wirm's body being taken out of the Superior's study and had been told that she had killed him. Jenur had no doubt that Darek was probably still traumatized by seeing his mother and fellow villagers all killed, but when he had hugged her upon seeing her and talked and played with her, Jenur figured that, for now, they would both be all right.

When Darek had been taken by Irliza to take his afternoon nap, Jenur had decided to take that moment to head out to Urma and bury her father. The Diogian student who had buried Braim offered to come with her and help, but Jenur had wanted to do this alone, largely because neither she nor Dad had been worshipers of the gods, so Jenur didn't want to bury Dad in accordance with a rulebook said to have been written by a god.

Jenur looked over at the hut in which she and Dad had lived. It looked as burnt-out and ruined as it had when she first arrived on Urma's shores a few hours ago. Digging through the debris to find Dad's remains had taken her a while, but in the end she had found what may have been his shirt, though it was so charred that she was not sure if it had been his or not. She had buried it anyway, however, as she didn't have his body or anything else with which to bury in his grave.

Dusting the dirt and snow off her jacket, Jenur tried to think of any rituals she needed to do to honor Dad's death. She could think of none. The Dark Tigers never had any special rituals for members killed on assignments. The only way they ever really noted the death of a Tiger was by tracking down and killing the idiot who had thought it a good idea to kill a Dark Tiger (unless the death was accidental, in which case they did nothing about it except retrieve the body). Beyond that, Jenur did not know of any rituals—human and aquarian—with which she could honor Dad that did not in some way involve the northern gods.

And there is no way in hell I am going to invoke their names at my Dad's funeral, Jenur thought. *None of them have ever been kind to us, except maybe Nimiko, but he's not here.*

Jenur decided that a fancy ceremony or ritual wasn't necessary.

Dad would not have wanted or expected it. He had been a heathen himself, as most Dark Tigers were, and to her knowledge there were no heathen rituals to acknowledge the passing of the dead. He would have been happy just knowing that she had given his remains a proper burial, rather than simply letting it sit out for some animal to eat at some point.

Then Jenur heard the sounds of boot-clad feet walking through the snow behind her. Wondering who it could be, as Jenur had gone to Urma alone, she looked over her shoulder and saw that it was the Magical Superior. He no longer wore his mage robes; instead, he wore a winter jacket and parka that looked similar to what Braim wore prior to his death, except they were pure white and had a stylized wand stitched into them. He used his actual wand like a walking stick, leaning against it as he walked.

Jenur was in no mood to talk to anyone, but she had some respect for the Magical Superior and she knew that he didn't usually come out of his study unless it was important. So she stood up, using her shovel for support, and dusted off the snow and earth on her clothes as the Magical Superior approached.

"Hello, Magical Superior," said Jenur, leaning on the shovel. "What brings you here?"

The Magical Superior stopped about a dozen feet away from Jenur. His old eyes focused on Dad's grave for a moment before he said, "I just wanted to come and give you my condolences. I never knew your father, but you did attend Braim's funeral and I felt it would be unkind of me not to return the favor."

"It wasn't a favor," said Jenur. "Braim was a friend of mine. You didn't need to come here, though I appreciate the thought."

"I know," said the Magical Superior. "But that is not the only reason I came. I came because I wished to discuss your and Darek's future. With Nijok dead, I believe that it is now safe to do so."

Jenur frowned and glanced at Dad's grave. "Yeah, right. Wirm might be dead, but the Dark Tigers are still around. Sooner or later the others will realize that Wirm is dead. Then they'll come after me."

"I would not be so sure about that," said the Magical Superior. "I am no Dark Tiger myself, but how many of the Dark Tigers do you think will go all the way to the Great Berg to avenge my brother's death? Very few, I would wager, considering how abusive and manipulative Nijok was to his men. Particularly if they suspect that we Academy mages had something to do with it."

"You've got a point," said Jenur. "Many of the Dark Tigers only listened to Wirm because they had nowhere else to go. Maybe the Guild will fall apart without Wirm leading it."

"Undoubtedly," said the Magical Superior. "That is what happens when you have followers who only listen to you based on fear. True loyalty can only be cultivated through kindness and fair treatment, but I digress. Your and Darek's future is the topic of discussion right now."

Jenur nodded. "I was thinking we could go to Carnag. Malock would undoubtedly give us a place to stay, because he's my friend."

"Actually, I was wondering if you would like to stay here," said the Magical Superior, gesturing over his shoulder to the north. "At the Academy. Young Darek has already shown a deep interest in magic. I have no idea what areas he might choose to specialize in as he gets older, but I would like to be able to cultivate his interest and see how he develops."

"Darek? A mage?" said Jenur. "I guess that wouldn't be so bad, but—"

"And Irliza and the students love him," the Magical Superior added. "They treat him like family. They are fiercely protective of him and would never even think of hurting him. He would be quite safe with us."

Jenur scratched her cheek in thought. "North Academy probably is one of the most secure places in the world, much safer than anywhere else. If Darek really likes the place and wants to learn magic, then I can't see any reason to disagree with that."

"You can stay with us as well, if you want," said the Magical Superior. "There is no age limit to attending the Academy. We've taught students as young as sixteen and students as old as sixty. The only requirement is that you be willing to learn magic and stick with us until you master whatever form of magic you are practicing."

"Doesn't mastering magic require devoting yourself to a god?" said Jenur.

"Yes," said the Magical Superior. "Magic flows from the gods, after all. It is possible to use magic without following the gods, but it is weak and ineffective. Devotion to the gods is a critical requirement for anyone who wishes to master magic."

"Then I'm sorry, I can't do that," said Jenur. "I'm ... well, I don't follow any god or goddess and I have no intention of doing so now. I'm not much interested in learning magic anyway."

The Magical Superior frowned under his parka. "Then I am

afraid there is not much room for you here at the Academy. Every student and teacher is a mage or a mage in training. We do not allow people who have no intention of learning magic to stay here, at least permanently, much less heathens like yourself."

"That's fine," said Jenur as a cold wind blew through. "I'll just go somewhere else. I can take care of myself."

"But what about Darek?" said the Magical Superior. "I was under the impression that you are highly protective of him. Of course, as I said, most of the students and faculty care about him, too, and would never, ever allow him to come under any harm or danger, but I thought you would want to stay here for Darek's sake, if nothing else."

The Magical Superior had a good point. Though Jenur was not Darek's mother, wasn't even related to him in any way, she still felt responsible for him. She couldn't just up and leave him here, even with Irliza and the others who would keep him safe. She thought about maybe just coming by to visit Darek every now and then, but it then occurred to her that she really did want to see Darek grow.

He doesn't have any parents anymore, Jenur thought, glancing at Dad's grave. *Nor do I. I'm not his mother, true, but I could still be there for him, still raise him and teach him. I know he'll have all of the students and teachers here, but they come and go. He needs someone who he can depend upon to be there for him always ... a parent.*

So Jenur, still leaning against the shovel, said, "You're right. Darek still needs me. I can't just go and abandon him like this, even if he will have you guys. He needs someone to be there for him, and that someone has to be me."

The Magical Superior nodded. "Then that means you, too, will have to enroll as a student here in the school."

Jenur groaned. "Looks like it. Guess I'd better figure out which god I hate the least."

"Don't worry," said the Magical Superior. "You don't have to choose right away. Many students spend years deciding which god they would like to devote their lives to. You will probably need to spend much time learning the basics of magic before you decide who to follow."

"All right," said Jenur. "I guess that's fair. But I'm only doing this for Darek, so don't expect me to become some loyal follower of the gods or anything."

"I cannot force you to change your opinion of the gods," said the Magical Superior, "but I can say that it will have to change at some point if you wish to become a mage. There is a reason history records very few heathen mages."

Jenur rolled her eyes. "Right."

The Magical Superior didn't comment on that. Instead, he said, "Now that your and Darek's future is set, do you wish to return to the Academy with me? I am heading back there right now."

Jenur looked at Dad's grave again. She just wanted to sit there and mourn him, but with the clouds in the sky getting darker and the wind picking up, becoming colder and sharper, she realized that staying out here in this weather would be suicide.

But I will return, Jenur thought. *To give Dad a proper tombstone, if nothing else.*

So Jenur nodded and said, "Sure. I need to bathe after digging out this grave anyway. Then maybe I'll take a nap, get some real sleep, something I haven't gotten nearly enough of in the last two weeks."

Chapter Twenty-Three

MALOCK STOOD IN FRONT of the mirror in his room, standing very still while the royal tailor fitted his coronation robes around him. They were made of a shiny gold-and-red silk, especially designed for Malock's body. Malock also wore a red doublet, which like the robes had been custom-made to fit his exact body size. The tailor was simply making some last minute preparations, as Malock's coronation was to start in a few minutes.

"This is your big day, Prince Malock," said the tailor as his long, delicate fingers made the tiniest of adjustments to Malock's clothes. "Or should I say, King Malock?"

Malock shook his head. "Wait until after the coronation to call me that, tailor."

"Yes, of course," said the tailor. "I'm just so excited and nervous. This is the first time I've designed robes for a coronation, so I am just trying to make sure that they are absolutely perfect, that they make you look like the king that you are about to become."

Malock didn't debate that. The tailor had based Malock's robes off of Father's old coronation outfit. Malock had wanted to wear that instead, but Father's old coronation clothes had not fit him well, which was why the tailor had been called in to design new ones. And Malock had to admit that the tailor had done a very good job, because the robes were neither too tight nor too loose and were easy and natural to move around in. It was almost like wearing air.

"By the way," said the tailor, glancing up at Malock as he adjusted the hemline of Malock's robes, "how did your night out with that pretty young woman go, Hana, I believe her name was? If it is all right with Your Majesty for me to ask."

Malock bit his lower lip. He was well aware that nearly all of the servants of the Carnagian Royal Family had been gossiping about Hana for the past week, though of course never when Malock was around. He suspected that Friyu must have told them about her, but the panamancer swore up and down, albeit not very convincingly, that she had not said 'much' about Hana to anyone else except to Mother. She was probably not telling the truth, but since he had no way to prove she wasn't, he accepted the explanation.

Malock wasn't one to encourage gossip, however, so he simply said, "It went fine. It wasn't very long, maybe only a couple of hours at most. Had to get back to Carnag Hall to speak with the Royal Event Organizer, you know. Don't have all the time in the world to go out with women at the moment."

"Are you going to be going out with her again?" asked the tailor, a silly grin on his face before he realized his impudence and took on a more somber expression. "Uh, I mean, are you going to go out with her again, Your Majesty?"

Malock thought about that for a moment. He and Hana had simply had a short walk around the Royal Garden, which he had mostly spent telling her about his game with Hollech, as well as Hollech's ultimate fate. Hana seemed to enjoy it, though Malock had not made any plans to get back together with her anytime soon. That was because she had had to leave for Stalf again, having been summoned by the Mechanical Goddess to help with something there. Hana had promised to return as soon as possible, however, though Malock had assured her that she could take her time and that she didn't need to rush anything (mostly for his own sake than hers, though he had tried to make it sound like he had said it out of concern for her).

Malock shrugged, though it was a subtle movement, as he had to stay as still as possible until the tailor was done. "We don't have any plans to go out again. She had to leave and go back to her home because she has some work to do."

"Oh, so she's a *working* girl?" said the tailor, standing up from straightening Malock's hem and looking at him intently. "I thought you were only interested in royal girls."

Malock glared at the tailor. "Are we done yet?"

"Ah, um, yes, Your Majesty, I believe we are," said the tailor. "Move around a bit. How does it feel?"

Malock moved his arms up and down. "Feels very good, tailor. You did a fine job, but I do have one tiny criticism to make."

"Yes, Your Majesty?" said the tailor, putting his hands together eagerly.

Malock leaned toward the tailor slightly and said, "Tell the other royal servants that I do not appreciate them gossiping about me and my private life behind my back. In particular, I do not want to hear another word about Hana. Do you understand?"

The tailor gulped, but nodded. "Yes, yes, of course, Your Majesty. I shall make sure that every servant in Carnag Hall hears this message."

"Good," said Malock. He glanced at a clock on the wall. "Uh oh. I need to get going immediately. The ceremony is about to start."

Malock turned from the tailor and walked over to the door, but before he could grab the doorknob, it turned and the door opened. Orel's round face peeked inside, causing Malock to stop before he could run into his servant.

"Prince Malock?" said Orel. "I was sent by Queen Markinia to come and get you. The ceremony is starting in three minutes."

"I was just on my way there," said Malock. "But you may lead. I shall follow."

Orel nodded and opened the door all the way, allowing Malock to emerge into the wide hallways of Carnag Hall. "This way, Your Majesty."

Orel led Malock down the halls, past the various statues and portraits of past Carnagian kings and queens, including a portrait of King Iryu the Second Most Just. As they passed the entrance to the Royal Garden, fear and anticipation gripped Malock's heart and he could feel his hands sweating, but he tried not to show it. Thankfully, Orel didn't seem to notice.

Finally, the two reached the doors to the throne room. They were currently closed and standing before the doors were a dozen Justice

Enforcers, captained by Banika Koiro, who stood at the head of the group in her golden armor. The Enforcers stepped to allow Malock to pass, but they also knelt, which Malock could not remember them ever doing to him before.

They always used to do that to Father, though, Malock thought. *When he was alive, of course.*

Orel put his hands on the doors to the throne room, then looked over his shoulder at Malock. "Your Majesty, are you ready for this?"

"Of course I'm ready," said Malock, wiping away the sweat from his forehead. "This is what I have been training my whole life for. Let's get this started."

Orel nodded and pushed open the doors. He stepped aside, kneeling just like the Enforcers, as Malock walked past him. Malock held his head high and his chest out, trying to look as kingly as he could as he entered the throne room.

The throne room had been decorated for the occasion. Red banners—with Grinf's hammer sewn into them in gold stitching—hung from the ceiling, while a long red carpet ran from the doorway to the steps of the thrones. A couple dozen people—largely Carnagian nobles, though a handful of foreigners, such as King Fabadi, were present as well—stood on either side of the carpet. They all turned to look at Malock as he entered, their eyes following his every move as he walked up to the thrones. He spotted a few Enforcers on the perimeters of the crowd, though he doubted that anything bad was going to happen today.

Not only that, but the throne room smelled different. It was the exact same smell—like roses and leather—that Malock had always associated with Father. He recalled having been taught once by Father that that scent, called the aroma of kings, had been worn by Carnagian kings since the founding of Carnag hundreds of years ago. No doubt Malock would have to wear it now, though of course he would not need to until he was officially made King of Carnag.

At the end of the room, standing next to Father's old throne, was Mother. In her hands she held Father's old crown, which looked as shiny and precious as ever in the sunlight streaming in from the windows. Due to the slight differences in head sizes, they had had to have the crown re-sized so it would fit Malock's head comfortably, but the crown still looked beautiful, courageous, and royal.

When Malock reached the throne, he turned and sat down in it, as was tradition. He had never sat on these thrones before, not even when he was a rebellious young child. Father's throne was comfortable, but something about the way it was designed—maybe it was the back, which stood erect and tall—made Malock sit up straighter than he normally did. Just sitting there, looking out on all of the guests, made Malock feel like a king.

As he looked out over the guests, Malock's eyes briefly met Fabadi's. Earlier that week, King Fabadi had apologized to Malock for the accusations he had made against Skimif. Fabadi had said that he no longer believed Skimif to be the corrupt tyrant that he had been led to believe he was and that he was now urging the other nations that distrusted Skimif to treat him like any other god.

When Malock had asked Fabadi what had caused this change of heart, Fabadi had said, "The truth was shown to me and I believed it." It was not a very satisfying answer, but since Fabadi reported finding some success in urging the other nations to drop their distrust of Skimif, Malock didn't question it.

Perhaps things will work out after all, Malock thought. *We just need to give it time.*

Then Malock looked up at Mother. She looked like she was going to cry, but of course she wouldn't. Tradition dictated that it was the oldest living female member of the Royal Family who would crown the new king, so Mother would just have to hold herself together, at least until after the ceremony was over.

"Prince Tojas Malock," said Mother, her voice firm and clear. "Son of I, Queen Jinaria Markinia, and son of my late husband, King Todar Halock, Crown Prince of the House of Carnag, and former Captain of the *Iron Wind*, in the name of Grinf and Justice, I crown you King Tojas Malock, King of Carnag."

Mother slowly placed the crown on Malock's head. It fit perfectly over his hair, sliding down over it as smoothly as water. The metal felt cold around his forehead, but at that moment Malock could care less about how it felt. He simply sat as still as he could, waiting until Mother finished placing the crown on his head.

"Now, arise, King Malock of Carnag," said Mother, stepping away from him. "Arise, and give a speech to your guests and, ultimately, to all of the citizens of Carnag."

Malock stood up and glanced to his right. Darfna Enux stood close by, paper and pen in hand. He looked ready to begin transcribing Malock's words as soon as Malock began, so Malock took a moment to think about what he wanted to say. After all, once Enux transcribed the speech, the royal scribes would write copies and distribute them all over Carnag to be read or heard by every man, woman, and child on the island. Therefore, Malock would need to be careful about what he said.

Looking out over the guests, Malock said, "Friends and servants of the Carnagian Royal Family, I stand here today, no longer as the Crown Prince of Carnag, but as its King. To be honest, I did not think I would wear this crown so soon. I believed my father, King Todar Halock, would live much longer, but alas, his sudden, unexplained illness took him well before his time. Sadly, that means he could not be here to witness the coronation of his one and only son."

Malock stopped for a moment. Anger and bitterness bubbled up inside him when he thought about how Hollech had spoke so glibly about poisoning Father. A thousand curses came to mind, but as this was not the appropriate time to be cursing the gods, Malock ignored his negative feelings and returned to his speech.

"Though King Halock is no longer among us, this does not mean that his influence is over," Malock continued. "I will always remember the lessons he taught me about what makes a good king. His thirst for justice, his devotion to helping the people of Carnag, his actions towards helping Carnagian businesses, and many other things besides, will all guide me as I grow into the King I am meant to be. And of course, my mother, Queen Markinia, will offer her wisdom and experience to guide me into making the right decisions for the people of Carnag as a whole."

For a moment, Malock was uncertain what else to say, but then he remembered that it was tradition for newly-crowned kings to announce their first actions as king. He didn't know what he would do first, however, until his eyes once again met Fabadi's, who nodded.

"My first action, as King of Carnag, will be to finish the peace talks with Shika," said Malock. "The two nations will no longer be enemies, but instead will be allies, even friends. I will work with King Fabadi of Shika to have our armies and Navies work together, both in times of peace and in times of war, to ensure that in times of great trouble both nations can come to each other's aid. This will be the first step into a new era of peace between Carnag and Shika, the first era of peace between our two quarreling nations."

Fabadi smiled, while the other guests muttered among themselves, yet Malock did not hear any complaining or negativity coming from the guests. That was good. The last thing Malock needed was opposition from the nobles, especially so early on in his rule.

"Not only will today be remembered in history as the day I ascended to the throne, but it will also be remembered as Peace Day," said Malock. "Both on Carnag and Shika. The two nations and the people within them shall forever be friends and shall use this day to remember and renew their friendship."

This time, there was no muttering at all. Instead, some of the guests started clapping, soon followed by every guest in the throne room. The combined sounds of so many hands clapping together at once in the confined throne room was thunderous, despite the small amount of people. Even Enux was clapping, his pen and paper on the floor at his feet, having apparently either finished transcribing the speech or simply being so moved by the speech that he had forgotten to do so.

But Malock paid little attention to Enux. He simply stood before the guests, feeling their excitement and approval flow through him like the blood in his veins. That was how he knew that he had what it would take to be King of Carnag, whatever challenges awaited him in the future.